THE BOILING SEASON

THE
BOILING
SEASON

A Novel

CHRISTOPHER HEBERT

HARPER

An Imprint of HarperCollins*Publishers*
www.harpercollins.com

This is a work of fiction. Although inspired in part by some actual events, the characters, places, and incidents presented here are products of the author's imagination.

A number of facts and several lines of dialogue appearing in chapter 11 are borrowed and/or adapted from the article "A New Retreat for the Rich—Surrounded by Tumbledown Shacks," published in the *New York Times*, January 6, 1974.

Faustin Charles's poem "Sugar Cane" appears with permission of Peepal Tree Press and is published in *Children of the Morning: Selected Poems* (Peepal Tree Press, 2008).

FIRST EDITION

Designed by Leah Carlson-Stanisic

Library of Congress Cataloging-in-Publication Data
Hebert, Christopher.
  The boiling season : a novel / Christopher Hebert.
    p. cm.
  ISBN 978-0-06-208851-2
  1. Caribbean Area—Fiction. 2. Political fiction. I. Title.
  PS3608.E727B65 2012
  813'.6—dc22

                                        2011021510

12 13 14 15 16 OV/RRD 10 9 8 7 6 5 4 3 2 1

for Margaret and Elliot
with whom I share everything

Green fields convulse golden sugar,
Tossing rain, outgrowing the sun,
. . .

The reapers come at noon
Riding the cutlass-whip;
Their saliva sweetens
In the boiling season.

"SUGAR CANE"
—FAUSTIN CHARLES

PART ONE

Chapter One

I was nineteen the year I came into the service of Senator Marcus. At the time he was still just a lawyer, the legislative elections three months away. But at the urging of his wife the staff had already begun to refer to him by his future title, so that by the time of the election the results seemed to us a foregone conclusion.

Like everyone else of their class and standing, the Senator and his wife owned a home high in the hills of Lyonville, a suburb east of the capital. In Lyonville one saw the figurative divide between the upper and lower classes made geographically literal, the dusty roads at the lowest altitude lined with the wasteboard bungalows of laborers and petty merchants, their skin invariably black; as one wound one's way up the hill, complexions grew lighter, the houses larger, and the garden walls higher. And as the walls generally shielded the houses from view, allowing only the spillover of bougainvillea blossoms, one was forced to judge the relative wealth of neighbors by the strength of their gates and the freshness of the tar on their drives.

The Marcuses were mulattoes, their families among the oldest and wealthiest on the island. From the Marcuses' house, perched atop a bluff on the southwest corner, it was possible to look down upon the houses below and see everything the lesser residents were able to hide from the rest of the world: blooming terraces and swimming pools and verdant gardens, all of it just a little bit less lush and blue and vibrant than the Marcuses' own.

The Marcuses' house was a marvel of mahogany and marble. The only metal they believed in was gold. The art they collected was unlike anything I had ever seen, heavy oil renderings of ballerinas and landscapes that seemed cold and lifeless compared to what one observed daily in the tropics. Every room boasted rugs and vases from the Orient and books in half a dozen foreign languages, English the only one I understood—and that just barely.

The staff consisted of a gardener, a cook, a maid, and myself, but only the maid and I lived in the house. My room was on the very top floor, in a corner just below the eaves, a tight space with a sloped ceiling, furnished with a small iron bed and a side table with a drawer barely large enough to accommodate my two handkerchiefs.

The room was by no means luxurious; despite the cool air that chilled the hills even on days when the city itself was sweltering, my room stayed warm and stuffy. Nor had Mme Marcus entirely removed the items she had long stored there. Boxes of hats and linens and old correspondence leaned crookedly up against the wall by the door, looking as if they had been placed there for just a moment, before being permanently forgotten. None of these flaws, however, meant anything to me. The room was the first I had ever had to myself.

The room's sole window was the size and shape of a dinner plate. Given its position, a half meter above the floor in the shadow of the overhanging roof, it allowed only the suggestion of light. In the evening, when I had completed my tasks, I liked to lie on my stomach, my chin atop my folded arms, and look out the window, feeling like a hawk observing the world from an alpine nest. High as I was above the trees, I could see not only the spires and rooftops of the city but, to the west, sixty miles of green, stippled cane fields slashed into lopsided rectangles by irrigation ditches—and beyond the plain, a line of patchy, mostly barren mountains that on hazy days appeared blue. Far down below, at the very base of the Lyonville hills—where as in a gutter the grime inevitably settles—was the home where I had grown up, where my father lived still. From this distance, the place looked almost welcoming, its filth and decay undetectable to the naked eye.

Senator Marcus had hired me as a footman, but I quickly became more than that. Among his staff of four I was the only one who had been to school; unlike the others, I had aspirations to live in a world better than the one I had grown up in. This difference was not lost on the Senator and his wife. Even from early on in my employment, Mme Marcus entrusted me with signing for any deliveries that came to the house. Occasionally in the evening, after a long day at the office, Senator Marcus called me in to his study to dictate a letter. On one such occasion I recall presenting a finished letter for him to sign, and as the nub of his pen touched the paper, he looked up to me and said, "I have rarely seen such clean and assertive lines."

"My father thought penmanship extremely important," I said, feeling the heat simmer at the base of my neck, trapped there by a stiff, high collar.

Senator Marcus added his name and spent a moment regarding it. "Your father was wise."

Caught off guard, I did not know what to say. "Thank you," I offered after allowing an awkward silence to elapse. "He was a good man."

The Senator was elsewhere as he nodded his assent.

Only as I passed into the hallway, closing the door behind me, did I realize we had been talking about my father as though he were dead. By then it was too late to turn back.

By profession my father was a shopkeeper. His store—a term far grander than the premises deserved—was a single room about the size of the Marcuses' pantry, with a pitted concrete floor he could not keep clean no matter how often he swept. A warped, distended curtain in the back corner poorly concealed his sleeping quarters—a nook barely larger than his pallet. The sum of his worldly possessions—aside from his meager stock—fit on a pair of shelves at the foot of the bed, which he kicked every time he rolled over in the night. I knew my father would jeer at the notion of Senator Marcus thinking him wise. Nevertheless, it was true that, after my mother died, the most important thing in his life was to get me through school. He had gone as far as to sell our old house to pay for tuition.

I had learned about the job with the Senator from my friend Paul, whose mother's cousin knew the Marcuses' cook.

"My mother wants me to take it," Paul told me after church one Sunday, as he ground his heel in the dusty street. The other parishioners were wobbling out around us, piously rigid in their least ragged clothes, which they habitually straightened and brushed at with the backs of their hands, as if such gestures could make the rest of us overlook the bloated knees and tattered lace. We were waiting for Paul's mother and my father. They had both gotten held up somewhere along the way.

"Are you going to?" I asked.

Paul looked at me cockeyed. He had been practicing this look on me all our lives.

"Where's the future in it? You think I want to be somebody's servant the rest of my life?"

"You have to start somewhere," I said, toeing a crushed can half buried in the dirt. Time and the traffic of countless feet had flattened it into an almost perfect disk. It bore no mark of its former contents. "It has to be better than this."

Pushing me aside, Paul picked up the compacted can. With a sidearm fling he sent it sailing. Like a bird caught in a headwind, the can banked suddenly upward, and then just as suddenly swooped back down, crashing into the side of the nearest house with a forlorn-sounding clank.

I spun around to make sure no one had noticed.

Paul had already moved on. "At least here," he said over his shoulder, "no one's always ordering you around."

Across the street, several guys I knew from the neighborhood—all of them just a few years older than me—squatted in their accustomed positions along the concrete wall of the depot, lazily passing back and forth the one lowly cigarette they had among them. This was not their well-earned Sabbath leisure; it was how they spent every day of their lives. I did not bother saying so to Paul, but it was hard not to think that someone to give orders was precisely what the place needed.

Paul had dropped out of school when he was fifteen, intending to get an early start on making his fortune. His ambition was no different from that of any other boy in the neighborhood; the guys pressed up against the depot wall all talked the same way. But Paul set himself apart with his determination. His plan had been to go into business for himself, and although he never specified what type of business, it was clear he would never settle for the life of a shopkeeper like my father. Instead, for the last three years, Paul had spent his nights loading and unloading unmarked cargo at a windowless warehouse by the docks, where sleek speedboats slipped in after dark without running lights, escorted by a pair of overweight police officers everyone in the neighborhood feared. Paul spent his days playing dice, trying to build up capital. At the time his mother told him about the job working for Senator Marcus, Paul had already begun a modest operation of his own, bringing in cases of name-brand toothpaste from the States, which he passed on to upscale drugstores downtown. His mother knew nothing about his side business. Although I knew little about it myself, I knew more than I wished. Paul was also making connections in the world of bathroom tissue and had his sights set on athletic socks. It was just a matter of time before he would run a warehouse of his own, but until then he made do with an empty closet in the basement of the telephone exchange, guarded by a blind man he paid in watered-down bottles of rum.

What Paul liked best about the work—more than the money—was having to keep it secret. What he liked best about secrets was breaking them, the awe they earned him among less adventurous boys, who knew no better than to believe Paul a major underworld operative. That Paul was in this regard his own worst enemy seemed to trouble him far less than it did me. He talked often of what might happen if his boss ever caught on to his entrepreneurship. The bigger his audience, the more elaborately he spun the repercussions.

"It's not a joke," I said whenever he let his imagination loose. "You could really get hurt."

He inevitably rolled his eyes. "You're worse than my mother, Alexandre. I don't know why I tell you anything."

Paul and I had grown up together, fewer than a dozen houses apart, and when I reflect upon our friendship I wonder if it was precisely because we had so little in common that we became so close. No doubt my timidity had a way of making him feel all the more daring and fearless. And for me Paul was a window into the wider world outside the neighborhood. His was a path I would never follow, but at least it was a path. The other boys I knew were content to idle on street corners until their fates caught up with them. Chasing schoolgirls. Always the same story. Not until it was too late did they see how it would end—that they would be trapped here forever, doing whatever desperate things they could to feed their unexpected families. Over the last several months, more than one of them had been discovered at dawn twisted in a ditch, face all but unrecognizable.

Like virtually every woman in the neighborhood—except those too sick or too old to do anything at all—Paul's mother cleaned houses higher up in Lyonville. And just as the altitude of a house on the hills signaled the status of its owner, in the neighborhoods down below we measured a woman's family by the houses she dusted and swept. On this scale, Paul's mother was toward the bottom, her clients ranging from factory foremen to low-level government functionaries.

Paul's father had disappeared when we were young. Seeking fortune and a new life somewhere else, no doubt. In doing so, he had followed a familiar route. But even though I was young, I remembered being surprised when I learned he was gone. It would be foolish to claim I knew him well, but in the few memories I retained of him he was always smiling, the most joyful man I had ever known. Whenever he came to see my father, he would squat down to talk to me about whatever I was doing, as if clacking together a pair of sticks were a vital occupation.

Like his son, Paul's father had been fond of schemes; he always had something to sell. And I can still remember the awkward sight of him pitching his ideas to my father. The thing I recall most vividly is the two of them sitting side by side on the stoop of my father's shop, Paul's father grand-marshaling a parade of impossible utopias, while my father stared off at the horizon, as if at any moment something might appear there to add interest to the endless blue. Paul's father was the only indulgence I can remember my father entertaining, and even now I have no idea why he did.

As a rule, the men in our neighborhood—at least those who managed to find work—enjoyed a greater variety of jobs than the women, but their wages were scarcely better. Some of them labored up on the hills with their wives, as gardeners or handymen or house painters or pool cleaners. Others worked in the few factories scattered across the capital, assembling imitation leather shoes and handbags for export. From what I had seen, few of them wasted time dreaming of anything better.

My father sold candles and oil and flour and thread and whatever else the people around him appeared to need. In theory it was a lucrative profession for a man of his class, but even though my father had little competition, he never made much money. As a matter of principle, he insisted on buying his goods from unreliable small suppliers, rather than the larger wholesalers. The costs were higher, and doing it this way meant more work, but none of that mattered to him.

"I'd rather go broke," he never tired of saying, "than give my money to those pigs." A pig, to my father's mind, being anyone of wealth. If ever a car—for he believed only a rich person could own one—stopped in the street outside his shop, he barred the door and pretended to be closed. In this way my father succeeded in being the only adult in our neighborhood making his living without ever having to consort with the mulattoes living above him in Lyonville, whom he contemptuously referred to as "the hill people"—which had a curious way of making them sound like primitive cave dwellers rather than millionaires.

Unlike my father, my mother had never discriminated when choosing her clientele. Until she died, when I was eight, my mother had been a seamstress, one of the finest in the city. There were others who worked more quickly or whose clothes were more practical, but no one could match my mother's eye for beauty. For weddings and funerals, rich and poor alike sought her out, and my mother turned no one away. The rich she overcharged; the poor she charged next to nothing. But since there were far more of the latter than the former, in actuality she barely broke even.

My parents' lives were thus a strange mixture of success and failure. Despite coming at things from different directions, they wound up at more or less the same place: well respected but poor, living the same desperate existence as everyone around them.

While my father aspired for me to receive the education he had never gotten—and that many of our neighbors considered useless to the practical affairs of their lives—he had no wish for me to join the ranks of the hill people. He wanted me to become a doctor, not in a hospital, of course, but in a muddy tent in the countryside, administering shots to tubercular peasants. Or I was to become a lawyer, but only so that I might fight to preserve the land rights of rural farmers. Unlike many people—the majority of our neighbors included—my father did not see these professions as stepping stones to a career in politics, for it was toward politicians that he felt the greatest contempt. It was axiomatic for him that no politician had ever brought the country anything but ruin, and as evidence he pointed to every man he had ever been foolish enough to help elect. It did not matter if he picked a liberal or a conservative, they all turned out to be crooks and despots. When I was still a child, he had given up voting once and for all, disposed of his radio, stopped reading the newspaper, and ceased to allow conversations on political topics in his presence. He made it a practice to mutter profanities at every government vehicle that crossed his path, daring the police to try to stop him.

Throughout my childhood, my father had done what he could to pass his values on to me, but in the end I had proven a disappointment, unable to emulate his bitter passions. Since politics in every form was banned in his presence, I had little occasion to learn what it was that I was supposed to reject. To me, as to every boy my age, the president was just another name in a textbook full of names we dutifully memorized, each one as irrelevant to us as the next. As each successive general or minister completed his coup, he replaced the songs and poems we had recited for his predecessor with compositions in his own honor. Not infrequently was the school itself christened anew. We could not have told the men apart if we had tried. They rarely lasted long enough in office to leave an impression.

When, years later, I leaped at the job Paul had passed up, it was not because I was trying to disobey my father, but because work of any kind was scarce, and this, at least, was not manual labor. And when, during the course of the interview that led to my hiring, Mme Marcus told me that her husband would soon become a senator, I never stopped to think about how my father might react. I merely thought about how exciting it would be to work for someone so important.

Coming back down the hill afterward, I was so pleased with having gotten the job that it was not until I ran into Paul on the street in front of my house that I realized what I had done.

"You think your father's going to let you work for the hill people?" he said with a smirk, gleefully anticipating the trouble to come.

"He'll understand," I said.

Paul laughed joyously. "He'd sooner kill you."

I had never lied to my father before, and what I told him, standing in his shop a few minutes later, was not exactly a lie. I simply told him I had gotten a job assisting a lawyer. Senator Marcus was, after all, still a lawyer.

"Assisting how?" my father said. For a shopkeeper, he was a huge man. As a child, he had worked in his father's bean fields, and he still bore the broad chest and shoulders of a farmer. The sun had wrinkled his mouth into a permanent frown.

"Just helping," I said. "I'll be living with him and helping him with whatever he needs. What better way could there be to learn to be a lawyer?"

"I see." But whatever it was my father thought he saw, it clearly left him dubious. "Where does he live?"

"He works downtown," I said. "Near the palace."

"I asked where he *lives*." I watched my father clench his fists, even the muscles grown soft in the years since he moved to the capital tensing and turning to stone.

I pointed up the hill.

Just then the shop door scraped open and an old woman hobbled inside, an old battered basket rocking under her arm like a pendulum.

"Can't you see we're closed?" my father shouted, not even taking the time to see who was there.

The old woman's stooped back nearly straightened in surprise. The only sound was the creaking of the straw handle as she pulled the basket closer to her chest. She looked over at me, and then at my father, and then at me again, a curse bubbling under her lips. She knew it was my fault she was getting turned away, and she wanted me to know that she knew.

"This is only temporary," I told him as the old woman struggled to slam the door behind her. "While I study for the exams."

"I won't allow it."

"But you want me to become a lawyer," I said. "How many lawyers do you think there are outside of Lyonville?"

"Then you'll be a doctor."

I said, "But the doctors live there too."

He knew I was right. And he knew we needed the money. What he understood less clearly was that my future as either a doctor or a lawyer was far from certain. Not only was I merely an average student, I had no aptitude for being a champion of the people. Nor the energy or ambition. What the peasants of the countryside needed was someone like Paul, albeit a Paul with a clearer conscience and purer motives.

But until I had a better idea of what I might more reasonably accomplish, I let my father continue to dream.

Chapter Two

In my four years as Senator Marcus's footman, I learned everything I could about running a household. I watched the way Mme Marcus supervised the staff, sternly but never unkindly. She was not afraid to punish insubordination, yet she did so in a way that inspired respect, not fear. She would never dismiss a servant without cause, and she was willing to reward ambition. By the end of those four years I was helping her to maintain the household accounts.

The more the Marcuses grew to rely upon me, the more responsibility I felt, not just for myself but for the rest of the staff as well. If one of us was neglecting his duties, it reflected badly on the rest. Of course, it often seemed I was the only one burdened with this concern. For the others, a job well done was a far lesser priority than a job done quickly—or better yet, a job done not at all, if they thought they could get away with it. As much as I could, I avoided them, but there were times when they simply had to be confronted.

One afternoon, as I was carrying some small packages in from the car, I happened to come upon the gardener engaged in an assault upon one of Madame's prized hibiscus hedges. From behind—his legs spread for leverage and his arms quivering with strain—he appeared to be trying to choke it to death.

"Look at what you've done," I said, setting down the paper-wrapped boxes and ripping the shears from his hands. The blades were s   thick with rust they could not be closed even without a branch caught between them.

He looked at me dully. "What business is it of yours?"

"I don't want to see these again until you've had them sharpened," I said.

He grabbed them back. "If you don't want to see them, go back in the house where you belong."

"What do you think Madame will say when she sees this?"

He came closer, pointing the blades at my chest. "Do you want to find out how sharp they really are?"

I pushed them away. "You're as ignorant as you are lazy."

"And you," he said, scissoring the blades together with a metallic hiss, "had better remember your place."

That evening before supper I was pulled aside by Mme Marcus. Like a woman mustering gratitude for a gift she found distasteful, Madame offered me a smile that was tight and uncomfortable.

"Of course you were right to have said what you did," she admitted, sitting me down in one of the upholstered chairs in the sunroom. "They're like children, always trying to get away with something. But it would be best if you left such things to me. No one enjoys being disciplined by an equal."

An equal what? I wanted to say, but I knew she was speaking only in terms of our employment.

"Of course," I said wretchedly. "I was only trying to help."

Without another word, without a glance in my direction, Mme Marcus rose, and I felt ill as I listened to her footsteps fade. Her disappointment was punishment enough.

Before going up to my room, I went to the kitchen to tell the cook not to set a place for me.

With what little daylight remained, I lay down on the floor and stared out my porthole. I tried to imagine what Paul would have done in my place. But of course, Paul would never have been in my place. Paul would never have confronted the gardener, because Paul could not have cared less about the hedge. Nor would Paul be hiding in an attic. No, Paul would at that very moment be lying on his back in the gardener's shed, holding the dregs of a rum bottle up to the fading light and boasting about the depravities he intended to perform upon the Marcuses' new maid. And as for Madame, Paul would sooner have quit than say he was sorry. That was why he felt so at home in the moldy, queasying docks, surrounded by gun-toting thugs who did not believe in regret. That was also why I knew it was only a matter of time before his mother would find herself in the city morgue, futilely attempting to identify his remains.

Darkness came down like a curtain, and I found relief in no longer being able to see the things down below that filled me with disgust. But then a new mire of dread accumulated in my stomach as I contemplated another sunrise and the continuation of Mme Marcus's disappointment.

The gardener, when he arrived in the morning, looked at me smugly. The cook burned my breakfast. All day it seemed that even the Marcuses were avoiding me. Otherwise, why would they have sent the maid, of all people, to deliver the message that the Senator wanted to see me—a message she delivered with a smirk?

The first thing I saw when the door to the Senator's office swung open was the pipe dancing on his lips as he mumbled for me to sit—or so I gathered when he followed the words with a finger aimed at one of his hard leather chairs.

When I was settled, he came around and lowered himself onto the corner of the desk. He was so close we could not avoid brushing knees.

He extracted the pipe with an inadvertent pop. "I think it's time we discussed your future," he said with a solemnity that suggested such a talk would not take long.

I could barely swallow.

"Madame Marcus and I have been talking," he continued, "and we feel you're ready for a more demanding position."

The pipe lay nestled in his hand like a small, contented pet.

I was speechless.

"We're going to be expanding the staff."

Although his first announcement came to me as a shock, this last bit of news was no surprise. After less than one term in the legislature, Senator Marcus had already established himself as one of the preeminent political figures in the country. Dinner parties, formerly once-a-month affairs, had recently begun happening weekly. Several days before I had overheard Madame telling one of her friends during tea that she was contemplating hiring a cook's assistant and a second footman. But I did not see how either one would be an improvement over my current position.

"Perhaps you've noticed," the Senator added, lifting a crystal decanter from the sideboard, "that I've been traveling a great deal."

I nodded.

He splashed some amber liquid in a glass, and with his finger he chased an errant drop down the side, disciplining it with an efficient swipe. "I'm in need of a valet," he said, pressing the wet finger between his lips. "And a driver. What do you say?"

"To which?"

"To both."

I crossed and then uncrossed my legs, trying to control my excitement. "It's my wish to serve in whatever way is of the greatest use to you and Mme Marcus."

He raised his glass in the air.

"Your father would be proud of the fine young man you've become."

"Thank you, sir," I said. "It's very kind of you to give me this opportunity."

"If only there were more like you." The Senator took a puff from his pipe. "So many young people these days are content to do nothing. They complain about how hard their lives are, but they don't do anything to change them."

"That's very true, sir," I said, feeling another surge of exhilaration. I wanted to tell him the exact same thoughts had occupied me all night. "Where I grew up, it was exactly like that."

"But your father showed you the value of hard work."

"My father was very stern."

"He would be very proud."

I said, "It would be wonderful to think so."

The next day Senator Marcus took away my nondescript footman's coat and slacks and replaced them with an only slightly used gray woolen suit. It was the first suit I had ever owned.

Of the two roles I had been given, the latter was the most difficult, for I had never driven before—had never even sat in the front seat of a car—and the steep, twisting roads of Lyonville were a less than ideal place to learn.

From the day I turned in my footman's uniform to the day I finally left Senator Marcus's service, five years later, I accompanied him virtually everywhere he went. Each morning I drove him to his office in the Legislative Palace. While he worked, I tended to errands downtown, always returning in time to take him to lunch. If I came back early, or if he had no errands for me to run, I waited in the anteroom. The wait was often long and dull, but there was a soft leather wing chair reserved for me, and I could sit there and watch cabinet ministers and ambassadors I recognized from the Marcuses' parties come and go.

And it was here, too, that I first saw President Mailodet.

That morning had been otherwise uneventful. I had just returned to the Senator's office after picking up some items at the market for Mme Marcus. Scarcely had I taken my seat when two enormous men in black mirrored sunglasses only a shade darker than their skin pushed through the door behind me. Instinctively I knew to lower my eyes. One of them was wearing mismatched socks, brown on the left, and on the right, deep burgundy with a grid of small gold diamonds. The diamonds above his outer heel were split where the sock had begun to run.

The men's arrival seemed to catch everyone by surprise. In my memory there was a collective, instantaneous intake of air as Senator Marcus's secretary and his clerks came to a sudden, speechless halt.

If the staff were trying to make themselves invisible, they apparently succeeded, for the only person the two men took note of upon entering was me. Seeing me sitting there, the one in mismatched socks came forward and ordered me to stand. When I hesitated, he reached down and lifted me by my lapel. While his partner watched, the man ran his hands roughly over my suit, pausing only when he felt the sharp edge of the car keys in my pocket. And then he was done, and again I must have been too slow to comprehend what he wanted, for he stabbed two fingers into my chest and I toppled back down into the chair.

That was the moment President Mailodet entered. He looked precisely as he always did in the newspaper: a slight, older man with a soft, mild face upon which perched a pair of black-framed eyeglasses so thick and unwieldy I wondered fleetingly if they alone might be responsible for the stoop in his posture. A crushed felt derby at least one size too small sat precariously atop his head. Whether it was his shabby clothes or his milky expression I do not know, but just as in the paper he looked not the least bit presidential.

By that point, M. Mailodet had been in power for only ten months. At this early stage of his term he still had the bearing of someone used to being hushed in the presence of more important people. Compared to many of the presidents who had served before him, however, M. Mailodet was in fact already well established. In the twelve months prior to his election, four different men had occupied the palace. There

had been six in all since M. Marcus joined the Senate. In his own quiet
way, President Mailodet so far seemed determined not to follow in his
predecessors' footsteps.

We were not unaccustomed to tempestuous political seasons, but
these recent ones had been extreme even by our standards. The first
president in the latest string had been a provisional replacement—a
judge—chosen to fill the vacuum left by the resignation of his predecessor, who had been exiled at the persuasive urging of the military.
Following the judge's appointment, a brutal campaign had commenced
among the four main candidates vying for votes in the upcoming elections. When the judge proved incapable of quelling the rioting among
the various partisans, the legislature chose to remove him, selecting
one of the four candidates to take his place. As for the second provisional president, his term ended less than two months later, when he
was placed under house arrest for allegedly plotting to assassinate his
rivals. The resulting vacancy led to two separate failed coups by competing factions of the military, following which the two camps settled
on naming one of the remaining three candidates as the third provisional president of the year. Less than three weeks later, another group
of army officers ushered him away.

Making a rare appearance on the radio the evening president
number four was swept away, M. Mailodet summed up the frustration
of the populace, declaring, "They have all gone mad."

By the time the elections finally arrived, most of the original candidates had either been removed or discredited. M. Mailodet's victory
thus brought about a reassuring calm.

Though he was always invited, the president had never attended
one of the Marcuses' parties. President Mailodet had been a doctor,
and I had come to understand he was a very private man, nevertheless
thought of as friendly. He was generally well liked, even behind his
back. After all the time I had spent within earshot of conversations
about him between Senator Marcus and his colleagues and friends, I
often felt as though I knew the president as well as they did.

As he made his unhurried way to Senator Marcus's office the after-

noon of our first encounter, President Mailodet glanced over at me, his
eyes small and sleepy. He smiled slightly and removed his hat, revealing a brush cut with a halo of white around the edges. His was a genuinely warm smile. Not calculated—not the empty gesture one might
expect from a polished statesman. I wondered if he meant the smile as
an apology for his bodyguards' bad manners. But his face was so placid,
it seemed to me impossible that he could have any inclination of what
they had done on his behalf. And I liked the way the president closed
Senator Marcus's office door behind him, so that I only just barely
heard the latch click. He was a man with nothing to prove.

The president and his bodyguards made several similar appearances over the next few months, and in truth I thought it odd that it was
always the president who visited Senator Marcus, and not the other way
around. But I took it as a sign of the Senator's growing importance. For
his part, Senator Marcus never mentioned the meetings. Not to Mme
Marcus—at least not where I could overhear—and never at any of their
dinner parties. He trusted me to do the same.

"You know how people gossip," he said.

Why raise suspicions when there was no need?

At the time I had little notion of what it meant to be a senator.
What Senator Marcus did all day in his office, and what transpired
on the Senate floor when they were in session, were mysteries I had
no hope of unraveling. I understood, of course, that Senator Marcus
was responsible for passing laws. But in my ignorance I imagined the
process being like what I occasionally witnessed in his study, four or
five dignified men discussing a subject over cigars and cognac and then
shaking hands, donning their coats and hats, and parting as friends. It
is a testament to the peacefulness of those years—and to my own na-
ïveté—that I could assume something so quaint.

Chapter Three

Senator Marcus had lunch each day with one or another of his colleagues, or with one of his many lawyer friends. His favorite restaurant—though I had heard him say it was by no means the best—was at the Hotel Erdrich. At the time, the Erdrich was the finest hotel on the island. Of course, there was little in the way of competition, but the hotel nevertheless took its prestige seriously.

Despite the relative peace following M. Mailodet's election, the few visitors the island managed to draw tended to be small-time businessmen who had failed in their own countries and were desperate enough to try their luck in ours. All of them stayed at the Erdrich. Occasionally Senator Marcus lunched with one of them, though always reluctantly. I often heard him complain to Mme Marcus and to his dinner guests about his encounters with these vulgar and pushy "captains of industry," a phrase he insisted on rendering in English, as though it were a concept foreign to his own language.

Senator Marcus seldom told me with whom he would be lunching, but I could always tell. If, as I drove him down rue Yvane toward the Erdrich, he asked me to turn on the radio—always merengue, to which he liked to tap his fingernails against the glass—I knew he was going to see a friend. But if he sat silently in the backseat, staring vacantly out the window, I knew he was anticipating unpleasant company. And I knew to adjust my own demeanor accordingly.

I quickly settled into this new life, and I would be lying if I said I did not enjoy the feeling of importance the work gave me. Each night when I undressed I picked every sliver of lint from my gray suit. Each morning, before putting the suit back on, I checked to make sure the buttons still held fast. In my breast pocket I carefully arranged my handkerchief.

My father, however, had not changed his mind about my employment. If anything, time made him only more opposed to what I was doing. Each Sunday when I went to his shop before church he greeted me with questions he had spent the week sharpening like knives: What kind of cases does this lawyer take? (All kinds.) How many meals do they feed you each day? (Three.) Are you studying for your exams? (Of course.) When will you take them? (M. Marcus says I should take my time if I want to do well.) What church does he attend? (The Church of the Holy Trinity in Lyonville.)

Church was an especially fraught topic. The first time I mentioned it, my father retorted bitterly that the Church of the Holy Trinity was a museum of antiquity, not a house of worship. He made me promise never to attend services there. The priests, he said, were more concerned with preserving privilege than promoting good works.

"But the masses are in Latin," I said. "I wouldn't understand what they say anyway."

"Exactly," my father shouted, as if I had made his point for him. "All they care about is collecting golden chalices."

But since I spent my Sundays with my father and not with the Marcuses, there was no point in arguing. I promised I would stay away.

As for the rest, I was lucky that my father knew even less about the law than I did; I was able to get away with the vaguest of answers. But I had no stomach for lies, and treating my father like a gullible child brought me only misery. Sitting beside him in the pew, it was hard not to feel as though the strict moral judgments at the core of each week's sermon were directed solely at me.

In truth, the sermons were probably intended for the benefit of Paul, whose vices were far more public than mine, and whose mother knew the priest personally. But though pious in his own way, Paul had no use for lectures. Every Sunday after mass he waited for me at the bottom of the church steps, and each week it was something else, some new shipment he thought I could help him "unload." Now that I was living on the hill, he assumed I had some sort of influence over the products rich people bought.

"I have six cases of shoe polish," he told me one week. "Premium stuff." He offered me a ten percent commission.

"Do you expect me to sell it door to door?" I asked.

"Just bring it up in conversation."

"What makes you think I have conversations with these people?"

"Then you can use it on the senator's shoes. And when people compliment him, you can tell them where you got it."

"Why would anyone compliment his shoes?"

Paul threw up his hands. "Maybe they would if you did a better job polishing them."

I had grown tired of his jokes about my supposedly servile existence. "I do more than polish his shoes."

"Of course," Paul said, grinning viciously. "I meant no offense, Alexandre. It's important work. Today you chauffeur his car, tomorrow maybe you'll be collecting bribes and necklacing unionists. Who knows—a few years from now you could be leading your own juntas."

"Very funny," I said.

Paul stuffed the shoe polish back into his bag. He knew no more about politics than I did, but he had spent enough time around the wrong sort of people to know how to bluff with authority.

"What makes you think I'm kidding?" he said.

"Senator Marcus isn't like that."

"They're all like that." He tossed the bag over his shoulder and turned to go. "At least the ones that want to survive."

"Not anymore," I insisted. "President Mailodet and Senator Marcus are different. They're looking out for the people."

"Please," Paul said. "They can look after you, if you want. I'm looking out for myself."

⸙

I first learned of Habitation Louvois from M. Guinee, the assistant manager at the Hotel Erdrich. As Senator Marcus's valet, I spent a great deal of time sitting by myself in the hotel lobby. I must have been a pitiful sight, every day from at least noon to two, struggling to appear neither bored nor overly interested in what was happening around me. After four years in Senator Marcus's home, I had learned to comport myself around a new class of people, but never before had I been asked to sit, if not among them, then in their midst.

It was on one such occasion, early in my time as Senator Marcus's valet, that I first met M. Guinee. I had seen him several times before. He was impossible to miss, scurrying about the hotel in his red jacket with the Erdrich crest. I knew he had noticed me too, and had perhaps wondered who I was, but we had never spoken. That afternoon he approached me where I sat in the lobby, and with a slight bow he said, "Welcome to the Hotel Erdrich." Nervously I had watched him come, worrying that I had done something wrong. But his tone was warm, and I sensed he wanted me to know I was not as alone as I thought.

Every day thereafter, M. Guinee was sure to greet me. Despite being several decades older than me and far more advanced professionally, he was always kind. Soon we were having conversations about our work and about the roads and about prices at the market. Most days we spoke in the lobby, the two of us standing; he was not allowed to sit. Sometimes, when business was particularly slow, I accompanied him as he delivered orders from the hotel manager to the rest of the staff.

"I'm merely a messenger in a suit," he often said. But it was a suit that demanded respect. And he was also responsible for seeing to it that the manager's orders were carried out.

My admiration for M. Guinee was understandable enough, but I never knew what he saw in me, a young man who had experienced so little of the world. I thought perhaps that I reminded him of his son, who had been killed when he was my age, under circumstances M. Guinee refused to discuss. I did not press. My mother's passing was something I rarely wished to revisit. Everyone lost someone, and the details were often best forgotten.

In addition to lunch, meetings also sometimes brought Senator Marcus to the Erdrich. Often the meetings took place during the day, but on more than one occasion I can remember him waking me softly in the middle of the night, telling me only that there was someone he needed to see. Although I never saw this "someone" myself, I always recognized his two enormous companions, wearing their identical mirrored sunglasses in the dark.

When he could, M. Guinee kept me company. If it was particularly late, he let me sleep on a pallet on his floor, with orders to the porter to wake me when I was needed. And so it was, one evening I was with M. Guinee in his quarters. It was late, but neither of us was tired. We were playing dominoes, as we sometimes did when M. Guinee's shift was over. For a change, I was winning. When M. Guinee suddenly asked, apropos of nothing, if I would be interested in going on a trip with him, I suspected he was simply trying to throw me off my game.

"A trip?"

"On Sunday," he said. "I assume you don't work?"

"That's true," I said, laying out my domino. "But I have other obligations."

"'Obligations?'"

I told him about my father. I had spent every Sunday with him since I was a child, attending church and neighborhood gatherings.

"I see," he said.

I asked him where he was going.

"It's not important," he said, "if you have 'obligations.' "

"Just tell me where," I said.

He tapped one of his dominoes on the table, uncertain whether it was the one he should play. He said, "I was only thinking it would be good for you to get away."

I sighed. "Just give me a hint."

With exaggerated ponderousness he stroked his chin. "I wouldn't know how. There's nothing I could say to describe it. You wouldn't believe me if I tried. . . . But if you're busy . . ."

"You're toying with me."

"That's true," he said. "But I'm also being honest." And then he laid a double five on the table. I had just one bone left, but now I had to pick six new ones before I came up with a five of my own. After two more turns, he played his last domino. As always, I was left with a losing pile.

"I'll pick you up at eight," he said, pouring himself a celebratory rum.

All day Saturday I wondered what kind of trip M. Guinee had in mind. He was not the sort of man to play a joke, but neither could I comprehend his need for such secrecy.

Early Sunday morning I waited outside the gate. I already regretted having sent word to my father that I was sick. Lying was bad enough; how much worse was it to be both lying *and* skipping church? And rather than asking for forgiveness, here I was getting picked up in a car in front of Senator Marcus's house, as if I were a man of leisure.

At eight exactly, M. Guinee pulled up in a sleek, dark sedan.

"One of the chauffeurs owed me a favor," he said with a grin as I got in.

In silence we wound down through the hills of Lyonville. I found it surprisingly disorienting, having so recently learned to drive, to ride for the first time in the passenger's seat, compelled to watch the road and yet powerless to affect our course. I did not distrust M. Guinee's ability, but here his authority seemed greatly diminished, owing more than anything else to his rumpled brown suit, vastly inferior in quality to the red jacket with the Erdrich crest that he wore at work.

We passed through the capital and south along the coast. Out here in the countryside it was a different world. The farther we drove, the more it felt as if we were going back in time. Soon oxcarts outnumbered cars. I was surprised by how little green there was to see. Along the dusty, disintegrating road, almost entirely free of landmarks, women and children bore their burdens however they could, the lucky ones leading donkeys loaded with heavy packs. There was nothing but brown, parched earth as far as I could see.

Beyond the bay there was more for living things to cling to in the soil, and the view improved slightly. Small plots dominated the landscape, daggered crowns of sisal and rows of corn and millet interspersed with tufts of vetiver. And then came the great swamps of rice, worked by peasants in wide palm hats, who looked up as we drove by, as if obliged to keep a tally. Yet despite the crops and laborers, this too was an oddly barren landscape. The fields, so lush in their confines, looked as if they had been artificially grafted onto the terrain. In stark contrast, the land left uncultivated seemed unable to support anything more than low, desolate shrubs and rust-colored grasses. There was scarcely a single tree anywhere in sight.

I had never been so far from the city, and yet there was something familiar about the surroundings. Perhaps I was remembering my father's stories of his youth, one of six children of poor farmers like these. But they could have been anyone's stories. The city was full of people who had fled the depleted countryside in hope of finding better lives and had simply found themselves wasting away somewhere else instead.

I was relieved when, after half an hour, we left the coast on a course due east into the mountains. The road here was rough, and we frequently had to slow so M. Guinee could ease the car over rocks and around holes sluiced out by recent heavy rains.

"I'm taking you to see a house," M. Guinee finally volunteered.

"A house?" I repeated, and I waited for him to smile, to say he was only kidding. Surely he would not have brought me all this way for a house. Every home we had passed so far appeared to have been lashed together from roadside detritus.

By this time we were halfway to the mountain village of Saint-Gabriel, and suddenly M. Guinee pulled over. I thought at first that something had happened to the car. On roads such as these, axles snapped as easily as bones.

"Impressive, isn't it?" M. Guinee said. He was looking past me out the passenger side window, and I turned in that direction. Only then did I notice the immense stone wall running parallel to the road, largely obscured by underbrush. We were parked on a pebbly shoulder that I now realized was the start of a private drive. Just a few meters away I saw a tall wrought-iron gate camouflaged beneath a tangle of weeds and liana.

The wall was perhaps two and a half meters tall. The sun, just barely filtering through the trees, reflected off dirty shards of glass cemented to the top. As I looked down the road behind us, I realized we had been following the wall for perhaps as long as a kilometer.

At the time, the area was largely uninhabited, but for a few rustic farms. The sugar plantations that centuries ago had claimed swaths of land all across the island had not extended into these inhospitable hills. And neither had the mango groves nor the bean fields nor the coffee plantations, which survived—however meagerly—at higher altitudes. The land, however, was anything but unspoiled. The only things growing here were things for which no one had any use. Furniture makers in the capital had long ago harvested all the hardwood they could find. Desperate peasants took care of the rest. Lacking electricity, they found other sources of fuel, cutting down anything that would burn, burying it in ditches covered with peat, turning trees into charcoal. One could see sacks of it for sale at the market, stacked in sooty piles. Briquette by briquette, the island turned to ash.

Everywhere I looked, I saw hilltops resembling the backs of starving dogs, stripped utterly bare.

"What is this place?" I asked.

M. Guinee reached into his pocket and pulled out a key.

At first, the lock refused to move. Flakes of rust crumbled as I forced the key a fraction of a turn. I nearly lost the skin on my thumb and forefinger. Then all at once it gave. M. Guinee had me open the gate and then close it again once he had driven the car through.

"What is this?" I said.

"I already told you."

Royal palms lined the driveway on both sides like sentries, rising out of the overgrown grasses. Nothing here was any different from what we had seen along the road. But then we turned a bend in the drive, following the faint impressions left long ago by other cars—or perhaps even wagons—and suddenly everything changed. A vast lawn spread out before us. Beyond it on every side rose the densest forest I had ever seen—like onrushing waves of green. All of it—every last leaf—had been hidden from the road.

It would be impossible to describe what I saw. It was as though everything formerly growing on the now barren hills had found sanctuary here.

The drive wound downward, bringing us ever closer, and all around us bougainvillea and yarrow and goldenrod and ferns and a thousand other plants I could not name burst outward against a tangle of trees—sabliers and gumbo-limbos, outstretched mapou and swollen tamarinds, all of it coiled with heavy liana vines—as if the jungle were so overstuffed it might at any moment explode. The landscape was so distracting, so overwhelming, I feared turning my head, lest the jungle instantly overtake me.

Not until we reached the end of the drive did I finally see the house. M. Guinee said it was a house, but it looked more like a fortress, two stories of stone and mortar built in the colonial fashion, wearing the jungle around its shoulders like a stole. Senator Marcus's house was dwarfed in comparison.

Suddenly I felt dizzy, and I realized I had been holding my breath.

The estate was situated in a valley nestled between the bay and the mountains, the same range that ran the length of the island, bald and gray and lifeless. Later I would learn that when viewed from the bluffs above, the grounds formed an enormous triangle, with the manor house at the base, built close to the cliffs behind it. To the west, the land sloped quickly downward, a series of stairs and stone paths connecting the manor house and the guesthouse to the undeveloped forty-five acres of the forest preserve, which formed the estate's westernmost boundary.

The house itself was as much a revelation as the grounds. The portico, three high, sweeping arches held up by columns, led directly into the foyer, no door to seal off the interior from the outdoors. Dirt and leaves and twigs coated the floors, dulling the marble's shine and texture to the point that it looked like concrete. The chandelier and the broad, winding staircase were encased in cobwebs. We had to stop every second step to swipe them away. Yet, even in this deteriorated state it was clear the house might once have pampered kings and queens.

With the shutters closed, the second floor was almost impenetrable: mahogany-paneled walls, mahogany trim, oak floorboards grown inky with age. The masonry had begun to crumble. M. Guinee explained the place had been unoccupied for nearly thirty years. I would have believed him if he had said a century. I was afraid to touch anything; I did not wish to cause even the most insignificant harm.

Back outside, M. Guinee led me to the guesthouse. It was as decadent as the manor house, only in miniature. We passed through it quickly and then followed a path into the forest. There was a fertility here that could not be stopped, trees growing out of other trees, wild orchids sprouting like weeds. We fought our way along the trail, and eventually we arrived at a small stone villa. The villa was far less formal than even the guesthouse—the ceilings lower, the rooms more modest—but the materials from which it was constructed were no less formidable; I was no less in awe.

And still there was more. How much more, I could not yet conceive. We spent hours wandering the estate, and we saw just a portion. Behind the manor house there was a compound of outbuildings, where a staff of servants had once lived and worked. M. Guinee told me of natural springs and a small waterfall buried deep among the trees, but he said even he no longer knew where to find them. They had been reclaimed by the forest. At that moment, I could imagine the same thing happening to me—the trees reaching out to abduct me with their gnarled arms—and I knew I would not fight it.

"I remember stories my mother used to tell me," I said as we paused to rest on the manor house steps. "They were stories my grandmother had told her. About how long before even her mother was born, a man could reach up wherever he stood and pluck a piece of fruit. The whole island was a garden. My mother said it was paradise. Until now, I never really knew what she meant."

M. Guinee nodded.

"I had no idea there was anything like this here."

"No one does."

Much of the rest of what I saw passed in a blur, as I reached and then surpassed my ability to take in new things. Despite the eagerness with which I listened to M. Guinee's explanations, I retained none of it. As soon as we got back in the car, I fell asleep in exhaustion. I awoke again much later, midway up the road to Lyonville, and I felt a sudden panic as it occurred to me that I had paid insufficient attention to the route we had taken to get to Habitation Louvois, and I had slept through the return, and now I would never be able to find my way back.

That evening, after M. Guinee dropped me off at Senator and Mme Marcus's house, I pressed my face to the glass of my small attic window and looked to the south, retracing as best I could our course along the bay and up into the valley, and for the first time I noticed a tiny patch of intense green on the otherwise anemic hillside.

I realized how small and cloistered my life up until now had been, how meager my ambitions, and it saddened me to think how modest even the lives of the Marcuses would seem to me now. I began to regret ever having gone with M. Guinee. Now that I had discovered a whole new world, how could everything that came after not be a disappointment?

Chapter Four

On Wednesdays, Senator Marcus and I left the office at ten o'clock in the morning for his weekly tennis match on the courts at the Hotel Erdrich. His opponents varied from week to week, but his doubles partner was always M. Rossignol, the minister of health. The minister of health was a singularly unpleasant man, cursed with a short temper and long arms and a comical tendency to wave the latter when demonstrating the former. Of the two, M. Rossignol was the better player, a fact Senator Marcus himself was never ashamed to admit. But Senator Marcus liked to say—and he said it often—that what he lacked in skill he made up for in heart. Senator Marcus scurried after every ball, regardless of his likelihood of catching up with it. The shots he did manage to return he hit with a grunt that seemed to contain all the strength he could muster, though the results seldom bore this out. No matter how many balls he returned into the net, nor how many glanced off the outer frame of his racket in unexpected directions, he never lost his temper. Not once can I remember him swearing, the way the minister of health routinely did, particularly when an opponent hit a shot that clipped the tape and fell in for a point. At such moments the minister of health had a way of glowering at the ball as though it had reneged on some sort of gentlemen's agreement. Upon retrieving the ball he would give it a squeeze, only to declare it flat, thereby having an excuse to replace it with a ball that had not yet offended his sense of decency.

The week after my visit with M. Guinee to Habitation Louvois, Senator Marcus and the minister of health played a long-awaited rematch against their oldest rivals, Father Grommace and Ambassador Twitchell. Father Grommace was the priest at the Church of the Holy Trinity in Lyonville, and I had no doubt my father would say he was in suspiciously good shape for a man who should have held himself above vanity and matters of the flesh. Nor would my father have approved of the expensive watch and the handful of rings Father Grommace stored in a velvet pouch in the hotel safe while he played. Then again, my father would have been more furious still just to learn I knew the man.

That his fiercest competitor was also his spiritual guide seemed to pose no problem for Senator Marcus. He often joked that winning was that much sweeter when you beat a man with God on his side. And when Father Grommace won—well, that was God's will, and there was nothing Senator Marcus could do to change it.

Ambassador Twitchell, in contrast to his robust partner, had the look of a man in the late stages of terminal illness. By common parlance, his skin was white, but in truth it was nearly transparent, like certain fish one finds clinging to life in the fetid pools of dank caves. No matter the weather, Ambassador Twitchell had a cold, and there was room in his pocket for only one ball at a time, for the rest of the space was packed with lozenges. For all that, though, Ambassador Twitchell possessed a remarkable grace with a racket. Even while he clenched a handkerchief in one hand, his other could return a ball with all the ease of an afterthought. He had the ethereal presence of a ghost.

At their last match, several months before, Father Grommace and

Ambassador Twitchell had come out the victors. For the minister of health, the loss had been particularly painful. Having twisted his ankle in the last game of the third set, M. Rossignol had to hobble through the final points as best he could, but his range was drastically reduced. The match had ended with a backhand from Father Grommace that—adding insult to injury—nicked the tape and fell in just a few centimeters from the minister's outstretched racket. Off balance and infuriated, he crumpled to the ground, howling in pain and rage.

Today's rematch turned out to be no less dramatic. In the last game of the final set, Senator Marcus and the minister of health were leading, having mounted an impressive comeback. It had begun to look as though they might actually win.

But then the minister of health, who had served flawlessly all day, double-faulted, driving both attempts straight into the net.

"Shit!" he yelled, swinging his racket as though it were a scythe. "*God*damn it," he declared, drawing out the first syllable for special emphasis.

Father Grommace frowned.

"Never mind about that." Senator Marcus squeezed his partner's shoulder. "We've got them right where we want them."

The minister of health's feet remained planted in protest.

"The net's not going to change its mind," the Senator said, gesturing for him to resume his service.

The minister of health glared back in silence as he stomped to his left, reluctantly getting into position.

As he bounced a new ball at his feet, M. Rossignol's eyes followed each movement with furious attention, as if he were performing some elaborate form of exorcism with his mind.

At the other end of the court, his opponents were growing impatient. Ambassador Twitchell coughed. Father Grommace twirled the racket around his finger.

The ball finally stopped bouncing.

The ambassador and the priest curled into their crouches.

I believe even his opponents let out a sigh of relief when the serve the minister of health produced was good.

But then came Ambassador Twitchell's return. His swing was effortless, and yet the ball shot from his racket like a bullet. As if its velocity were not enough, the ball arched through the air with a tremendous slice, gliding like a butterfly from one side of the court to the other.

Lunging to his right, the minister of health made a desperate swat. The ball leaped feebly from his racket into the net.

"Fuck!" With all his strength, M. Rossignol drove his racket into the clay. There was a chilling crack as the neck snapped in two.

"It's okay," the Senator cooed. "It's okay."

When the minister's back was turned, Senator Marcus waved me over. "He keeps a spare in his trunk," he said softly, and he gave me a pat on the back.

It took me several minutes to find the minister of health's car. In describing it, the Senator had left out the most important detail: his was the only one in the entire lot of virtually identical sedans that was not black. Perhaps I should have realized sooner that the minister of health would opt for fiery red—a color to match his temper.

Opening the trunk, I discovered not one spare but at least half a dozen, some wood, some metal, all of them brand-new. Mixed among them were several other odds and ends: a small collapsible shovel, a bar of soap, a pale plastic doll with corn-silk hair and a pink party dress. The doll looked miserable, smeared with dirt and grease. Casting it aside, I glanced again at the rackets. I had no idea which one I should take, but I knew the rage that would greet me if I chose incorrectly.

As I was moving things around, I uncovered a brown canvas bag partially buried behind the wheel well. Its zipper was undone, and inside I could see the dark handle of another racket. Unlike the others, this one was somewhat smudged, showing clear signs of use. I took that as a sign that it was the one M. Rossignol preferred.

I reached out to grasp the handle, but the moment my fingers touched its surface, I realized something was wrong. It was not the thin aluminum of a racket I felt, but something made of dense, heavy steel. I recoiled as if it were a snake, pulling my hand back from its bite.

Several drops of sweat coursed down my back. I was alone in the parking lot, shielded from the hotel by the raised trunk. The air was so hot it seemed to buzz along with the cicadas.

Once my hand had stopped shaking, I reached out again toward the bag. The metal of the shotgun barrel was warm and faintly clammy, like everything else in the trunk. As I ran my finger along the inside of the rim, I found myself wondering if the minister of health had ever fired it. Or was it, like so much else about him, just another prop to make the people around him ill at ease? Senator Marcus had no need for such crude measures. That was why, of the two, he was the one President Mailodet trusted.

I chose another racket at random. Jostled in the process, the doll bobbed her eyelids, signaling her approval.

Back at the court, I handed the new racket to the Senator. I wanted nothing more to do with it.

The minister of health frowned when he saw what I had selected, but I no longer cared. For several minutes, while the other players watched in weakly concealed amusement, M. Rossignol paced back and forth, angrily clubbing the air, grumbling under his breath.

"Well, what are you waiting for?" he spat.

All at once the other men tucked away their mirth, moving back into position.

Standing stiffly with one foot on the baseline, the minister of health bounced the ball before him on the clay. He seemed to scowl with every rebound.

When at last he felt both ball and racket had proven their readiness, M. Rossignol tossed the one into the air and reared back with the other. The minister of health hit the ball with more force than I had ever seen before, roaring with the effort.

But the priest was waiting, and his return was ferocious, a wicked, sinking backhand. Father Grommace's shot would undoubtedly have fallen in for a point, tying the score, had Senator Marcus not been standing so far out of position. Seeing the ball coming straight toward his head, the Senator ducked, raising his racket only to protect himself. Miraculously, the ball caromed off and crossed back over the net, landing squarely on the line two meters from a dumbfounded Father Grommace. Senator Marcus was the last to realize what he had done. His celebration, though belated, was nonetheless joyous.

But not even victory brought any comfort to the minister of health. He had already stomped off the court, mumbling invective at the net.

W hile M. Rossignol and Senator Marcus showered and changed back into their clothes, I went to the front desk to ask after M. Guinee. The morning after we returned from our trip into the country, M. Guinee had come down with a fever, and that afternoon when I brought Senator Marcus to the Erdrich for lunch, M. Guinee was in bed, not to be disturbed. He was no better on Tuesday. Today his condition remained unchanged, but to my relief the clerk reported that M. Guinee had asked to see me.

M. Guinee's room was tucked away in the same outbuilding behind the Erdrich that housed the laundry. Aside from the manager—who lived in the hotel itself—M. Guinee was the only staff member with a room of his own. But the room was cramped and airless and oddly shaped, giving the impression of having been created out of space left over from more important things. The room was far beneath what a man of his dignity deserved, and I disliked seeing him there as much as I sensed he disliked having me there. But if we wanted to talk in relative peace, it was our only option.

I had just started along the path when I saw up ahead a man coming out of M. Guinee's room, shutting the door softly behind him. The man stood for a moment on the paving stone, turning around and around, as though uncertain where he was and how he might have gotten there. A dark-skinned man in dirty khakis and a white shirt with a tear at the elbow, he looked like a gardener. As I drew closer, I noticed the bag he carried was made of leather, though it was dark and misshapen, as if it had spent the night in a puddle. One of the handles appeared to have recently fallen off and been stitched back on, the thread much brighter there than on the other.

As I arrived at M. Guinee's door, the man looked at me suspiciously.

"Where are you going?" he asked.

"To see M. Guinee."

"Oh, no you're not." The dirty little man reached out and grabbed my arm. He began leading me back the way I had come. "I'm afraid he's not well enough to see anyone."

"M. Guinee asked to see me," I said. "I'm a friend."

"And I'm his doctor," the man said.

"*You* are a doctor?" I said, making no secret of my disbelief. I knew the doctor the hotel called on to treat its guests, a mulatto with whom the Senator sometimes lunched.

He regarded me severely.

"I would like to look in on him," I said. "I want to make sure he's all right."

The doctor took my arm again, a bit more gently this time. "He's as good as can be expected. Let him sleep. And let's hope it passes."

It had never occurred to me that it was anything other than a simple cold. "Is it something serious?"

"That depends on how strong he is."

For a moment I could only shake my head in puzzlement. "How strong does he seem?"

The doctor stopped, pausing to look me in the eye. "Only time will tell."

"I don't understand," I said. "How much time?"

But the doctor was already walking away, and I was too distraught to chase after him.

Back at the hotel lobby, the doctor screwed on his soiled hat and left, and I found myself even more worried than before. Did he not realize that waiting was the hardest thing of all?

A table of white men, alone in the Erdrich's otherwise empty club room, looked up from their glasses when I came in. Though I paid them no attention, their eyes continued to follow me as I made my way to the bar, their conversation gradually sputtering into silence. There were several cameras lying among their drinks, and the men appeared bored, the tennis court the only scenery outside the adjacent window.

By now I had worked for Senator Marcus long enough to understand the basic algebra of white men: in groups of two or three, they were either diplomats or businessmen, and one knew the latter by the cheapness of their suits. Any more than three, and they were journalists, whose suits were cheaper still. The journalists were the most rare, but also, Senator Marcus said, the most distressing, for their presence meant one of only two possible things: that some sort of political crisis had occurred, or that it was about to. They had use for us only when we offered them coups and bloodshed.

Under President Mailodet, neither of those any longer applied.

I had not yet reached the bar when I heard one of the men call out to me from behind. The man wore a tan linen suit, badly rumpled at his knees and shoulders. Despite the ceiling fan swirling above the table, he had loosened his tie and popped the top button of his shirt, and I could see the sweat blooming beyond the fold of his collar. He had a busy mustache and a nose that sloped down directly from his forehead, and both of them twitched slightly when he asked if I spoke English.

"A little," I said.

He smiled. "We've met before, haven't we?"

I assured him we had not. He said he wanted to ask me a question. I comprehended too slowly to decline and excuse myself.

"Is it true," he began, "that President Mailodet is pressuring the legislature to approve a new constitution?"

I said I knew nothing about it.

"It's been said," he added, "that this new constitution would allow the president to appoint nearly half of the Senate and rule by decree when the Senate isn't in session."

"I don't know," I said.

He gestured out the window, toward the tennis courts. "Wasn't that Senator Marcus I saw you with?"

I admitted it was.

"Senator Marcus has been a loyal supporter of President Mailodet."

"Of course," I said.

"How does Senator Marcus feel, knowing this new constitution could allow the president to dissolve the legislature at will? Will the senator vote to put his own job in jeopardy?"

It was for Senator Marcus to say what Senator Marcus felt. I simply shook my head and said I had no idea.

"Do you believe Mr. Mailodet's presidency is headed down the same path as those of his predecessors?"

"Of course not," I said.

"Will this end in violence?"

"Of course not," I said, ready now to be on my way. "We elected President Mailodet because we trusted him to do what was best for us. Now we owe him our allegiance." To show him the conversation was over, I turned to walk away, but in my haste I failed to notice Senator Marcus and the minister of health, dressed once again in their suits, standing in my path.

The expression on Senator Marcus's face was peculiar—both bemused and perplexed. He looked at me as if I were someone he recognized but could not quite place.

"Did you hear that?" he said to the minister of health, clapping his hands together for a brief applause. "I couldn't have put it better myself."

I must have been the last to notice their arrival, for by now the rest of the reporters and photographers had risen from their seats, standing in a circle around Senator Marcus and the minister of health. The reporters were tossing out questions, and Senator Marcus was speaking loudly in his near-fluent English. I marveled at the ease with which he held them there.

The reporter with the bushy mustache repeated to the Senator precisely the same questions he had asked me, and I understood now that he had rehearsed them in advance.

"This," Senator Marcus said, "is an all-too-familiar instance of feckless agitators working to stir up unrest for their own ends. Such rumors as these," he said with a gentle smile, "are not worth the attention of intelligent men.

"As my colleague has said"—and with a grand, sweeping gesture from Senator Marcus, the reporters' heads turned my way—"we stand united. Now if you'll forgive me, gentlemen, I'm afraid that's all the time I have."

At that, Senator Marcus took the minister of health by the arm, leading him to a table in the corner. The reporters dispersed, returning sullenly to their seats and their glasses, and the conversation I had interrupted when I came in appeared to pick up where it had left off.

A minute later, when I brought over their drinks, Senator Marcus and the minister of health were in the middle of a conversation of their own. I was hoping to slip away without their noticing. But Senator Marcus glanced up when I set his glass on the table, and he pointed to an empty chair and motioned for me to sit. I did so willingly, knowing what was to come, that I was about to receive the punishment I deserved for speaking so foolishly of things I knew nothing about. I thought to apologize, to show Senator Marcus I regretted having embarrassed him, but I was too ashamed to speak.

Senator Marcus nodded toward the tennis courts and said to the minister of health, "We're damn near unbeatable out there."

The minister of health swished the sweet drink in his mouth with the face of one prepared to swallow something bitter. "We would have beaten them in straight sets," he said, "if the net had been regulation height."

Senator Marcus rolled his eyes. "There was nothing wrong with the net."

The minister of health brought his glass down so suddenly, it was as though he meant to crush a fly. "They'd been playing for an hour before we got here. They'd monkeyed with the net, and they were practicing so they'd be used to it."

"You should hear him when we lose," Senator Marcus said to me with a wink.

"Joke if you will." The minister of health tugged irritably at the cuffs of his shirt, fishing them out of his jacket sleeves and lining them up with the tops of his wrists. I was amazed they reached that far. Given his odd proportions, they had to have been custom-made.

In an effort to pacify him, Senator Marcus changed the subject, but he continued to make gentle fun of the minister of health, who had recently come under scrutiny after funds intended for several rural clinics had gone missing.

"Don't insult me," said the minister of health. "If I had that sort of money, do you think I'd be playing at these miserable courts?" He snorted viciously. "I'd build my own."

When Senator Marcus and I left an hour later, having finished lunch, the minister of health was still grumbling, and I was still at a loss to explain what had happened. I had made a fool of myself, and yet Senator Marcus had asked me to sit at his table and take part in a conversation, as if we truly were colleagues, not master and servant.

Chapter Five

In the beginning of May, just a few weeks after Senator Marcus's victorious rematch, I learned that the reporters in the club room of the Hotel Erdrich had been correct in their assertions about the existence of a new constitution. But they were wildly wrong about its contents.

At a surprise press conference in the library of the palace, President Mailodet held up the hefty document, cradling it like a fragile treasure. To a cascade of applause he listed five new reforms, one for each of his gentle fingers, which he unfolded in order, starting with the smallest: a fairer tax code, certain legal protections, expanded electoral reform, the elimination of several unpopular government offices, the naming of a special committee to oversee police activity.

"The people have spoken," the president said. "And now I am giving them what they asked for."

The following Sunday, the day before the constitution was to be put to a public vote, my father and I went after the morning's mass to a gathering at a neighbor's house. Except within earshot of my father, whose intolerance for politics was well known, everyone was talking about the vote. Even though no one but Paul knew I was working for a senator, the fact of my living now in Lyonville was enough for people to come to me for advice. I felt proud to be able to tell them with confidence that the new constitution was a necessary step toward progress.

"The president is a very kind man," I said again and again.

"Have you met him?" one of my father's neighbors wanted to know.

"I see him often," I said. "He's a very gentle man."

"Are you voting for it?" asked another.

"Of course," I said, though privately I doubted I would have a chance. The Senator and I had a great deal to accomplish on Monday.

Only Paul seemed unimpressed. As the afternoon turned to dusk, we finally had a moment to ourselves. Ducking behind a pair of towering reed baskets, Paul produced a glass flask and uncorked the top.

"He's just another tyrant," Paul said between sips. "No different from any of the others."

Across the yard a calico cat, its fur spiked with grime, tore into the tough, stringy flesh of a snake, pinning the limp brown body with one of its paws.

"President Mailodet isn't like the others," I said, refusing his offer of a drink. "He's a good man."

"How do you know?" His voice echoed from the mouth of the bottle. "Did the senator tell you so?"

"You don't know the slightest thing about either one of them," I said.

Without even glancing, Paul tossed the empty bottle over his shoulder. "What do I know? I'm just a humble businessman." Then he reached down into his tattered bag and pulled out something square wrapped in heavy paper. There were words in gold script on the label: LAVENDER SOAP. He handed it to me.

"Just in case your senator doesn't turn out to be so clean after all."

The following day, as Senator Marcus knew it would, the constitution was approved by an overwhelming margin. On Tuesday, the measure came before the Senate, and after several more days of contentious debate—led on one side by Senator Marcus—the new constitution passed. The margin was three votes.

That evening, when we pulled into the driveway, Mme Marcus was waiting at the top of the steps with the rest of the staff. I opened the door of the car, and the Senator emerged to a chorus of cheers.

Inside, the new footman poured champagne.

At the Erdrich the next day, every table in the club room and every stool at the bar was taken. Never had I seen so many white people in the same place. The international press corps had arrived. Overnight their numbers had multiplied exponentially, and we were turned away for lunch. There was nothing left from the menu to serve.

"Think how disappointed they'll be when they don't get their bloodshed," I heard Senator Marcus say.

"Make no mistake," scoffed the minister of health, who met us there. "They'll get it. One way or another. Even if they have to provoke it themselves."

※

It was university students who took to the streets first, much to Senator Marcus's bemusement. "They'll take any excuse they can to cut class," he said, flipping through the morning paper.

He predicted they would grow bored of it soon enough.

All that week, one could not drive through the capital without running into the students and their picket signs and their songs and the tracts they batted at every passing car. And everywhere one looked one saw sweaty white faces, tongues curling in concentration as they tried to write down every gritty detail. I learned that if I sped up when I saw the protesters coming, they knew enough to get out of the way.

One night, as I was bringing Senator Marcus coffee, I spotted one of the tracts on his desk, a piece of shoddily mimeographed propaganda. They had replaced President Mailodet's suit and derby with a general's khakis and stripes, but the contrast between the outfit and the president's milky expression was so extreme the image came off as not sinister, but absurd. The message accompanying it, that President Mailodet was maneuvering to secure himself a dictatorship, struck me as laughable. I was as likely a dictator as he.

For most of the week, President Mailodet permitted the protests, allowing the schools to remain closed. Through radio broadcasts, a few of which I overheard while passing in the corridor outside Senator Marcus's study, the president urged calm.

At breakfast one morning, face hidden by the paper, the Senator confided warily to his wife, "I'm afraid it will get worse before it gets better."

He was not mistaken. When another week passed and the unrest still showed no sign of abating, the president called on the police to restore order.

The morning the riot troops appeared on the streets, we were in the Senator's office, two blocks away. Through the one small window facing the square we could hear the frenzied chanting, but we could see nothing other than a corner of the building next door. Still, the noise was enough to paint a picture of the mob of well-dressed students frothing with righteousness, and the smaller mob of their admirers, with sunburned faces bent over notepads ballooning with heroic adjectives. Out of the sea of sound an identifiable slogan would occasionally rise, but then it would be madness again. What was the point of such hysteria? Surely they could not have expected anyone who mattered to listen.

When at last the police burst through the din with their bullhorn, the protesters only seemed to grow further inflamed.

"If you do not disperse, we will have no choice but to fire," the same stern voice commanded three and then four and then five times. We heard it clearly. How could the protesters have not? Or did they not believe it? Or had they driven themselves into such a state that they were no longer capable of reason?

The first shots must have been drowned out by the chants, and then by the screams. By the time the Senator opened his door, a few seconds later, all we could hear were the wails of police whistles. Here and there were pops, like a child running a stick along a picket fence. After the mania of the protesters, it was surprising how innocent the guns sounded.

Senator Marcus glanced at us with heavily lidded eyes and shook his head. "What did they expect?" he asked no one in particular.

Although there was nothing to see but a fog of gas slowly dissipating toward the roofline, no one in the office seemed willing to leave. We were still clustered by the window, perhaps twenty minutes later, when the one clerk who had briefly slipped outside returned.

"They say six of them are dead," he reported, struggling to catch his breath. I thought perhaps that he had been running, but there was scarcely any blood in his cheeks.

The Senator laced his fingers atop his head. "What a waste," he sighed, and with an uncharacteristically tired shuffle he slipped back into his office and closed the door.

We had no place to be until lunch, so I returned to my seat in the lobby, still not entirely clear about what had happened. It all seemed vaguely unreal. Why could they not see where this would lead and simply return to their classes? What did they possibly think they would gain?

It was only eleven o'clock when Senator Marcus appeared in the doorway and announced it was time to leave.

"Where are we going?" I asked.

"An appointment," he muttered. His hat sat crookedly upon his head.

Even once we were in the car, the Senator would not say where the appointment was.

"Just drive," he said, but when I started down the road away from the palace, he made me turn around.

"Perhaps it would be best if we avoided the square," I suggested, but the Senator mumbled that I should go.

The police were mostly gone, although a few remained, smoking with their backs to the iron fence surrounding the grass and the fountain. As we drove past, they barely lifted their eyes. At their backs a single blue balloon tied to the fence tried to tug itself free from its tether.

It was as if nothing at all had happened, as if the bodies still lying on the blood-stained cement were entirely in our imagination. I counted four, but there could have been others. They lay as they had fallen, uncovered, baking in the sun. And there was more blood still, clots of it splattered in the street, but whomever it belonged to appeared to have gotten away.

"The reporters got their wish," Senator Marcus observed as we went around the bend. "Plenty of bloody photos to send back home to their editors."

All I could think to say was, "What a waste."

Despite the coverage of the student deaths, over the next several days the protests spread. Several unions joined the students. There were so many people in the streets surrounding the National Palace that it became nearly impossible to drive, and I had to seek out lengthy alternate routes whenever we needed to go anywhere.

Stores along the waterfront, many of them favorites of Mme Marcus, closed out of fear of looting.

Within Senator Marcus's household, we had always been able to sense when something was wrong, even when we were uncertain what it might be. Perhaps the same could be said of most households, for servants are invariably the first to feel the effects of a master's foul temper. But what made Senator Marcus unique was that he threw no fits or tirades. With him, the signs were always subtle: the amount of food untouched on his plate; the severity with which he knotted his ties. They were signs that, had the Senator been less kind, we never would have noticed. That he displayed none of these during this period I took as an indication that everything was as it should be.

Yet over the next few weeks conditions continued to worsen. One afternoon toward the end of May there was another violent clash be-

tween protesters and police, and that night I heard the Senator inform
Mme Marcus that the president was shutting down the newspapers and
all but the government-run radio station until the state of emergency
was over.

The next day, President Mailodet made use of another of his new
constitutional powers—one never mentioned in any of his speeches—
calling in the army to patrol the streets.

On the first Wednesday in June, I was sitting in the anteroom
of Senator Marcus's office, waiting to drive him to his tennis match,
when one of his clerks—a thin, forgettable young man—came rushing
through the door. Seeing the dazed look on his face, the secretary came
forward to see what was wrong. Someone went to get the Senator, and
the clerk was rushed into the offices.

I watched everyone disappear into one of the back rooms.

When they came back out a few minutes later, everyone looked
ashen. "It's just temporary," Senator Marcus said from the doorway
behind them, betraying no sign of worry. "Consider it a vacation."

He did not say it, but I understood. The legislature had been dismissed.

When everyone else was gone, he picked up his briefcase. "Come
on," he said to me, "we don't want to be late." He seemed determined to
go about his day as if nothing had changed.

At the Hotel Erdrich a few minutes later, the minister of health was
waiting, sunk into one of the overstuffed chairs in the lobby. He made
no move to extract himself as we approached.

"Well," he said with a faint nod toward Senator Marcus, his tone
even more caustic than usual, "at least now you'll have more time to
practice."

It was the first joke I had ever heard him make. It seemed an odd
time for him to be trying his hand at humor.

Senator Marcus chuckled all the same.

"If you'll excuse me, gentlemen," the Senator said with a smile.
Taking from me the bag containing his tennis clothes, he went off to
the locker room to change.

Five minutes passed. Then ten.

After fifteen minutes I went in to check on him.

On a bench in front of his locker, still dressed in his suit, Senator Marcus sat with his head in his hands. Suddenly I too felt faint, and I wished I could sit down beside him and wait for the dizziness to pass. But then I thought of the reporters in the club room, laughing into their glasses of rum.

"Senator," I said, more sternly than I would have imagined myself capable.

Linking his arm with mine, I pulled him to his feet.

Over the next three weeks, the state of siege finally subsided. We waited anxiously for the legislature to be restored.

"The time is not yet right," President Mailodet said at the first of his evening addresses. "Soon."

He said the same thing a week later.

And again a week after that.

Through it all, Senator Marcus stayed in the house, and I stayed with him. He saw no visitors, and even Mme Marcus approached the door to his study with trepidation. The tension within the household grew almost unbearable.

And then one day in the middle of July, following almost two months of relative quiet, I was idly pacing in the back garden when the footman came outside to tell me a message had arrived.

"The Senator is in his office," I said.

"The message is for you."

At the front door stood a boy with a small folded note stained with grubby fingerprints. I recognized him as one of the urchins always loitering outside the Hotel Erdrich, and I realized the note must be from M. Guinee. I was hopeful, as I opened it, that the note would say he was at last fully recovered.

"Habitation Louvois is sold," the note said. "Come immediately."

Chapter Six

I never knew the nature of the business that brought Mme Freeman to the island. I knew only that as a powerful executive with little time for exploring, she had not come out of any particular curiosity about the place. At the time of her arrival we were a republic under dictatorship, a tropic with little to offer even the most adventurous tourist. Anyone who did not absolutely have to be here—especially foreigners—had already fled. Embassies were clandestinely receiving enemies of the state desperately seeking asylum. M. Guinee later told me that Mme Freeman was the only guest at the Hotel Erdrich without a press pass, which meant she was the only one there who had not come to watch us crumble.

Nor did I know what it was that captured Mme Freeman's interest once she arrived. She could not have seen much, trapped as she was at the hotel, just as we were in Senator and Mme Marcus's home. By now the worst of the violence had ended, and a calm had settled in, but disfigured corpses were still being discovered each morning in dumps on the outskirts of the city, and no one trusted the government-run radio station's reports that life had returned to normal. The other radio stations—as well as the newspapers—were still closed by decree.

Somehow Mme Freeman remained oblivious of what was going on. Or perhaps just indifferent. Despite her considerable talents, it could not have been easy for her as a woman to have achieved the success that she had; perhaps she had grown to accept conditions such as these as the cost of doing business.

M. Guinee said he often found Mme Freeman strolling the hotel grounds, admiring the modest gardens. One afternoon he came across her seated on one of the stone benches beside the fountain, hands folded in her lap as she gazed at the treetops. They had spoken a few times before, always of insignificant things, especially about the weather and her continual astonishment that it never changed. She had always been pleasant, and on this afternoon, he told me, he would not have minded speaking with her again, but he knew it would be inappropriate for him to approach her without cause or invitation. The hotel had strict policies regarding interactions between staff and guests.

As it happened, however, Mme Freeman called out to him as he passed.

"What's the name of this tree?" she asked, pointing to a cluster of golden yellow flowers dangling from a branch above her head.

"It's a trumpet tree," M. Guinee said. She nodded admiringly.

"As you can see"—he reached out for one of the blossoms—"its shape is like the bell of the instrument."

"It's beautiful," she said. "Everything here is beautiful. I've never seen flowers as wonderful as the ones you have here. At home in the States I have a rose garden I tend to myself. I won't let the gardener near it. The rest of the gardens are his, but that one's mine."

She and M. Guinee spoke for a few minutes more, and—as M. Guinee would later describe it to me—he had already wished her good day and turned to continue on his way when suddenly he stopped. He said the idea struck him just like that, without any premeditation.

"Mme Freeman," he said, turning back toward the bench, "I know of a place I think you would like very much."

And so M. Guinee told her about the road to Saint-Gabriel, and about the stone wall and the estate beyond it, about the forty-five acres of unspoiled tropical rainforest, the last of its kind on the island. Of course, he did not suggest taking her there himself; such an idea would never have occurred to him. But so enchanted was she with his description of Habitation Louvois that, after they parted ways, Mme Freeman found the hotel manager and demanded M. Guinee be given the rest of the day off to do just that. Both the manager—himself a mulatto—and M. Guinee said it was impossible. A black native man and a white foreign woman alone together—never.

Of course, M. Guinee and his employer were each too well mannered to explain the reason.

"Perhaps my wife could escort you," the manager suggested. "M. Guinee could tell her driver the way."

Mme Freeman would not hear of it. "Either Mr. Guinee takes me," she said firmly, "or I'll go alone."

M. Guinee related all of this to me with a sheepish grin, as if to say, What can you do with a woman like this?

Seeing no alternative, the manager arranged for a car, and M. Guinee brought it around front. As Mme Freeman came down the steps, he hurried over and held open the door to the backseat, as he had seen the chauffeurs do many times before. But Mme Freeman had other ideas. Upon reaching the drive, she brushed past him and let herself into the passenger seat.

"Madame," M. Guinee said, reopening the door she had just closed. "I'm afraid I cannot allow—"

Mme Freeman looked up at him over her sunglasses, fatigued and annoyed. "I don't understand what the point of all of this is. Am I to assume by all of these safety precautions that you feel some uncontrollable urge to do me harm?"

M. Guinee was horrified. "Of course not, madame."

"And I think you'll agree I'm quite harmless myself," she said. "So let's get on with it. We're wasting time." She yanked the door from his grip, letting it slam shut between them.

M. Guinee never mentioned what they spoke of during the drive. It was the first time Mme Freeman had seen the countryside, and I imagine she was struck—and perhaps even shocked—by the sight of the peasants and their roadside shacks. Nor did M. Guinee provide me with the details of the tour he gave Mme Freeman upon their arrival at Habitation Louvois, but I suspect it was much like mine—descending down the drive to the swollen jungle below; cutting a swath through the weeds and thistle as they circled the manor house; her wonder upon stepping inside; the pools and fountains on the grounds; down the winding paths and stone steps to the villa; a brief walk into the preserve, to the point where the trails, long overgrown, finally disappeared.

Every tree, every structure, even the laundry room and stables, Mme Freeman declared "magnificent." And yet, while M. Guinee acknowledged that she seemed awed by everything she saw, he said her awe was always tempered by a calm practicality. Businesswoman that she was, she appeared to be calculating what it all might be worth.

Of course, M. Guinee had been right about her. Even before they got back into the car to return to the Hotel Erdrich, Mme Freeman announced that by this time tomorrow the estate would be hers.

In retrospect, the fact that Mme Freeman, a wealthy white woman—a foreigner—would buy land in a black republic seldom acquainted with peace surprised me less than M. Guinee's confession that he had told her about it in the first place. Why volunteer such a secret? For that matter, why had he even shared it with me?

I asked him that on the day I received his note and went to see him.

"The moment I saw you in the lobby and came over to shake your hand," he said, "I knew I would tell you."

"But why?"

"I remember seeing you in that chair," he said. "I must have watched you for a week before I finally spoke to you."

"I cannot imagine what you saw that was so interesting."

"There was a stillness about you," he said. "It seemed you were waiting for something. And by that, I don't mean the Senator."

I tried to remember that day in the chair in the lobby, but there had been so many others just like it, so many days notable only for their blankness. I had always wished to belong in such a setting, where handshakes and nods determined the fates of countless lives. But once I actually arrived there, I felt most of all an inclination to disappear. Were anyone to notice me, I knew I would be called out as an impostor. And so I often did everything I could to clear my mind of even my own presence, hoping to become as inconspicuous as an amber ashtray on a crowded table.

Still, I did not doubt M. Guinee's recollection. In fact, it seemed not unreasonable to suppose that there were numerous ways in which M. Guinee knew me better than I knew myself. So many of the people in my life—Paul, Senator Marcus, even my father—seemed to be endowed with a remarkable clarity about what they believed and who they believed themselves to be. I was all too well aware that the same could not be said of me. Maybe that was what M. Guinee saw, that I was waiting for that clarity of purpose to be delivered to me.

And now it had.

Whatever it was that he saw in me, M. Guinee evidently saw it in Mme Freeman too. The only thing left to do, after having introduced each of us individually to Habitation Louvois, was to introduce us to one another. And this he accomplished by convincing her to take me on as the manager of her new estate.

⌗

Even though M. Guinee's fever was now weeks behind him, traces of it remained—in the grayish pallor around his eyes, and in the way the red jacket with the Erdrich crest slipped slightly from his reduced shoulders. He was more easily winded now, as he made his rounds, his pace much slower, and I felt as though he were following me, rather than I him. When he had finally delivered the last of the manager's orders, we sat for a few minutes in a corner of the kitchen, where M. Guinee could safely rest, out of sight of his superior. Without his having to ask, one of the cooks brought him a cup of coffee.

"It's been this crazy for months." As M. Guinee raised the cup to his lips I noticed his hand twitching slightly; the coffee rose to the rim and a few drops slipped away.

M. Guinee saw where I was looking and quickly lowered the cup, causing it to clatter and spill upon the table.

"There's no end to what these people need," he continued, nodding in what I supposed was the direction of the club room, where the international press corps was at the moment gathered, adding still more drinks to their expense-account bar tabs.

"Do they drink this much at home?" he said. "Or is it something we drive them to?"

I shrugged. "I don't know."

M. Guinee batted away his own question, indicating his lack of interest in an answer. "We had to buy more pillows," he added. "Every one of them needs at least two pillows. What do they use them for? How many heads do they think they have? It's the same with towels. I've never seen anything like it. They go through three or four of them a day. How wet can a person get?" All of this he said with a smile, but the smile failed to hide the true depths of his fatigue.

"It's time," he said, letting out a sigh as he slowly rose to his feet. "Let's not keep Mme Freeman waiting."

Mme Freeman and her lawyers had needed a week to complete the sale for Habitation Louvois. It turned out the estate was owned by a family for whom M. Guinee had once worked. M. Guinee had never actually worked there himself; by the time he came to know of it, the place had been uninhabited for years. But he had gone there once with his employer to remove a few pieces of furniture that had been left behind. His reaction upon seeing the place, M. Guinee said, had been virtually identical to mine. So moved was he by the experience that he had risked his job—and who knows what more severe punishment—by stealing the key to the gate. It was an indication of the disinterest with which his employer regarded the property that he never noticed that the key was missing.

In the two decades that had passed since, M. Guinee had tried to visit Habitation Louvois at least once a year. But since coming to work at the Hotel Erdrich he had found it difficult to get away. When he decided to take me, nearly ten years had passed since he had been there last.

"If you kept it a secret all those years," I asked that same day I received his note, "why did you suddenly decide to tell someone?"

"It wasn't sudden," he said. "I'd given it a great deal of thought." We were in his room, and he had gone over to the small table by his bed and opened its one small drawer, picking through the few objects inside until he found what he was looking for. He held the key out to me, saying, "There's very little I can pass down."

"Maybe you should give it back to its rightful owner."

"I've decided," M. Guinee said, pressing the key into my palm, "that you are its rightful owner."

"But why?" I said. "Why would they want to get rid of it?"

"They didn't know what else to do with it."

"Isn't it enough just to preserve it?"

M. Guinee shrugged. "For who?"

I thought of my mother's stories about the long-lost island she would never get to see. For her, I wanted to say. And for everyone else who needed to believe that in this world such a place was still possible.

I do not know what I expected in Mme Freeman. I had encountered few white people in my life, only the occasional reporter and a few ambassadors and visiting dignitaries at the Marcuses' parties, interactions largely limited to the refreshing of drinks. In my experience, white men were always distant, regarding me—when they regarded me at all—with annoyed distraction. Their wives, on the contrary, tended to be anything but distant. Undernourished and overpainted, they clung to their husbands' sides, twitching at every sudden sound and movement with the precautionary terror of rabbits. They would rarely hand over their wraps and purses when they arrived. Dinner became an excruciating ordeal, watching the women struggle to operate fork and knife without simultaneously spilling their belongings from their laps. Even before dessert was served, one inevitably saw them whispering into their husbands' ears that it was time to go.

M. Guinee found Mme Freeman in the club room, and as soon as we entered the room she rose from her seat with a smile.

Mme Freeman was a slight woman in what I guessed to be her late forties. Her hair was blond, but it appeared to be in the early stages of turning something else, brown or gray or silver. It swept across her head in a bold, purposeful wave, curling at the bottom so that it cupped her pearl-studded ears. She wore a cream-colored skirt and a matching jacket, trimmed with black and closed with brass buttons.

"I'm very pleased to meet you," she said, stretching out her hand to greet me. Her perfume bore the faint, sweet trace of heliotrope and peach blossoms, but there were darker undertones, too, of something I could not quite identify.

I do not recall what I said in return, or if I said anything at all. I was distracted just then by the realization that the table she had chosen, in the corner of the club room, was the very same table Senator Marcus and the minister of health had favored after their Wednesday tennis matches. It was more than just a coincidence, I decided; it was a sign, and it immediately caused me to wonder what on earth I was doing here. Was I really considering leaving Senator Marcus? If I had any conscience at all, I told myself, I would thank Mme Freeman for her kindness and then excuse myself and never again would I think of treating Senator Marcus so unjustly.

"I've been looking forward to this," Mme Freeman said, and before I could apologize and explain my own change of heart, she had pressed me into a chair. A waiter appeared at my elbow with a drink, which he set down in front of me with a disapproving frown he intended for only me to see. I wished M. Guinee would take a seat as well, but he continued to stand beside the table, concerned, no doubt, about being seen socializing with a guest.

Mme Freeman had kind eyes, their lids lightly dusted a rosy peach, and the way they looked into mine, I could see she felt no discomfort. This to me seemed both odd and inappropriate, for there was nothing normal about our meeting like this. I could feel—and in some cases see—the reporters crammed into the surrounding tables watching Mme Freeman and M. Guinee and me. M. Guinee's Erdrich jacket made it clear who he was. But who was I? As on the day they had seen me here with Senator Marcus, the reporters must have assumed I was someone significant—someone, perhaps, with inside information concerning the "constitutional crisis" they had come to cover. Perhaps they thought they should have been speaking with me themselves. I could have taken pleasure in their attention, savoring the pride it gave me to have worked my way into a position where I might be mistaken for someone important—but instead every eye reminded me how easily the story of my being here might find its way to Senator Marcus's ear.

"Mr. Guinee tells me you're familiar with my new estate," Mme Freeman said.

"Oh, yes," M. Guinee cut in. "Almost as much as me," and grateful though I was to have him speaking on my behalf, I could not help worrying about other things he might have told her, and how many of them were similarly lies. Sensing perhaps my temptation to confess the truth, M. Guinee quickly added, "And he knows precisely what needs to be done."

"I'm so glad to hear it," Mme Freeman said, and I nodded miserably, accepting the part I was playing in this deception. "When can you begin?" she said.

I felt what little English I at the time possessed trickle away, leaving me with only, "Yes."

With a nod she showed that this, the only word I had managed to utter over the course of the conversation, was the very one she had been waiting to hear.

I had not known, until the moment I gave it, what my answer to Mme Freeman would be. During the week leading up to our meeting I had thought about little else, but my thinking was seldom the same from one moment to the next. Down at the base of the hills of Lyonville where I had grown up, a man my age was lucky if he found any work at all. If he did, the best he could hope for was a job paying him just enough to feed his family. And yet somehow, without ever having worked toward this end, I found myself in the position of choosing between two jobs, each of which was infinitely better than any job held by anyone I had ever known. Assisting an influential politician or managing the estate of a rich foreign businesswoman? Contrary to everything my father had tried to teach me to feel about people of wealth, I liked and respected them both. Senator Marcus and his wife had shown me great generosity, far greater than I deserved, and that was part of what made the decision so difficult, for it seemed to me that by going to work for Mme Freeman I would be repaying their kindness with ingratitude. But how could I refuse an opportunity like this? It was a job even Paul would have given up his toothpaste and bathroom tissue to take. And what greater honor could I pay to the memory of my mother than to dedicate myself to saving a piece of the island she had believed to be extinct? As for my father, I could think of no better way to satisfy his wishes than to take leave of the hill people and say good-bye forever to the world of politics.

Leaving Senator Marcus was not easy, but it would have been far harder had he not been so distracted. Even now that the state of siege had ended, President Mailodet seemed reluctant to restore the legislature or give up his emergency powers. Nor was there any sign that the legions of recently arrested political prisoners—students, unionists, journalists— might soon be released. If anything, all indications were that their cells would soon be filled to bursting, now that owning a radio had been added to the list of crimes against the state. The president's newly created security forces were busily confiscating every transistor they could find.

Despite all this, Senator Marcus appeared suddenly rejuvenated. It was as if this crisis had given him a new sense of purpose. Men were arriving at our door early each morning, even before Mme Marcus had risen, and they were staying until long after she had gone to bed at night. I had no way of knowing what was being said behind Senator Marcus's study door, and that was as I wished.

It was on one of the few nights when Senator Marcus did not have guests that I delivered the news of my resignation. We were in his study, and I had brought him his coffee. His first reaction was to set down the papers he had been examining.

He removed his reading glasses and squinted at me with a pained expression. "What will you do?"

"There's an estate." Until now I had not realized how nervous I was. "A forest preserve. It needs to be protected."

He leaned back with a sigh. "It sounds wonderful."

"It is." And I almost told him then of my mother's stories about the way the island once had been, before the endless turmoil. But how could I, given what had happened, given the trouble we once again found ourselves in, with Senator Marcus caught in the middle of it?

He was silent, and I felt him regarding me with a detached kind of scrutiny, as if he were looking not at but through me. "I envy you."

"Not at all, sir," I said, fearing I had gone too far.

"There are times I wish I had a place like that I could disappear to." I watched his eyes flutter closed. "I don't know what happens to us. We want to make things better, but we always make them worse."

"No one has done as much as you," I said, striking a more defensive tone than I had intended.

He opened his eyes at the sound of my voice, as if he were surprised to find me still there.

"But we can't all just escape."

"No, sir."

"Someone has to stay and see things through."

"Of course," I said.

He looked at me strangely, and I worried again that I had said the wrong thing.

"I hope you don't expect me to let you go without a fight," he offered, not unkindly.

"I'm sorry for any inconvenience this might cause you."

He folded shut the earpieces to his glasses and then sprang them open again. "Of course it's a terrible time for this to happen," he said, and in truth I found myself hoping he might try to talk me out of it. But rather than finish his thought, he propped the glasses back upon his nose and resumed reading the papers.

By the next morning, he had forgotten all about the promised fight. He spent the next few days locked in his study with his most trusted advisers.

I had been looking forward to telling my father. On the Sunday following my meeting with Mme Freeman, I hurried home hours before the start of mass, not wanting to wait until after church. It being Sunday, the shop was closed, but when I got there my father was dusting his shelves, already dressed in his starched shirt and pants. He looked me over cautiously as I came in, alarmed to be seeing me so early.

"I brought you something," I said, handing him a small box.

He opened the lid and tilted the box slightly to look inside. Nestled within a paper wrapping was a pineapple cake—his favorite. I had gotten it the day before at the Marcuses' bakery.

"You shouldn't be wasting your money on luxuries," he said, setting the box aside without closing the lid.

"It's a treat," I said. "For a special occasion." My saying this seemed to confirm his worst suspicions.

"What occasion?"

His dread was so palpable I nearly changed my mind. I contemplated lying, fabricating an occasion. Where did this come from, I wondered, this need of his always to expect the worst?

"I got a new job," I said, and my father instantly lowered himself onto his stool, clutching the dust rag in his hand.

"What new job?"

"I'm not going to be working for hill people anymore. Isn't that great news?" I said, and his demeanor was such that I honestly no longer knew if this news was good or bad or something else altogether. What would constitute great news for my father? What calamity would need to befall the National Palace for him to so much as smile? I realized as I stood there in his shop, my own excitement rapidly dissipating, that my father had oriented his life in anticipation of disappointment. I believe this had not been a conscious decision on his part, but a consequence of things having worked out the way they did—the loss of his father's land, the early death of his wife, the venality of politicians, the failings of his son.

"I'll be working in the countryside," I said. "Just as you always wanted."

His eyes narrowed in on me. "Doing what?"

"There's a forest preserve. It's the most beautiful place I've ever seen."

"What about your studies?"

"This is better."

"A forest preserve?" He laid down his dust rag and looked at me with consternation.

"It's a sanctuary for trees and plants," I said nervously. "And there's a house—"

"But what's it for?"

"It's an enormous garden," I said. "It reminds me of Mother. It's the sort of place she would have loved. You would like it, too. When you're there, you forget about everything else. All the chaos."

"What makes you think I want to forget?"

"Wouldn't you love to get away from all of this?"

He suddenly looked exhausted. "You only hear the things you want to hear."

"That's not true. All my life you've told me how much you hate all of this: the politics, the violence."

"You've never understood," he said with a shake of his head. "Being disgusted is not the same as being indifferent. I never taught you not to care."

How could he so quickly change his mind? It was as if he were willing to say anything in order to find a way to disapprove, even if it meant contradicting himself.

I said, "But I won't have to work for the hill people anymore. I thought that was what you wanted." He could not possibly deny that it was.

"Trees can take care of themselves," he said.

"People will destroy them."

"People are just trying to survive." My father got up from his stool and pushed past the curtain separating the shop from his bed. He returned a moment later, wearing his hat.

"And I suppose you'll be too far away to come back for church?" He opened the door and stepped outside, not bothering to wait for an answer.

Throughout the service, my father would not meet my eye. But for once he seemed scarcely aware of the priest either, failing to respond with the rest of the congregation to any of his usual flourishes. It seemed my father had not come for the mass, but to have a moment alone—even amongst this crowd—with the one authority he believed could show him the way forward. By now my father must have understood the impossibility of changing my mind with any kind of appeal to a higher power, but perhaps he still hoped he might be able to beg some kind of favor. Maybe a fire rained down upon Madame's preserve. Or even locusts, if all else failed. It was difficult to watch, knowing he would only be adding to his disappointment. It was harder still to sit silently, unable to plead my case.

Looking for distraction, I allowed my thoughts to wander, and soon I was back again in the marble foyer of Habitation Louvois, straining my neck to gaze at the crystal chandelier hanging dustily overhead, like a jeweled cocoon. I could hardly believe it was real, that in just a few days I would be calling it home.

The service was almost over when we heard the clamor out on the street. It started with shouting, and then there was the thud of feet running on the hard-packed dirt. Outside, a woman screamed and the priest fell silent, cutting himself off mid-sentence. The shouting grew louder, and I could hear it getting closer. The gunshots, when they came, were not especially loud, but still everyone started at the sound. We all knew what it was. A couple here, a couple there. And then two more in quick succession, somewhere very close by.

"The doors," the priest shouted, "someone get the doors." There was scrambling in the back, and first the metal gate and then the wooden inner doors slammed shut, sealing out most of the light.

"O God," the priest spoke, lowering his head, "Who knowest us to be set in the midst of such great perils, that by reason of the weakness of our nature we cannot stand upright, grant us such health of mind and body, that those evils which we suffer for our sins we may overcome through Thine assistance. Through Christ our Lord. Amen."

Around me spilled an echo of *Amen*s, some whispered, some shouted. For once my father's was among the quietest.

In the end, it appeared that the priest's prayer fell upon a more sympathetic ear than my father's. We waited a few more minutes locked inside the church, until it seemed the danger had passed. The same men who had closed the doors went back and opened them, and a few at a time, the congregation crept outside.

On both sides of the street it was the same—faces peeking out of doorways, peering down from rooftops. The body in the street belonged to a young man. He lay facedown on the ground, shirtless, his gray pants already stained purple. The blood ran in veiny streams from his head, following whatever depressions it found in the dirt. I could not believe how much of it there was. It appeared he had been blindfolded, but the cloth had slipped down and I could see his eyes. I recognized him instantly. His name was Thierry. I knew him from the neighborhood, but not well. I had seen him more than once with Paul, and thinking of Paul, I looked around for him. He would know what to do. But neither Paul nor his mother were there.

A sobbing woman rushed forward, Thierry's sister, I thought, though I could not be sure. She was screaming, but it was impossible to make any sense of it. Perhaps there was no particular sense, just rage and sorrow. Another woman came forward and took her by the arm. By then the crowd had pulled closer, and all around me people were shouting about what they had and had not seen. Two men with a gun. Maybe more. Someone claimed it was the police. Or the army. Or thugs. They had dragged Thierry out. No one seemed to know why. What did it matter, really? There was no possible explanation that would give anyone even a sliver of relief. How could this be anything but madness?

"Do you see?" I said, turning to my father. "Now do you see what I mean?"

From a nearby house a sheet was produced, and an old woman came forward to drape it over the body. My father knelt down and crossed himself. It was as if I had not spoken.

We walked back to his shop in silence. The silence was almost more than I could bear, but out of respect for my father and for Thierry I knew I should say nothing more. What could I have said that all that blood had not said already? This was no longer a place for civilized people. How could my father not understand why I had to leave?

Mme Freeman hired a car to come out to the Marcuses' house to get me. The morning she arrived, the Senator was in his study, not to be disturbed. Mme Marcus was out shopping. I had reminded them the night before that I would be leaving, and I could not help taking their absence now as a sign that they were not yet prepared to forgive me for abandoning them. Most of all, I regretted not having a chance to thank them for all they had done.

It took me just a few minutes to collect my few possessions, and then Mme Freeman and I were on our way out of the city, following a route I was surprised to find I remembered perfectly. Mme Freeman seemed different now, more distant and distracted, and I wondered if she was having second thoughts about me. Seemingly to break the silence, she began asking questions; she wanted to know about my family, and as best I could in my limited English I told her about my father and his shop.

"He must be very proud of you," she said, and for a moment all I could do was stare back at her, my mind as blank as the sky. What could I possibly have said to give her that idea?

"My father has always had his own ideas about what I should do with my life."

Mme Freeman smiled. "Don't they always?" And then she added, "What about your mother?"

I told her she had died when I was eight, and Mme Freeman let her fingertips curl upon my arm.

"I'm so sorry," she said.

In the rearview mirror the driver's eyes danced with each bump, never once looking back. I held my breath until Mme Freeman had moved her hand.

"What was she like?" Mme Freeman wanted to know.

"She was very kind," I said. "And pretty. And patient. My father was the practical one. My mother was the opposite. He would send her to the market for food, and she could come back with flowers. She bought food too, but he complained about the flowers. She would plant them, and before the day was done they would be trampled or somebody's goat would eat them. Or my father would buy fabric to sell and my mother would take it and make him a shirt and he would complain because he already had a shirt and why would he need another?"

Mme Freeman smiled again. "She sounds wonderful."

"I think you would have liked her," I said. "She would have liked you."

"I don't know." Mme Freeman shook her head. "I fear I may be more the practical sort, like your father."

"She loved my father," I said, more adamantly than was probably necessary. "Despite their differences, they loved each other very much."

Mme Freeman curled her fingers against her chin. "Which of them do you think you take after more?"

I imagined that she believed it to be a simple, maybe even frivolous question, but it caught me unprepared. Having lived without my mother for so long, I had rarely stopped to consider the ways in which I saw her reflected in me.

"All my life," I finally said, "I've been surrounded by poverty and ignorance. All my life I've wanted something better, and I've worked hard, like my father taught me. He wanted me to have a better life, too, but he wanted me to remain where I was, with the same people, in the same world, the same struggles. But I've had enough of that world. I want a world more like my mother's, with flowers and new shirts. With beauty."

Mme Freeman reached out to pat my knee. "That's the world I want, too."

For several minutes after that, we rode without speaking. I did not know how much of her silence grew out of the things I had said and how much of it was a reaction to what she was seeing outside. By then we had reached the countryside along the coast, where a certain darkening of one's mood becomes inevitable.

We passed over a narrow bridge, below which the river was nearly dry. At the lowest points, a few still pools remained, and there a crowd had gathered. We saw a half dozen women in calico dresses squatting in the hard-packed mud, rubbing at their laundry with stones. How such an effort could result in cleanliness was impossible to fathom. In the shallows along a sandy bar a man had parked a small bus emblazoned with "God Is Good" across the windshield. He stood in the water stripped to his waist, washing the vehicle down with a rag. An old woman riding sidesaddle on a donkey looked up at us and waved. Between her sunken lips she clutched a smoldering pipe.

This was not the first time Madame had seen these sights, but I could tell she was still struggling to make sense of them. In her country, I understood, there was no such poverty. In her country, cars did not share the road with animals. Adults did not wallow in mud. What

THE BOILING SEASON 69

must all of this look like to her? I wondered. What must she think of us? And I felt shame, sitting there, watching the peasants outside my window. Everything about their struggle for survival seemed to me a manifestation of their deadly ignorance. How could you help not looking down on these people when you knew a world where none of this existed?

After several minutes, in an effort to ease her discomfort, I said, "It's a disgrace."

My voice appeared to shake Madame from whatever thoughts were preoccupying her.

"It makes me wish I could do something," she said.

"Yes," I said. "But what can you do with people like these?"

"Surely they can be helped?"

"Of course," I said. "But they must help themselves, too."

"Are there schools?"

"Yes," I said. "But not all the children go. How can you expect to improve your life if you don't go to school?"

"Why don't they go?"

"Their parents don't think it important enough. They save no money."

"School isn't free?"

"Of course not. Everyone pays."

"What if you can't afford it?"

"One must find a way," I said. "My father did. It's the most important thing."

She continued to look out the window, seemingly deep in thought. And then she turned to me with a puzzled expression. "I'm surprised you don't have more compassion. These are your people, after all."

"My people?" I said. Could she really not see the differences between them and me? I stammered on for a moment, but I saw no way to correct her without giving offense. All I shared with such ignorant people was an island. I did not see how the accident of my birth in this time and place compelled me toward loyalty with others simply because they shared the same fate. If I must be assigned a people, why could

those people not be Senator and Mme Marcus instead? Or even Mme
Freeman herself? People who had worked hard to achieve their success.

I was relieved when we turned inland again and began heading up
the road into the hills, which would lead to Habitation Louvois. From
here, peasants were few, and only the remains of century-old plantations testified to their ever having been here. Within a few minutes our
conversation was forgotten.

I knew we were almost at the estate when we passed a footpath
twisting down the hillside to a small clearing, where two plaster shacks
with thatched roofs squatted in the shade of acacia trees.

Madame exhaled. "How picturesque!"

I nodded, withholding my thoughts about the filth one would undoubtedly find inside.

A few minutes later, we pulled up to the manor house and Madame
dropped me off alone. She would be staying at the Hotel Erdrich into
the foreseeable future, until we were able to get her room in the manor
house restored. The room she had picked out for herself was on the
southern end of the second floor, with a corner balcony overlooking
the pool and the gardens—or rather what had once been gardens. Aside
from that room, Madame graciously offered whichever one I wished.

After she left, I spent an hour going from room to room, but none
of them seemed suitable. They were too large, much larger than I
would ever need, the smallest the size of the Marcuses' bedroom, with
a balcony and shutters extending from floor to ceiling. A glass door
connected this room to a slightly smaller space, which was not itself a
proper room, since it was accessible only though the larger room. Nevertheless, it was in here that I laid my pallet.

Later, when the renovations were complete, this would become
my office, and the attached room my sleeping quarters. By then the
memory of my former space in the Marcuses' attic had begun to fade,
and these new rooms no longer seemed quite so large. I learned quickly
that there is nothing easier to grow accustomed to than luxury.

Chapter Seven

As I had hoped, upon taking up my new life at Habitation Louvois, the world I had become acquainted with through Senator Marcus quickly disappeared from view. I was able to go days and weeks at a time with no other preoccupation than exploring my new home—its endless paths and vast, empty rooms and disguised, secret cupboards. I had been left alone to discover the relics of a lost civilization, the island trapped in time. As far as I was concerned, the entire world was contained within the borders of our stone walls and iron gate.

Yet, however separate I was from the latest upsetting incidents in the capital, there was nothing I could do to entirely shut out the rumors. They slipped in like stowaways whenever I received an occasional visitor, sent by Mme Freeman to perform one or another task. In this way, I learned that a few days after I arrived here two journalists foolish enough to attach bylines to work criticizing certain allies of the president had been beaten nearly to death.

A week later, the interior minister—a vocal opponent of M. Mailodet and a friend of Senator Marcus—was gravely wounded in a mysterious bombing.

Still, however awful the news, it was easy to believe these things were happening somewhere far away. Here we received no visits from ambassadors and government ministers. Here no bodies were deposited along the road. In fact, the road went almost entirely untraveled. Politics were not only irrelevant, they would have been an unwelcome distraction from the work at hand.

In addition to the violence and terror, I was also finally free of the nagging reminders of the place I was from, the most hopeless place I had ever known. And behind me now were the hours I had wasted in the lobby of the Hotel Erdrich, content to listen to the buzz of important men with engagements to keep.

In my own way I had become one of those important men myself.

On those rare occasions I cared to look, the capital existed only as distant lights sparkling through the trees beyond the balcony.

One morning about a month after I took up residence at the estate, I awoke to discover legions of laborers waiting at the gate. They had been dispatched by Mme Freeman's architects to begin the renovations. There were masons and carpenters and plasterers and steel workers and gardeners armed with scythes and machetes. Madame's architects were there too, a pair of light-skinned mulattoes who zipped down the drive in a sleek white convertible with a brown leather top folded in the back. One was directing the restoration of the manor house, the other the recovery of the landscape. In a circle around those two gathered the foremen of the different trades.

That first morning, standing on the balcony, I watched the men disperse from their separate camps and converge on the manor house, and I felt as though I were watching colonies of ants descend upon a fallen crumb.

In the coming weeks and months, work on the manor house progressed slowly. Electricity was no less erratic here than everywhere else; if anything, our remoteness made it even worse. Sometimes we went days without power. The telephones were dead, too. President Mailodet had recently introduced a special tax levy to pay for modernizing the phone lines. The money had been collected in full, but not a penny had been spent.

Much of the manor house's foundation needed to be rebuilt. After nearly two hundred years of exposure to the elements, significant portions of the mortar holding together the stone had turned to dust. Matching the original construction without the original materials proved an unending challenge. For many of the crumbling columns and balustrades we had to make new molds before we could recast them.

The weather also slowed us down. Generally it was dry—too dry— but when it rained it rained enough to unbury the dead, and we often lost several days of work at a time. One afternoon a storm unexpectedly tore through, reducing the masons' scaffolding to a pile of firewood.

Stone, cement, and wood arrived by the truckload. Mahogany, oak, pine, cherry. I did not know where it came from, but I was certain there were not enough trees left on the entire island to supply it. The trucks never ceased. They brought food, too—sacks of rice and beans and fruit by the crate, and cages of chickens and dozens of small pigs. I spent days doing nothing but running back and forth to the gate to let the trucks in, and I could not remember when I had been more happy.

Three old women did the cooking, peasants from Saint-Gabriel. They also brought the men water as they worked, going from one to the next with a bucket and gourd.

At night, sleeping mats covered nearly every patch of lawn, giving the grounds the appearance of an army encampment. The three women slept inside the manor house, in the room next to mine. I slept lightly in those days, my ears attuned to any sign of trouble.

During this time I saw little of Mme Freeman. She continued to stay at the Hotel Erdrich, only occasionally coming to the estate to check on our progress. Sometimes she brought with her the architects, but most of the time she came alone, and we strolled for hours along the paths and the forest preserve. This was to be Madame's second residence, a retreat from her frantic work life back home. For me it was no less important an escape, albeit one of a different sort.

But a month into the construction, it was finally time for Mme Freeman to leave. From the start I had understood she was a successful businesswoman in her own country and that business would often keep her away. The day before she departed, she came to the estate for a final inspection. With the two architects at her side, she walked inside and around the manor house and across every accessible meter of the grounds. Together they made note of the things still to be done.

"We have a long way to go," she said when we met in her office that night. "But I have every confidence that you'll be able to see it through."

"Thank you, Madame," I said. As sad as I was to see her go, I too felt not the faintest doubt. "I will not disappoint you."

"Is there anything you need?" she asked as she walked me to the door.

"Not a thing."

A flicker of worry came into her eyes, but I could not understand what I might have said to put it there.

She touched my arm. "Maybe you should take some time off. You haven't had any time to yourself since you got here. Perhaps you'd like to go visit your family?"

"I'm very happy here," I said, relieved that it was nothing more substantial than that. "It's peaceful and the work is rewarding."

I could tell by her look that she was not yet convinced.

"I never hear you talk about your father or your friends," she said. "Don't you miss them?"

"Yes, of course," I said quickly. But Madame was still looking at me strangely, and I could not explain why I suddenly felt so uncomfortable.

Was it not enough that I wished to stay at the estate and complete the work she had hired me to do? "I love my father—"

"Is there no one else you're close to?" she added after a pause. "I've heard you mention someone named Paul. And what about M. Guinee?"

"I like them very much." But did I also need to explain that they were a part of my old life, two of the many things I had gladly left behind when I came here?

"And is there no one else? A girlfriend maybe?"

"I prefer to avoid distractions."

"I see." Her face wore a worried look. "Not even just for fun?"

"Maybe later," I said. "When there's more time."

"I don't mean to press." Her tone had turned apologetic. "It's just that I don't want you feeling stuck here." Then she peeked at her watch. "I have to go, but I'll be back soon. We'll talk more then." She reached out and took my hand. "This place seems to attract lost souls. Soon we shall see what else it brings."

※

However hard I tried to remove myself from the political dramas still unfolding in the capital, they continued to find ways to reach me. If the worst of it was over, there was still plenty of bad news to be had. Truck drivers delivered the stories with the rest of their cargo; the other men brought back gossip from visits to their families. Everyone agreed that President Mailodet was showing no signs of letting up. He crushed the unions that dared come out in opposition to his new constitutional powers. In response to a supposed conspiracy involving a small group of students, he abolished all youth organizations, regardless of philosophy and affiliation. Everywhere he looked, he saw a plot. Knowing all too well where coups and assassinations were bred, he shut down the military academy. And the first task he assigned his new security forces—whose members he picked by hand—was to keep an eye on the few army officers he had not already removed.

Although he, too, was a reminder of a past life I had been glad to put behind me, the one person I did think of often, particularly during

Mme Freeman's absences, was Senator Marcus. Whenever I had trouble with the men, or when the construction faltered, I imagined myself back in the Senator's study, watching him dissect problems with his always flawless composure.

By this time I had fashioned an office of sorts, a desk made of an old oak door balanced atop two rusty barrels, and it was from here that I handed out orders. Whenever one of the foremen came to me for an answer, for instructions as to how the men should proceed, I thought back to the times Senator Marcus and his colleagues retired to his study after dinner to discuss matters unsuited to the dinner table. No matter how impassioned the conversation grew, Senator Marcus always sat calmly in his chair, the last to respond. I often suspected he purposefully held back what he had to say, savoring it like cigar smoke, until the time was right to let it out. The weight of his deliberation had a way of nullifying everything that came before it and rendering useless anything that might follow. His way of speaking with finality was something I tried to emulate, and slowly, over time, I began to feel comfortable as the man in charge.

The majority of the problems had to do with the men. I forbade alcohol, but the men drank anyway. And they fought. Who knows what they fought about? It hardly mattered. They welcomed any excuse for picking up a knife. These were the sort of men I had spent my life avoiding—crass, vulgar, lazy, and violent. They would gladly have smuggled guns or drugs instead of hammering nails, if only they had been offered an invitation.

One evening I heard them yelling out back. Fearing the worst, I went to investigate. Against my better judgment I had been allowing the men to build a fire each evening in the pit by the laundry. Joseph, the foreman of the carpenters, had assured me that it was an easy way to keep them entertained.

"At what cost?" I asked on the day he brought his proposal.

"They're men," Joseph insisted, "not children."

To which I had replied, "I hope you're right."

That night, beside the fire, two dozen men stood in a circle, shoulder to shoulder. From within came the shouts I had heard from my office.

"What are you waiting for?" someone in the circle said. "Hit him."

Pushing my way through was like rolling heavy logs stuck in the mud.

"What's going on here?" I yelled.

As if they were slowly waking from a dream, the two scuffling men in the center came to a belated stop. One had a torn shirt, the other a cut above his eye. The two men looked at each other and then at their feet.

"What is this about?"

The one with the ripped shirt looked up, but he would not meet my eye.

"I caught him," he said. "It's his fault."

The other winced, shaking his head. "I didn't do anything."

Several of the men in the crowd pointed to the man with the bloody eye. "It's true. He caught him red-handed."

"Enough," I said. "Both of you."

The two in the center looked up warily.

"You're done here. Pack your things." And then I turned to face the others. "Let this be a warning to you. I will not tolerate this behavior. There are thousands of men out there who would give anything to have your jobs. If any of you step out of line for any reason, I will throw you out without giving it a second thought. I have no time for childishness."

"We didn't do anything," protested someone at my back.

I turned around, but it was too late.

"Who said that?"

Everyone fell silent.

"You," I said, pointing to a tall, weak-chinned young man who was trying to hide behind the others. "Was it you?"

"No."

"Was it him?" I asked his neighbor.

He averted his eyes. "Yes."

"You're fired too. I want you out of here now."

He stomped off into the dark, cursing under his breath.

I looked to the others. "Do any of you want to join him?"

They answered with silence.

"Then put out the fire. It was your last."

There was grumbling, but no one was foolish enough to complain. They may not have been happy as they dispersed, lumbering back to their mats, but they understood I was not to be trifled with.

Naturally, everything took longer than we expected and cost more than we had hoped. Every time the men fixed one thing, they discovered something else in need of repair. Still, the renovations continued, and no problem was insurmountable. We worked sunup to sundown, and at night I studied an old English grammar I had found on my last trip to the capital. I wrote Madame long letters each day, detailing our progress and outlining what remained to be done. I was sorry I could not do so in person. The phones remained unreliable, when they worked at all, making the mail our only means of remaining in touch. These letters seldom required a response, and seldom received one, though Madame always arranged for more money when we needed it. She always expressed her gratitude and announced her intention to return shortly. I kept waiting for that day to come.

The worst part of my life was the degree to which the work kept me from my father. As time passed, I felt a growing sense of guilt about enjoying a life of relative tranquillity while he continued to be exposed to the ever-worsening conditions of his neighborhood. Yet what could I do? He had chosen his life and I had chosen mine, and there no longer seemed to be anything either one of us could say to change the mind of the other.

Although no work was done on the estate on Sundays, I was seldom able to get away. There were always matters for me to attend to. Having no car, I had no easy way to get to my father's shop. Nevertheless, once a month I woke up early and caught the bus from Saint-Gabriel. By now most of the roadblocks and obstacles thrown up during the recent strikes had been cleared away, making the drive at least bearable, if not pleasant. After transferring to another bus in the capital, I could reach my old neighborhood just in time for church. But in order to get on the return bus, I had to leave before the neighborhood gatherings.

I think it was in large part because of the infrequency of these visits that I began to notice differences in my father. One afternoon I arrived to find him slumped on his stool, struggling to catch his breath.

"What happened?" I said, rushing to his side.

He waved me off, but several moments passed before he was able to tell me he was all right. Eventually I got him to explain what had happened.

He had woken up that morning with the idea that he should rearrange the shelves of his shop. Just before I arrived he had begun taking down some of the boxes and tins, but he had not gotten far. Knowing his stubbornness, I was glad he had been wise enough not to try to push himself further.

"You have to take it easy," I told him.

"And who," he said raspily, "is going to take care of the store while I'm sitting around with my feet up?"

"I never said you shouldn't take care of the store. But why did the shelves need to be rearranged? Why was that so important?"

"Because that's the way I wanted them."

We continued to argue throughout the day, finally coming to an agreement that he would avoid any physical labor not strictly necessary. It became clear, however, that we had different definitions of what qualified something as necessary. For my father, anything he might decide to do was by its nature necessary; otherwise, he argued, why would he decide to do it? All I had accomplished was to convince him not to do things he would never have wanted to do in the first place.

"I've been thinking," I said that afternoon as we sat quietly together in the yard, he on an old wooden chair and me on an overturned pail. "You should come to the estate. You could sell the store and come live with me. I'm certain Mme Freeman would not mind. There would be plenty of work, if you wanted to have something to do."

It was a still, quiet day. Next door a young woman was clearing brush from around her house with a bamboo rake.

My father looked at me as if I could not possibly have meant what I said. "What makes you think I want to leave?"

Across the street two small children—a boy and a girl—squatted in the dirt beside a muddy ditch full of mango pits and orange peels and sewage. They appeared to be rooting for some kind of treasure.

I said, "I thought it would be nice for us to be together."

My father's arms settled across his chest like a wave dissipating into the surf. "We're together now."

"We would be together all the time. Besides," I said, "it's not safe here."

"I've lived here forty years."

"But things are getting worse." I could not fathom how he failed to see it. "It's filthy. And there are more guns than ever."

My father smirked. "Do you expect me to be afraid of my own neighbors?"

"I'm not talking about your neighbors. I'm talking about the entire city. The thugs. The police. The army. They would just as soon shoot you as anyone else."

"Let them. I'm not leaving."

"I don't understand," I said, rising to my feet. "What do you think you owe this place? Look," I said, pointing to the children, who were now poking at something at the bottom of the ditch. In their concentration they looked like doctors performing some delicate surgery. "Look how disgusting it is. You cannot possibly tell me things aren't getting worse."

My father shook his head. "You start hanging around with rich people, and suddenly the things you've known all your life aren't good enough for you anymore."

"Why should I not offer you something better, if I can?"

In the corner of my eye I saw one of the children across the street rise with a joyful cry. Holding the stick far out in front of him, he carefully turned, as if he were in danger of losing his balance. The little girl shrieked and started to run, and the boy with the stick came chasing after her, laughing as he leaped across the open drain at the roadside. Only now could I see that the weight at the end of the stick was a dead rat.

"You deserve better than this."

He gave another shake of his head. "Not if I'm the only one who gets to enjoy it."

"What are you saying?" I asked, sitting down again in defeat. "The only way you'll come is if I invite everyone else?"

He thought about that a moment.

"Yes," he said. "Then I would come."

I had hoped a walk would help me clear my thoughts, but on a street such as my father's it was impossible to find any peace. The houses were piled up next to one another like discarded boxes, so tightly it felt as if not even air could get between them. It was difficult to breathe, let alone think. If I had not gotten away when I had and found sanctuary at Habitation Louvois, I knew I would have grown just as bitter as my father. His bitterness I understood, but I could not fathom where he found this sense of loyalty, this absurd principle he alone upheld. While everyone else around him did whatever they could to look out for themselves, my father clung to his idealism. It was as if he saw something noble in suffering and the unending struggle. What was noble for him was for me deadening. I knew my mother, if she had lived, would have come to see it that way too.

Everywhere overhead sagged knotty twists of power lines. No one here could afford electricity, so they stole it instead, tapping into taps that had already been tapped. It was a wonder the entire place had not burned down. No doubt my father saw the twisted wires as further proof of his neighbors' solidarity.

A man leaning on a low cement wall in front of a windowless house nodded as I went by. He wore a clean white shirt and pressed black trousers. On one of his feet I could see a newly soled shoe. We were just three doors down from my father, but I had never seen the man before. The distant, thoughtful expression on his face gave the impression of someone who knew he did not belong here. Like me, I thought, he must be visiting. Perhaps he had family here, too.

He nodded and I nodded back, and then I found myself wondering if maybe I knew him after all. He could have been someone I had met at the Hotel Erdrich. Or was it somewhere else?

Without meaning to, I stopped.

"Hello," he said.

"Hello."

"How are you, monsieur?"

"Fine, thank you," I said. "I was hoping to get some fresh air," I added. "I had forgotten how little there is to be had here."

"Oh?" He pushed himself away from the wall, brushing the dust from the seat of his pants.

"Have we met?"

He shook his head. I was surprised by his certainty.

"I'm here visiting my father," I said.

"Which one is your father?"

I pointed back in the direction from which I had come. "The shopkeeper."

The man gave a knowing smile. "Ah, I've heard a lot about you. You're rebuilding that old estate."

"How did you know?"

"He talks about you all the time."

"Really?"

"Of course. If you have a son moving up in the world, you don't keep it secret."

He stood at the side of the road, and I stood in the middle. Between us remained an awkward distance good manners dictated I should cross, but my feet felt too heavy to move. I could not believe any of these words had come from my father.

"Well," he said. "I don't want to keep you." He turned away, back toward the house. "I'm sure you have important things to do."

I understood then, as I should have from the start, that the house was his and that the clothes, which were so much nicer than his neighbors', were merely part of a uniform. That was why he had looked so familiar. With his cap and his jacket, which he must already have hung up inside, he would be identical to the dozens of chauffeurs I used to encounter each day while out on business with Senator Marcus.

"And I hope you find your fresh air," I heard him mumble.

I had offended him, and perhaps I deserved the mocking tone, but I could not understand why it was so hard for anyone else to see all the things that were wrong here.

Paul's mother's house was the same cinder-block square as my father's. But she had done her best to enliven the unpainted cement, planting two scraggly green shrubs in the hard earth outside her door. She had painted the plywood covering her windows blue, a hopeful approximation of the sky.

Inside, there were cartons everywhere, stacked to the tin roof along every wall. Paul's mother sat on one in the center of the room, hunched over a steaming bowl. Another carton served as a table.

Paul was sprawled in the corner, his legs buried in a mound of metal canisters. As he jumped to his feet, the canisters spilled across the floor.

"Alexandre! It's about time you paid us a visit," he cried, opening his arms as he rushed toward me.

I had to look carefully around my feet before taking a step. "I see business is expanding."

"You never believed me." Paul grinned, gesturing around us with satisfaction.

"If it gets any better," I said, "you'll have to sleep on the roof."

Paul gave a generous laugh. "We should be so lucky."

His mother blew a cool, tired breath into her bowl. "I can hardly wait."

Begging her pardon, I asked Paul if we could go outside to talk. I could no longer stand being in that cramped space.

"I need to ask you a favor," I said once we were out in the yard.

"Sure. What do you need?"

I started walking, and he followed me back up the street toward my father's shop. "I need you to check in on him," I said. "He needs help, but he's too proud to ask for it."

A smile unfurled on Paul's face. "Of course!"

I had expected him to be willing to help, but I was surprised by how eager he seemed. Knowing Paul as well as I did, I could not help feeling suspicious. He had a knack for working the angles. But what sort of angle could such a request possibly offer?

"You know how stubborn he is," I said.

Paul gestured for me to say no more. "You don't have to explain. This is the least I owe him."

"There's nothing you owe either one of us," I said. "This is a favor."

"No," Paul said, "it's a debt."

"A debt?"

"You've seen how well business is going," Paul said. "Those boxes in the house, that's just part of it. There's more. Lots more."

I resumed walking. "I'm glad."

"Everything is about to change," Paul said.

"I'm happy for you."

The way he looked at me, I could tell he thought I was being insincere. But in fact I meant it. We were both doing well, and that was no small thing. I still could not agree that the risks he was taking were worth it, but I knew there was no longer any point in trying to change his mind.

"What is it now?" I said. "Shaving cream? Razor blades?"

Taking me by the arm, Paul stepped into my path. "I don't think you understand. I'm being serious."

"As am I."

"I'm saying it's time I paid him back."

"Paid whom back for what?" I still could not figure out where he was heading with this, and I was growing tired of guessing.

"Your father."

"Why?" I said. "Has he been helping you sell your shoe polish?"

Paul looked stunned. "I thought you knew."

He could tell by my irritation that he had been mistaken. "Knew what?"

Paul scratched his cheek and raised his eyes briefly toward those wires dangling eerily above our heads. When finally he turned back to me, his expression was uncharacteristically grave. "You don't know about the money?"

"What money?"

"Every week," Paul said. "For food or whatever we needed."

He was still looking at me as if at any moment he expected me to confess that I knew more than I was letting on. "What are you talking about?"

"Your father."

"Are you saying my father gave you money?"

Paul responded with a nod. "Ever since my father left. I thought you knew."

"*My* father?"

"Your father."

"That's impossible." It was not that I doubted my father being capable of such a gesture. But how could something such as this have gone on for so long without my knowing?

"But that was"—I had to stop and count—"almost twenty-five years ago."

"My mother didn't ask," Paul said. "He just gave it to her. Your father is a good man."

"Yes," I said. "I know."

We were almost at my father's door, and I was the one who made the move to press on. And yet, as each step brought me closer, I felt at even more of a loss. I was not angry—I was baffled. What was I going to do when we got inside? What was I going to say? All I had planned was to tell him that Paul was going to lend him a hand. Instead I found myself in the middle of a family secret that apparently everyone had known but me.

We walked in, and my father was lying on his bed in the dark. He heard our shoes skating on the dusty floor and opened his eyes. Turning his head, he looked at me and then at Paul, and his expression was no different than it had ever been. Why had he not told me? It was like so much else with my father. He was as protective of his deeds as he was of his thoughts and feelings. So too the motivations that fueled them. He was a devoutly religious man, but even his moral code was something I had never heard him discuss. Unlike politics, religion was not forbidden in his presence, but neither did he encourage it as a topic of conversation. He had little tolerance for righteous speech divorced from righteous acts. Was that it, I wondered? Was helping Paul and his mother a simple act of Christian charity? And his refusal to take credit an effort to ensure the purity of the gesture? Even with him sitting before me, I understood it would be impossible ever to know.

My father had come to his spiritual awakening relatively late in life, after he was already a grown man. I never asked what drove him to it, and I doubt he would have told me if I had. The most obvious impetus would have been the passing of my mother, but by that point she had already been dead for more than a year. I was nine years old the first time he took me to church. It was not at all what I expected. Instead of one of the glorious stone-and-stained-glass cathedrals in the capital, he chose a place in the neighborhood made of cinder block. It looked like a schoolroom. The altar was constructed of old crates. The priest was a tiny man whose black pants were constantly smeared with chalky handprints. Each Sunday, from his rickety pulpit, he thumbed through his Bible in search of passages promoting the liberation of the poor from unjust social and economic conditions. The priest called it liberation theology, but to me his sermons sounded a lot like the sort of thing my father no longer tolerated from the radio and newspaper. It seemed my father saw it differently. I supposed the crucifix—a wooden monstrosity that appeared to have been hacked into shape with a dull machete—provided the assurance he needed that such inflammatory rhetoric came down with the authority of God himself.

Over time I had come to see that this was how it would always be. When it came to my father, the only choice was to follow where he led. And that meant that if he wanted his support of Paul to be a secret, I would never dare to break it.

"I was outside," I said, hoping he would not detect my discomfort. "I ran into Paul."

My father pulled himself up into a sitting position.

"He is starting a shop of his own. Of sorts," I could not help adding.

My father was still and silent. He seemed to sense there was a point to what I was saying, and he would not commit to anything until I had made it.

"He would like to learn from you how to run a shop."

My father turned to Paul, as if looking for verification.

"Would it be all right," I said, "if he stops by every now and then to help out?"

With a groan my father started to get up. Paul reached him before I had a chance, extending his hand. My father took it. "I'm glad at least one of you decided to do something useful."

Useful? I wanted to say. Did he really believe that Paul's contribution to mankind was greater than mine? Did he really have such high regard for black-market toiletries? But then I remembered what the man I had met in the street had said, and I realized my father must have decided that any pride he had in me should be kept secret, too.

"You have a good head for business," my father said to Paul. "I always thought so."

Had he? I found it difficult to believe he had ever bothered to form any kind of opinion of him at all.

Paul looked at me and smiled. I had gotten what I wanted. What right did I have now to complain that they had taken to each other too well?

"We'll leave you to your rest," I said.

My father finally let go of Paul's hand. "Come over whenever you want," he said. "I'll teach you everything I know."

Never had I been so glad to leave my father's shop. Even the still, dead air outside brought welcome relief.

"Thank you," I said to Paul. The way things had turned out, perhaps he should have been thanking me.

"Like I told you," Paul said. "I owe him. I owe more than this. Besides, friends help each other out. They look after one another—"

"I appreciate it."

"—Friends give each other support," he continued. "By the way"—he gestured back toward his mother's house—"Did I mention what I got in the other day? A fresh shipment. Some very nice stuff. Quality merchandise. Floor wax. Imported. Expensive stuff. Extremely rare. But since you're a friend. . . ."

I headed back to Habitation Louvois with three cases' worth. At least it was something we could use, even if the supply lasted a lifetime.

We had estimated it would take a year to complete the renovations to the manor house. As that year stretched into eighteen months and then twenty-four, Madame began to grow impatient. Finally she wrote to give us a new set of orders. We were to begin work on the hillside villa east of the manor house. She reasoned that the villa could be completed more quickly than the manor house, and it would give her a place to stay while we finished the rest.

During this time, I rarely left the estate and very little news reached us, and as a consequence I lost what little grasp I had once possessed of what was happening in the capital. Whether or not the radios and newspapers continued to be shut down I could not say, nor did I have any interest in finding out. The men were satisfied with the morning-to-night merengue on the state-run station, and as long as it inspired them to work, it was good enough for me.

But then one afternoon in mid-September one of the architects arrived in a strangely frantic state. I was on the balcony when I heard his convertible race down the drive, skidding on the loose gravel. M. Laraque was not the sort of man to be so reckless, and I could tell something had happened.

As I reached the front steps, he was springing from the car, his collar loose and necktie askew. The others sensed something, too. They had dropped their tools and gathered around.

I arrived just in time to hear M. Laraque utter—with a hesitancy suggesting that he resented the burden he had been forced to carry here—"an attack on the palace."

I assumed I must have misheard, but when I looked at the other men, I saw that they were equally bewildered.

"What happened?" asked Joseph, standing at the head of his troupe of carpenters.

"All I know," M. Laraque said, his voice rising defensively, "is what I heard." He glanced at the crowd closing in around him as if he were trying to separate friend from foe, but it was impossible to know, and consequently it looked as though he wished we would all go away. He could not risk saying the wrong thing. Men had been killed for less than taking the wrong tone when delivering news of an attempted coup.

With a wave of his hands the architect tried to indicate he would say no more, but he must have realized no one among us would leave until we had heard the rest.

M. Laraque loosened his tie another notch. "They came on a fishing boat," he said with a sigh.

"Who?"

Again he seemed irritated by our interest. "Three former officers," he said reluctantly, carefully choosing his words. "And a handful of mercenaries."

"How many?" someone demanded, not bothering to hide his impatience. Either he had forgotten the man before us was his superior or he was too agitated to care. But M. Laraque appeared not to notice the offense.

"Eight," he said. And then again with fading breath: "Eight."

"Eight!" one of the gardeners shouted, and then he quickly held his tongue. It was not clear whether he was disgusted the president could have so many enemies or distraught that he had so few.

"They got past the guards at the garrison," M. Laraque said quickly, as if hoping to cut off any further questions before they could arise. "Disguised. The officers had the mercenaries cuffed, pretending they were prisoners."

"That's impossible," Joseph gasped.

The architect showed no sign of wanting to disagree. "It was late. The rest of the soldiers in the garrison were sleeping."

"My God," said one of the masons. "What did they want?"

Disgust was written across M. Laraque's face. "What do you think?"

We knew. All of us knew. We had known from the moment he first opened his mouth. But no one could be blamed for wanting to hear him say it, the forbidden words, that they had come to topple President Mailodet.

"What did *he* do?" one of the older men finally asked. We all knew which *he* he meant, and we were grateful the old man had spared us from having to ask.

M. Laraque sighed. "He thought it was an invasion. After all, they'd taken over the garrison. The president assumed there must be an entire army. He had an airplane ready. I don't know where he thought he'd go, but he knew he couldn't stay."

High above our heads a woodpecker hammered his way into the upper trunk of a pine tree, relentlessly chasing his lunch. For me—as I could only imagine it was for the other men, too—the sound mirrored the rush of blood to my head as I tried to consider the possibility. I had thought I no longer cared about what happened in the capital, but I realized now that when it came to President Mailodet, I still cared very much.

What if he were gone? What if President Mailodet were really gone? The more I thought about it, the more I hoped no one would ask. I wanted to retain the possibility as long as I could, not letting it be spoiled by the truth.

M. Laraque closed his eyes. When he opened them again, I saw the depths of his regret. A dapper, confident man, he suddenly looked like a miserable child forced to confess to some misdeed. "One of the officers wanted a smoke," he said, slowly and cautiously. "So he sent a hostage out for cigarettes."

It was more clear than ever that he wished he had not taken up this task. The way he looked at us, with weary expectancy, he assumed we already knew what came next.

"The hostage told them as soon as he got outside," M. Laraque sighed. "He told the security forces. He told them there were only eight men. It wasn't an army, just eight men."

From all the gathered mass of men, who had run from across the grounds in the sodden heat to get here, there was not a single sound. It appeared they would sooner cease to breathe than allow their disappointment to be known.

"They took pictures," M. Laraque said, his voice nearly breaking. "So everyone would see." Though he was standing in the sun, he suddenly looked as if he had been struck with a cold fever. "They all died a dozen different ways."

Even among friends there was no exchange of glances. In silence we drifted away from each other, like shipwrecked castaways clinging to whatever bit of flotsam we could find, knowing we had no choice but to face our common fate alone.

That night at dinner the silence remained. By then the news had trickled down to the rest of the men. Not knowing who was listening, no one was willing to risk so much as whisper. But we did not need to speak to understand we were all thinking the same thing. How could they have come so close and been such fools? If only we ourselves had been one of the eight, I could see the men thinking, everything would have turned out differently.

In the following days, we had no choice but to move on, which we accomplished—as if by mutual agreement—by pretending we had never heard the architect's story. President Mailodet was still with us, just as he always had been, just as he always would.

Three months after we began work on Madame's villa, we were done. I wrote to let her know, and within a week I received a response. She was coming for a visit, she said, perhaps for as long as a month. She asked that I make arrangements to get her what she would need to plant herself a rose garden.

Chapter Eight

For nearly two months we had been without rain, and the relentless sun had reduced the lawns surrounding the manor house to coarse, brittle straw. Even in the parts of the estate protected by dense canopies of trees the ground cover had turned brown and crisp. Not until the evening before Madame's arrival did the rains come again, and then for hours the rain fell without cease.

Just after dinner, as the men were spreading out their mats on the lawn, we saw the black clouds gathering above the mountains at our backs. But at the top of the cliffs they seemed to halt, like an army awaiting orders to advance. The foremen circled around me, and Joseph asked what was to be done. But there was no time to decide; there were no tentative first drops. The clouds fell upon us like a blanket. The only sound louder than the thunder and the pounding of water against the hard earth were the shouts of the men as they gathered their filthy belongings.

"We need shelter," Joseph shouted.

"The stables," I said.

"Too small."

"There is no place else."

Joseph was looking over my shoulder at the manor house.

"Out of the question," I said.

But he was already signaling for the men to follow. "We have no choice."

The men charged inside like cattle into a pen, trampling one another and everything in their path. Beneath their sopping feet and mats the floor took on the texture of mud and manure.

"Be careful," I yelled.

No one listened. They were already making space for themselves among the piles of rubble. Others had started up the stairs, and I had to run, pushing my way past, to head them off.

"The second floor is off limits," I yelled, spreading my arms from banister to banister. I could smell them below me, an odor of sweat and wet and hay.

Back down we went, me herding from the rear. But as soon as we reached the lobby, it was clear how little room remained. Everywhere one stepped, one tripped over a man or construction debris. We tried the ballroom, the dining room, the library. Not even in the kitchen was there a spare corner.

We quickly ran out of places to look.

"Very well," I said. With me at the lead, we headed upstairs again, and I showed them into the room two doors down from mine. "I don't want to hear a sound."

It was not so much the noise of the men that kept me awake as their physical presence. There was a palpable difference in the air, a compression as if from a single collective breath. If they were making noise, I would not have heard it anyway. The rain fell like stones upon the shutters and the balcony.

I was still awake when the first drop hit my chest. By the time I understood what was happening and had sprung out of bed, the papers at one corner of my desk were soaked through, heavy as a brick. There was a knock on the door.

"Monsieur," one of the men shouted, "it's not our fault."

The leaks sprung slowly at first, slowly enough that we—the men in the other room and I in mine and the three old women next door— were able to keep up with them, running from drip to drip with buckets and pots and cups and gourds. Sleep became impossible. The echoes of hundreds of tiny splashes made my rooms throb and groan.

The leaks multiplied, and soon we ran out of vessels. The water was coming down so heavily there might as well have been no roof at all.

"Downstairs," I yelled to the others as I rescued the ledgers and other important records.

The men on the first floor were anything but pleased to see us. First aroused from sleep by the commotion, next they were getting kicked and stepped on as we tried to find our way in the dark. As I should have expected, nothing came from the lamps when I pulled the chains.

I do not know where the others ended up. We were all on our own. I finally thought of the perfect place to settle myself in peace, but one of the men had beaten me to it. I saw his dark form as soon as I opened the pantry door.

"Out."

He opened his eyes, blinking in confusion. "This is off limits." He spilled out into the corridor, and I barred the door shut with a heavy sack of rice.

When I awoke the next morning, the storm had passed, but everywhere one looked one encountered its grim remains. Every depression in the earth, no matter how shallow, hosted a still, murky pool. Across the grounds it appeared as if the sky had opened up and let loose a hail of kindling. Madame's investment looked like a ravaged swamp.

But then the sun came out and the pools of rainwater turned to steam. By mid-afternoon, even some of the grass had come back to life. Inside the manor house, however, the damage was not so easily erased. We had no choice but to sacrifice the morning's work to drying out the rooms, mopping up with whatever we had at hand, carrying what we could outside to set in the sun.

In the midst of all this disarray, Madame arrived. The car was magnificent, as long and glassy as a sailboat. It even moved like one, bobbing and swaying with each dip and turn in the drive.

As the car came to a stop, I froze, realizing with dread that almost nothing was ready.

Through the window I noted Madame's eyes opened wide and her mouth agape, caught in mid-exclamation. I rushed to her door, wishing to shield her from disappointment.

"It's incredible." Her eyes swept past the furniture and household goods spread across the lawn as if they were invisible. "I had almost forgotten how breathtaking it is here."

Two years had passed and she had scarcely changed, though her blond hair had more clearly begun to favor gray. I wondered if she would think I was different. It had been nearly three years since we had first met. I was thirty-one now, no longer a boy, but Senator Marcus's suit still fit as it always had. I seldom had a reason to look in the mirror, but when I did, I sometimes thought I saw a face that had grown leaner and coarser. I hoped the men saw it too, and understood that I was a man to be taken seriously.

Madame wore a yellow dress, the outfit I would come to associate with her visits. She had arrived by ship the day before and had waited out the storm at the Hotel Erdrich. Yet somehow she did not look at all exhausted by the days of travel. "If only you knew how badly I've wanted to come back," she said. "I never meant to be away this long."

I said, "I've been looking forward to this day since the moment you left."

The driver lifted Madame's luggage from the trunk of the car, and I took it from there.

"It's been too long."

"It's just as well," I said as we started down the stairs toward her villa. "You would not have had much peace."

Though they had made little progress anywhere else, the gardeners had managed to attend to the path leading from the stone stairs beside the guesthouse to Madame's villa. After months of careful pruning and weeding and planting, this small stretch of jungle had finally come to resemble a civilized garden.

"Anything would have been better than where I've been," she said, following along behind me. "Here, at least, at the end of a long day you can go out and breathe fresh air. Do you know that the windows in my office don't even open? And do you know why?"

"No, madame," I said. "I can't imagine."

"To stop me from jumping out."

"You, madame?" I said, genuinely alarmed.

"Everyone. If ever there was a sign of the imminent collapse of civilization, that's it. This is what thousands of years of progress has gotten us: we conquered plague and pestilence only to succumb to the eight-hour workday. Who am I kidding? The twelve-, fourteen-hour workday. For the last two months the sun hasn't risen or set with me not behind my desk. The only rest I have is the twenty or thirty seconds I get every now and then between meetings and phone calls. In my mind I've learned to stretch that into hours. I can take a whole vacation in the time it takes my secretary to announce an appointment and open my door. And do you know where I come for those twenty seconds?"

We had reached the courtyard, and I was about to go on ahead to open the door when I realized she had stopped somewhere behind me.

She was gazing up at the treetops. "I come here. And it gets me through."

And then her eyes fell back on me, and then on our surroundings, and I heard a sharp intake of breath. "It's beautiful." She rushed to the door before I had a chance to open it.

Her mouth fell open again as she stepped inside. Gesturing in several directions at once, she seemed unable to decide on what she wanted to look at first: the cream-colored leather settee, the low teak table, the rosewood escritoire.

"My God," she said, touching the desk, "the grain is like marble."

And then she turned the corner, stepping into the doorway to the bedroom. Needing to catch her breath, she sat down on the edge of the bed, parting the silk canopy. She kicked off her shoes, stretching out her toes against the hand-glazed terra-cotta tiles. "It's like a cold drink for your feet."

I felt her euphoria spreading to me, and I looked for more things to show her. I pointed out the tub in its elevated alcove across the room, and then I drew open the curtains, filling the room with daylight.

When I looked again, she was lying flat on her back, horizontally across the mattress, moaning with delight.

"Is there anything I can get you, madame?"

"Nothing," she said. "Not a thing in the world."

That evening, following a long rest, Madame came to my office to invite me to dinner.

"I wish I could," I said. "There's still so much to do."

She folded her arms across her chest. "I insist."

With the manor house in no shape for entertaining, the three old women from Saint-Gabriel served us in the villa, a modest meal of roast pork and rice, which Madame savored as if it were a rare delicacy.

"This is exactly what I was hoping for," she said, pouring herself another glass of wine. "You're going to make it impossible for me ever to go home."

I said, "I wouldn't be doing my job if you did."

"What about you?" she said.

"Me?"

"Are you content?"

"Of course, madame," I said.

"You don't miss the excitement of the city?"

"Not at all. This is a very good life. It's very peaceful."

"For some people there's such a thing as too much peace."

I shook my head. "Not for me."

She squinted at me. "I don't think I've ever known anyone as inscrutable as you."

"Pardon me?"

"You never show emotion," she said. "You're never upset. You're never happy. I never know what you're thinking or feeling."

I felt my face flush. "I am happy. I'm very happy here."

"Why? Why is this the one thing that makes you happy?"

"It makes *you* happy, doesn't it?"

Her grin was an admission that I had caught her squarely. "It makes me feel I've escaped from the rest of the world."

I nodded. "As my mother would say, it's like paradise."

"But you're so young," she said. "What do you have to escape from?"

I could see no easy way of telling her. How could she possibly understand what it was like to grow up in a place where people were so hungry they sometimes sought sustenance in cakes of mud, where houses were made of things that people such as Mme Freeman routinely threw away?

I said, "I always felt I was meant for something else."

"Life on the island isn't always easy," Madame said. "Is it?"

I was surprised she had to ask.

She raised her glass to her lips with grim determination, as if to suggest she would require more than a little wine before she could discuss this any further. "You must think me crazy for buying a place like this."

"Not at all." Even knowing the dangers as well as I did, I would have done the same. In fact, knowing what life was like on the island made the estate that much more vital. There was nothing we could do to fix the rest, but this was something we could save.

"I knew it was a risk," Madame said. "But I like risks. I decided it was a risk worth taking. Don't you agree?"

"Yes," I said. "Of course."

Madame picked up her fork and took a small bite, before gently returning the silverware to her plate. Feeling suddenly self-conscious, I looked around my plate and realized I had eaten everything I had been served, like a ravenous dog. I might have escaped the place from which I had come, but I had not yet learned to be someone better.

"We need to believe that paradise is possible," Madame said with a blot to her lips. "Without that, life would be unbearable."

It was as if she could read my mind. It was remarkable how wise M. Guinee had been to bring us together. How could it have been otherwise but that we would share this place and all the good it would bring?

The women came to take our dishes away. While we drank our coffee, I told Madame about the storm. The damage from the leaks was substantial, but ultimately inconsequential: the ceilings were going to be torn out anyway, the floors refinished. The roof, however, would need to be inspected immediately. Already the builders had indicated that repairs would be costly. But no amount of bad news could spoil the pleasure Madame felt at being here.

"Better that we discover this now than later," she said, stifling a yawn.

"You must be tired."

"I just hope I'm not too excited to sleep."

I began gathering together our cups and saucers.

"Were you able to make the arrangements I requested?" Madame said, bringing her hands together in anticipation.

I was relieved to be able to say yes. At least one thing had worked out as I had hoped.

"They will be here in the morning."

She held open the door, beaming at me as I passed through. "I can't thank you enough for everything you've done."

"There is no need," I said. "There is nothing I would rather do."

I had almost reached the edge of the courtyard when I heard her call out to me. "I nearly forgot to tell you," she said. "Monsieur Guinee sends his regards. I was able to tell him about all the work you've accomplished here, and he was very pleased."

"Thank you, madame." It brought a smile to my face to think of him again. "I've been meaning to write to him."

"I'm going to have to keep an eye on you," she said. "It is possible to lose yourself too much in your work."

There was no need to disagree. Despite what she might say for the sake of appearances, we both knew we were in this regard exactly the same.

She tinkled her fingers in the air to wave good night.

Madame wasted no time. Early the next morning, after a hurried breakfast, she set to work with the two boys I had hired to help her with the garden. When I left them to attend to the roofers who had just arrived, they were clearing the ground Madame had picked for her roses, just beyond the villa's terrace.

With the grounds and the manor house at last dried out from the storm, things felt as though they had returned to normal. I was looking forward to a day in which Madame's enthusiasm would take the place of the usual chaos.

I was thus more than a little distressed when, several hours later, I was sitting in my office and heard a series of shouts coming from down below. Rushing out to the balcony, I saw an unfamiliar vehicle in the drive. I thought at first that it was an army jeep, but what would the army be doing here? Looking more closely, I noticed the jeep bore none of the army's markings. Still, I could not imagine whom it might belong to.

There were more shouts, and I hurried down the stairs and out to the grounds. On my way to Madame's villa I came across two of the masons eating lunch in the shade of an avocado tree. I ordered them to come with me. "Something is wrong," I said. "I may need your help."

They got to their feet slowly and shared a furtive glance as they brushed at the seats of their pants. By the time I had reached Madame's pool, they were no longer behind me.

On the newly cleared earth behind Madame's villa stood four large, dark-skinned men dressed identically in khakis and sunglasses, pistols holstered on their hips. The two boys I had hired to help Madame were nowhere to be seen.

"This is my property," Madame was yelling, "and I want you to leave. You have no business here."

The men shifted uncomfortably. I could see they were confused. No doubt they did not understand a word of what Madame was saying, though her tone was unambiguous. The man standing closest to her—the biggest of the four—seemed to be their leader, if only because of his size. His right hand hovered in the vicinity of his weapon.

"I have asked you to go," Madame said. "If I have need of your services, I will let you know."

The big man turned to me then, acknowledging my presence for the first time. "Who is this white woman?"

His sunglasses—all of their sunglasses—were dark-lensed and thoroughly obscured his eyes, making it impossible to judge his intent.

"She owns this property," I said.

"She owns nothing."

On Madame's face I saw no fear. I knew the same could not be said of me. But then again, she had the benefit of not knowing what he had said.

"What's going on here?" The big man glanced at the building materials still scattered around the villa.

"Nothing," I said. "We're just rebuilding."

"Why?"

"So she can live here." I nodded toward Mme Freeman, who in return raised her eyebrows, curious to know what I was saying.

"Why would she want to live here?" the big man said, coming another step closer.

"Why not?"

"It isn't safe."

I took another step back. "Why isn't it safe?"

The big man smiled, and the effect was anything but friendly. "Because I said so."

"I see."

"We might be able to make it a little safer," said one of the smaller men. "It's something to think about."

With my attention turned to the man who was speaking, I did not see what happened next until it was too late. I heard shuffling behind me and I spun around to find Madame striding toward the big man, fists raised as if to strike him. I reached out to stop her, but not before she had pushed her hand against his chest.

"Leave!" she yelled. "Now."

In what felt like slow motion, the big man lowered his head, regarding the thin fingers pressed into his white shirt. He could have broken every bone in her hand, if he had wished. I do not know what stopped him.

The big man merely turned, letting Madame's arm fall to her side. He nodded wordlessly toward the path, and four sets of heavy boots tramped their way back up to the drive.

Madame and I stood silently side by side until we heard the jeep start, and then the crunch of loose gravel as they sped up to the road.

"Who do they think they are?" Madame said. Her face was flushed, her eyes wide with wrath.

Above us I heard something rustling, and I looked up to find one of the boys emerging from a cover of banana leaves on the roof of Madame's villa. At the same moment, the other one returned from somewhere in the trees, whistling nonchalantly to himself as he picked up his shovel and returned to work, as if nothing at all had happened.

It took me several hours to arrive at a satisfactory answer to Madame's question. I started with the two masons, reading into their timely disappearance that they knew something I did not. I brought them into my office one at a time.

"Who were they?" I asked the first, hunched in a chair opposite me, his clothes stiff with mortar.

With his fat, dirty fingers he pulled a penny nail from his pocket and began to clean his cuticles. "I don't know."

"What's your name?"

He looked at me sideways, half squinting, as if he could not quite remember. "Roro."

"Who were they, Roro?"

The dirty little man twirled the nail between his fingers. "I don't know."

"Then why did you disappear?"

He began to work on the cuticles of his other hand.

"You knew there was going to be trouble."

He glanced at me quickly, and then once again he lowered his eyes.

"How did you know?" I said, losing patience. "Was it the jeep?"

He sighed, letting the nail tumble in his open palm.

"How did you know the jeep?"

"Everyone knows it."

"Everyone but me," I said angrily.

Once again he gave me that sideways look.

"Where have you seen it?"

He shook his head sullenly. "Around. In town. Everywhere."

"Why will you not just tell me who they are?" I said. "Must I treat you like a child? Are you afraid they'll come get you if you do?"

"How do you know they won't?"

"This seems not to be much of a secret," I said in exasperation, "if everyone knows but me."

He put his hands on the arm of the chair and started to push himself up. "Then ask someone else."

I was up first, and I pushed him back down. "I'm asking *you*."

Hearing my voice shaking with anger, he slumped back down and the cushion deflated with a hiss. "Who do you *think* they are?" He threw up his hands in frustration. "They work for President Mailodet."

"Doing what?"

"How should I know? Whatever he tells them to."

In disgust I shooed him toward the door. "Send in whoever is next."

Each in turn, the others confirmed what the first mason told me. The men in khakis and sunglasses were part of President Mailodet's personal security force. In recent months, men like these had been appearing throughout the capital, as well as in the slums where most of the workers lived. It was not the first I had heard of them, but I was surprised to find them circulating so far from the palace. What I had thought to be a small contingent of bodyguards, however, had apparently swollen into something inconceivably larger. There were rumors the security force's ranks now outnumbered the army's. One had to give the president credit: he had finally found the perfect solution to the threat with which the military had plagued his predecessors for more than a century. There could be no coups as long as his army was larger than theirs.

It seemed everyone had heard of the president's new protectors. One after another, virtually every man on the crew supplied me with a third- or fourth- or fifth-hand account of what these so-called security forces had done to one or another of President Mailodet's enemies. Everyone believed Madame had been lucky to have treated them the way she had and to have escaped with her life. Had she not been a white woman, a foreigner, they were certain things would have turned out much differently.

As for why the president's security forces had come here in the first place, no one could say for sure. Madame was certainly not one of the president's enemies. Perhaps they had been ordered to find out what we were up to. Perhaps they were annoyed that from the road they could not see what was going on beyond the wall. I could imagine they had simply been exercising their right to go anywhere they pleased. Or their motive could have been even baser still—to frighten us into paying some sort of bribe. Either way, they had underestimated us. Madame was not to be intimidated. The same could not be said for the gardener—threatened, he said, at gunpoint—who let them in.

That evening, Madame called me to her villa. "What have you found out?" she said, skipping her usual pleasantries.

"I think they were security forces, Madame."

"And what," she said, "were they securing?"

I took a deep breath. "President Mailodet."

"And why," she said, pouring herself a glass of water, "does the president need to be secure from me?"

When I failed to answer—when I could not answer—she added, "I wish you had told me in your letters about what's been happening here. I need to know."

Most painful to me was the disappointment in her voice. How could I tell her that I had not known myself? How could I face her, knowing how badly I had failed?

"I'm sorry," I said. "It won't happen again."

She waved me out of her office, and the door crashed shut behind me.

The next morning, before anyone else was awake, I caught the bus coming down the road from Saint-Gabriel. It took an hour to travel the twenty kilometers of tortuous roads to the capital. At the central market I hired a taxi and directed it up the hills to Lyonville.

About halfway up, the taxi arrived at a wooden barrier blocking both lanes of traffic. Two men dressed in khakis sat lazily at the side of the road. With their identical clothes and their eyes cloaked behind dark sunglasses, there was nothing to distinguish them from the men I had encountered just the day before. I could see now how their interchangeability made them appear that much more ubiquitous and menacing.

When we came to a stop they rose slowly to their feet and ordered us to get out. One of them held a pistol between my shoulder blades while the other searched the car. The driver lit a cigarette, leaning up against a whitewashed garden wall. The three of them chatted casually, while I did everything in my power to become invisible. The man with the gun to my back complained about a toothache. The driver recommended a woman he knew, who made a special poultice.

The man who had been searching the car inched out of the backseat. "Would that work on a sore shoulder?"

"Don't know," the driver said. "Maybe."

While he explained where the woman could be found, I felt the gun twisting against my spine. I tried to imagine I was somewhere else, but the pain was too specific, and it kept pulling me back.

"Tell her I sent you," the driver said.

"I will."

From around the bend came the sound of a downshifting car.

The driver flicked his cigarette over the wall. "Well?"

The man behind me slid his pistol back into its holster. Apparently we were done.

"What was that?" I allowed myself to ask once we were a safe distance away. I did not dare look back.

"Security." I detected in the driver's tone a disturbing calm, as though what we had just experienced required no explanation. As though we had been dealing with checkpoints all our lives.

The only person I knew I could trust to tell me what was really happening was Senator Marcus. As we rounded the last bend at the top of the hill, I felt at last that everything—however bad it seemed—was going to be all right. I only hoped he had forgiven me for abandoning him.

When we reached their drive, I was surprised to find the gate was open. It was not like the Marcuses to be so careless. Only later, as I thought back on it, trying to make sense of what I had seen, did I realize the driver had shown no alarm as I rushed from the car; he had not bothered to call after me, demanding his fare. It was as if he had known all along that I would be back.

At the center of the circular drive, the three stone children in the fountain swung as always around their maypole, happy and carefree. Beyond them, at the top of the broad front steps, a scorched hole marked where the front door had once been. On the floor above, the windows stared out like a dozen black eyes. The smudge of my own small window, just below the eaves, was almost indistinguishable from the ring of soot circling the roof.

I might have stood there the rest of the day, frozen in shock, had the taxi driver not pulled forward.

"Ready to go?" he said with the same tone he might have used to discuss the weather.

As I lowered myself unsteadily into the back of the car, I managed to ask, "What happened?"

He looked up past the gate, saying offhandedly, "Looks like a fire."

Upon my return, I did not tell Mme Freeman what had happened to Senator Marcus's home. Even so, she had seen enough for herself. Two days after my trip to Lyonville, she boarded a plane. She could not say when she would return.

Her rose garden remained unplanted.

Chapter Nine

It was the solitude that took the most getting used to. Solitude was something I had grown to recognize in my time at Senator Marcus's house, but I had gotten little direct experience of it myself. When she was not entertaining—or preparing to do so—Mme Marcus had often liked to read, and I frequently came upon her in her favorite chair in the sunroom, enjoying the warm wash of light soaking through the windows. When she was not reading, Mme Marcus could be found in the ballroom, practicing her minuets on the grand piano.

Until I began working for the Marcuses, I had never seen a piano, except in pictures, and in fact I was not at first certain the instrument in the ballroom *was* a piano. Contrary to everything I thought I knew about pianos, this one was ivory white. For several weeks—before I ever heard anyone play it—I eyed the piano from a distance, and once or twice I thought to ask Mme Marcus what it was, but it seemed best whenever possible not to remind her of my ignorance.

One day I happened to be passing through the ballroom alone, and with no one in sight I went over and touched the cold white finish, so glossy it felt like water flowing over a stone. I lifted the lid, and there were the keys, the big, thick white ones and the skinny, stunted black ones. Gently I pressed the very last key, and it made a sharp, hollow sound, less like music than like something clattering to the floor. Scarcely had the note stopped echoing through the room before I had returned the lid to its place and quickly stepped away.

Not long after that, I heard Madame play for the first time. Although I had no true means for comparison, I knew I had never heard anything so beautiful. I rarely had a chance to actually watch her, but whenever she played the sound resonated throughout the house, and I stopped whatever I was doing to listen. Sometimes, when it was just the two of us alone together and I knew I would not be seen, I stood in the corridor where, at just the right angle, a mirror allowed a view of her sitting at the bench, her slender fingers bouncing along the keys. Even during the most complex movements, Mme Marcus appeared at peace, the music serving only to emphasize the silence surrounding her.

This image I had of Mme Marcus was something that returned to me often in the months and then years following the renovation of the manor house at Habitation Louvois. Six months after Mme Freeman's visit to the estate was interrupted by President Mailodet's security forces, our work was completed. Rolling up their tools in their mats, the men returned to their wives and girlfriends—their small lives. The three old women who had done the cooking made their way back to Saint-Gabriel.

The painters were the last to go. On the day they finally folded up their protective sheets, I wrote a long letter to Madame, telling her the news. I led her from room to room, writing down everything I saw. By now my English was greatly improved, and I was able to fill pages with details, describing the ballroom with its floor of oak parquet in interlocking strips and squares that looked almost woven; around the windows the gold silk curtains in panels that fell like cascades from the valence; and in the dining room, the walnut coffered ceiling.

I told her about the day the plasterers working on the high ceiling in the foyer had sent the crystal chandelier crashing to the floor, destroying the fixture and chipping the marble beneath, and how after several months of searching, the interior designer had finally been able to find an identical fixture—actually in much better shape—in an antique shop oceans away. And how one of the masons knew of another long-abandoned home elsewhere on the island that had been built around the same time as Habitation Louvois and had similar floors, and one night, under cover of darkness, several of the men broke in and swapped marble slabs, and to look at the floor in the foyer now, no one who had not been there at the time would be able to say which piece had been replaced.

Although I had begun the letter filled with satisfaction over the things we had accomplished, I finished it with a sense of sadness. The letter was eleven pages long, impossible to fit into an envelope; I went through to shorten it, but there was nothing I could bear to leave out. There was already so much I had skipped over, so much that one simply had to see for oneself. I realized how hard it was going to be to live here now, having accomplished so much and having no one with whom to share it.

In addition to Madame, the person I would have most liked to share the estate with was M. Guinee. Although M. Guinee had never fully recovered from his illness, he had for the last several years been able to continue working at the Hotel Erdrich in a slightly reduced capacity—a shorter schedule, fewer tasks that required traversing stairs. The manager had reduced his pay accordingly and had recently begun threatening to revoke the privilege of M. Guinee's private room. He undoubtedly would have followed through, moving M. Guinee to one of the crowded dormitories where the waiters and gardeners and porters lived, but around the time the construction at the estate ended, my old friend's condition began to deteriorate even further.

M. Guinee was the only one I had told of what had happened to Senator Marcus. At the time, some of the president's circle had continued to frequent the Hotel Erdrich, and I had hoped that M. Guinee might be in a position to overhear if one of them were to let something slip. Although I had not seen him since, M. Guinee and I had kept in close contact, exchanging letters at least once a week. I told him about the state of the renovations, and he let me know what he had learned of Senator and Mme Marcus. But while I had been able to go on and on with details about the construction, M. Guinee's responses had often been no more than a few lines: "I'm afraid life here carries on as usual, with nothing new to report."

In the year since the Marcuses' house had burned, no one had said a word. Either no one knew or they knew enough to know they should keep quiet. The closest M. Guinee ever came to openly mentioning the thing neither one of us was willing to risk naming was when he wrote, after months without news, "Do not let yourself be consumed by guilt."

But it was not guilt I felt. If someone as powerful as Senator Marcus could not save himself, what could I possibly have done? If anything, the terrible event was proof that I had done the right thing in seeking to escape when I had. I felt no guilt, but I still had my loyalty, and how could I help Mme Freeman avoid a similar fate if I did not know how Senator Marcus had met his?

I often thought of going to see M. Guinee so that we could speak in person of the things we could not discuss in letters. A visit was the least I owed him after everything he had done for me. But it was hard to get away and harder still to see him at the hotel, where one could do nothing but watch while he was treated with so little respect.

Still, I knew I could afford to put it off no longer. Lately, M. Guinee's letters had grown more infrequent, his penmanship more unsteady. Even before I received word of his turn for the worse I feared his health—like my father's—was rapidly failing him.

M. Guinee was alone in his room when I arrived, and I was pleased to see a plate and glass on his side table. Someone was taking care of him. He was lying in bed, and as I came in he tried to raise himself. The best he could do was lift his chin.

"There you are," he said with a smile.

"I wanted to come sooner."

"It doesn't matter." He turned his head so that his eyes fell upon the chair beside the bed, and I followed the invitation to sit.

It had been a long time since he had shaved, but the beard did little to hide the hollows in his cheeks. Looking at the coarse, gray whiskers, I tried to remember how old he was. I had recently turned thirty-two, which meant he was in only his early sixties. And yet he looked two decades older.

"We just finished," I said. "The estate is complete."

He nodded. "I knew you would."

I said, "I cannot wait for you to see it." He smiled again, and it seemed to me, when I saw him like that, that it was not at all unreasonable to expect that he *would* get to see it.

"Tell me what it's like."

I edged the chair closer to the bed, and I told him about my bedroom, with its wallpaper of textured blue roses, and my office, done up in wainscoting of rich, dark mahogany. And I described my polished maple desk, with its black leather inset and brass locks.

"It sounds beautiful," M. Guinee said. "Just as I'd imagined."

"Can I get you anything?" I checked to see that his water glass was full. "Something to drink? Something to eat?"

He closed his eyes. "I have everything I need."

"You look tired," I said, and he rolled his head away.

He took a slow, deep breath. "I'm sorry I wasn't more help."

"Not at all." I squeezed his arm. "It was foolish of me to think we could ever find out."

"They might still be alive."

At one time it would have comforted me to hear him say so. I had spent months thinking about what might have happened to the Marcuses, considering every possibility. If they were dead, I had been quick to reason, we would have heard. The paper would have said they died in the fire. It would have been the perfect cover-up. But they never said that, and the only possible reason I could see was that the Marcuses were still alive. I had needed it to be so.

Following their disappearance, a long period had passed in which everything I did, everything I saw, everything I heard, reminded me of the Marcuses. With everyone I encountered—every plumber and electrician, every deliveryman at the gate—no matter the topic of conversation, I found myself desperate to mention the Senator and his wife. Knowing how dangerous it was only made the urge that much more unbearable. It was as if recklessness alone might somehow preserve them. And the more I distrusted the man with whom I was talking, the more my pulse pounded, the more I had to struggle to resist. But I always did. Instead of saying their names I might say instead, "*A former employer of mine* smoked that very same tobacco," or "I once knew *a woman, the wife of a lawyer,* who detested cats." In that way, I forced even strangers to become bearers of the Marcuses' memory.

Of late, however, as the reality of what had happened settled in, the urge to remember had begun to diminish, and in its place I felt a new and equally strong urge to forget.

M. Guinee closed his eyes.

"I'm sorry," I said. "I can see how tired you are. I should let you sleep."

"I think I will sleep for a while."

His breathing was labored. It was as though there were not enough air in the room for both of us. I got up from the chair and moved away from the bed. Standing against the wall, I watched him until my legs grew tired, and then I lowered myself to the floor, where eventually I too fell asleep.

It was dark when the chambermaid came in to check on him. She woke me with a touch.

"He's asleep," she said.

I stood groggily. "Is he getting any better?"

She shook her head kindly.

"What does the doctor say?"

She picked up the empty plate from the side table, avoiding my glance.

I reached into my pocket and pulled out several bills. I handed them to her. "Please call the doctor," I said. "Call him now."

"I don't think it would do any good."

I pressed the money into her hand.

"I have to go," she said. "I can't let the manager find me here."

"Promise that you'll call."

She refilled his glass with water and said, "For when he wakes up."

I spent the night on M. Guinee's floor. The discomfort felt less like a punishment than a duty. I reminded myself that as a boy I had known children who slept standing up because there was no room on the floor of their cramped houses for everyone to lie.

In the morning the doctor arrived, the same ragged man I had met before. It had been more than four years, and he seemed to have aged without changing his clothes. Rumpled and dusty myself, I had few grounds for complaint.

The doctor took M. Guinee's pulse and listened to his chest.

"I'd say he's as good as can be expected," he told me as we stepped outside.

"Is there nothing you can do?"

"About death?" he said, picking up his decrepit bag. "Only the same things anyone can do."

"We have to do something."

"You can make him as comfortable as possible."

After the doctor left, I spent a few minutes cleaning up M. Guinee's room. No one had dusted and swept for months. I took the extra blanket outside to air it in the sun. I had just gone back inside when there was a knock on the door. I hurried to answer it before M. Guinee awoke.

Outside on the step, glancing disdainfully down his pimpled nose, twitched a gaunt young man in a crisp, red blazer bearing the Hotel Erdrich crest on its breast. Everything about him made me want to close the door and go back inside.

"You have to leave," he said brusquely.

"Who are you?"

He sniffed at the question as if its smell offended him. "The manager says you are to leave. Now."

"He's dying," I said, gesturing indignantly toward the bed.

The young man glanced sourly over my shoulder.

"You can leave now, or you can wait for the police to take you away."

"What have I done wrong?"

"It upsets the guests to have doctors around."

"What guests?"

His eyes seemed to quiver.

"If they dislike doctors," I said, "I imagine they'll be even less pleased to see the police."

"I wouldn't worry about that." His eyes suddenly sparkled. "The police know how to be discreet."

I felt the anger rising in my throat, and there was nothing I could do to stop it. I stepped outside, closing the door behind me. "Have you no decency?"

"Have it your way," he said as he spun unsteadily on his heel. "You can tell it to the police."

Watching him stride back up the path, I was sorry I had not struck him when I had the chance. What was it about living under tyranny that encouraged even imbeciles to turn into petty tyrants themselves? I wondered if President Mailodet was pleased to know how many pretenders he had inspired.

After the young man had gone I remained there for another few minutes, trying to coax my heart back into my chest.

When I stepped back inside, I discovered M. Guinee was awake. "I'm sorry," I said. "I didn't mean to make so much noise."

"You should go," he said softly. "I appreciate your coming."

I went over and kissed him on the forehead. "I'll be back."

The next day, I could not get away, and hardly a minute passed when I did not worry about my old friend. The day after that, the rains were terrible and it was impossible to go outside.

But the following day was sunny and clear, and I went to find the doctor. As it happened, he lived not far from my father. His house had two rooms, and in a chair in the first sat a pregnant woman with a little girl on her lap, whose twisted jaw hung partially open. The place was a mess, even worse than the doctor's clothes. How desperate would you have to be, I wondered, to allow such a man to stick his dirty hands in your mouth?

I heard a rustling in the corner. A dented brass birdcage was wobbling from a hook in the ceiling. Inside, a dingy, hunched red parrot shuffled awkwardly along its perch, watching me with its one good eye. The other was just an empty socket, and the bird's expression seemed understandably bleak.

An old woman in a brown frock parted the curtains. "The doctor is ready now."

"I must talk to him first," I said, pushing past her.

The nurse tried to stop me, but I had no time to waste.

The doctor rose from his stool when he saw me come in. There was blood on his shirt and his arms and his fingers.

"We must bring him to the estate," I said. "He can rest there."

The doctor hung his head wearily. "He can't be moved. Even carrying him, he wouldn't make it out the door."

I had not come all this way to be told no.

I handed the doctor all the money I had, just as I knew my father would. "Get an ambulance. I'll be waiting."

The lunch rush at the Hotel Erdrich was no longer what it once had been. Glancing into the dining room as I hurried past, I saw only a third of the tables filled. In the hall outside the entrance, where in years past lines had often formed, a waiter with his tray pressed to his side ran a finger along the arm of a chambermaid, who coyly twisted a towel with her long, thin fingers. She looked up as I went by, and the waiter shot me a glance full of venom, warning me not to interrupt.

There was no sign of the manager or his underling. Aside from the lovers in the hall, no one saw me make it out back.

M. Guinee was asleep, and he did not awaken as I came inside and closed the door. His breathing was labored and uneven, his skin cold and slightly gray. And yet, I thought he looked relatively peaceful. Ill, certainly, but perhaps it was not as bad as the doctor said. Who knew what kind of schooling the man had. To dress so raggedly and work in such filth, how good could his training possibly be?

What I saw in M. Guinee did not look like death to me.

I was eight years old when my mother passed away, and for all but a few hours of her illness I had refused to leave her side. My father had tried to keep me from her, no doubt wanting to shield me from her suffering. But I had not understood, and I wanted to be near her. Even at eight I was no stranger to the disease. I had lost a cousin and one of my aunts to malaria, and I had known others who had contracted it and recovered. But it had never occurred to me that such a thing could strike my mother, the person I loved best in the world. Nothing bad could ever happen to her, because then who would take care of me? It was impossible. That was what I told myself as I watched her sweat and shake, barely able to open her eyes. And then, after a few days, the convulsions and the vomiting set in, and I told myself she was purging herself of the disease, even as her sisters and aunts and neighbors swept in and out of the room, clutching compresses and herbal remedies that made the entire house reek of wretched things.

And where had my father been throughout all of this? He was

trying to get the drugs—the real medicine, he said—that he had heard could save her. He went all over the city, to the hospitals and clinics, demanding the pills. Eventually he got them, but not in time. Or maybe he could not get enough. Or maybe they had taken his money and given him something worthless instead.

All the while I had been sneaking in to sit at my mother's side and hold her frigid hand and tell her stories. I recall feeling as though the most important thing in the world was that I keep talking, and the thing I most clearly remember talking about was a carved wooden butterfly we had seen at the market only a couple of days before. A tiny, fragile creature smaller than the palm of my hand, and yet incredibly detailed and painted a deep, ruddy orange. My mother had held it for a long time, marveling over the delicate trio of small silver dots accenting each wing. She had told the woman selling it that the butterfly was the most beautiful thing she had ever seen, and I remembered how sad she had looked when she handed it back, how much she would have liked to make a home for it on the high shelf in her bedroom where she kept the few other precious things she owned, pictures and several pressed flowers and a small gold locket she had once found on the street. But such a purchase was the kind of indulgence my father would never allow.

Sitting at the edge of her bed as my mother shrank further and further from life, I told myself that if only I could get that butterfly for her, everything would be okay.

And so one day when the fever briefly broke, I slipped away and went to the market. I had no money, of course, but I thought there had to be something I could offer in exchange. All I could think about— and the way I remember her still—was how she looked that day at the market, holding the butterfly, how happy it made her just to touch it.

But that day the old woman was not at the market. No one had seen her. And that evening my mother passed away as I clung to her arm.

Even now there was a part of me that thought there must have been something I could have done to help her. Perhaps not the butterfly, but something.

On M. Guinee's walls hung a crucifix and several icons of the saints in cheap balsa-wood frames. There was the virgin in a long, flowing dress, glancing bashfully to the side. Another wore a disheveled cloak slipping off one shoulder, a smooth yellow flame circling his head like a bonnet. Was this Saint Jude? He had always been one of my father's favorite saints. I was surprised they had this in common. My father loved nothing more than a lost cause, but from M. Guinee I would have expected something more hopeful.

"Come to my assistance in this great need—" Standing beside M. Guinee's bed, I repeated the words over and over again, wishing I could remember the rest. Would it really have been so difficult to listen to the sermons, instead of simply letting them wash over me? Why had I not done as my father asked, just this once?

And then it came to me: "that I may receive the consolation and help of heaven in all my necessities and sufferings, and that I may praise God with you always."

How strange that in all the times I had visited M. Guinee here, I had never noticed the icons. Looking around now, I saw other things too: a wrinkled photo leaned against the base of the lamp on his side table. I did not recognize the woman, but the young boy was obviously his son. The eyes could be no one else's. Why had he never shown this to me? I had known he had a wife, but I could not remember him mentioning her name. Of his child I knew only that he had died, but not the cause. I had told M. Guinee everything about my family, but only now did it occur to me that I had learned almost nothing of his life. All we had ever talked about was the estate. Was it that I had never asked about anything else?

Why were these things so easy for everyone else, that came so hard to me? It had been M. Guinee who chose me, and not the other way around, but still I had never meant to be so poor a friend.

The darkness and quiet of the room made me sleepy, and I sat down in the chair beside the bed. I was sitting there still when I awoke sometime later to find the doctor bent over M. Guinee's bed, his ear pressed to my old friend's chest.

"I'm sorry," he said.

I scrambled up from the floor, grasping the doctor by the arm.

"I'm sorry," he repeated. "You did everything you could."

"No," I said. "Everything is fine. He was fine just a minute ago." I looked at my watch. How was it possible that three hours had passed?

The doctor smoothed out his dirty, rumpled sleeve. "Sometimes a minute is all it takes."

In the morning I alone accompanied the body to the cemetery, where the priest was waiting to say a few words. It was just the two of us and the two men with shovels, lurking impatiently a few paces away. Even though the hotel was almost empty—the reporters having left long ago—no one who worked at the Erdrich was permitted to attend. Their time was too precious to be wasted.

It had never occurred to me that M. Guinee might have no one else but me.

The diggers came, and the sound they made was like drumming, until the dirt muffled everything and soon there was nothing left of the hole.

❊

There were times I felt like a ghost, alone in the abandoned estate. The only reminder I had that I myself was still among the living was the echo of my footsteps as I walked the vacant corridors. In the days following the funeral, I spent my time fighting off cobwebs and rearranging mementos from M. Guinee's life—his balsa wood saints, his virgin, and of course his key—which I displayed on the shelves in my office.

I found comfort wherever I could. I took long walks, exploring the grounds more thoroughly than I ever had before. I discovered two of the natural springs M. Guinee had told me about and several of the places in the preserve where the fruit trees grew. I went twice a week to gather what I needed.

I saw no one. I talked to no one. In my solitude, I spent a great deal of time thinking about M. Guinee and Senator Marcus, but most of all I thought about my father. It had been more than four years since I had asked Paul to keep an eye on him, and Paul had made good on his pledge, sending me regular updates and calling when the phones were in order. My father was still in relatively good health, but there were greater and greater limits to what he could do on his own. Whenever I did make it back home, generally for just an afternoon, my father spoke of Paul as if he were the son my father had always wanted.

There could be no doubt that Paul was serious about repaying the debt he felt he owed my father. But while it eased my mind that he was there to help, it did nothing to ease my guilt over not being there myself. As Paul's debt to my father shrank, mine grew. I had already decided that M. Guinee's passing should serve as a reminder of the importance of maintaining ties, even ones that sometimes felt impossibly strained.

Despite what my father might think, I had not abandoned him.

"Despite the sadness I have experienced," I wrote to Madame, "I continue to feel only hope and optimism about our undertaking here. We will fill the holes left by this loss with something new, something that will outlast us all."

❊

Two weeks after M. Guinee's funeral, I received a delivery from the capital. Inside the truck were several tables Madame had ordered almost a year before, at a time when she still believed this would be her second home. Despite the optimism I had alluded to in my letter, the arrival of the furniture was a depressing reminder of all that had changed. The driver was a man who had brought us wood and bricks many times during the construction, and this was the first time he had been back since we finished the work. As we walked one of the tables up the winding staircase to the second floor of the manor house, he could not stop commenting on everything he saw.

"Is that real marble?" he said. "Is that crystal?"

Each time I nodded, thinking how hard it had become to appreciate these things now that it seemed no one but me would ever get to see them.

At the top of the stairs we rested. Noticing the silence for the first time, he asked if I was here alone. I told him I was.

"Well, maybe that will change now," he said, offering me a cigarette. I declined.

"Why would that change?"

He shook out the match, considered dropping it on the floor, and then thought better of it. "I expect a lot will change," he said, "now that he's dead."

"Who is dead?"

"But don't you know?" he said, pushing out a cloud of smoke. "President Mailodet."

Chapter Ten

Given her background, it was perhaps inevitable that Madame would come to realize the financial potential of the estate. It was likely, in fact, that she had known all along and was merely waiting for the right opportunity. But I do not think it vain to believe the work we had done to restore the place played the greatest part in showing her what was possible, that within the walls of the estate we could build a sanctuary.

The same day I learned of President Mailodet's death, I sat down to write Madame a letter, eager to tell her the news. But the reply I received, a week later, was not the ecstatic one I had expected. Everything I had been able to tell her, she already knew. And I immediately began to fear that following my earlier failure, she had decided to seek out a more reliable source for information.

It was clear, in fact, that Madame knew more of the details than I did. Not until I read her letter did it even occur to me that I had forgotten to ask the deliveryman how the president had died. I had simply assumed an assassin had finally caught up with him, or that he had been cut down in the midst of a bloody coup, as had been the case with so many presidents past.

Only thanks to Mme Freeman did I learn that, being as defiant of history as he was of everything else, President Mailodet had the audacity to die in his bed. Before doing so, however, he was able to push through one last constitutional amendment, this time granting himself the power to name his own successor. The man he chose was named Duphay. For quite some time, that was all I knew about him, all I cared to know.

But that spring, after almost a year of silence, I received a second letter from the States. In it Madame mentioned encouraging news she had been hearing about our new president. In his very first speech, on the day of his inauguration, M. Duphay had boldly announced the end of the "revolutionary phase" begun under President Mailodet. His role, he said, was to usher in a new era of democracy.

Madame also made references to a great number of other things I knew nothing about: a new airport, new roads, plans to complete the construction of the hydroelectric dam, a project begun and then abandoned more than ten years before, which promised to supply us—for the first time—with dependable electricity. It was also from Madame that I learned that the independent newspapers and radio stations had been restored.

But Madame remained cautious. She was not going to take a chance on coming back until she knew for sure the danger was over.

Over the next year, I received occasional letters. Her tone remained optimistic, but she continued to avoid setting a date for her return.

Despite what was happening in the capital, life for me remained the same. I had the maintenance of the estate to keep me busy. So busy, in fact, that I was able to visit my father even less often than I had before. For months I had been planning an extended visit, perhaps as long as a week, during which I would help with the shop and lend a hand with anything that might need to be done. It was time for him to see that

Paul was not the only one eager to be of assistance. It had occurred to me that the shop could do with a fresh coat of paint, and there was quite a bit left over from the renovations at the estate that I was sure would not be missed.

But first there was an emergency rewiring project that needed to be completed in the lower north wing of the manor house. We had initially anticipated that it would take no more than a week or two, but that was before the electricians discovered the problem extended into the second floor as well. I had no choice but to put off the visit to my father until they were done.

Although I still spent most of my time alone, I was no longer as isolated as I once had been. There were more carts and donkeys outside the gate than ever. Even the occasional car and bus. But more signifi- cant than any of that was the cluster of shacks that had begun to appear at the western edge of the estate. It seemed to me an odd place for a person to choose to settle. I could not imagine what about that parched, treeless valley might seem inviting. President Duphay's recent pledge to entice new factories to open in the capital had apparently unleashed a torrent of desperate peasants from the countryside, and I feared many of them were ending up here, hoping to escape the overcrowded slums closer to the city.

For now, the trees and the wall kept them from spoiling our view, but nonetheless I could see only trouble coming from their proximity.

In the late fall, after the rains had ended, a crew of men from the capital came to fix the road, and the only bus service available to me was temporarily suspended. Once again I had to put off my plans to see my father.

※

The day after I received Madame's note that I was to ready the guest- house, the money she had wired arrived. I spent it as she instructed, hiring the necessary help—a chambermaid, a man to straighten up the grounds, a footman, and a chef.

It was a week later, and I was standing on the steps of the manor house, when the taxi came down the drive. As I watched the space between us close, I felt a sense of calm descend upon me. One at a time they stepped out of the car, Madame and the three white men she had described in her letter.

"It's a wonderful airport, isn't it?" she asked, glancing nervously from one to the next. "So new, so clean?"

Overwhelmed by everything around them, the three men seemed not to hear.

It had been three and a half years since I had seen her last, and I was surprised to find Madame so unchanged. Her hair was different; much of the remaining gold had given way to grayish white, and curls had come to replace the waves. Soft, shiny bangs swept over her brow. In her mid-fifties now, she was still fit and trim, and her face was aglow. Maybe it was just the excitement of the moment, but she seemed more youthful and vibrant than ever.

From a few steps away I watched as she directed the men's attention to one or another feature of the landscape. They were trying to follow the trajectory of her finger as she pointed here and there, but I could tell they found it impossible to keep up. At last I was able to witness someone else seeing the place as only I had been able to see it before.

"Down there," Madame said, gesturing vaguely beyond the guesthouse. "They will all go there. There will be paths connecting them. And the trees will provide privacy."

It seemed an eternity before she finally took note of me and came over to shake my hand. But the smile she brought along with her made the wait worthwhile.

"How wonderful, wonderful, it is to see you again," she nearly sang.

"Madame," I said, regretting we had to break our grasp, "it's a delight."

The first of her companions, a dignified gentleman with gray at his temples, blew out his cheeks in response to the heat that greeted him. He and the second man had come attired in dark, heavy suits poorly suited to the climate. The third was a man of considerable girth, who wore a tan linen suit and a pith helmet covered in matching fabric. In a schoolbook I had read as a child there had been a photo of a man dressed like this stalking tigers in the jungle. I feared this man had come seeking some similar sort of adventure. The outfit may have looked absurd, but he wore it with conviction, and I could see he was a man who committed to endeavors either wholly or not at all.

As the three men looked out over the grounds, I could feel their eyes seeking out the flaws, and it pleased me to think that though they would be here several days, they would be unable to find a single detail we had neglected; they could have months, and still they would find nothing.

After lunch, Madame took the three men on a tour of the estate, briefly inspecting the manor house, the guesthouse, the pavilion, her own private villa, and the various outbuildings, including the servants' quarters and the stables. They walked the gardens and as far as the top of the stone steps leading down to the preserve, which was as close to the forest as they were willing to go.

During the three days that followed, I saw little of Madame and the three men. Each morning they came to the manor house, and Madame received them in her office upstairs. Somehow the time I spent waiting for them to emerge for dinner seemed longer to me than the three years of silence and solitude leading up to this.

The meals were lavish affairs, expertly prepared. The chef was a man I had met years before, when he worked for an accomplished surgeon who was a friend of the Marcuses. We were both so busy with the arrival of Madame's guests that it was difficult to find time to talk, but that first afternoon I stopped briefly by the kitchen while he was preparing dinner.

On virtually every burner a pot was simmering. The stovetop was ablaze. The counters balanced pyramids of vegetables in a rainbow of colors. Amid the chaos he seemed perfectly at home, enveloped in a crisp, white apron.

"It's good to see you again, Michele." I offered him my hand, but he indicated with a wave that his was dirty.

"I'm glad you were able to come," I said. "I could think of no one better."

He gave me a nod of thanks, selecting a peeled potato from a bowl beside the sink.

"How have you been?" I said. "What have you been doing since I last saw you?"

He shrugged. "The same."

The hand holding the knife moved like a hummingbird's wing. The potato collapsed in shreds.

"But you have a new employer?"

"Yes, of course. But they're abroad."

With the back of the knife he scraped the potato into a bowl and went back for another.

"I was wondering," I said hesitantly, "whatever happened to your former employer, the doctor?"

Michele gave a distracted shrug. "I haven't seen him since I left."

"But is he okay?" I persisted.

"Why wouldn't he be?"

He turned around to attend to some onions sizzling in a skillet, and for a moment I considered giving up. The part of me that felt an obligation to ask had lately lost almost all of its ground to the part of me that did not want to know. But I was here and I was speaking these words, I reminded myself, so that I could know I had tried, so that it would be okay hereafter to let it go.

"How long ago did you leave him?"

Michele paused to wipe his hands on his apron. "Six or seven years. Something like that."

"That's about the time I left Senator Marcus." To my surprise the name caused no change in his expression.

Again, a single swipe of the knife pushed the fresh slices into the bowl. As he reached for another potato, I moved around the counter until my shadow fell across his cutting board.

"By any chance," I said, "did you happen to hear anything about Senator Marcus? Have you ever heard your new employer speak of him?"

Michele looked up impatiently. A drop of potato juice slid down the blade. "What would I hear?"

"I just thought—"

"If you'll excuse me," he said, moving to the stove, "I still have a lot to do."

With a nod, I turned to go, my relief far greater than my disappointment.

From the kitchen that evening it was impossible to see or hear how Madame and the three white men were doing. The moment he returned from the dining room, I pressed the footman for details.

"What are they talking about?"

"How should I know?" he said, brushing past.

"You told me you knew some English."

Back turned to me, he picked up another dish.

"Do they seem happy?" I asked.

"They don't seem angry."

On the morning of the fourth day, the car that had dropped the three men off returned for them, and as soon as they were gone Madame shut herself up in her villa. I did not see her for two more days.

They were two of the most difficult days of my life. I had grown accustomed to living with a body of water between us. A few mere footpaths, however, proved almost unbearable.

Michele's employer was returning from abroad, and he had to get back to the capital. From then on the chambermaid took responsibility for our meals. Each morning, afternoon, and evening she left a tray outside Madame's door.

I passed the second day of Madame's absence working in the vegetable garden I had recently begun planting. I was already preparing for what I assumed was to come—for Madame to go back home and for me once again to be left here alone. I would be disappointed, of course, but a return to normal would at least mean that I could finally pay that long-overdue visit to my father.

When the chambermaid came that evening to tell me Madame was waiting for me in her office, I assumed it was time to say good-bye.

"I wish to thank you," Madame said, even before I had closed the door behind me. She was standing beside the open jalousies, looking out upon the pool below. She seemed unusually anxious, and I wished she would sit down.

"I must confess," she said, "there have been times when I feared the best we could ever hope for was to keep the place from crumbling any further." She gestured for me to join her, and together we walked out to the balcony.

I was so nervous my hand streaked sweat upon the railing.

"But you haven't just halted the destruction," she said, "you've actually reversed it. The men who were my guests these past three days couldn't believe what a paradise it is. Even more than I'd described." Madame smiled. "Today I've received word that they've agreed to invest in us. Do you know what this means?"

I was afraid to guess.

"We will have our hotel," Madame said with a sigh that seemed seven years in the making. "It will be like nothing this island has ever seen. The Hotel Erdrich will be a mere country inn by comparison. People will come from around the world. And I couldn't have done it without you."

I knew in an instant that this was the moment and these were the words for which I had waited my whole life. It all seemed so familiar, just as I had imagined it. And that was why I could not explain the feeling suddenly coursing through me—not the elation I had expected, but a strange kind of sadness.

Only once the sensation had passed did the understanding come, gradually and at first uncertainly. I had not foreseen that such a moment would remind me of my mother, and how much I missed her. More than I had ever allowed myself to say. It was not for her alone that I had come here, but how could I not feel sorrow at the thought of her never getting a chance to know?

And then Mme Freeman reached out to take my hand and I, light-headed and trembling, brought her hand to my lips and gave it a kiss.

※

The workers were not all the same as the ones we had hired before, but it nevertheless felt very much like a homecoming. This time there were even more of them. There was more of everything. So extensive were the plans for expansion that the chief engineer and M. Laraque, the architect, decided they would need to set up temporary quarters. We arranged rooms for them upstairs in the manor house, along the corridor where Madame and I had our offices.

In the library they unfurled the blueprints. To me they were indecipherable, nothing but lines and smudges. Even if I had understood, I suspect Madame would have been unable to stop herself from explaining them to me, such was her excitement.

Given the difficulty of the terrain, she said, M. Laraque had been forced to place new villas wherever he could, and it was this necessity that led to the step-style effect on the jungly hillside. She showed me where each would go; the villas would be clustered in groups of three and four around central swimming pools, arranged in such a way that each would be isolated from its neighbors. Every villa was to be unique, its dimensions determined by the lay of the land both beneath and around it, but all would contain luxurious bedrooms, baths, and dining and sitting rooms, as well as private terraces.

"Like mine," Madame said with a wink. "But mine will still have the best view."

And then there were the attractions: the pavilion would be torn down and rebuilt, expanded to include a bar and a bandstand. Next to the pavilion would be the casino—the best on the island—and then the discotheque, designed to be identical to a famous one in the States that Madame spoke of in reverential terms. The tennis courts were to go adjacent to the manor house, just past the drive, on the flattest piece of land on the estate. The new restaurant, conceived as an addition to the manor house, would have two dining rooms, one inside and one out, the former with stone walls and a stone bar, the latter open on three sides, the roof supported by plaster columns. Next to it would be the back terrace and the manor house pool.

On the second floor, workers were going to knock down walls in order to create larger spaces for Madame's office and for an office with an adjoining bedroom for the hotel manager. At this stage, Madame said, delighted at the degree to which they had worked out every detail, M. Laraque and the engineer would move out of the manor house and into separate villas, as would the interior designer Madame had hired to furnish and decorate the entire estate.

"Of course," she said, patting my arm, "you won't be disturbed."

And then there were the gardens. Madame was ecstatic about the gardens. They would be planted in the vicinity of the manor house, with paths connecting them. She wanted an orchid garden and a cactus garden, and the fountain near the pavilion was to become a water garden.

"I will supervise the plantings myself," she said, eyes turning electric with the thrill of it.

Although the new construction was far more extensive than the earlier renovation, the work was estimated to take less time to complete, just under two years. It seemed starting fifty or so small buildings from scratch would be easier than repairing two very old and very large ones.

Except for a few month-long absences when she had to attend to business at home, Madame was at the estate throughout the construction. She was thus able to take upon herself many of the responsibilities I had held during the initial renovations. All problems—architectural, financial, disciplinary—came to her, and she dispensed with them with the ease of someone who had been making important decisions all her life. Seeing her like this often brought to mind memories of Senator Marcus, and for the first time since my conversation with Michele not only did I not push such thoughts from my mind, I allowed myself to feel genuine hope that I might see him again. If President Duphay was as good a man as Mme Freeman said, there would be nothing for President Mailodet's old enemies to fear. Back they would come from exile and from hiding. I could even imagine Senator Marcus regaining his seat in the legislature. All could be as it was before. It was not far-fetched to imagine Senator Marcus and Mme Freeman becoming friends. I could see Mme Freeman seated at the Marcuses' dining room table, discussing the future of the island with ministers and bankers. He might begin playing his Wednesday tennis matches here, rather than at the Hotel Erdrich. I would see to it that the courts would satisfy even the minister of health.

It is hard to remember a time when I was happier than when we were building the hotel. The telephone system was working, tourists were arriving, and nowhere was there any trace of President Mailodet's security forces. Everything we had worked for was coming together, and anything we might imagine seemed attainable. Even in the midst of the construction the estate became more beautiful by the day.

From month to month, I watched the villas rise, each one perfect and distinct. And when they were whole, it was Madame who gave them names: Villa Bardot, Villa Bernhardt, Villa Moreau . . . There were more than forty of them, each named after one of Madame's favorite actresses.

I spent my time going from place to place around the estate, watching what the various crews of men were doing, the masons and carpenters and gardeners. I was sorry the days passed so quickly.

In retrospect, I realize the days not only went by quickly, they went by without my taking much note of them. Weeks and months melted away, and I managed to forget that anything else existed. The estate was itself an island, and I its oldest inhabitant. I had been here before anyone, even before Madame. How could it be that I was born anywhere but here?

And in time I forgot the single most important thing I had pledged to do.

I was in my office one afternoon, taking a rest from the relentless

activity below, when I heard the blast of a car horn coming from the top
of the drive. I assumed it was just another delivery of building materials.

Standing at the gate was perhaps the last person I expected to find
there. I barely recognized Paul, dressed in a crisp blue button shirt and
pressed tan trousers. Except for the sunglasses, he looked like a boy
dressed up for his First Communion. Behind him a weathered black
sedan idled roughly. There was a man behind the steering wheel whom
I had never seen before. The butt of a pistol rose just above the dashboard, tucked into his shoulder holster.

"This is quite a surprise," I said, trying and failing to read the awkward expression on Paul's face.

I opened the gate and he stepped through, and when he reached out
to embrace me I was more than happy to receive him. Maybe it was just
because of how well things had been going, but I was genuinely pleased
to see him. In that moment, an unexpected visit felt like a delightful
treat, and I was already imagining all the things I would show him.

By now it had been close to five years since I had asked him to keep
an eye on my father. Although I had been back to the neighborhood pe-
riodically, Paul and I had seen little of one another. Most of our contact
recently had been over the phone, calls that invariably consisted of him
shouting over a background cacophony of strange industrial sounds—
heavy clanks and thuds and a chorus of other voices almost as loud as
his. Paul had moved out of his mother's house and found a place for
himself slightly higher up the hill in Lyonville, making it that much
harder for me to see him even when I was able to get away for a visit. He
knew that for a long time I had been planning on an extended stay with
my father and that the sudden change of affairs on the estate had made
that impossible. Since then I had been forced to count even more on
Paul. I had been assuming that the arrangement suited the two of them
just fine; Paul got to pay back even more of his debt, and my father got
the company he preferred.

"He's going to be someone important," my father had informed me
on more than one of our infrequent afternoons together. Since when,
I was always tempted to ask, did criminal behavior meet your criteria

for success? Either my father remained ignorant of the source of Paul's increasing power and prestige, or he chose to ignore it. Whichever it was, he was clearly willing to give Paul the latitude he had always refused to give me.

When Paul removed his glasses, I saw that his eyes bore an unaccustomed somberness, like a child experimenting with the mannerisms of an adult. "I wanted to be the one to tell you," he said.

So this is how it happens, I said to myself, and all that time came rushing back. My legs lost their grounding, and I felt myself begin to crumble. Just then Paul came forward and put his arm around my shoulders.

"I was just about to visit him," I said, my voice thin and hollow. "I had it planned. I was going to stay for a week."

Paul squeezed my shoulder. "There's no way you could have known."

"I asked him to come here. I begged him. He was too stubborn."

"You did everything you could." Paul's tone offered no reproach, but I did not need one to understand I had finally failed my father in the most unforgivable way of all.

Paul stood on the balcony, talking to me through the open jalousies as I packed a change of clothes. A light breeze swept through, carrying with it the dissonant percussion of countless different construction projects.

"I had no idea you'd done so well for yourself," he said. "My God, look at all that. And these women—these maids in their little skirts!" He let out a slow whistle. "You must be taking them by the dozen."

I continued to fold a shirt into my bag.

Paul glanced at me over his shoulder and gave a snort. "Tell me at least one of them."

I rolled my socks into a ball.

"I don't get you," he said. "You're not a bad-looking guy. Why are you so afraid of girls?"

"I'm not afraid," I said.

"What is it, then?"

I looked around the room, trying to figure out what else I might need. "We just don't have anything in common."

Paul threw his head back and laughed. "All of them? You don't have anything in common with a single one of them?"

"You'd know better than me," I said. "You're the one they talk to."

Paul gave a defeated shrug and turned back to the railing. "It's incredible. You have your own fucking kingdom. This place makes Duphay's house look like a chicken coop."

In the corner of my eye I saw him watching me. I was surprised that his mourning had suddenly turned so lighthearted. Then again, Paul had never been able to maintain a facade of seriousness for long. It did not matter to him that I was in no mood for talking.

"Have you been to the president's house?" I asked.

He winked. "You're not the only one moving up in the world."

"None of this is mine," I reminded him. "I just work here."

"You have to start somewhere."

I could see he was determined to keep the conversation going. "Like with bathroom tissue?"

He laughed, loudly and generously. "Exactly."

It was disorienting to have him in my rooms, talking and joking as he used to, while at the same time he was someone entirely unfamiliar. The old Paul had been complicated enough, but this new one thoroughly baffled me. I was grateful that he was here, even for his efforts to cheer me up, but his heartiness and newfound confidence made it feel as though he had gone from childhood friend to rich, chummy uncle.

As we made our way down the stairs, he eyed the floor with satisfaction. "I see you've made good use of that polish."

"And we have enough left," I said, "to last a thousand years."

Paul's driver got out to open our doors. I thanked him, and he said nothing in return. I wondered if he was under orders from Paul to remain invisible in the presence of important passengers.

Paul made no effort to introduce us. Whatever understanding there

was between them seemed to require no direct communication. Without need of instructions, the driver turned around and headed back
up the drive and onto the road. He knew exactly where he was going;
within a few minutes it became clear that I did not.

After about a kilometer, the driver turned off the main road onto
a small unpaved side street. We were still close to the estate—indeed,
I guessed we were only just past the western wall—and I was surprised
by the number of houses here. Not just the dozen or so I had been
aware of, but hundreds. And those were just the ones I could see. Farther down the hill, connected by twisting dirt paths, were hundreds
more. Though to call them houses was an act of charity. They were
little more than dingy shacks patched together from concrete and metal
scraps. Together they looked like a pile of tin cans tossed inside a dirty
cardboard box. There were even a couple of small shops, or so I gathered, spying as we passed an assortment of dirty black-market goods
through a few open doorways. And yet I could not comprehend why
people would choose to move here. Other than clear ground, what did
such a squalid place have to offer?

"Where did all of this come from?" I asked. "Last time I was here
there were just a couple of shanties."

"You've been busy," Paul said. "It's all gone up in the last year or so."

"Why would anyone want to live here?"

Paul smiled playfully. "Disappointed that you won't have the place
to yourself anymore?"

He may have been joking, but it was true. The remoteness of the
estate was a large part of what made it so appealing. Its purity came
from having remained so untouched. The last thing we needed was
more people to threaten its fragile existence.

"Don't worry," Paul said. "They'll be good neighbors."

"They had better be." But even as I said it, I felt a twisting unease.
Even if they could not be seen or heard from within our walls, their
presence would require constant vigilance, especially with the hotel
nearing completion.

Paul chuckled quietly to himself. "I'd forgotten how much you dislike being around black people."

With a glare I showed him I was not amused.

"Or is it poor people?"

"Have you forgotten where we grew up?" I said. "Have you forgotten who we are?"

Paul opened his palms to demonstrate his innocence. "I'm just saying it's hard not to notice your bosses keep getting lighter. And richer."

I made no effort to hide my anger. "Do you really think this is an appropriate time to be talking about such ridiculous things? Besides, you're not exactly slumming it yourself."

In an instant, the mischievous glint in Paul's eyes flickered away. "I apologize." He reached over to pat my knee. "I thought it might help to talk about other things."

We followed the road for another minute before pulling over in front of a shack that looked to me like all the rest. The driver got out and went up and knocked on a piece of flaking plywood strapped to a post. Apparently this was the door. I thought to ask what we were doing here, but the answer was all too clear. Only Paul could use a death as an opportunity to make a sales call. There was no point in getting upset; it was beyond him to understand.

As we were waiting, I looked around inside the car. For the first time I realized it was the same model Senator Marcus had owned. I shifted in my seat to get a better look at the front. At ten and two the leather steering wheel was stained black with grease and oil. The knob had fallen off the shifter. In the back, where we sat, the ashtrays were gummy and discolored, and one of the window cranks was missing. The fabric in the middle of the roof had come loose, pressing down on us like an overfilled bladder.

I never would have let the Senator's car reach such a condition.

"It gets the job done," Paul said. "I'm in the market for something newer."

"Business has been going well?"

He nodded. "Very well."

"I wouldn't have thought there would be such demand for floor polish, especially out here."

He let loose another of his enormous laughs. "We've expanded a bit beyond floor polish."

Just then the driver came out of the house, walking briskly to the car. But instead of getting back behind the wheel, he opened the rear door and leaned down to whisper something in Paul's ear.

"I'll be right back." Paul sighed as he slipped out of the car.

The two of them went up to the house together, passing into the darkened interior. Almost immediately the shouting began, Paul's voice louder than any of the others. And then suddenly a man stumbled out through the doorway, tumbling into the dirt. There was blood running down his face, and his hand was pressed to the top of his skull.

Paul and the driver strode out after him. The driver held a brown leather attaché case. In his hand, Paul gripped a pistol, his fingers wrapped around the barrel. When they reached the man, curled up on the ground, Paul knelt calmly down and with a face virtually free of expression he pounded the butt of the pistol once and then twice and then three times into the side of the man's head. With the first blow, the man flopped down onto his belly. After that he was still.

Paul stood up and brushed the dirt from his knees. Without a word he started back toward the car.

As Paul settled back into his seat, he placed the attaché case at his feet. He had traded with the driver, giving him the pistol in exchange. Several spots of blood were already drying in the cracks of his knuckles.

Paul saw me staring at his hands. He must have registered my horror, too, but he knew better than to try to explain. He had not wanted me to see this any more than I had wanted to myself. It was not the first such scene I had ever witnessed, but it was the first time I had witnessed someone I thought I knew taking part.

"Let's go to your father's now," he said, and he reached out again to pat my knee.

A purple shroud hung over my father's front door. The neighborhood women had lit candles and laid out my father on his bed, washed and dressed in his suit. These were some of the same women who had come to prepare my mother for her funeral, clothing her in one of her favorite handmade dresses. After the ravaging effects of my mother's death, I was surprised to see my father so little changed. It was clear how quickly and painlessly the end had come. Even in death he had lost none of his dignity, but such was my shame that I could bear to look at him for only the briefest of moments. Through his closed eyes I could feel him staring back at me, his disappointment now frozen for eternity.

"We'll let you be," Paul said as he ushered everyone out. How was it, I wondered, that when he cared to he always knew the right thing to do? Somehow he always seemed to be in control, even when he was beating a man almost to death.

Unlike my father's room, the shop was in disarray. My father had always been a fastidious man, and it was upsetting to see how bad a turn things had taken. The shelves at eye level were clean, and everything on them in straight rows and columns. But the shelves above and below were sticky with dust, the cartons and tins a jumble. On the floor a trail of unswept sugar circled one of the sacks, and another lay tilted toward the side, spilling a stream of rice. Was this Paul's idea of help? Was it for this that my father had chosen him as his favorite? And yet I knew it was me the neighbors would blame for having let things reach this state.

By the time everyone arrived, near dusk, I had the shop back in order. The neighbor women came in first; they had prepared food and tea, which they arranged on the counter, before several of them went into the other room to sit with my father.

Out in the yard some of the men set up a table and chairs and settled in for a game of dominoes. René, one of my father's oldest friends, was croaking in his gloomy monotone, eyes fixed upon his hands. He had a way whenever he told a story of seeming hopelessly bored by his own narration. It was a mood that tended to spread quickly. I was in no hurry to join them now.

But for a change, everyone around him seemed captivated by whatever René was saying.

"He never missed one." René tapped the table decisively with each passing word. "Every meeting. No one was more serious than him. Those university boys had never seen anything like it. He was a one-man revolution."

As I edged closer, René glanced up, his eyes alighting warily on my face.

"It's good to see you, René," I said.

The old man took my hand and squeezed it.

"I don't mean to interrupt, but I happened to hear you talking," I said. "I was just wondering—that isn't my father you were talking about, is it?"

René's face showed no change in expression. "No, no," he said with a toss of his head. "No."

The other men, who had been listening with rapt attention before, had suddenly turned their fascination toward the dominoes spread out before them.

"I see," I said. "Someone else then? That was what I assumed."

"Yes," René said, running his fingers through his beard, "it must have been someone else." He tapped a domino on the table. "It was a long time ago."

"Well," I said, "it's good to see you again. Thank you all for coming."

One after another the men said how sorry they were about my loss. I could tell their sorrow for the loss was sincere, even as I suspected it hid something else they were less eager to share.

Back in the shop, the women were drinking tea and talking. There was a uniform look of pity on their faces as I came in, as if they had been practicing. I had not eaten since morning, but as I moved toward the plates on the counter I could sense the women watching me, and I wondered if it was not another failing of mine that I could feel something as base as hunger at a time when I was supposed to be in mourning.

Excusing myself, I stepped out again into the yard, wishing there was somewhere I could go to be alone.

Paul had not yet arrived. Strange that he, who earlier had proven incapable of offering any sort of comfort—short of antagonistic distraction—was the only person I now felt I could bear to see. However much the distance between us had grown, it was nothing compared to what now existed between me and the rest of my father's neighbors and friends.

A tall young woman in a thin brown dress stretched tight across her belly approached from up the street. At the gate she rested a moment before turning in toward the yard. Seeing me there, she looked ρ and smiled. At last I recognized her.

Marie-Hélène and I had gone to school together. She had been Paul's girlfriend when they were younger. For a time I had thought I was in love with her myself, but it was pointless to pretend she would ever have me. I was not the sort of boy a girl ever noticed; certainly not the kind for whom she gave up what she had. There was nothing I could offer that someone like Paul could not easily trump. I had learned to settle for the brief moments we had together when Paul brought her around, watching the curl of her lip when she laughed. Even now, despite everything I had accomplished, I knew it would not be enough. The Pauls of the world always had something more: the swagger, the coarse edges, the certainty about what they deserved, and the confidence to take it.

"I'm sorry," she said, kissing me lightly on the cheek.

"Thank you for coming." I stepped back to get a better look at her belly. She was due at any moment, and yet she looked more lovely than ever. "It's nice to have some good news too," I said. "I hadn't heard."

She smoothed out her dress. "It's been a while since you were here. I haven't seen you at church."

"I've been wanting to come," I said, but I could see by her expression that she did not believe me. No doubt she had heard the same stories as everyone else.

"It can't be easy to come back to a place like this."

"It's not that—" I began.

"I don't blame you," she said. "I hear you've made quite a success of yourself. They pretend they wouldn't"—she nodded vaguely toward the men playing dominoes—"but they would do the same if they had the chance."

I appreciated her saying so, but I knew it was a lie. The difference between me and the men playing dominoes was that they belonged here, and they always would. Just as my father had. My world was the one my mother had imagined. I had taken it as my own.

Suddenly Marie-Hélène turned away, glancing over her shoulder. Paul's car was pulling up out front.

The driver got out first, adjusting his holster as he reached for the back door. I noticed the other heads in the yard swivel as Paul's smiling face appeared over the roof of the car. With a wave he led his driver up the path, the latter holding a large box in his arms. The domino players must have heard the clinking of the bottles, for they were instantly on their feet. Even René, old as he was, came forward to clap Paul on the back. Marie-Hélène watched adoringly, hands folded across her belly, as Paul handed out the rum. Given their choice of prodigal sons, it was clear which one they preferred.

"Come and play a game with us," René said, tugging Paul by the arm. One of the other men got him a chair.

"In a minute." Paul took the last bottle from the box, and as he carried it into the house I heard the women inside call out his name.

Some time later, after several rounds of dominoes with my father's old friends and solicitous chatter with all the old women, Paul found me hiding in the long shadows at the back of the house.

"How's it going?" he said with a squeeze to my shoulder.

"Losing my father was hard enough," I said. "Being here is almost impossible."

Paul sat down beside me. "I know what you mean."

"You?" I said in disbelief. "They treat you as if you were the mayor."

Paul shrugged, less flattered than I had expected. "Your father was a good man. I'll never forget what he did for me and my mother."

I had never seen him be so diplomatic. This just a few hours after I had watched him beat a man unconscious. I was glad to see he was still civilized enough to have washed the blood from his knuckles.

"For someone who never cared much for people, he had a lot of friends," I said. "Far more than me."

Paul nodded. "He was like a father to me, too."

He took a sip from a bottle I only now realized he had brought over with him. Then he offered it to me and I took it.

"This must sound terrible," I said, "but I always liked your father better than mine."

"That's because you had to live with yours. Who knows what mine would have been like if he'd stuck around?"

The rum tore at my throat. "No one ever really told me why he left," I said between coughs.

"Who knows." Paul took another sip and let out a sigh. "Who cares."

It was my turn again. This time it went down more smoothly. "Paul," I said, passing the bottle back, "what happened today? What did that man do to deserve what you did to him?"

"It's an ugly world," Paul said with a shrug. "What did any of us do to deserve anything?"

In the morning, the hearse came to bring my father's body to the church. Paul had made the arrangements, hiring the nicest car he could find—black paint polished so that it shone nearly as brightly as the chrome.

At the service it was the neighbor women who cried the loudest, but nevertheless I felt everyone's eyes on me. I wondered if they remembered me as a child at my mother's funeral, standing paralyzed at my father's side, refusing to believe that what they had told me was true. It made no sense that someone so vibrant, someone so full of appreciation for the beautiful things of the world, could be taken so quickly, so brutally. And here I was again, now an adult, but still wholly unprepared.

Were there others equally ill equipped for death? Looking around the church, I sensed it was only me. Every gesture I made, I was sure it was the wrong gesture. There was nothing I could do to show them how much I had loved my father—nothing I could say to prove I had not abandoned him.

Afterward, I went over to shake the priest's hand, thanking him for his kind words.

"Your father was a good man," he said, distractedly nodding at the others as they went by. "He deserved our respect."

"He would have been pleased with the service."

"I'm glad," the priest said. "Speaking of services, I hope we'll be seeing more of you."

Just then an arm fell around the priest's shoulder. He looked over, and there was Paul, smiling back at him as if they were old friends. Of all the things I had seen in recent days, this was the most odd and incongruous. This was the same priest who—when we were children— had written sermons inspired by Paul's many and various sins. All of that animosity had disappeared.

With a practiced ease, Paul folded several bills into the priest's hand, and the two of them exchanged kisses on the cheek.

The morning after his burial, I sold my father's shop to a newly-wed couple for half what it was worth, and late that night I was back at Habitation Louvois. At that hour I had to pay twice the usual fare to go so far up into the mountains, but I would have paid anything. As much as I could, I encouraged my thoughts to race toward the work left to be done on the estate, hoping I might forget what I was leaving behind. Not my father, but certainly my father's world.

⌘

Without the hotel to return to following my father's funeral, I do not know how I would have gotten through the devastation. And yet the hotel was not without its disadvantages. As I looked upon our progress, feeling the end come ever closer, I could not help but think with sadness about the people who would never know what we had accomplished. M. Guinee would never get to see the place he himself had made possible. And my father died without understanding why I had made this my life. And then of course there was Senator Marcus, who would never know that so many of his dreams for the island were finally coming to pass. But there was one exception—one person whose memory brought me comfort.

When I first arrived here, nothing had grieved me more than the thought of my mother and how much she would have loved this place that I would never get to share with her. But over time, as I began to feel more at home, I came to see her presence in the things around me: the flowers and trees and the carvings in wood and stone made by long-dead craftsmen whose equals the world would never again know. In fact, I saw now that Habitation Louvois brought my mother and me closer than we had ever had a chance to be in life. I felt I knew her better now than I had ever known anybody.

During the final week of construction, Madame's investors returned, and she spent her days rushing around the grounds like a woman half her age. I think she needed to feel that no detail, however insignificant, was escaping her attention.

The investors were staying at the Hotel Erdrich, and the afternoon the last of the tables were installed in the casino, Madame brought the three men to the estate. Perhaps as a testament to how civilized the island had become, the large man had left his safari clothes at home, opting instead for a light summer suit. The four of them went off alone on a tour, Madame nervously clutching her walking stick—which she had recently begun to favor—too high above the ground for it to be of any use.

I was standing by the front desk when they returned, perhaps half an hour later, ascending the stairs near the tennis courts, the three men in the lead. Madame's stick dragged at her heels as she followed behind them. I could not tell if she was defeated or relieved, but as she passed me on her way up the stairs to her office, she managed a smile to let me know that all was well.

That evening, our new chef—an acquaintance of Michele's— prepared his first meal in the new kitchen, and Madame and the three investors settled in the restaurant for a feast of twelve courses. Afterward they went out to the pavilion, where a band awaited, and Madame and the large man in the light summer suit danced until the last of the ice in the servants' buckets had melted, and then they went to the club room for one last, unchilled drink.

Chapter Eleven

Despite our preparations, no one was quite ready when the first guests arrived. For me it was not a matter of things we had neglected to finish; I had simply lived alone for so long I had perhaps forgotten how to be decorous. Instead of plumbers and carpenters getting in the way, suddenly it was ladies and gentlemen trailing porters overloaded with luggage. In all my time in the service of Senator Marcus, and even during my stays at the Hotel Erdrich, never had I seen such luggage—leather so thick and shiny it seemed almost alive.

As I watched our guests arrive—nearly one hundred of them in two days—I wondered if they had traveled here together; they seemed remarkably well acquainted, calling out to one another by name and trading flamboyant kisses when they intersected in the lobby. I imagined an enormous ship adorned with thick red carpet and polished brass fixtures transporting them around the world, from port to tropical port—

dining with the ship's captain at the head of a table long enough for all of them to sit together. I tried to imagine myself there with them, but I was not so naïve as to believe they would accept me as one of their own. Not yet, but I could see the distance between us closing.

Although we had gone to great lengths to anticipate every problem that might arise with the opening of the hotel, there remained one troubling detail we had been largely powerless to address. In the nearly two years since the first shacks had appeared to the west of the estate, they had quickly grown from a small cluster to a sprawling ghetto, complete with a squalid market. As before, most of the new residents continued to be migrants from the countryside who had been squeezed out of the capital's overcrowded slums or came here hoping to escape the violence. For each one of the factory jobs made possible by the new hydroelectric dam, there were at least a hundred untrained peasants. The other ninety-nine ended up here: Cité Verd. A name so false it rose above irony to cruel mockery. Never was there a place less bestowed with green.

One afternoon a few weeks before the opening of the hotel, I went to see Madame in her office, wanting to share my concerns. As loath as I was to be the bearer of bad news, I could not afford to repeat the mistake I had made years ago, failing to warn her of potential dangers.

"Just to be safe, I thought I should mention it," I said, closely attuned to any sign of anger. "Maybe it will turn out to be nothing. But I worry about having so much squalor so close by, and the effect it will have on the hotel and the guests."

Madame sat at her desk, thoughtfully folding her hands together. "I know what you mean."

"I apologize for raising this now," I said. "It all happened more quickly than anyone expected."

"They can't be moved," she said with a sigh, "so for now we'll just have to hope for the best."

She pushed her chair back and got to her feet. I did the same.

"I would be grateful to you, however," she added as she turned toward the window, "if you would continue to monitor the situation for me."

"Of course."

She tapped a finger against her cheek. "Something like this requires the eyes of a native, someone sensitive to the ways of his people."

"Certainly, Madame. Although"—I hesitated as I moved toward the door—"I would never consider these to be 'my people,' exactly, and perhaps I don't know them as well as—"

"You know what I mean." With a stiff, false smile, she showed me we were done.

Since there was no way to reach Habitation Louvois from the port or the airport without having to pass by Cité Verd, we had to do what we could to minimize the shock. After our conversation, Madame ordered the street-front houses painted, the colors coordinated by the hotel's interior designer. But not even a rainbow of reds and oranges and yellows and blues could hide cheap concrete and rusted sheet metal. It was embarrassing to imagine our guests' first impression upon seeing the gawking peasants standing along the road in their rags.

Yet I had to admit that this too was part of what made Habitation Louvois so astonishing a sight, for having cleared the gate and begun the descent down the drive, one felt as though one were on a bridge to another world. It had been nearly eight years since Madame had purchased the estate, and even I—despite having been here every moment since—found the transformation incredible. I could not get enough of the look on our guests' faces, the same expression—as if it were a mask they took turns wearing—of awe that such a place as this could exist. They had traveled around the world, visiting places I had only read about. Madame had visited them too, and she knew there was nothing anywhere as beautiful as Habitation Louvois.

On the day the last of these initial guests signed the ledger, M. Gadds—whom Madame had hired to manage the hotel—showed me their names, appending to them the details he was aware I did not know: he was a famous actor, she a world-renowned singer. There were painters and poets, businessmen and brokers. There was a tennis player, a producer, and many more about whom he could say only, "And *she—she* is *very* famous," without being able to say precisely what she was famous for.

And then M. Gadds showed me the ledger where he tracked future reservations. He turned page after page. There seemed to be no end in sight.

"How far in advance does this go?" I asked.

"That was for this year." He put the ledger down and picked up another. "This one is filled up for next year."

It was only then that I truly began to understand what we had made, that this was to be not just another resort, a place like countless others that travelers looking to get away might choose. For the people in the ledgers, choice had nothing to do with it. We were an essential stop on their migratory path. And perhaps that was why Madame was able to get away with charging what she did. Hundreds of dollars every night, an amount someone like my father would find inconceivable. But some of the guests, those whose presence Madame wanted to ensure, were staying for free. She had even paid their airfare.

"It's an investment," M. Gadds told me. "The whole world will be watching to see who comes."

Madame and M. Gadds had been working for months on a guest list for the party to commemorate the opening. In addition to the guests in residence, Madame had invited dignitaries from every foreign embassy, every man of note from our own government, and members of the island's most prominent families. The first invitation had gone to President Duphay himself, and Madame had been ecstatic to receive, via the president's personal messenger, a gracious note of acceptance.

In the week leading up to the party, even the chambermaids came to life. Rather than loitering in doorways, chatting to one another with dust cloths over their shoulders, they could be seen scurrying along the paths with piles of fresh linen.

Madame had hired a woman from the States to oversee the party preparation. Together with Jean, our new chef, she coordinated a buffet of local dishes.

"They can get caviar anywhere," Madame said. So instead we would have chicken and rice and beans and roast pig. A long table was set up by the manor house pool for the food and the champagne and the crystal bowl of rum punch. Workers strung the trees with lights, and the gardeners—having seen to it that the grounds were immaculate—dedicated themselves to gathering flowers, which a florist from the capital arranged into native bouquets. And a band came to rehearse in the pavilion, and the party planner from the States personally saw to training the waitstaff.

The night of the party, the three white men, Madame's investors, appeared in tuxedoes. Soon the local guests began to arrive. I stood for a time watching an almost unbroken string of headlights bob down the drive. Black sedans, parked nose to tail on the lawn, reflected the moonlight on their shiny hoods, making the grass appear like a glassy pond. A constellation of lit cigarettes showed where the chauffeurs had gathered, shooting dice near the stables.

A few at a time, the other guests made their way from the villas to the manor house, attired in silk and satin. There was a casual grace to them, as if they were unaware of what was happening here—as if they had stumbled upon the party by accident. The locals, on the other hand, appeared stiff in their suits and their punctuality. I watched the two groups merge and then separate, gravitating toward their own kind. The patio began to look something like a chessboard, alternating clusters of light-skinned visitors and dark-skinned island dignitaries.

Unlike the rest of the staff, outfitted in identical uniforms of red and black, I was given a tuxedo with a white jacket. It was yet another welcome sign that my days of passing out drinks were far behind me. I was free now to walk among these men and women not as a servant but as someone equally worthy of respect.

Madame, in an elegant yellow gown, was leading tours of the estate, down the lighted paths to the villas and the garden and the pavilion—where the band played merengue—and the casino and the discotheque and the manor house and back to the pool, where the waitstaff stood by with ladles of punch. In between excursions she mingled near the verandah, where she could keep an eye on the incoming cars. I knew she was nervous that it was getting late, and there was as yet no sign of President Duphay.

Yet even with the absence of the president, the gathering did not lack for luminaries. I was told the prime minster was in attendance, as was the secretary of the treasury.

Standing beside the marble fountain that lapped into the pool, I was drawn into conversation with a distinguished gentleman of perhaps sixty, who introduced himself as Justice Charles. His beard was elegantly streaked with silver.

"A judge?" I could not hide my delight.

In response he grunted and gave the bottom of his glass a swirl.

"It must be extremely difficult to become a judge." I was eager for him to understand that I was not unfamiliar with his profession.

"I suppose so," he said with a yawn.

How pleased my father would have been to see how far I had come.

I said, "I am the manager of Habitation Louvois."

At that, Justice Charles turned toward me with a grin. "You work here, then?"

"Why, yes," I said with pleasure, as he draped his arm around my neck. "I helped to build everything you see."

He gave me a nod and squeezed my shoulder.

"Excellent," he said. "Excellent." And with a quick glance to ensure we were alone, he led me a few steps away.

"Maybe you could tell me," he said, leaning in toward my ear, "where a man might go for a special treat?"

"Well," I said, lowering my voice until it matched his, "what kind of treat did you have in mind?"

"So many lovely women," the judge said with a wink. "But it's so hard to tell which ones are available."

Just then—at the worst possible moment—I spotted one of the houseboys cresting the top of the stairs. A look of panic was on the boy's face, and he was heading straight toward me.

I tried to wave him off, but the moment he arrived, he reached out to grab my arm. "Monsieur," he whispered hoarsely, "Monsieur."

I did my best to pull away, but the boy would not let go.

"Would you pardon us for just a moment?" I asked Justice Charles.

And then I dragged the boy a few steps away. "What is it? What's going on?"

"You have to come," he said, oblivious of my anger. "You have to come right now. There's trouble at the gate."

I turned toward the judge in embarrassment. "I'm terribly sorry," I said. "It seems they cannot do anything without me."

The judge raised his glass to his lips, allowing a single ice cube to slip past.

"I'll be back in just a moment, and then we can finish our discussion."

With a flick of his wrist, he signaled that he understood.

I grasped the houseboy by the sleeve, leading him up the stairs. I said, "This had better be important."

The moment we reached the drive, I could hear the trouble for myself, a vast commotion of voices up above us.

"Who are they?" I asked.

"Villagers."

"How many?"

He paused, struggling to come up with a number.

"What do they want?"

From where they stood, I doubted they could see much—the floodlights around the pool, perhaps, and the strings of white bulbs swaying from the trees. Did they really have nothing better to do?

We found the guards crouched in their booth, passing back and forth a bent cigarette. For a moment they seemed to consider springing to their feet and pretending I had not caught them hiding here. But then they appeared to remember what was happening outside and decided it was wiser to stay where they were. What did they think would happen, with a wrought-iron gate between them and the crowd?

"Get up, you cowards!"

From the counter above their bowed heads I picked up one of their flashlights. The metal felt slick in my hand, and I realized I was sweating.

Despite the moon and the lamppost, shadows prevailed. At the gate

I could detect movement, but the forms were a blur, like animals camouflaged under a cover of trees. But there was no cover, just a jumble of bodies, a mass of arms and legs and heads and torsos that appeared to have fused together. It was as if all of Cité Verd had descended upon us. So many eyes were on me as I approached that I did not know where to look.

Above my head I raised the dark flashlight, aiming it at the sky.

"He has a gun," someone shouted.

"He's going to shoot."

As the message traveled backward into the crowd, panic spread with it. There was a frantic scramble as the people in front tried to flee—but they continued to be pressed forward by the people behind them.

"You have ten seconds to clear away," I shouted.

There were screams and scuffles and pushing in every direction. Coming closer, still wielding the flashlight, I saw faces jammed up against the bars growing twisted with desperation.

As I began to lower the flashlight, an elderly woman threw herself against the man behind her, trying to get him to move.

When it was over, more than ten seconds had passed, but no one among them had bothered to count. Huddled together across the road, stretching down toward Cité Verd as far as I could see, they looked to one another for confirmation that they were safe now. There must have been hundreds of them, young and old. As if standing at the end of a drive were the most fascinating opportunity ever presented to them.

"Not a word of this to Madame," I said to the houseboy. "Just let me know if they return."

"As for you," I said to the guards, "if I have to do your jobs for you again, you'll be joining them. Do you understand?"

With pitiful nods they showed they did.

As I hurried back to the pool, I wondered what I would have done if they had refused to move. The advantage of dealing with people like these was that they were easily fooled. But there was a danger as well— one never knew what they might do. Even the most well-trained dog will sometimes bite. President Mailodet had understood this better than anyone, and perhaps that was why his first response had always been brutality.

My greatest fear, upon returning to the party, was that word of what was happening at the gate had already reached the guests. To my added distraction, I could find Justice Charles nowhere. My only consolation was that our conversation, however brief, appeared to have made just as big an impression on him as it had on me.

Beside the buffet, a thin white man in wire-framed glasses was talking with a tall blonde in a bib of diamonds. "I can't stand the poverty back home," the man was saying, "but at least here they can always pick fruit and vegetables if they get hungry."

The woman nodded in agreement. "It's tropical poverty as opposed to cold poverty. In a place like this you hardly even feel it."

A heavyset mulatto in a tuxedo leaned in behind the woman, skewering a shrimp with a firm, sharp jab. His thin, elegant lips were perched upon a long, prominent chin, and when he smiled he looked like a tulip blossoming. He swirled the shrimp in a pot of sauce. "If we are to postpone indulgences and luxury until the very last person on earth is fed and clothed," the man pronounced in heavily accented English, "it would be a very boring world indeed."

Thinking of the people I had known growing up, I nearly added that it would be a world in which no one would bother to feed or clothe himself, preferring to depend on handouts.

At the other end of the patio, Madame came walking up the steps from Villa Bacall, the remains of what must have been a small tour group trailing behind her. As she passed in front of one of the floodlights, I noted with worry the flush in her cheeks. She was carrying on a distracted conversation with the man walking beside her. In a few more steps they reached the pool, and the man suddenly turned in my direction. The moment I saw his face, I knew he was someone I had met before, but I could not place him. He was short and well rounded across the middle, looking weary and curiously uncomfortable, as if uncertain of the company in which he found himself.

For several minutes, I watched the man from afar. He kept tugging at the sleeves of his tuxedo, as if they were trying to escape to higher ground. Madame was called away, leaving the man standing by himself, surrounded by men and women in conversation, none of whom appeared to invite his participation. A waiter balancing a tray of glasses filled with punch stopped to offer the man a drink, and the man watched as the waiter lowered his tray. He took a long time considering the punch, staring blankly at the glasses, so long that the waiter's arm grew tired and he needed to use the back of a chair for support. When still the man was unable to decide, the waiter selected a glass for him, brusquely raising the tray back above his shoulder and rushing off.

Alone again, the man lifted the glass and took a small, indifferent sip. As he looked around at the crowd gathered on the patio, searching, it seemed, for a familiar face among these strangers, his eyes met mine. He looked at me as he always had, with condescension and a touch of boredom. But then in an instant—it must have been the moment he recognized me—the look turned to trepidation, and I saw just how badly the minister of health had aged.

He looked away from me then, reaching out for the elbow of a small mulatto woman who at that moment came up beside him. His wife was not a particularly attractive woman, but she had a kind face and she glanced up when he touched her, her fingers brushing against his. The gesture, it seemed to me, was meant to be comforting, and there was more behind it, I guessed, than I would ever know.

"Monsieur." The same houseboy reached up to touch my arm. Did he have no idea how to comport himself around superiors?

"What?"

He froze at my glance.

"What do you want?" I repeated, losing patience.

He was almost breathless. "The president is here."

The motorcade was still winding its way down the drive when I reached the front steps of the manor house. A few dozen people had gotten there before me, including some of the foreign guests, who stood in a clump, chatting with bored, lazy gestures, uncertain why they were there, regretting now that they had followed the rest of the crowd.

There were three cars traveling together down the drive, identical black sedans as graceful as cats. They slowed so gently—in perfect unison—that it was impossible to tell when they finally stopped moving. Even the foreigners halted their conversations.

The front and rear cars released their passengers first, eight bulky, unsmiling men in identical black suits and striped ties and sunglasses, pivoting their heads on rigid necks, like periscopes scanning the crowd.

Leaving her three investors at the top of the steps, Madame came forward alone. As she approached the middle car, one of the bodyguards reached out and opened the back door. An immense smile appeared on Madame's face. And then, in an instant, the smile cracked, like a delicate pane of glass. From out of the limousine emerged not the president but a pretty young mulatto woman with a string of pearls around her neck. Recovering quickly, Madame took the young woman's hand as it was offered and kissed her cheeks, each in turn.

The young woman was the president's niece, sent on his behalf. Mlle Duphay wore a sleeveless gown of cream-colored satin, accentuating the slightly darker hue of her skin. She was an elegant young woman of twenty-two, just returned to the country after several years studying abroad.

With two of her bodyguards at her side, Mlle Duphay joined Mme Freeman on a tour of the estate. Madame appeared distressed as they left, wringing her hands behind her back. I followed from a distance, hearing nothing of what passed between the two women. Mlle Duphay appeared to say little, merely nodding as Madame described what she was seeing.

From the manor house they went on to the guesthouse, and then down the steps to Villa Bardot. Presumably not wanting to exhaust the president's niece, Madame skipped the rest of the villas, leading her instead to the tennis courts and back around the manor house to the casino. I waited outside while they went in to see the tables. Then they came back out, moving on to the gardens, and I was halfway down the path behind them when one of the bodyguards suddenly stepped out from behind a bush and grabbed my arm.

"Who are you?" he said, crushing my bicep with little effort.

Looking into the lenses of his sunglasses, I saw only the reflection of some distant light. "I manage the estate." As he offered nothing in response, I added I was eager to see that everything met Mademoiselle's approval.

"If it doesn't," he said, giving my arm one final, painful squeeze, "I will personally make sure you're the first to know."

Thinking I heard footsteps, I turned. The houseboy was running up the path.

"Monsieur," he shouted. "I've been looking all over for you. There's been an accident."

I nodded to the guard. "It was nice talking to you."

Instead of releasing my arm, he did his best to throw it back at me, as if it were not attached.

The crowd at the gate began to thin as I approached, leaving only a few bodies huddled around a dark form sprawled in the gravel. In the beam of the flashlight I saw it was a young girl. Beside her an old woman was weeping as she held some sort of rag to the girl's head. The cloth was soaked in blood.

"It was one of the cars," the houseboy said. "They didn't see her."

"Where's the car?"

"They left."

"Call an ambulance," I said. "Quickly." He took off running toward the manor house.

"I hope you're pleased with yourselves," I yelled to the crowd. Once again, they had receded down the road, pretending they were not to blame.

Extinguishing the beam of the flashlight, I turned to the guards, watching from the doorway of their booth. "I warned them," I said. "They have no one to blame but themselves."

This far from the hospital, there was no chance the ambulance would arrive quickly enough. Soon our guests would be preparing to leave, and we could not let them see what had happened.

"We must move her," I said to the guards. Along the shoulder, a few meters up the road, I found a patch of grass and cleared away the loose gravel. I ordered the houseboy to fetch a blanket.

"You can stay with her," I said to the old woman. To the guards I said, "Get rid of everyone else. I don't care how."

The manor house was silent, but for the murmur of the party down below. When I reached my office, I did not turn on the light. I merely sat at my desk, listening to the laughter and the tinkling of glasses. The shutters were open, and as I watched the treetops sweep against their starry backdrop, I thought about everything we had done to make Habitation Louvois possible. It had cost all of us—me, Mme Freeman, M. Guinee—but nothing important ever came cheaply. My father, with his stark morality, never understood. Sometimes things had to be sacrificed to achieve a greater good.

I do not know how long I sat there. It was the buzz of the telephone that brought me back. I immediately guessed that the ambulance had arrived. And I was relieved that they had come so discreetly, without lights or siren.

But I was mistaken; it was one of the guards calling to let me know the girl was dead.

The hotel is magnificent," Mlle Duphay said, arriving at poolside after the tour was over. "Finally we have something no other country has."

Breathless and dusty, I got there just in time to see Madame's smile. I think it no coincidence that the first person she turned to in search of a witness was me. She knew as well as I did that the credit went to both of us, that we had done all of this together.

In that instant, all the evening's complications evaporated.

Mme Freeman was so pleased she seemed to forget her disappointment—that it was the president's niece and not the president himself she was speaking to. They were words that over the next several months I would hear Madame repeat upon the arrival of nearly every guest at the hotel. "I think you'll see," she would say, "that we have something here that you'll find nowhere else in the world."

Mlle Duphay did not stay long that night, and her departure marked the end of the evening for most of the local guests. Madame and the three white men in tuxedoes stood at the top of the manor house stairs, receiving thanks and congratulations as the chauffeurs readied the cars. I was off to the side, watching the procession, when I happened to glance over and see someone standing on the darkened tennis courts.

I do not believe the minister of health saw me coming, for he seemed surprised to hear my voice.

"As you can see," I said, "they're not quite done. The surface is far too pebbly."

The minister of health nodded, allowing a long silence to pass. "I hadn't noticed until now."

"Do you still play?"

He turned his back to me, making his way slowly to the net. I saw him frown as he tested the tautness. Even in so simple a gesture I detected a hesitancy that had never been there before. It was clear, I realized, looking at him now, that he had aged far more than the eight years that had passed since his weekly matches with Senator Marcus. There was no going back to the man who cursed at any ball that dared score against him.

"Do you see much of Senator Marcus?" I asked.

The minister of health sighed. "I should get back to my wife. She's waiting."

We started back together, but by the time we had arrived he had far outpaced me, and he never looked back. His wife was on the steps speaking with Madame, and the former minister of health went up to join them. He and Madame brushed cheeks, and then he was gone.

Chapter Twelve

It was still dark when I awoke the next morning. Not wanting to break the silence, I dressed slowly, leaving the lights extinguished. Crossing the corridor to the stairs, I could scarcely see. But I already knew the way, step by step. At the door to M. Gadds's room I paused, turning my ear to confirm that he was still asleep.

As I descended, following the curve of the stairs, I took in the lobby below, lit from without as if by a bulb draped in thick, black felt. From a distance the evening's disarray appeared to have been set to order: the floors shone as if newly washed; the trays and plates and glasses had been returned to the kitchen. After the party ended, before going up to bed, I had offered to oversee the cleaning. M. Gadds had refused, insisting it was his responsibility.

However clean the lobby had looked from the top of the stairs, from the bottom I could see everything they had missed. Beside the entrance a thick black smudge climbed the plaster, left by the shoe of someone casually leaning against the wall. Several broken flower stems poked out of the vase beside the front desk. I could see where someone had pulled out a blossom, dislodging the others in the process, so that now they stood inches taller than they should have. And how careless, I thought, as my eyes fell upon the two chaises longues—the maids had incorrectly paired each with the other's pillows.

In the library and the ballroom and the restaurant I observed a number of similar oversights. But they were nothing compared to what I found outside. The buffet tables were still in place by the pool. Mounds of cigarette butts huddled in the underbrush, as if swept there on purpose. Reaching into a gaping hole in a shrub behind the pavilion, I discovered an empty bottle of champagne, smears of frosty pink lipstick circling the mouth.

The courtyard outside Villa Bardot was a mess. Not a single piece of patio furniture was where it was supposed to be. At the door, someone had abandoned a red sequined dress. The tables and chairs I moved one at a time, careful not to make a sound. I folded the dress as best I could.

In the other courtyards I found more of the same.

With the first true light of dawn at my back, I followed the last of the paths to the end, reaching the entrance to the preserve. In a glance I could see the party had not made it this far.

There was a bench at the fork just up the trail, and I decided to take a moment's rest before heading back. Soon everyone else would be awake, and the day's business would begin in earnest.

I had gone just a few steps into the preserve when I spotted someone up ahead, sitting on that very bench, head slightly tilted, staring absently at the trees. I could scarcely believe my eyes. In all my time here I had never encountered anyone this far from the manor house. The light was poor, and I could make out little more than a silhouette. I moved a little closer. Hearing my footsteps, she looked over and smiled, and I was relieved to see it was Madame.

"You don't look happy to see me," she said.

"Just surprised."

"I should have known you would be up at this hour," she said. "Even the birds are still sleeping."

"I wanted to make sure everything was in order before the guests arise."

She slid over on the bench, patting the space beside her. "It was quite a party, wasn't it?"

Not long ago I might have been reluctant to sit, not wanting to give her the wrong impression, but it was clear that of late our relationship had begun to change.

"It looked like everyone was having a very good time," I said, sitting down.

"It was a success. A wonderful success."

"I couldn't be more pleased."

"You must think them strange," she said.

"Not at all."

"They're good people," she said. "I don't know them all, of course, but I know their type. Some people think them shallow."

"The few I spoke with were very kind. Justice Charles, for instance."

"They enjoy the things other people don't have. They can afford to pay to experience things other people can't."

"Anyone would do the same, if they could."

"There's a certain value in such people," Madame said, leaning back comfortably. "Taken to excess it can seem decadent, but without people like these there would be no preserving things of value. What would happen to the great art of the world if there was no one who could afford to collect it? Who do you think gives the museums their money?"

"Yes, of course," I said. "Art would not survive."

"What would have happened to this place," she said, "if we had not come here? You only need to look around to see what we're up against."

From where we sat it was impossible to see the barren hills surrounding us or the slum to the west, but I knew that was what she meant. And then there were all the things beyond, the capital and the

National Palace, the garrisons and endless ghettos, the violence—the things I had left behind that she scarcely knew.

"So tell me," she said, "is everything in order?"

I wished in that moment that I could tell her everything was fine. But how could I lie, after she had just spoken to me with such honesty?

I told her about the smudge on the plaster and the cushions and the things I found outside. She winced when I showed her the champagne bottle I was still carrying, which I had filled with cigarette butts. But I left out my discovery of the red-sequined dress lying in front of Villa Bardot.

"I don't know what I'd do," Madame said, "if I didn't have you looking out for these things."

"I consider it my duty."

For several minutes more we sat in silence, each of us enjoying the majesty of the jungle spread out before us. However imposing it seemed, we could never afford to forget its true fragility, that we were the only thing standing between it and oblivion.

When it was time to go, I walked Madame back to her villa, and I went on to the manor house. M. Gadds had only just come down from his rooms, his hair wet with tonic. On the front desk I deposited the bottle and its filthy cargo.

M. Gadds glanced at it with disgust. "Get that off of there."

"It's for you," I said. "I would never want Madame to think you missed anything."

That M. Gadds and I were not destined to be friends was made clear early on. He had come to us highly recommended, having worked for more than two decades at some of the finest resorts in the world. I never knew where M. Gadds was from originally; in addition to French, he spoke German and Italian and English, all of them with an accent I could not quite place. M. Gadds was a generation older than me, and I could tell he felt it impertinent for me to ask him personal questions.

He had fair skin and glassy blue eyes and short, thinning hair he slicked back and parted through the middle, creating a broad path straight to the bald clearing at the back of his head. He was always immaculately dressed in silk shirts and cashmere jackets, and he was never seen without a brightly colored handkerchief arranged in his breast pocket.

He had tried to negotiate, as one of the terms of his contract, that my rooms—the largest in the manor house—be given over to him. Of course, Madame would not hear of it. I was not someone who could simply be cast aside.

Whether it was because of this or some other injustice, I do not know, but thereafter M. Gadds let it be known that he saw me as a rival, and he sought out every opportunity to try to undermine me. Whenever Madame was present, M. Gadds found an excuse for pointing out some gap in my knowledge of the hotel business, an expertise he had spent his entire life attaining.

"Fear not," he bravely offered whenever he had a chance, "I shall take him under my wing."

The first few times this happened, I took him at his word, for I was eager to learn everything I could. But of course, he had no intention of teaching me anything. In fact, M. Gadds enforced a strict separation between his responsibilities and mine, hoping thereby to preserve my inexperience. If that was as he wished it, there was little I could do, other than remind him that I was not the only one with something to learn.

Although I found satisfaction in what we had achieved with the opening of the hotel, there were parts of my old life I grew to miss.

It soon became obvious, for instance, that my quiet days spent exploring the estate—and my hours of restful contemplation—were gone forever. Now my days were a constant string of demands. No matter how much help we had, it was never enough. There was always one group of men doing this, another group doing that, and a dozen more projects standing by. To me, every task was important, because behind each of them was a guest we could not afford to disappoint. To that end, our greatest obstacle was the men themselves, whose every task, no matter how simple, had to be carefully supervised. It was the only way to ensure they did as they were told, and did it without dallying. I had no choice but to spend my days—and quite often, my nights—rushing from one corner of the estate to the other.

I often spent the few minutes of free time I managed to secure resting in the chair on my balcony. In the afternoon I could count on there being a tennis match or two to watch on the courts below. We were too long a drive from the capital to attract many regulars from the island, so our players mostly changed from week to week, as new guests arrived and old ones left. But there was one man, a local, who played with some regularity. Unlike most of the others, he displayed little seriousness toward his matches, often standing at the net joking when he should have been serving. His play was lackadaisical and he was always first to congratulate his opponents whenever they scored a difficult point. He was older and portly, skin a light shade of brown, and each time he stepped onto the court I imagined I was seeing my old employer, Senator Marcus. Even though I knew it could not be him, the sight always brought me comfort, for it carried to mind a picture of the Senator as I remembered him best, and it helped me to believe that, wherever he was, he had found happiness and a new kind of peace.

Aside from tennis, most of the activity at Habitation Louvois came at night, as our guests descended upon the manor house in their evening attire, ready to feast. After dinner there was always a band at the pavilion and champagne by the lighted pool. The discotheque was a favorite of our younger guests, who went inside to dance and then snuck back out later to entwine themselves under the starlight. Sometimes I awoke in the night to the sound of their laughter.

But they were not the only ones staying up until dawn. Not infrequently did my morning inspection of the grounds bring me upon middle-aged businessmen struggling to make it back to their villas with their jacket pockets stuffed with chips. There were guests who spent their entire trip hunched over craps tables and roulette wheels, never seeing the sun. We learned to accommodate whatever our guests wished, no matter how peculiar. Although most of the staff never knew who our guests were, they knew to treat everyone with deference. Because of my position, I was often aware of who had arrived and who we were expecting, and occasionally there were faces I recognized from a magazine.

My principal disappointment was that I saw so little of Madame. She came to Habitation Louvois whenever she could, but business back home more often kept her away. Through regular letters I let her know what was happening here. From M. Gadds she received financial reports, but she counted on me for the details of daily life, which was what kept the place alive for her in her absence. She understood that no one knew the estate like I did, and there was no one she trusted more. That was why, when she was here, she made a point of meeting me each morning at our bench in the preserve, before she went to see M. Gadds.

Never on these mornings did we see anyone else in the preserve. For the guests, it was too wild a place; they preferred their pools and the cultivated garden paths. Since only the two of us ever visited it, the preserve grew to feel like our private sanctuary. We joked about it sometimes, saying that if anything were to happen to us there, no one would ever find us. But of course, nothing bad could ever happen there. As only the two of us understood, it was the most peaceful part of the entire estate.

While the hotel itself continued to cater mostly to foreign visitors, within months of opening, the restaurant had come to be regarded throughout the capital as the finest on the island, far eclipsing the Hotel Erdrich. Chef Jean and his menu were the talk of Lyonville. On any given night, half the tables were filled with politicians and businessmen negotiating deals over oysters and escargot.

One summer night toward the end of our first year, I was passing through the dining room and out of the corner of my eye I saw someone waving at me. It was dark in the corner where he was sitting—the table lit by a single flickering candle—and as I approached, he bounded up from his seat and met me with a crushing embrace.

"Look who it is," Paul cheered as he clapped me on the back. "This is Alexandre, the guy I was telling you about." As he turned us toward the table, he stumbled, misjudging where the floor should be.

A pretty young woman wearing a sour expression glanced up reluctantly. Disturbed from their meals by Paul's outburst, many of the diners at the tables around us sat with their forks midway to their mouths, watching us with curious displeasure.

I gestured for Paul to sit.

"This is Claudette," Paul said in a voice that was much too loud. The young woman extended her fingers. She could have been no older than twenty-two—more than a decade younger than he—but she seemed not the least bit uncomfortable here, as though she had spent her whole life eating in restaurants like this. She was dressed in an expensive purple satin dress, and her ears held diamond studs. Well above her plunging neckline a gold chain rested against her bronze skin. Her complexion was much lighter than Paul's. Her features were both delicate and firmly precise.

"She didn't believe me when I said I knew the guy who ran this place," Paul said, winking at me when Claudette looked away.

"Paul," she said sharply, "the food is getting cold."

"Let it," Paul burbled, signaling to Georges, one of the waiters. "More champagne. And another glass."

"No, no," I said. I managed to catch Georges by the sleeve and gesture that he should forget the glass. I immediately wished I had vetoed the champagne, too.

"This is my oldest and dearest friend," Paul said, grasping Claudette's shoulder. She shrugged him off. "We've known each other since we were kids."

"A long time," I said. A time that I had lately found it increasingly easy to forget.

He grinned. "A *very* long time. How have you been? It's cruel of you not to keep in touch with your friends." His voice kept rising, and the people at the neighboring tables were eyeing us again.

"Don't go," Paul said, seeing me begin to back away. "Let's get you a chair." He was looking around for an empty seat, and finally he found one, a few tables away. I saw him reach into his pocket. The roll of bills he produced was so thick he had trouble getting it out. But once he did, he proceeded to snap several off the top. As he reached out for the chair, he let the two fingers holding the folded bills stray in the direction of one of the men sitting at the table.

Even in the dim light I could see the man's face redden. He was a regular customer, an official of some kind. "Take the chair," he said through clenched teeth, careful to enunciate every syllable, "and sit down."

Paul waved the bills once more, but the man had already turned away.

"I can't sit," I said, pulling Paul away from the empty chair.

Claudette was gone from the table. I spotted her across the restaurant, making her hurried way toward the restroom.

As I helped Paul to his seat, I saw M. Gadds watching from the doorway.

"Promise me you'll come visit," Paul said. "Promise." Perhaps it was just an effect of the champagne, but the way he looked up at me, his eyes red and glistening, I could not possibly say no.

In the kitchen, I met M. Gadds's scowl with one in kind.

"We cannot afford this kind of embarrassment," I said, nearly shaking as I passed. How could I ever have imagined such a friendship could endure?

"We must make sure," I said, "that he never be allowed to come back."

Chapter Thirteen

As with everything else, the idea had been Madame's. I first learned about it the day we received the airmailed carton full of crisp, shiny brochures printed on heavy stock. "The Wedding of Your Dreams," it said in elegant script on the front panel, above a black-and-white photo of the manor house front-lit by the setting sun. And inside, the orchid and the rose gardens, the pavilion done up in flowers and silk. On the back were the packages, the most decadent of which delivered bride and groom by horseback to the altar. We would provide everything: the minister, the banquet and champagne, the string quartet, the floral arrangements, the children bearing baskets of petals, even—if one wished—the handmade dress. Nowhere was there any mention of price.

Almost immediately, the dates began to fill. M. Gadds would permit only a single wedding each month. We could have managed more, but I think he enjoyed being able to turn people away. So desperate were so many couples for one of the few available slots they were willing to sign onto a waiting list in the faint hope that ill fortune might strike someone ahead of them. I remember it happening just once, a young couple flying across the ocean on two days' notice to step into the plans someone else had already set in motion.

In the spring of our second year, a musician from the States famous enough to be known even here rented out the entire estate for his wedding party.

"It's what everyone will be talking about," Madame wrote elatedly from back home. "If he leaves happy, we'll have more business than we ever dreamed of."

In truth, it was difficult to imagine how we could accommodate any more business than we had already, but even still I could not help sharing in her excitement.

"We will not let you down, Madame," I wrote in return. "We will see to it that everything is perfect."

The next afternoon, I went to speak with M. Gadds.

"We should call a meeting of all the staff," I said, standing before his desk. "We need to make it clear how important this is. They should know our expectations will be higher than ever before."

M. Gadds could barely be bothered to glance at me over the top of his glasses. "We shall do no such thing." He turned back to the document he had been reading. "The staff don't need to be told to do their jobs."

"But Madame—"

"Need I remind you," he said, snapping off his glasses, "that I am the one running this hotel? Not you."

He may have been the one running the hotel, but it was clear to me that I was the one who truly cared about Habitation Louvois. For M. Gadds, it was just another job. For Mme Freeman and me, it was the most important thing of all.

During the few days remaining until the guests arrived, I stayed out of M. Gadds's way. If he wanted to do everything himself, who was

I to argue? But even if he was willing to ignore the importance of the occasion, I was taking no chances. I had my reputation to be concerned with; the hotel might have been his, but the estate was mine. I personally went through each villa myself, making sure there was nothing in need of repair. And I walked every inch of the grounds with the gardeners in tow, pointing out every twig and leaf that needed to be clipped.

Despite his optimism, the first sign appeared early on that things might not go as smoothly as M. Gadds had hoped.

The arrival of the wedding party passed without incident—no small feat, considering its size and the fact that they all came at once. But as the taxis pulled away and the guests crowded into the lobby to collect their keys, I watched the blood drain from M. Gadds's face.

He had made a gross miscalculation.

Even without taking the time to count, I could see there were more than two of them for every bed.

The musician was tall and thin, with deep-set eyes of mossy green. Propped against the front desk, he looked like an ivory statue of some ancient nobleman, radiating a warm, placid glow.

M. Gadds threw back his shoulders and took a deep breath. "I'm terribly sorry, but I'm afraid there are far more of you than we expected." He looked from one to the next, as if hoping someone among them might be prepared to accept the blame. "Had we known," he said, shaking his head with regret, "this could have been avoided. What I would propose, as a courtesy—"

"What's he saying?"

Without even turning to see who had spoken, the musician lifted his hand for silence.

M. Gadds raised his voice so everyone would be able to hear. "I will personally make the arrangements at the Hotel Erdrich for those of you we cannot accommodate here."

I recall the musician smiling as he ran a finger over the contours of his chin. He had not shaved in days.

"We don't mind sharing," he said in a tired baritone, reaching out for the key.

The other members of the wedding party, draped over each other on the lobby furniture, began to stir. With their identical long hair and denims, it was hard even to tell the men and the women apart. I had no idea which one might be the bride.

Never had I seen a wedding party in which everyone was so young. I doubted there was anyone among them a day over thirty. At the time I remember thinking it strange that someone would choose to exclude his family from so important an occasion. I quickly came to see, however, that this was the least of the conventions they were intent on breaking.

Less than an hour after the musician and his friends checked in, a maid sent to deliver extra towels returned to the manor house in a state of distress. I found her in the kitchen, chewing on her thumbnail.

"What is it?" I asked. "What's wrong?"

She would not speak until we had reached the privacy of my office and I had closed the door.

"They're not wearing bathing suits," she whispered. It was not clear who she thought might overhear.

I turned to the window. "Surely that can't be." Did I expect proof to be sitting out on the front lawn? Did part of me hope it was? "Perhaps someone forgot to bring one."

She grimaced and shook her head. "Not one. All of them."

Somehow word had already reached M. Gadds. I heard footsteps rushing down the corridor. He burst in without knocking.

He could not have heard a word we had said, yet he immediately grabbed the maid by the arm, pulling her out of her seat.

"This is not your concern," he said to me.

"Nor do I wish it to be."

When they reached the door, he turned back. "I don't ever want to catch you meddling in my business again."

"There is nothing I would like more," I said, "than to be able to do my job without having to do yours as well."

There was rage in his eyes, but I knew I could not be blamed for putting it there.

An hour later, as I sat on my balcony minding my own business, a topless young woman showed up at the front desk wanting an aspirin.

However much they may have adored his music, the maids complained the loudest. Soon they flatly refused to go to the villas. The rumors appeared to have the opposite effect on some of the younger waiters and houseboys, who showed uncharacteristic dedication to their work. That first night, half of them continued to volunteer their services even hours after their shifts were supposed to have ended.

It had long been Madame's motto that luxury meant catering to every conceivable need and whim—and doing so with gusto—but by the second day of the wedding party's stay it became clear by the smiles on the houseboys' faces that we were satisfying some desires she had never intended.

Being unwilling to reprimand the guests and too weak to properly discipline the staff, M. Gadds resorted to reassigning as many of the young men as he could to the kitchen and the stables. I had to put the rest to work on the grounds. And so by default my regular crew of gardeners were promoted to houseboys and waiters. But of course they had no experience with the work, and no idea how to properly interact with guests. As anyone but M. Gadds could have predicted, they wasted no time in displaying the same proclivities as the others. Hardened by their labor on the grounds, they were perhaps even more popular. From the moment they started their new positions, they were constantly disappearing, abandoning even the pretense of doing what we asked of them. It was no mystery where I would find them. But much like the maids, I could not bring myself to look.

On the morning of the third day, having reached the limits of my patience, I called them all together. Looking into their bleary eyes, I could see at least half of them had not slept at all the night before.

"Have you no decency?" I asked as they tottered like reeds, barely able to stand erect. "Have you no self-respect?"

I could hear snickering in the back. Even the men right in front of me seemed to be struggling to suppress smiles. No, it was clear they were quite pleased with themselves. These were not men, they were feral dogs in heat.

"Prude," one of them whispered.

"If you want a boss who approves," I said, "go find yourself a pimp. This is a hotel, not a brothel."

They were silent.

I looked them over once more in disgust. "You're fired," I said. "All of you."

They eyed one another then, unable to believe what they had heard.

"Let's go," I said. "Now."

They were too surprised to resist. I had not expected such an orderly march to the gate. They must have believed I would change my mind, give them another chance. But then we arrived, and I ordered the guards to let them through. When the first of the men hesitated, I took the automatic rifle from one of the guards' shoulders and aimed.

With the men on the other side and the gate once again closed, I sent the weaponless guard to collect their belongings.

"Dump it all in the street," I said. "That's where they'll be working from now on."

As for the men themselves, I had nothing more to say, nothing to prove.

That same night, one of the fired gardeners tried to sneak back onto the grounds. But this time he had something other than himself to sell: vials and pouches of powder stuffed in his pockets.

When the guards brought him to me, I told them how pleased I was to see this uncharacteristic display of competence. Then I picked up the phone and called the police. He was their problem now.

By then, a little more than two years since our opening, it was beginning to become clear how difficult it was going to be to entirely seal off the estate from the less savory aspects of life on the island. Even with the violence and unrest kept in check, there were always new problems. Lately it was drugs. The island had become a way station between the two hemispheres, and so far President Duphay had proven unable to do anything about it.

And then there were also the difficulties that in all fairness M. Duphay could not be expected to control. Foremost among them was the drought we had been suffering through for months. The effect on the grounds was bad enough, as everything green inevitably began turning brown, but the lack of rain also meant the newly constructed dam was failing to keep up with demand. Large swaths of the island had already experienced blackouts, and more were guaranteed. Although we had our own generators, it was nevertheless a worrisome reminder of the fragility of things. And the reports I had been hearing of failing crops and the resulting rise in prices and hunger across the countryside were familiar signs of trouble to come. The exposure of most of our guests to the outside world was limited to the time it took to drive from the airport to the hotel and back, but no one could say how long we could keep them isolated.

As worrying as all of that was, however, I was far more concerned with our immediate troubles. By the day of the musician's wedding, the interactions between the guests and staff had grown so unacceptable that M. Gadds and I were running from villa to villa ourselves, serving everyone at once, while the head housekeeper saw to it that no one among the staff left the manor house. Neither of us got more than a few minutes' sleep.

Much to our surprise, the ceremony itself turned out to be a subdued affair, the bride in white and the groom in a fine black suit. Although there were secular options as well, they had requested a minister to perform the ceremony, which their friends attended in quiet reverence, fully dressed and genuinely sober.

And when the bride and groom exchanged their vows and kissed, there were even more tears than usual, including among the men, many of whom were as carefully jeweled and beflowered as the bridesmaids.

※

After what we had been through together leading up to the wedding, it seemed to me that M. Gadds and I should have been able to make peace. For days we had been so busy that we had no choice but to set our arguments aside. But with the return to normal business following the musician's departure, M. Gadds resumed his usual antagonisms. If anything, they increased. Rarely did a day pass in which I was not accused of transgressing some supposed protocol. Not satisfied with insisting that I leave to him all matters relating to guests, he similarly decreed—despite lacking the authority to do so—that the same be true of any business involving the staff. He felt only the gardeners and occasional repairmen—about whose work he preferred to remain ignorant—should remain within my jurisdiction.

As best I could, I kept my distance. Let him think what he wished. Madame had been correct, and so, by extension, had I. Our success handling the wedding party had raised our profile even higher than it had been before. Demand surged, even though there was little we could do to meet it. We had already been filled to capacity.

Madame, it seemed, was busy, too. Nearly six months had passed since she was here last. Her letters had also grown less frequent. I could only assume it was business back home that kept her from attending to what was happening at Habitation Louvois.

Madame was so distracted, in fact, that she never even thought to warn us when, less than a month after the musician and his friends left, we received our most important guest yet.

In the registration book he was listed as M. Swallows. I did not realize, until the day he arrived, that this was the name of one of Madame's three investors, the large man who had shown up the first time wearing a pith helmet.

M. Swallows stepped out of the limousine attired as only a man on vacation could be, in long plaid shorts of such peculiar dimensions they had to have been tailored especially for him. They were enormously broad across the back, with thin legs to cover his disproportionately skinny thighs. The shorts looked something like an overstuffed otto-man. Gone was the jungle apparel. Gone the linen suit. His shirt was a vibrant blue, but numerous other colors too, featuring toucans and palm trees and coconuts in a festive array. This time he came alone, without his companions, Madame's other two investors.

He was standing at the front desk when I entered the lobby. I was caught off guard when he seemed to recognize me.

"How are you, monsieur?" he asked, giving me a friendly nod.

"Well," I said, fumbling for words. "And you? How are you?"

"Excellent!"

"Wonderful," I said, trying to produce a smile equal to his. "Let me know if there is anything I can do for you."

"I will!" he boomed. "I most certainly will."

As he walked away, I realized the feeling had gone from my fingers and toes.

We gave M. Swallows the guesthouse. It was far more space than even a man of his girth would require, but the accommodations were luxurious, and their proximity to the manor house meant we could more easily ensure he received everything he needed.

That first night, at dinner, M. Swallows refused the menu. In-stead, he sent Georges to fetch Jean from the kitchen.

"I would like to eat," M. Swallows announced to the startled chef, "whatever you would like to cook."

Jean pivoted on his heel, impressively unshaken. "As you wish."

M. Swallows sat at the head of a table of ten. I do not know how he managed to make so many acquaintances so quickly, but they all seemed happy to be there. With two fingers he signaled for the sommelier.

"Do you have any Château Montelena?"

"Of course."

"Bring us a case."

There was escargot to start. M. Swallows declared the snails "remarkably plump."

The echo around the table concurred. "Incredibly plump." "I've never tasted anything so plump."

If M. Swallows knew his companions' names, he preferred not to use them. It was, "You, more wine," and "You, pass the bread."

When Georges delivered the filet mignon, M. Swallows moaned as if he had been struck a blow. "It's so tender you don't need teeth."

The woman to his left produced a horsey smile. "A baby could eat it."

"You could spread it on a cracker," someone else offered with an overeager laugh.

The meal went on so long that Georges was found asleep in the pantry when it was finally time for dessert.

During the week he was here, it seemed there was nowhere I could go without hearing M. Swallows's laugh, like a car engine turning over and over and over. And everywhere he went—the restaurant, the pool, the club room—M. Swallows's laughter spread to everyone else. He was a different man from the one who had visited us before.

Within a day of his arrival, he had become the figure around which everything seemed to revolve. Everyone was talking about M. Swallows—or Freddy, as he preferred to be called. Although he had come here alone, everyone was instantly his friend. Each night he dined with an entirely new entourage. We had to send to the capital for an emergency resupply of wine.

Second only to his love for food and drink was M. Swallows's fondness for dancing, as I remembered well from one of his earlier trips. But whereas Madame—his dance partner then—had liked to go to bed early, M. Swallows's new acquaintances seemed to care as little for sleep as he did.

But not everything M. Swallows did was in the same grand fashion. For someone who had made his fortune investing in risky ventures, he proved to be a modest gambler. From several different croupiers I heard that M. Swallows spent his time in the casino walking the floor with the same few chips, lingering now and then at a table but rarely putting any money down. But wherever there was a high roller on a streak, M. Swallows could be found cheering, orchestrating the waitresses' trays of drinks.

He must have slept sometime, but it was not clear to me when. On one of my early-morning walks, just as the sun was rising, I spotted him on his patio enjoying a cigarette. He did not appear to see me.

A few days later, as I was leaving the restaurant following break-fast, I discovered M. Swallows sitting alone on a lounge chair beside the manor house pool. Wearing a bikini swimsuit that nearly disap-peared beneath his belly, he was casually watching a houseboy skim leaves from the water.

"How long has he been out there?" I asked a waiter who was pass-ing by.

"Since I got here," he said.

That afternoon I began a letter to Madame in which I remarked upon her investor's sudden transformation. Although the phone service had improved enough that we could talk when necessary, I still pre-ferred the intimacy of the written word. Only on the page could I take my time in formulating the precise things I wished to say.

"We have achieved more than I ever thought possible," I wrote. "A perfect paradise. Being here is like being enveloped in a dream. The scent of the gardens is a greater elixir than man ever made. When one is here, the outside world dissolves like a sugar cube in water. As for M. Swallows, you would not have recognized him. I hope you do not think it impertinent for me to suggest that he could find no place for his bur-dens here and simply let them go."

Chapter Fourteen

In the weeks leading up to Mlle Miller's arrival, the actress's representative was in constant contact with M. Gadds, checking and double-checking to see that everything his client would need during her two-week stay had been attended to. It was imperative that her time at Habitation Louvois be restful. Mlle Miller was taking a break between the shooting of two films, two very demanding roles. The project she had just completed was a historical epic set in ancient Rome, in which the young woman played the favored mistress of an aged emperor threatened by challengers to his throne. In one of our guests' discarded magazines I had read of the film's devastating final scene, in which Mlle Miller fights her way through a mob to reach the side of her lover, who has just been cut down by assassins. In the article, Mlle Miller spoke of the scene being so emotionally exhausting she could not stop crying until long after the director had declared it "a wrap." The photo accompanying the article showed a thin young woman sitting in profile upon a marble bench, gazing out over the ocean. She wore a toga and dark glasses, and her blond hair was aglow under the midday sun.

To ensure peace and quiet during her stay at the hotel, Mlle Miller had reserved not just one villa but an entire group of four, and Madame set aside for her the most remote spot of all, south of the manor house, where traffic from other guests was lightest.

By this time the hotel had been open only a little more than three years, yet Madame nevertheless ordered that Mlle Miller's four villas be entirely repainted, inside and out. I personally went through and tested every stone in the courtyard and along the paths she would be most likely to travel, ensuring that none were loose.

A few days before Mlle Miller's arrival, we received a wooden crate upon which the word FRAGILE had been stamped so many times we had trouble determining which way was up. Inside was a box of candles scented with sandalwood and a bag of soaps individually wrapped in brown paper and tied with a pink ribbon. At the bottom of the crate rested a cedar case lined with velvet, inside of which nestled a set of bed sheets so soft and supple they seemed to be woven of feather.

However much these preparations were intended to set us at ease and guarantee that everything went smoothly, for me at least they had the opposite effect. Each of Mlle Miller's special measures felt like a reminder of the things we lacked—of the potential for the visit to go wrong. I wished it were not so, but in truth the precautions were not entirely unwarranted; there were still too many problems on the island over which we had no control.

Although the worst of the drought had ended, food shortages persisted. At Habitation Louvois we had from the start relied on imports of virtually everything but the produce brought each morning by market women from Saint-Gabriel. But with so many of the island's crops devastated by the long months without rain, even sweet potatoes had grown increasingly scarce. Rice had become almost as expensive as petrol.

At a time when so many people were struggling just to eat, however, perhaps the most troublesome problem were the rumors coming out of the palace. One morning Mme Freeman—who was here for a brief visit—brought to our bench in the preserve a clipping she had made from a foreign newspaper. Following a brief but nevertheless damning overview of our political past—written in a tone oozing with condescension—the article carried the claim, based on unnamed sources, that over the last year half of all government revenue had been diverted to special private accounts, including some linked to the president himself. The author closed with a self-satisfied smirk: "A new kleptocracy is born."

"Is it true?" I asked.

Madame shrugged, making it clear I was missing the point. "It doesn't matter if it's true. What matters is that it was printed in a newspaper that people actually read. That our *guests* read."

"What can we do?" I asked.

"Hope there are no more surprises."

I doubted even she could summon the optimism to support such a wish.

The afternoon Mlle Miller's plane was due to land, the boy I had sent to clean her pool came back to tell me he had discovered a problem. The water pump was showing signs of strain. He did not think it would last.

"Why didn't you mention this before?"

"I don't know, monsieur." His hand went *tap, tap, tap* on his knee.

"You were supposed to have checked it a week ago. Did you?"

He looked away. The tapping increased. "Yes, monsieur."

"Don't lie to me. I have no use for people who cannot tell the truth."

"I'm sorry, monsieur," he said. "It won't happen again."

"No," I said, rising from my desk. "That's for certain. I want you gone by the time I get back."

To be sure, I had to inspect the pool for myself. But even before I opened the door to the shed behind Mlle Miller's villa, I could hear the motor groaning. With just a glance it was clear nothing could be done. A replacement, I knew, would take weeks to arrive.

As I was making my way back to the manor house to tell Madame the news, one of the gardeners met me on the path.

"What now?" I said, detecting on his face yet another impending annoyance.

He stepped aside, sweeping off his hat. "I thought you should know, monsieur," he said, "there are three men outside the gate."

"What do they want?"

He shrugged. "I don't know."

"Why not?"

"They are white men, monsieur."

"Very well," I said. The news about the pump would have to wait.

At first I saw just two of them, sitting on the ground with their backs to a tree, similarly attired in wrinkled brown pants, scuffed brown shoes, and white short-sleeved shirts, one of them accented with pinstripes of pinkish red. Around them radiated a scattered array of garbage and assorted belongings—cigarette packs and bottles, a necktie, a comb, notepads, and swollen paperback books. It looked as if the men themselves and everything else in their possession had been dumped out of a sack.

The shorter of the two had removed his shoes and rolled his already shortened sleeves. His tie hung askew of his collar. They were playing cards, and the tall one—even with them seated, there must have been half a meter's difference in height—kept looking down over his companion's shoulder to see what sort of hand he held.

The short man discarded, flicking a black face card onto a small pile in the dirt. Even before the dust had settled, the tall one pounced.

"Aha!" he exclaimed, scooping up the card.

"Bloody hell!" the short one cursed as his friend fanned his winning hand along the uneven ground. He slammed his own cards down in disgust. "I thought I had you that time."

"You're always giving it away," said the tall one with a shrug. "I can read you like a book."

From out of the leather bag at his side the small man removed a silver flask. After a long swallow he wiped the mouth on the tail of his partially untucked shirt and offered a drink to his companion.

The tall one drew a cigarette out of a badly crumpled pack. Along the tracks of his suspenders sweat seeped like water from a bog.

"May I ask what you're doing here?" I said, stepping out of the shadow of the gate. The short one looked up from his flask with a smile, but it was the tall one who rose to his feet, his long legs unfolding like a crane's. "You must be from that big house down there," he said as he came forward to greet me. "Quite a home."

"It's a hotel," I said.

"Is it now? See, I never would have guessed." And then the tall man turned to his companion to check his reaction, as if this had been a matter of contention between them.

"Marvelous, lovely place," said the short man, nodding his approval.

"Do you gentlemen have business here?"

"Not as such," the tall one said. "Not as such." He gestured for me to wait as he retreated back to the tree and began rooting through his bag. "You could say," he mumbled around the cigarette, "it's more a matter of pleasure." And then he rose again, and around his neck he lowered a strap, to which was connected the biggest camera I had ever seen, the lens nearly the size of a man's forearm. "We're birders."

"That's right," said the short one, stuffing the flask back into his bag. "We love the bloody things. The colors, all that. Marvelous animals, birds."

"There are no birds here," I said. "Not many, anyway. Mostly just crows and pigeons."

"Crows, cardinals, cockatiels," the tall one said from his spot at the base of the tree. "They're all equal to us. Real bird lovers don't discriminate. If it has wings and flies—"

"Or doesn't fly," added the short one pointedly. "Some don't, you know." He had pulled on his socks, and now he was working on his shoes. "We don't discriminate."

"Perhaps you could do this elsewhere?" I said.

"Of course," said the short man, "of course. Here, there, every-where. We'll go, we'll come back. You have to be flexible. Let the birds be your guide."

"Right now the birds are here," said his companion, looking off into the distance. "There goes one now." He pointed excitedly toward a stand of trees beyond the wall, quickly taking aim with his camera. "Too late," he said, lowering the camera in disappointment. "Elusive buggers."

"Unfortunate, that," said the short man as he removed a similar camera from his own bag. "Just have to wait for it to come back."

It was then that I noticed something on the other side of the tree—a third pair of brown shoes, crossed at the ankles. From that angle they appeared unattached to anything, as if they had sprouted from the earth. Only as I moved along the gate to get a better view did I see the shoes were indeed connected to feet, and the feet to legs. The rest, however, was hidden behind the trunk of the tree.

"Is something wrong with him?" I said.

The short one shrugged. "A touch of something or other. It'll pass."

"Could I ask a favor?" I said. "I understand if you wish to photo-graph the birds, but we're expecting a very important guest."

"Is that so?" said the tall one.

"Would you mind going somewhere else for a few minutes, until after she has arrived?"

The two men glanced at one another, silently conferring.

"Of course," said the tall one.

The short one began gathering together the cards spread out in the dirt. "Think nothing of it."

"I appreciate it," I said.

Back at the manor house, I told the gardener who the men were.

"You might see them taking photographs," I said. "I told them it would be okay."

A short time later, M. Gadds came looking for me. From the opposite end of the hall I could see the smirk on his face.

"Birders?" he said with a laugh. "Is that what they told you?"

"I told them there aren't many birds here," I said as I tried to pass by.

He sidestepped to block my way. "They're here," he said with evident enjoyment, "to take pictures of Mlle Miller."

"You must be mistaken."

Never had I seen him so giddy. "They work for those magazines you're so fond of."

"What magazines?"

M. Gadds folded his arms across his chest, his lips pursed with condescension. "The ones you keep in your office."

"I keep them for the guests."

"In that case," he said, "perhaps you should consider putting them in the library, where the guests will be more likely to find them."

At that moment, two of our guests were passing through the lobby— a foreign businessman and his wife—and I turned to greet them.

"If this is true," I said once the couple was gone, "we have to stop them."

M. Gadds was already turning to leave. "This isn't your concern. Security of the hotel is my responsibility. Your job is to change the lightbulbs."

I should not have been surprised that Mlle Miller's visit brought out the worst in him. I had long ago observed this tendency, that his insults grew in direct proportion to the importance of whoever happened to be around. The presence of Madame made him cruel. The presence of a well-known musician made him unbearable. The presence of a world-famous actress made him intolerable. It did not seem to matter that I was usually the only direct witness to these displays. The satisfaction he found in being so unpleasant would likely have been the same with no audience at all. What point would there have been even trying to deprive him of this pleasure? Besides, it was easy to see that it all came down to simple jealousy. He knew it was me Mme Freeman looked to first, my opinions she sought out, not his.

In the days following the young woman's arrival, I was so busy I very nearly managed to forget she was here. The first time I went down to Mlle Miller's villas to check on her pool, she was already several days into her stay. It was a little after noon and a collection of deck chairs lay in the sun, but there was no sign anyone had recently been using them. I supposed Mlle Miller had gone to the manor house for lunch.

The pump's motor had gotten neither better nor worse. It was impossible to say if it would survive until its replacement arrived. Resigning myself to returning the next day to check on it again, I closed the shed door behind me.

Over the moan of the engine, I had failed to hear her coming, and I was caught by surprise when I stepped outside and found the young woman standing alone at the edge of the pool, staring at the placid water, her right arm weighed down by a tumbler filled with an amber liquid.

Outside of a magazine, it was the first time I had ever seen her. Mlle Miller looked older than I had expected, and yet somehow younger too. Her face was both dull—as if worn down by age and the elements—and also soft and gently chubby, like a child edging toward adulthood. Hair more brown than blond, it failed to absorb the sunlight swelling on the cement at her bare feet. She was as tall as I had supposed, and thin, her open bathrobe revealing a slim figure in a two-piece swimsuit—green with white spots. I would still have called her pretty, but I sensed she would take no pleasure in such a compliment.

"There's no beach," she said, her voice so soft and quiet I was scarcely sure I heard it. I realized belatedly that she was talking to me.

"Pardon me?"

"There's no beach here. I expected there to be a beach."

"It's not far." Thanks to the new roads President Duphay was building all across the island, everything was closer than it used to be. "Just twenty minutes."

She turned to look at me, the ice clinking in her glass. There was about her a sadness I would never have guessed someone so famous and successful could feel.

"Is it pretty?" she asked.

"Beautiful."

"I'd like to go there."

"Of course." Suddenly aware of the grease on my fingers, I folded my hands together behind my back. "There's a car at your disposal. The concierge at the manor house will be glad to arrange it." I turned to start back up the path.

"It's a long walk," she said to my back, "and I'm not really dressed." She sounded tired, and I found myself feeling sorry for her, this young woman of whom so much was demanded, for whom simple rest away from the eyes of the world was impossible.

"I'm on my way up there myself," I said. "I'll make the arrangements. Your car and driver will be waiting."

The wings of her nose wrinkled when she smiled. She was once again the breathtaking young beauty from the magazine. "You're very kind."

Sitting with his back to the tree, the tall man looked up from his companion's cards when he saw me coming. It had been days since I had last spoken to them, and it appeared they had not moved.

"Any luck with the birds?" I said.

The tall man threw down a card. "They're very quick."

"Elusive," said the short man as he regarded his hand and his companion's discard with disappointment.

"I thought you might be interested in something I saw."

The short one barely glanced at me over the tops of his cards. "What's that?"

"Something very rare," I said slowly, enticingly. "It had a bright red belly and a long blue tail and I think its back was green. I thought you might want to come in and take a look."

"You mean in *there*?" The short one pointed past the gate.

"We should hurry," I said, waving them on. "Before it gets away."

The two men dashed into each other as they rose, and I could hear them whispering as they rustled through their bags. When they were ready, the short one went around to the far side of the tree.

"Come on," he said. He bent over, and when he came back up again he was dragging along the limp body of the third man, a gaunt figure with gray skin and yellow eyes circled by steel washers. The third man staggered forward as though both legs had fallen asleep, his clothes wrinkled and twisted around him like a candy wrapper.

"Lead the way," the tall man said.

I stepped aside to let them through the gate.

Once the sick man got moving, momentum seemed to take over, for he quickly outpaced his companions. Down the drive we went. As we neared the manor house, I could see the three of them looking at the car waiting out front. Mlle Miller's driver sat on the hood, smoking.

"This way," I said, and the three men followed me down a path away from the drive. Soon we were behind the manor house, winding our way among the outbuildings. It was brutally hot, even in the shade, and the men were growing tired. We passed the garage and the stables, and we lingered several minutes by the laundry while I made a show of trying to remember where I had seen the bird.

"I think it was this way," I said, and I led the men beyond the maids' quarters and the storerooms. By now perhaps twenty minutes had passed. The sick man had grown wobbly.

"Maybe we should try that direction," the short one said, pointing back toward the manor house.

"It must have flown away," I said, feigning disappointment.

The tall one mopped up his forehead with his sleeve. "Right."

So we turned around, following the same route back. I apologized again. Behind me the short man and the tall man grumbled, while the sick man struggled to keep up, and just as we were about to reach the drive, I spotted Mlle Miller's car up above us, closing in on the gate. The men were too far back to have seen her.

"Look!" I stopped just in time and pointed up into the trees. As the three men raised their heads, Mlle Miller's car cleared the gate.

"Never mind," I said, relieved that we could finally bring the game to a close. "I guess it was nothing."

I continued up the path, and the short man and the tall man followed, but the sick man remained where he was, head thrown back at the trees above him.

"I see it," he said, pointing toward the sky.

There, in the crook of a giant locust tree, preening its black-and-white barred wings with its yellow bill, sat a small bird with a red belly and blue tail. It was beautiful, like nothing I had ever seen. Was it possible, I briefly wondered, for four people to share the same hallucination?

The sick man raised his camera and clicked a shot. "It's splendid."

Speechless, I barely managed to nod.

"I knew you would like it," I finally thought to say.

Although she insisted it was true, I found it hard to believe that Madame's long-overdue return just happened to coincide with Mlle Miller's visit. Who could blame her for being starstruck?

That night I arrived at the restaurant to find Madame in the dining room going from table to table, greeting her guests with an uncharacteristically distracted air. In a glance, I noticed Mlle Miller was missing, and I feared Madame was growing impatient at the continued absence of her most famous visitor.

At the other end of the restaurant, glowering beside the swinging doors to the kitchen, stood M. Gadds. Seeing me come in, he gave me one of his testy waves, ordering me over as he disappeared inside.

When I reached the kitchen, he was standing beside the walk-in refrigerator with his arms crossed, his reddened face seemingly radiating as much heat as an oven.

With a pinch he grabbed my arm. "Where have you been?"

"Working," I said.

We went up the back stairs to his office. For a moment after closing the door behind us, he stood behind his desk with his back to me, staring out the window.

"Sit," he said.

"I don't wish to sit."

When he turned around, his face was swollen with rage.

Leaning forward, he planted his hands on the leather blotter. "Did you arrange for Mlle Miller to go to the beach?"

"She asked—" I began, but M. Gadds cut me off to interject, "How many times have we talked about this?"

"I was only trying to help," I said.

"We don't need your help."

I knew nothing could be further from the truth. "She asked for my help."

"How many times have I told you to leave the guests to me? It couldn't be any more simple. You get the toilets. I get the people."

I turned to leave. "You cannot talk to me this way."

"Her car was stopped," M. Gadds said. "At *gunpoint*," he added for emphasis. "Mlle Miller was taken from the car, terrorized, and made to pay a toll."

He appeared to enjoy the silence that followed.

I lowered myself into the chair. "Does Madame know?"

"I tried to explain to Mlle Miller that it was all a misunderstanding," M. Gadds said, continuing to stand.

"How is she?"

"She is packing." M. Gadds picked up the phone and dialed the front desk. I heard him tell the clerk to fetch Madame from the dining room.

"How was I to know?"

"You're not," he said. "That's why we have a concierge."

The wait, which we passed in silence, was interminable. When Madame finally arrived, she entered without knocking, and it was clear as she regarded the two of us that she was not happy to have been interrupted.

"What is so important?"

I had to endure another telling of the story. M. Gadds was careful at every opportunity to stress my involvement, and I did not try to protest, knowing it would only make matters worse.

"Were they security forces?" Madame said, "or some sort of bandits?"

"I don't know," M. Gadds said, at which Madame snapped irritably, "Well, find out!"

While M. Gadds was on the phone, locating the driver and ordering him to come up that instant, I heard Madame grumble, "He promised me nothing like this would ever happen."

But it was unclear whether Madame was talking to me or to herself, and I was afraid to ask to whom she was referring.

The driver was out of breath when he reached us, and he looked terrified even before M. Gadds began to speak.

"Tell us who the men were," M. Gadds ordered, motioning for him to sit. "You've done nothing wrong. Tell us what they looked like."

The man slowly lowered himself into the seat, just as I had a moment before, looking nervously from one of us to the next.

Madame leaned in closer. "What did they wear? Did they wear khakis and sunglasses? Were they the president's men?"

He nodded hesitantly.

With a smile to show him he had done well, Madame thanked and dismissed him.

As soon as he was gone, she stood, her face contorted with fury.

"This cannot be permitted." Her voice carried a disturbingly false note of calm. She was careful not to slam the door as she left.

During the next two hours, as I waited for Madame to emerge from her office, I tried to contemplate what might happen. I would be fired—that much was clear. I had always thought that to be my worst fear, but now that it was upon me, I realized what worried me more was what this might mean for the hotel. As M. Gadds said, once word of what had happened got out, we would be ruined. And I thought of the photographers outside the gate, who must have been there when Mlle Miller returned. I could imagine the story that would appear in the magazines, with photos of the terrified young beauty dramatizing her ordeal. After all our struggles, all our effort, could we be undone by something like this?

It was late and I was pacing on my balcony when I first heard and then saw the black car come speeding down the drive. Directly below me, it came to a screeching stop. Out of the back stepped a man in a dark suit and a narrow-brimmed hat. At the bottom of the broad stone steps he paused, reaching toward his throat to adjust his tie.

With my ear to my office door, I heard a phone ring—the front desk calling up to Madame's office. And then, a minute later, came the footsteps, two sets, as the desk clerk led the man in the narrow-brimmed hat to Madame's door. He went inside, and the other set of footsteps trailed away back downstairs.

I tried to guess who the man might be, but it was impossible to know. He might have been someone the president had sent, or maybe someone from the embassy.

After half an hour, I could no longer wait. I knocked on M. Gadds's door. He was out. I went downstairs, hoping he might be at the front desk, but he was not there either, and neither was the clerk. The porter who was temporarily covering for him did not know where they were.

"Did they say anything about the man who came to see Madame?"

"No," he said, and then he nodded past my shoulder. "But you could ask her yourself."

Descending the stairs in matching steps, both of their mouths molded into polite smiles, were Mme Freeman and Senator Marcus's old friend, the minister of health. The sight was so strange, these two pieces so puzzlingly placed together, I could only stare.

At the bottom, before separating, Madame and the minister of health shared a few quiet words and then shook hands, and I watched the minister of health return to the car waiting below.

"It's going to be okay," Mme Freeman said once he was gone.

"That was the minister of health," I said.

"Of course not," she said. "That was the minister of tourism."

I was taken aback. "I wasn't aware we had one."

"We do now." And then she wished me good night.

Chapter Fifteen

As far as we could tell, the incident did not appear in any of the papers or magazines. Madame had people keeping an eye on them in the States. I was careful to peruse everything I found lying about the manor house. Within days of her return home, Mlle Miller's photo resumed appearing in the weeklies, but the captions never said anything about us. There on those glossy pages, the young actress was her radiant self again. It was hard to believe any misfortune had ever been visited upon her.

Despite the promises of the minister of tourism, for the next several weeks we were cautious, discouraging guests from excursions beyond the gate. It seemed we were not the only ones complaining about incidents involving the security forces. For an organization supposedly disbanded, they suddenly appeared to be everywhere. The president denied it, going so far as to make a televised speech assuring us it was not so.

"We are experiencing the greatest peace and prosperity we have had in decades," he said. "Let us not jeopardize this with irresponsible and upsetting rumors."

The next day, a reporter thought to be a source of some of these rumors went missing.

Having been forced to close our guests off from the rest of the island, we had to do what we could to bring the island to them. In addition to the usual evening performances at the pavilion, we hired a rotation of bands to play all day long. The estate began to feel as though it were in the midst of a party that never ceased.

At M. Gadds's suggestion, around lunchtime each day craftswomen from the Cité Verd market came and spread their beadwork purses and hand-carved wooden icons on blankets around the manor house pool. Anything our guests wished to buy we added directly to their bills.

Yet however much we tried, it was impossible to keep the troubles outside from sometimes seeping in, especially as those troubles began to spill beyond the island's shores. Food shortages resulting from the drought persisted. For reasons as numerous as they were intractable, the economy was in collapse.

In the middle of May, just as tourist season was beginning to pick up again, stories started to surface in the foreign press about coast guard vessels intercepting refugees fleeing the island in homemade dinghies.

"Boat people," one of the articles quipped, had "become the island's main export."

With each new article, we received more cancellations.

One morning a few weeks later, at our bench in the preserve, I shared my concerns with Madame. As her most trusted confidant, what choice did I have but once again to be the one to deliver the difficult news?

"If this doesn't stop soon," I said, more bluntly than I ever had before, "I don't know how much longer we can survive."

"I know," she said. Never had she sounded so defeated.

"Have you spoken with M. Rossignol?"

"Of course."

"What does he say?"

Madame threw up her hands. "We're on an island," she said. "They can't patrol every inch of shore."

However deep her frustration, I could not be sure she truly appreciated how dire the situation was. Under President Mailodet she had watched as things went from bad to worse, but she had seen too little to understand that those had not been isolated events. Those conditions were always with us, and unless one did something to stop them, they would forever return.

"There is one other thing we could try."

Her head hung low as she turned it toward me.

"Sometimes," I said, "it's not enough to tell them how important something is. You have to show them, too."

"And how do you do that?"

"You hand them a briefcase," I said, regretting the words even as I knew I had no choice but to say them. "And inside the briefcase you place whatever you think the thing is worth."

"Never," she said. "Absolutely not."

Without another word she got up and walked away. My breath left me as I watched her go.

For the next two mornings, Madame was absent from our bench. Whenever I saw her in the manor house, she turned the other way. I could not blame her for her reaction; mine would have been no different. But we both knew there was no other option. Nor was there any time to waste.

On the third day she called to make the appointment. I do not know what finally changed her mind. What could it have been but desperation?

M. Rossignol's office was only a block from where Senator Marcus's office had been, and it would have been impossible as I entered not to look at the chairs in the lobby and see myself sitting there quietly for hours, waiting for the moment the Senator would need me to take him somewhere. Given how much time had passed, the thought was more upsetting than I would have expected. But time had done nothing to lessen the pain.

There were the same young secretaries and clerks, the same shiny, opulent desks. The world should not be permitted to go on, unchanged, as if such terrible things had not happened. A man such as Senator Marcus should not disappear without his absence being everywhere preserved.

The receptionist offered me coffee, and when I declined, a seat.

My wait was brief. Scarcely had I settled in with the briefcase at my feet than she was standing before me, saying the minister was ready.

There was a time, not long ago, when I could not have walked down a corridor such as this, lined with dark paneling and gilt frames, without feeling I did not belong. But I was no longer the shopkeeper's son, nor the boy sleeping in a stuffy attic. I was a man with an opulent office of my own. I was a man with a briefcase full of money.

When I arrived in his doorway, the minister of tourism was standing behind his desk with his hands behind his back. He looked far better than he had at the party. The paunch was still there across his middle, but in his new suit he seemed solid and substantial instead of old and worn out. The ferocity was back in his eyes as well, as if the new post had greatly improved his sleep.

With a bow, the secretary ushered me in and then stepped away.

I had assumed M. Rossignol would be expecting Mme Freeman, but he seemed not at all surprised at the sight of me. Nevertheless, I could not say he was pleased—but when had he ever been pleased?

"Monsieur," he said, lowering his eyes and gesturing toward a chair.

"Thank you for seeing me," I said. "I know how busy you must be." But as I came around to take a seat, I noticed the cleanliness of his desk, the almost complete lack of files and papers. Remembering the mess

I had found in the trunk of his car all those years ago, I would never have expected him to be so tidy. Then again, with tourists fleeing the country even faster than the boat people, perhaps there was not much work to be done.

There was just a phone, a silver pen in an ebony stand, and a framed photograph of his wife.

"I suppose this was inevitable," he said.

I looked up from the case at my feet. "Pardon?"

"Your being here like this."

I shrugged. "How do you mean?"

"I've known you a long time," he said. "I know it's no accident, your being here today." Then he leaned forward, and I could smell the bitter coffee on his breath. "Let's be clear. I'm not looking to judge. It's no accident that I'm here either."

In the days leading up to the meeting, and even during the ride into the city, I had endlessly rehearsed exactly what I would say and how I would say it. I had even practiced the handing over of the briefcase. Perhaps it was because I had worked out so careful a script that I felt so disoriented now. With his eyes boring into me, my confidence began to flag, and I turned again to the picture on his desk.

"Your wife," I said. "I saw her at the party. She seemed very kind."

He looked at her and then at me. "That's another thing we have in common," he said. "We choose our women well."

I said, "I don't have a wife."

"You have something better," he said. "Your Mrs. Freeman is here only a few months a year. You get the benefits she brings, and you also have your freedom."

"I'm very fond of Mme Freeman," I said, hoping to bring that line of discussion to an end. "I like her very much."

"And I like my wife, too, although that's not why I married her." M. Rossignol sat back with a smirk on his face. "You don't know why I married her, do you? You don't know who she is."

I shook my head.

"You might know her by her maiden name," he said. "Duphay."

"I see," I said, and in fact it was the first time since I sat down that I felt I understood anything.

"Obviously the marriage has brought me certain benefits," he said, and the sweep of his hands conducted my eyes over the amenities of the office. "But in the long run," he added, more somberly now, "I wonder which of us is better off."

"I'm sure Mlle Duphay—that is, Mme Rossignol—has a great deal more influence."

"I'm sure you're right," he said. "But around here you never know how long anything will last."

I could see he was enjoying the long silence that followed and the discomfort it caused me. Was he waiting for me to say I felt certain President Duphay would be around for a long time to come—that his patronage was safe? Or did he imagine I was one of the many waiting for his downfall? If I had truly felt free to share my thoughts, I would have said I did not care. Let them rise, let them fall, as long as they left me in peace.

"As for you and me," he said, "we'll do whatever it takes to survive." As he got to his feet I felt a wash of relief, knowing the moment had finally come.

Without bothering to open it, he accepted the case and set it down behind his desk. However glad I was that it was over, I still shared Madame's disgust.

"Think what you will," he said, scrutinizing my face. "I know you better than you realize. You've worked hard to get where you are. I know where you started out. You're not about to give up the things you fought so hard to get. When your time comes, you'll do exactly the same as me."

I decided I would rather let him think what he wished than remain there a moment longer, arguing the point. All I could think was how distraught—though perhaps not surprised—Senator Marcus would be to see how low his former friend had sunk.

I knew enough not to expect Madame to be happy with the outcome of my meeting with the minister of tourism. However well we succeeded, for her the ends would always be tainted by the means. For that reason, I took the burden of it upon myself, sharing with her nothing of what had transpired. I did not enjoy her disapproval and continued absence from our bench in the preserve, but I knew it was necessary. I could only hope it would pass. In the meantime, I had to ignore the knives piercing my stomach whenever I saw her across the room, pretending not to see me.

The results came more quickly than I had imagined. Even with our contribution, M. Rossignol could not afford to patrol every meter of shore, but the boat people were immediately made to understand that the coast guard and the rough open waters were no longer the only dangers they faced. The minister of tourism finally found a way to put the security forces to good use, raiding beaches and docks where launches were known to occur and making arrests of ferry operators hiring themselves out for smuggling.

Within a month, the number of newspaper stories, both here and abroad, had dwindled to such an extent that some sources were already claiming the government crackdown complete.

But we had little time to savor our success; problems continued to pile up faster than we could solve them.

More and more I was overhearing the maids and bus boys murmuring about trouble in Cité Verd, where virtually all of their families lived. Security forces had recently begun showing up at the market there, collecting "taxes" and demanding bribes. In a place as poor as that, it was hard to imagine why they would bother. What could those few pennies buy? The tiny return would seem like disincentive enough, but I had also been hearing about a growing resistance, a gang of men and boys armed with rocks and bottles who were fighting back, building barricades to keep the security forces out.

In late June, four months after Mlle Miller's ordeal, the problem became a crisis. One afternoon, several members of the security forces—out of drunkenness or boredom or sport—beat a pregnant woman unconscious with a brick. And then they stabbed her in the stomach and left her to die.

Minutes later, a mob gathered at the market, bearing machetes and whatever guns they could find. That night they caught a man from the security forces by surprise and strung him from a telephone pole.

This time I did not bother going to Madame or M. Gadds. There were some things, it had become clear, that I would need to take care of myself.

The next afternoon, passing by two of the gardeners resting under a tree by the stables, I heard one of them say, "If it's war they're after, they're going to get it."

"You," I said, rushing over before they could say any more. "Both of you. I want you out of here at once."

They looked at me as if I were crazy, but when a moment passed and they still had not moved, I kicked the one sitting closest to me in the leg. "Now!" I shouted. They stood up, and I grabbed each one by the arm and led them toward the gate.

"Our things," one of them said. "We need our things."

"You should have thought of that before."

"Before what?"

By then we had reached the gate, and I ordered the guards to open it. "If you're so interested in the revolution," I said, "you're free to join it. I don't ever want to see you here again."

The guards were mystified, standing off by their shack, not wanting to get too close. "If I ever hear that you let them back in," I said, pointing at their chests, "I'll throw you out just as quickly."

The guards looked at the gardeners and then at their feet.

"Do not test me."

That night I called a meeting of the day-shift staff. For once, they all showed up on time, squeezing into the largest of the servants' quarters. I was aware that the silence of so many people crammed into so small a space could only mean the story of what had happened to the gardeners had spread. Who else could have spread it but the guards?

Not only did I not mind, I was glad.

"I trust," I began, "that all of you have heard about what happened here today. Let me assure you that the same will happen to each and every one of you if I hear even a single word about gangs or guns or security forces or resistance or anything else. We are running a hotel. What do you think will happen if the guests hear you?"

Someone in the back murmured, "They wouldn't understand what we're saying anyway."

"Who said that?" I shouted, and everyone fell silent again. "One more outburst, and I will fire every single one of you. I could stand outside the gate, and within five minutes I would have a replacement for every person in here." I paused to let that sink in.

"Our guests understand more than you think," I continued. "They may not understand the words, but they don't have to. All they need is to see the whispering, and they will know something is wrong. That's all it takes. As soon as they start thinking something is wrong, it's over. Think about that," I said. "Unless you wish to join the ranks of the starving and unemployed, keep your thoughts to yourselves. I want to see nothing but smiles."

I dismissed them then, pleased with their quiet and orderly retreat. I did not care if they liked what they heard—I needed only for them to absorb it, and I had no doubt they had.

That night I could not sleep, and in the morning I met with the smaller night-shift staff and told them the same thing I had told the others. They made no outbursts and offered no complaints. They had already been warned.

I was aware that for the next several weeks everyone on the staff did whatever they could to avoid me, but I was everywhere, making my rounds at all hours of the day and night. My ears were attuned, and I heard nothing more about any resistance in Cité Verd.

For a time, it almost seemed as if things were finally settling down

again, and I looked forward to the day when we could return our ener-
gies to running the hotel, instead of constantly managing crises. Still, I
was not so foolish as to think our troubles were past. As was always the
case, as soon as one thing was dealt with, something else—something
even worse—came along.

It was late July when the warnings first began appearing in the
newspapers and the radio. A tropical storm was moving in from the
southwest. With its torrential rains and gale-force winds—phrases that
quickly became as familiar to our guests as "gin and tonic" and "white
wine spritzer"—it had already decimated several other islands in its path.

If nothing else, the storm gave the staff something new to worry
about.

We took precautions, stocking up on supplies and testing the generators. But despite our assurances that Habitation Louvois was perfectly safe, most of our guests insisted on cutting their visits short.

For those few who stayed, it was as we had expected. The first hour
or two, each drop of water felt like a bucket, and the winds bent the
trees as if they were drinking straws. But the floods went right around
us, leaving us unscathed. Aside from some minor damage to the roof
of the guesthouse and a few of the villas, the estate survived perfectly
intact.

But while we were strong enough to withstand the storm, Cité Verd
was not. All those shacks built of nothing blew away even before the
worst of it hit. With no vegetation to hold down the soil, the hillside
streets of dirt became an ocean of mud, and who knows how many
people washed away. There were estimates of anywhere from a few
dozen to a few hundred. No one knew. How could they? These were
people who had been like ghosts even when they were alive.

It did not take long for the murmuring to return. On the streets
of Cité Verd there were protests and clashes with the security forces.
Not just gangs this time, but old women and children and everyone
else as well. They blamed it all on President Duphay. As if there were
something he could have done—some vast umbrella he could have held
above them until the storm had passed.

For our part, we were able to make it clear that despite whatever problems existed elsewhere, Habitation Louvois remained open for business. With few exceptions, the guests who had been waiting for the skies to clear hurried to claim their villas. Within a week of the storm, everything at the hotel was back to normal.

Everything beyond the gate, however, continued to grow worse, especially the constant clamoring in Cité Verd. More than once, M. Gadds had to phone the office of the minister of tourism, complaining of blocked streets that threatened to keep guests from reaching us. Each time, M. Rossignol proved himself as good as his word. The security forces came through and cleared the way.

But no matter how hard we tried, there were some things we could not shut out. Late one night in the second week of August—six months after all the trouble started—I awoke to the pops and cracks of gunfire.

Given how routine the sound would later come to be in my life, it seems odd to remember that initially I did not know what it was. Yet even as I got out of bed and went to the shutters to listen for the laughter of late-night revelers uncorking champagne, the rigid fear in my body told me it was something far more sinister.

If the guests heard it that first night, they said nothing. In the morning, wearing sunglasses as they sipped sparkling wine and orange juice, they grumbled about their losses at blackjack and craps. Perhaps the casino had muffled the sound. Or perhaps the vast quantities of rum they had been drinking had allowed them to sleep more soundly than me.

I knew the same could not be said of M. Gadds. He had heard it all, and throughout the morning just the sound of silverware clattering in the kitchen was enough to set him on edge.

The following night, everything was back to normal, and yet the memory of what I had heard refused to leave me. It was as if some part of me already knew what was about to happen and wanted the rest of me to be prepared for when it did.

I did not have long to wait.

Two nights later, at an hour when even the most committed gamblers were asleep in their beds, I awoke to the stuttering crackle of machine guns. I could do nothing but listen as everything we had worked so hard for fell apart.

This time, Madame, down in her villa, heard it too. When I saw her at our bench in the preserve the next morning, she looked as though she had also been up all night.

"They attacked one of the newspapers," she said. "The security forces burned it down."

As always, she wore a yellow dress, but this one appeared unusually faded. Madame looked older, too. But then I realized it was just that she had not applied her makeup that morning. I was surprised to see what a difference it made. There was almost no color in her cheeks, and her eyes were nearly lost within the encircling creases. The fingers fretting in her lap bore chipped polish in pomegranate red.

"I thought all of this was behind us."

"M. Rossignol will fix it," I said.

Madame sighed, shaking her head at the trees. "You were right—you said there would be trouble."

It was kind of her to say, even if it was the sort of thing I could feel no satisfaction in being right about. More than anything else, I was simply glad she was once again looking to me for advice.

Together we got up, and in silence I walked her back to the manor house.

Throughout the rest of the day, despite her claims of optimism, the strain of smiling began to seem as if it were more than Madame could bear—as if the fragile scaffolding holding up the corners of her mouth might at any moment collapse.

At dinner, a guest who had stayed with us several times—a writer traveling with a male companion—stopped me as I was on my way to the storeroom to ask if what he had heard about the assassination of an opposition leader was true.

"Certainly not," I said. It was the first I had heard about there even being an opposition. "The reports are always exaggerated. There's really nothing to worry about."

That night, the gunfire unfurled in one tremendous, interminable explosion. For twenty minutes it rumbled without cease. Closing my eyes, I focused my ears not on the battle but on the sounds of doors and shutters opening and closing down below and voices in English asking each other what was going on.

In the morning, the writer and his companion were gone.

Chapter Sixteen

They appeared first in the register as thin black pen strokes discreetly paralleling the rule on the page. The lines were so subtle, it was as if we were not supposed to see them there, our eyes drawn instead to the prominent names beneath. If you looked quickly, you might think nothing had changed. So too in the restaurant, where unless you stopped to count you might not notice there were fewer tables than before.

In their individual stations, the staff must have noticed other differences. The dishwashers went through their work more quickly than before. The laundresses needed fewer lines to hang the sheets.

The villas surrounding Madame's were the first to be taken out of use. They were the most out of the way, the least likely to have their vacancies noticed.

A few weeks later, we closed up four more.

There were one or two maids who got sick or pregnant. That still left us with far too many. We had no choice but to start letting them go. So too the gardeners and chauffeurs and houseboys and waiters.

It was not long before the lines in the register were replaced with blanks. By late October, six months after Mlle Miller's visit, we had more empty villas than full. In light of what had happened since, even M. Gadds had to recognize that the part I had played in that incident no longer mattered.

I was on my way out of the manor house when I saw the taxi arrive. I do not know what it was that made me stop. Taxis were not an unusual sight, although it is true that by this point it had become rare to see one bringing passengers to us, instead of simply taking them away. We were down to a half dozen guests. I suppose a part of me had begun to wonder if there would be any more.

I was standing on the bottom step as the car came to a stop. The driver got out first and removed a suitcase from the trunk. Then he opened the rear door, and out stepped M. Swallows. Gone were the shorts and the toucan shirt, gone the safari gear, gone the white linen. This time he wore a dark, heavy suit. Somehow he was not sweating. There was a new fierceness about him, a look that suggested he would not allow something as banal as heat to distract him from whatever purpose had brought him here.

As he climbed the steps to the manor house, he did not once turn around to look at the grounds. He made not even a cursory glance toward his investment.

"What are you waiting for?" he growled as he passed me.

Upon reaching the lobby, he immediately ascended the stairs to the second floor, and I could only assume he knew Madame would be awaiting him in her office.

M. Gadds had let the last of the porters go. In their place, I picked up M. Swallows's suitcase and brought it inside.

That evening, despite our vacancies, M. Swallows declined his former accommodations in the guesthouse, preferring to stay at the Hotel Erdrich. I later heard he remained in his room all night, not even venturing downstairs for dinner. He checked out early the next morning, mumbling to the porter, the desk clerk, the doorman—to anyone who would listen—that this was a godforsaken country and that he would never again return.

The day of M. Swallows's departure, Madame called me to her office. Even as she gestured for me to sit, she was turning her back to look out the open shutters. The view appeared to do nothing to settle her nerves.

"I'm leaving," she said.

She turned to look at me then, and just as quickly she glanced away. "Tomorrow. I have no choice."

"I understand."

"I have urgent business at home." She was frazzled, turning around and around, unable to decide what to look at, what to do. "I've put it off for too long. I have to go now."

"I understand," I said again.

She walked over to her desk and idly picked up a pen. Then she put it back down. "Don't worry," she said without conviction.

It was hard to feel reassured when she could not bring herself to look me in the eye.

"We'll get through this."

"Of course," I said, daring the faintest of smiles.

Something came across her face, something that I thought looked a little like hope.

By now, our only remaining guests were an American couple on their honeymoon, who for the last three days had crept about the otherwise empty estate as if afraid of being seen. They had arrived warily too, and I could not help wondering if their presence on the island was some sort of accident, as if they had climbed aboard the wrong plane and had no idea where they had landed.

M. Gadds had dismissed all but a few members of the staff. The chef had obtained a visa and fled to the States. With the gunfire in Cité Verd getting worse each night and the bodies more plentiful in the streets each morning, I believe the only thing keeping the American couple here was fear that what they might find outside the hotel would be even worse.

Finally, on the day after Madame flew back home, it came time for the American couple's departure. That morning, the last remaining gardener carried their bags up from their villa. M. Gadds, who at this point was serving as desk clerk, settled their bill. I do not know why it was that so many of us happened to be in the lobby just then—one of the chambermaids paused on her way out to the laundry room; Georges and the sous-chef who had taken over the cooking stood watching in the entryway to the restaurant.

The American couple were clearly uncomfortable with all the attention. The woman was small and skinny; there was almost nothing to her. Even her hair was thin and light, as if she were wasting away before our eyes. Her husband, a tall, lanky blond, spoke to M. Gadds in barely above a whisper.

Judging by the contortions of the woman's lower lip, she seemed to find the presence of the staff almost menacing, but M. Gadds made no move to dismiss them. Nor did things improve when the couple went outside to get into the idling car. Everyone followed, gathering at the top of the steps as the gardener loaded their bags into the trunk. The other remaining chambermaid appeared just then on the lawn by the tennis courts, as if summoned.

As the gardener came around to the side of the car where the American couple was standing, the poor woman seemed to tremble. The gardener opened the back door, and when he did so, the woman let go of her husband only long enough to sweep up the back of her dress and duck inside.

The gardener let himself into the front seat. In the absence of anyone else to do the job, he was chauffeur as well. We watched as the car made its way up the winding drive, but it was not the grand exit I believe many of us were expecting. At the top, the gardener had to stop, for there was no longer a guard to open the gate. And once they reached the street, I imagine the American couple were disappointed to discover they still were not free. After pulling the car forward a few meters, the gardener had to stop the car again and go back to close the gate behind him.

And then the car was gone, and when I looked again, the rest of the staff had already dispersed. M. Gadds was back inside, rummaging around behind the front desk. I watched him lift the guest registry, which had been lying open atop the counter, and close it, sliding it onto a shelf beneath the counter. Without a word to anyone he went upstairs to his office.

As I made my way across the lobby, the sous-chef called out to say that my lunch would be ready in a moment. In the restaurant, one of the regular tables had been set.

"Here you are, monsieur," Georges said, placing a small vase of lavender orchids in the center.

"What is this?" I asked.

"It comes compliments of M. Gadds."

"What do you mean?" I said.

"We prepared a special lunch for you."

"I'm perfectly content to have lunch in my office, as usual."

"I understand, monsieur," he said, gesturing at the table he had set so carefully, "but since it was M. Gadds's idea . . ."

"Why would M. Gadds suggest such a thing?"

"You would have to ask M. Gadds," Georges said as he headed off to the kitchen.

A moment later he was back, carrying a silver tray loaded with dishes.

"This can't all be for me?" I said.

"It was M. Gadds's request."

"I cannot eat all of this," I said. "Take some of it to the others."

One by one, Georges removed the dishes from the tray, setting them before me.

"But there are no others, monsieur."

"I meant the staff, Georges," I said, beginning to lose my patience. "I realize there are no more guests. There's no reason I should be the only one eating."

"I understand," Georges said, "but of course they're gone too."

"They haven't gone anywhere," I said. "M. Gadds is upstairs. I saw the others outside not five minutes ago. Call them in. We'll eat together."

"I don't mean to contradict you, monsieur," Georges said. "I too saw them just a few minutes ago, but they've left. M. Gadds went upstairs to gather his belongings. The others did the same. Madame gave the orders. She was kind enough to provide a month's wages."

"That can't be," I said. "She would have told me."

Georges was untying his apron. "Will there be anything else before I go?"

"Won't you eat first? There's so much food."

Taking off his apron, he folded it once, draping it over the back of the chair beside me. Empty-handed, he walked toward the lobby.

It occurred to me then that this was just a joke, that everybody was somewhere outside, waiting to spring upon me and have a laugh at my expense. If Madame had made such a decision, I would have been the first to know. I was her confidant, her friend, her adviser.

I reached the drive just in time to see Georges close the gate behind him and pass out of sight beyond the wall, heading toward Cité Verd.

The casino and the pavilion were empty. Up and down the paths and staircases connecting the villas I saw no one. Only a little more than four years had passed since the hotel had opened. Petals and leaves had already begun to collect in the pools.

Chapter Seventeen

That night the rain caught me by surprise. I was sitting at my desk, staring past the open jalousies, when suddenly the sky opened up. In an instant it was as though I were staring into a waterfall. I got up to close the shutters, and just then the wind sent one of the stone pots crashing off the balustrade to the tiled floor of the balcony.

I secured the shutters of the manor house first. Then I rushed from villa to villa, but there was no way for me to get to all of them in time. Rain raced down the cobblestone paths as if along a riverbed, the stairs like so many rapids. By the time I reached Madame's villa, the rain still had not let up. Soaked and muddy, I sought shelter inside.

✠

Madame had always claimed privacy as her reason for choosing to live in the villa. In truth, however, it was clear she would have found just as much privacy—and far more space—at the guesthouse. Even after the estate's expansion—the addition of forty-three more villas—Madame continued to stay, despite the loss of her private pool and garden. Nor did the newness and amenities of the other villas lure her away.

What I think drew Madame to this particular villa—what over-shadowed its numerable disadvantages—was its history, which M. Guinee had told me only after I had begun to work here.

M. Guinee did not himself know who originally built Habitation Louvois. One can only assume that in the early days of the colonial settlement it was the home of a wealthy plantation owner. Given the distance of the estate from the cane fields, it is also possible the property served as a mountain retreat, rather than as a year-long residence. What M. Guinee did know for certain was that—more than a century and a half before—the estate had come into the hands of General Louvois, who arrived on the island as commander of a forty-thousand-man colonial army. General Louvois had been sent here to quell an uprising of slaves, the human chattel imported from a distant, savage continent for the purpose of harvesting the empire's sugar fortune. Their sudden rebellion threatened to destroy everything the general's countrymen had spent decades building.

Perhaps the general was expecting an easy engagement, for he brought along his young wife and newborn son, as if the trip were a day's outing to the countryside.

M. Guinee knew few of the facts concerning the general's life at the estate. What had been passed on to him were merely stories. It was the very gruesomeness of the stories that made them so hard to believe. Was it true that General Louvois once ordered a servant accused of having stolen a gourd of cornmeal to be buried alive in the doorway to the storeroom? The truth is difficult to know. During construction of the hotel, the old storeroom was torn down and a new one put up. The excavation produced no remains.

The war slogged on for more than twelve years, at the cost of tens of thousands of lives. The general's army, despite its muskets and can-nons, was decimated, worn down by disease and the fierce resistance of a people fighting for their freedom.

In the end, this small piece of the empire was lost, never to be regained. But it was not just the general and his countrymen who found themselves defeated. So too was the loss felt by the island's mixed-blood offspring, born from the unsanctioned unions of settler and slave. Despite their lower caste, they had by virtue of their lighter shade sided with those whose divine right it was to rule, whose ranks they would have done anything to join.

Shortly before General Louvois and the remnants of his forces fled—along with whatever white settlers they could fit on their warships—the general was said to have held a party in honor of the wives and sisters of the collaborating mulatto officers, a fête to show his gratitude, even in the face of defeat, for their efforts in undermining the black cause. The evening was full of fine food and dancing, and at the end of the night the women were invited out to the garden, where they were greeted with a sight none of them at first understood. Along the paths, lit by oil lamps, a group of figures cloaked in black robes were leading a procession of coffins. When the women were invited to come closer, they saw inside the coffins the freshly slaughtered remains of their husbands and brothers.

Thus it was said that if ever there had been uncertainty about the distinction the empire made between the various shades of black and brown, there could be no longer. No matter how diluted, the taint of color was absolute. Only to us did the differences between light and dark matter, and with time this preoccupation would only continue to grow, until finally its shadow hung over all our daily pursuits.

Were I to accept the story, I would never have been able to set foot in the manor house; I would have been unable to cross the threshold of the gate. But in following the fate of Senator Marcus, I had seen how easily truth could be manipulated, how a man could be made into something other than what he was. To the extent that it was within my power, I would not allow legends to trap us forever in the past. Of everyone who worked at the estate, only Madame and I knew of its origins, and we never spoke of them. Nor did we ever discuss intentionally keeping these stories from the rest of the staff. But I think we both realized we were saving them from something they would not have wanted to hear.

If any place on the estate was free of the bloody legacy of General Louvois, it was Mme Freeman's villa, which had originally been built for the general's wife. Unlike her husband, the career soldier, Mme Louvois was said to have been a spirited young woman, active in the arts. She had made the long journey here against her will, loathing politics and all things military and dreading the unremittingly sticky climate. Upon arriving she had immediately set out to distance herself from the entire undertaking.

It was said that Mme Louvois chose to have her villa built in that particular location both for the view it commanded of the bay above the tree line as well as for its distance from her husband and the comings and goings of his advisers and underlings. The general's wife was an artist—a painter, though she dabbled in music as well. The bay provided the inspiration for many of her landscapes, and the seclusion assured privacy for painting portraits. As subjects, she was said to have favored her husband's male slaves.

Whenever I try to imagine such a scene, I cannot help thinking it likely that the general was aware of what was happening in his wife's villa. Mme Louvois reputedly made no effort to hide her work. And one cannot help but wonder about those men as they sat for portraits in an airy poolside villa with the general's wife. What sense could they have made of it? They had to know her husband would mutilate them if he ever caught them together. Perhaps they feared she would have them killed if they refused. Then again, maybe an opportunity to sit for an afternoon in relative leisure was worth the risk.

When she moved in, more than a century and a half later, Mme Freeman took care to furnish the villa with restored pieces from the colonial period, including an armoire thought to have originally belonged to the general's wife. But the object of which Madame was most proud was an original painting signed by Mme Antoinette Louvois, which hung in the sitting room. It was perhaps the only painting by Mme Louvois to have remained on the island after she and her husband fled.

In delicate strokes of oil carefully turned and daubed to capture every realistic detail, Mme Louvois had re-created the very view of the bay one could see outside even now, and more than once during Mme Freeman's absences I had carried the painting out to the terrace where Mme Louvois must have painted it all those years ago. To stand where the general's wife stood and to see what she saw was to have been present at the birth of the nation. Some of the trees were different—old ones having fallen and new ones having taken their place. But the bay had not changed, although it was true that naval frigates, such as the ones in the painting, were long gone. By now so too were the ocean liners that had been anchored there just a few weeks before. Soon there would be no ships at all, except the occasional lilting barge bearing peasants and charcoal from the north. Whether or not it was a good painting, I was unqualified to say; I had no basis for making such judgments. But if the purpose of art is to make us feel pleasure and pain, then it was a very great work indeed.

The night of the storm, while stranded in Madame's villa, I spent a long time sitting on the sofa looking at the painting, and I thought how peculiar a coincidence it was, finding myself here in Mme Louvois's former sanctuary on the very day our hotel came to its end. I wondered how Mme Louvois had felt when she learned her husband's army had faced its last defeat, and if, as her maids loaded her clothes and jewels and paintings into crates to be hauled to the hold of the ship that would return her to her proper home, she felt any regret or nostalgia for what she was leaving behind. I cannot help thinking she truly did come to love the island, and perhaps she even loved some of the men who had sat for her and let her capture their likenesses on canvas. Perhaps that was why she had taken those canvases with her, so that she would be able to remember the men when she was back again in her own country and the island itself became a long-forgotten dream.

I awoke the next morning with the sun in my face. I opened my eyes to find a woman standing above me, the jalousies open behind her.

"I trust everyone is gone?" she said.

The light at her back made her seem to glow. I gave no thought to answering her, for it seemed impossible to me that what I was seeing was real. Was she Antoinette Louvois, come to paint me? The woman reached out and touched my wrist, which dangled from the edge of the sofa.

"I trust everyone is gone?" she said again.

"They are."

She went out to the terrace and returned a moment later with her bags, and as she closed the shutters behind her, the light faded and I saw that it was Mme Freeman. Panic brought me to my feet, but I had only half risen when the pain in my head knocked me back down. From the bedroom, Madame called.

"Is there anything to eat?"

"I'll bring you something," I said, and I had just enough sense to grab the empty bottle as I stumbled outside.

As one's mind does in such moments, mine immediately sought to repeat the events of the last few minutes. But no matter how much I wished to be able to recall every nuance of Madame's expression upon finding me on her sofa, I could not. I could only assume she had been furious. No doubt she had seen the bottle. And how could I explain about the storm of the night before, now that all trace of it had evaporated in the morning sun?

I was still so upset and distracted when I reached the kitchen that I actually called out to Georges, and I felt a moment's anger when he failed to respond.

I was surprised to note they had taken care to clean up before they left. The pots hung from the hooks in rows above the butcher knives and ladles, which were themselves arranged according to size. Had this, too, been M. Gadds's order?

There was no food. This should not have surprised me, for I knew we had received no deliveries in days. But I was in no mood for more setbacks.

On a table in the dining room I found the dishes Georges had brought me the day before, all of which I had left uneaten. Everything had spoiled.

I had to make do with what I could gather outside, assembling a breakfast of mango and papaya.

"I'm sorry," I said when I returned to Madame, sitting at the table on her terrace. "We seem to have run out of pastries. And I don't know what happened to the last of the coffee."

She regarded the tray with a flicker of displeasure.

"There's water in the pitcher," I said apologetically.

Madame seemed neither angry nor pleased. "Why don't you sit down and have some of this?"

Although I wanted nothing more than to join her, I suspected she would be more likely to forget the morning if I were not here to remind her.

"I should get to work."

Madame poured herself a glass of water. "There will be plenty of time for work."

With her foot she pushed out the chair opposite hers at the table, and indeed, Madame seemed to believe what she said. We spent the rest of the afternoon on the terrace, looking out over the bay. Several times I went to fill the pitcher, but she would otherwise not allow me to leave her side, though neither did she seem to have anything in particular to say to me. Not once did she ask about my presence in her villa that morning. She gave every indication of having forgotten.

As the sun touched the treetops to the west, she turned to me and said, "What should we have for dinner?"

I recalled having seen one last chicken in the yard, and I told her about it, glad at last to have something to offer. "I'm afraid, however, that I'm not a very good cook."

"And I'm not much of a butcher," she said. "If you'll do that, I'll take care of the rest."

So I did as she asked, and I plucked the bird, too. By necessity her preparation was simple. In the herb garden behind the kitchen she picked sprigs of thyme and tarragon. With the chicken roasting in the oven she went back to her villa to freshen up. For me it was an occasion to get out of the clothes I had been wearing since yesterday. By the time she returned, I had set a table in the dining room, with a bouquet of her favorite bee orchids arranged as a centerpiece.

"It's been years since I did anything like this," Madame said as she opened the oven, "but I believe it's done."

"I have no doubt it will be delicious."

While I carved, she went to see what sort of wine we had left.

For a meal assembled so quickly and with so little, it came out remarkably well. What the chicken lacked in seasoning, it made up for in tenderness. I complimented her.

"Oh, I'm not helpless," she said. "I know my way around a kitchen. I used to enjoy cooking quite a lot. But of course it's hard to find the time. And since my husband passed away, I've lost my motivation. It rarely seems worth it to go to such trouble for oneself."

"I can see how that would be so."

"Have you never been married?" she said.

"No."

Madame tilted the wine bottle over her glass, only to discover it was empty. Aside from the single glass she had poured me, which remained untouched, she had drunk the rest herself.

"If you don't mind my asking—," she said.

"You may ask me anything."

"I was wondering why you never married."

I had not been aware that my thoughts were drifting, but suddenly I felt my pulse quicken. "Married?" I said, and I shook my head, trying to dislodge the image that the word had planted there. And then I was instantly paralyzed by the thought that somehow she had seen it too. I did not mean it, I wanted to say. It was unintentional. Between Madame and me there could never—should never—be any such thing. I respected her more than anyone I had ever known, but we were partners in a different sense. Anything more was distasteful even to consider.

"When I was growing up," I said, "too many of the boys I knew wound up with wives and children without ever really meaning to. It just seemed to happen, and then they were trapped. Suddenly they had families to take care of, and they were stuck in the neighborhood forever. Or, in order to leave, they had to disappear, leaving their families behind. I could never do that."

"Maybe some of them were happy," Madame said. "Maybe some of them didn't want to leave. Maybe they liked raising families."

"Perhaps," I said. "My father never wanted to leave. But what kind of life is that?"

Madame clenched her napkin and brought it up to her chin. "Maybe you'll want to now, now that you've left and you have a new life. Maybe now you're ready."

"Now there is more to do than ever. We have to be ready when the guests return."

Madame set her elbows on the table, folding her arms together. "Did you never wish for something more?"

"Like what?"

"Like some other sort of work?"

"My father wanted me to be a lawyer," I said. "Or a doctor. He wanted me to help people."

She smiled somewhat distantly. "I think you have. People need a place like this to come to. Even if they don't come, they need to know it exists."

"Thank you," I said, "although I don't think my father would agree. He would have approved only if we had torn down the gate and let everyone in."

She rolled her eyes. "Back home we have a name for that sort of thing."

"Oh?"

"Out of respect," she said, "I'll keep it to myself. It's obviously not a philosophy I subscribe to, but I think people should be free to think whatever they want, however naïve it might be."

"I still loved him," I said, "even though we agreed about almost nothing."

Madame's gaze regained its warmth. "You've told me what your father wanted. What about you? What did you want to be?"

"I never really thought about it," I said. "I just needed to get away. Opportunities came, and I took them."

"And are you glad you did? Don't say yes just to avoid hurting my feelings."

"Of course," I said. "I cannot imagine things being any different." And in truth just then I found myself wondering what it would be like if it could always be just like this moment, the two of us here together, enjoying what we had made. There need be nothing impure about it. Merely two friends who understood one another. We did not need guests. We both knew no one had ever been able to appreciate the place as she and I had.

"You wouldn't have chosen another path?" she said.

I shook my head, sorry to have to abandon my reverie. "There was no other path. It was either this or the world I grew up in. I wanted something different."

Madame lowered her eyes, but there was no hiding the sadness they contained. "I wanted something different, too."

And then she placed her hands abruptly on the table, signaling a sudden change in conversation. She glanced toward the kitchen. "I don't suppose there's any coffee?"

I shook my head.

"You must think me a terrible coward for not being here yesterday." She had turned away from me, as if she were speaking to the tapestry on the wall.

"Of course not."

"It would have been too much," she said. "I couldn't bear to see everyone leave."

"You could have done no differently."

"My only comfort," she said, "is that they'll have no trouble finding work. Their experience here will be invaluable to them."

"Of course."

"It's getting late," she said, rising suddenly from the table. "I've enjoyed our conversation. Tomorrow at eight I'll take breakfast in my office."

And I found myself unexpectedly disappointed, as she crossed the lobby and stepped into the darkness, that she did not suggest that in the morning I should join her.

After it had been clear all day, the evening sky brought with it a blanket of clouds. By the time night fell, the stars had disappeared, and even the moon was little more than a hazy suggestion of light. I washed the dishes, and afterward when I went outside I could barely see my way up the drive to the gate. Once there, I found the road equally dark. But I knew it could not be clouds obscuring the market, less than a kilometer down the road, nor the houses along the way. It seemed equally impossible that a blackout had struck everything but the estate. Almost nobody in Cité Verd had electricity to begin with.

The only possible explanation was that they had extinguished their kerosene lamps and fires on purpose. I wondered if life had grown so dangerous out there that even people locked inside their houses found the greatest safety in not being seen, either in the flesh or as shadows.

A curfew had been in effect for a couple of weeks, though I doubted it was necessary. Anyone with any sense did not need to be told it was unwise to go out at night. And anyone who did need to be told was unlikely to listen.

Distantly from up the mountain road I heard an engine, a car coming slowly, its shocks straining over the gullies and ruts. It was an army jeep, and in the flare of the taillights as it passed I could make out a man kneeling in the back with a machine gun in his hands.

No longer, it seemed, were the security forces fighting alone. Now the gangs of Cité Verd—the supposed resistance—had the army to contend with, too. Perhaps President Duphay had finally decided to bring an end to this foolishness once and for all.

The jeep rumbled its way through Cité Verd. Not until its sound had faded did I at last hear footsteps on the gravel. On the far side of the road, walking in the black, I saw a figure too small to be a soldier. I called out in barely more than a whisper.

The footsteps stopped. "What do you want?"

"Over here," I said. "At the gate." The boy crossed the street tentatively, and when he reached the gate, I went into the guard booth and turned on the light. Though just a bare bulb, it was strong enough that I could see the boy's dark face, and he mine. He was at most fifteen, wearing a red-and-white jersey.

"What's your name?" I said.

"Hector."

"Hector," I said, "I need you to run an errand for me."

He glanced down the road toward where the jeep had disappeared. And then he glanced past me to the manor house at the bottom of the long drive, drawn like a moth to the lights.

"I need you to go to Etienne's Bakery and pick up some croissants."

"Some what?"

"Never mind," I said, handing him a slip of paper. "I've written it down. Just give this to Etienne, and he will give you what I need."

"What does it say?"

"Never mind. Afterward you must stop by the market and get a kilo of coffee. Here is the money, and here is the fare you'll need for the bus. You must deliver it first thing in the morning. I will be waiting here at six. I'll give you twice as much when you deliver it. If you do well, there will be other jobs."

Again the boy peered over my shoulder. "Do you live here?"

"Yes," I said. "You'll need to get an early start in the morning."

He folded the paper and put it in his pocket. "What's it like in there?"

"If you do well," I said, "I'll show you some day."

"Show me now."

"It's dark now. There's nothing to see. Remember," I said, "I need these things by six. No later."

That night, instead of sleeping, I waited for the army jeep to find its target. But for once all of Cité Verd lay in peace.

In the unaccustomed quiet I unexpectedly found myself entertaining a peculiar thought. From the start I had wanted nothing more than for the turmoil to cease, and I knew only President Duphay could make that happen. But I realized now that he could not prevail on his own. He needed the security forces, or the army, or both, to crush the resistance. But how could I align myself with the security forces, whose existence had caused me nothing but trouble? And the army? Success for them would inevitably be just another excuse for a coup. Who knew what even greater trouble that would bring. But was there more to hope for in the victory of a gang of peasants and slum dwellers? Not that I could see. The only truly acceptable ending was the impossible one—that somehow all three would manage to wipe each other out, leaving us in peace.

The next morning at six, after gathering a small basket of fruit, I stood at the gate and waited. With every passing minute I felt a fool for having trusted a stranger—a boy no less—with such an important task. But what choice did I have?

A market woman approached, balancing a basket atop her head.

Did she have any coffee?

No.

Nor did the woman following after her.

"Did you see anyone along the way with coffee?" I asked.

"I don't know," she said. "There's some at the market."

But I could not risk leaving the gate.

In a couple of minutes, two boys strolled by, one of them walking a bicycle with a bent front tire. I called them over and asked if they knew Hector.

"We know lots of people," said the boy with the bicycle.

"Hector," I said. "He wears a red-and-white jersey."

"Hector is his cousin," said the boy with the bicycle. There were bruises all over his face and arms.

"He is not," the other boy said. He was tall and thin and covered with a pox of acne. "My cousin is in the army."

"He's not in trouble," I said. "I gave him money to buy something for me."

"I'll buy it for you." The tall boy took a step forward. "Give me the money. What do you want? I can get you a gun."

"No, you can't," said the boy with the bike.

"I can too. From my cousin. He can get anything."

"Your cousin's not in the army. He's just a thug."

I looked at my watch. It was now almost seven. "Do you know where Hector is?"

The boys looked at one another with uncertainty. "We don't know any Hector."

"And if we did," said the tall boy, "we don't know where he is. Give us money. We'll get you what you want. I can get gasoline."

"No, you can't," said the boy with the bicycle.

"My uncle can. Give me some money. I'm hungry."

"If you find Hector and bring him here in half an hour, I'll give you money," I said.

"We'll find him," they said, and down the road they went, the bent bicycle tire squeaking with every rotation.

I knew I would never see them again.

I swept the front steps and then the lobby. I swept my way up the stairs and down the corridor to Madame's office. There was just enough time to clear the stones on the terrace of leaves. I made sure Madame's favorite table was clean, in case she wished to lunch there, as she often did when she worked in her office. The pool below was also cluttered with leaves, but there was nothing I could do with the little time I had left.

I did not know how I would explain to Madame that for the second morning in a row I had failed to bring her a proper breakfast. I could offer only the same plate of fruit.

Hearing footsteps in the house, I hurried inside. "Please go up and get yourself settled, Madame," I said. "I will be right up with your breakfast."

I turned the corner, and there, leaning against the reception desk, his head thrown back in wonder, stood Hector.

"How did you get in here?"

"What is that?" He pointed up at the high, domed ceiling.

"A chandelier."

"What's it for?"

"Light."

He looked at me suspiciously, as though I could not possibly be telling the truth.

"Do you live here?"

"Yes," I said. "Did you bring what I asked? Where is it?"

Without looking, he swung his arm toward the reception desk, where I saw two small wrapped packages.

"These are not croissants," I said, opening the larger of the two. "They're just rolls. And they're not even from Etienne's."

"Etienne's is closed."

"What time did you go by?"

"How should I know?" The boy had wandered over toward the staircase. "Don't you know all the shops have closed?"

"You must not have gone to the right place," I said. "His shop is by the embassy."

"I know where it is," Hector said. "My sister was one of your maids. Marie."

There were Maries everywhere; it did not mean he was telling the truth.

"You see," he said, "everything closes."

"We are not closed," I said. "But tell me how you got in."

"You owe me money," Hector said. "And you said you'd let me look around."

I grabbed him by the arm and led him to the exit. "I said no such thing. I said I would show you the grounds, that's all." I handed him the money. "Now I will walk you to the gate, and you will tell me how you got in."

But of course there was no time. I turned him around and led him the other way, down the corridor and past the dining room to the terrace.

"I have another job for you," I said. "You must clean the leaves out of the pool."

I showed him the long-handled net for skimming the water.

"Get started," I said. "I need to prepare the coffee. When I get back, I expect you to be done, and then I will take you to the gate, and you will show me how you got in."

As I sliced the fruit and brewed the coffee, I worried I had been a fool again to allow the boy to stay a moment longer on the estate. These were dangerous times.

I walked out to the terrace and I could immediately hear splashing.

"What are you doing?" I yelled down to him.

As I leaned over the balustrade, I could see Hector floating in the deep end with a fist full of leaves and petals.

"What you asked."

"I didn't invite you for a swim," I said. "There are tools. I meant for you to use them."

"What's the difference? I'm getting it clean, aren't I?"

"Get out and finish up," I said. "I'll be back for you in a few minutes."

Madame's coffee was ready. I assembled a tray, adding one of the lumpen rolls to the plate of fruit.

Upstairs in the corridor, I knocked on the door of Madame's office, and she asked me to come in. She sat behind her desk in her reading glasses. A ledger of some sort was open before her.

I set the tray down on her desk and poured her a cup of coffee.

"Please have a seat," she said.

After the events of the day before, I felt a sense of failure at this sudden return to formality.

"I'm going to be leaving in two days," Madame said. "I've been away too long, and as there's no longer business to keep me here, I must attend to business at home."

There was nothing I could say.

"I need to ask you to do something very important."

"Anything," I said.

"I need you to take care of the estate."

"But madame," I said, "is that all?"

"This is no small task," she said. "This time I don't know how long I'll be gone."

"But you will be coming back?"

"Of course," she said. "Of course. Just as soon as things return to normal. And as soon as I've taken care of things at home."

"Madame," I said, "I consider it my duty."

"You have no idea what a relief it is," she said, "to have someone in whom you can put your trust."

I had not noticed until now the change that had overtaken her, the sadness in her voice. Its effect on me was devastating. I felt as though we were discussing not the management of an estate but the death of an intimate friend.

"You should not think of it that way," I said. "It would be a privilege. It's always been a privilege."

"You won't be alone," she said, straightening up quite suddenly in her seat. The emotion was gone from her face. She was a business-woman again. "You will need help. The estate is too large for one person to manage. Of course," she said, "this will be far too little help to maintain the current state. But you must do the best you can. We will close the villas and the casino and whatever else we can."

"I will keep up your villa, madame," I said, and I was pleased to have made her smile. "I will trust that responsibility to no one but myself."

"I have a few things I need to do before I go," she said.

I stood up and poured her a little more coffee, and then I went downstairs to get rid of Hector once and for all.

Chapter Eighteen

The road into Cité Verd had never been paved, and aside from the shacks visible from the main road leading up to Habitation Louvois, almost nothing had ever been painted. From up close it was clear that what had been painted needed to be again.

The scenery, such as it was, consisted of naked cinder block and cardboard and old scraps of rotten wood and corrugated metal. So uniform was the dusty gray below my feet and on all sides that it was as though a fire had rained ash down on everything. About the only other color to be seen was the sloppy spray of red on nearly every available wall spelling "Down with Duphay" and "Duphay Must Go."

What had once been not even a town, just a couple of desolate shanties attached to meager plots, had exploded during the five years the hotel had been open into a vast slum city of more than a hundred thousand. As I had known it would, the place had become the very ghetto its inhabitants had come here to escape. And there they squatted in seemingly every open doorway, their faded T-shirts advertising products in English that they had never even heard of, let alone purchased. And I felt the eyes of their potbellied children following me, faintly hoping I had brought something—anything—to give them. Little did they know that I had nothing left.

The hotel was gone. Mme Freeman was gone. At last I understood how it must have felt to be Senator Marcus, finding himself stripped of not just money and power, but even dignity.

I had not been in Cité Verd since before the hotel had opened. I had hoped never to have to come back. And yet here I was. Suddenly the world I thought I had escaped proved to be the only world left, and it cared nothing for the things I had lost.

In Cité Verd, everything destroyed by the recent storm had been rebuilt, and just as poorly as it was originally. Every corner was taken up with cement squares topped haphazardly with tin. Trash was everywhere underfoot, as if to substitute for paving stones. Open drains dribbled inconceivably foul waste. The heat did nothing to dampen the smell. The handkerchief I had brought to wipe the sweat from my eyes was drenched. Never had I felt so unclean.

A truck rattling down the road from the opposite direction slowed as it approached, choking in what appeared to be its death throes. All the glass was missing from the windows. Had it been shot out? Or perhaps just stripped? In the bed hunkered three young men in nylon running suits who looked as if they were on their way to the gym. Two of them held rifles pointed at the sky. The other, with a thick, gold chain swinging around his neck, lifted his pistol to aim it at my head.

"Who are you?" They were just three words, yet they somehow managed to cover the full spectrum from menace to boredom.

I considered telling him it was none of his business. "I'm offering work."

"Good for you."

With a percussive cough the truck jerked forward, kicking up dust and stones as it sped off, swerving toward a three-legged dog humping its way across the street.

Apparently my interrogation was over.

Was this the resistance, the force that would free us from dictatorship? A gang of idle teenagers harassing people from a crippled truck? As they drove away, I looked around, certain I would find a soldier on patrol or a jeep in pursuit. There was nothing. And if I had found someone, what would I have done? As much as I did not care who among them won, I could not conceive how a force like that could possibly fight back against both the army and the security forces. That they had lasted this long could only mean President Duphay was still exercising restraint.

The market was not far from the turnoff from the main road. It too had grown, from a few women spread out on blankets to a complex of rickety stalls selling everything from millet to radios. The place was both crude and frail, the roofs of the stalls made of cloth and scraps of metal, and many of the tables were nothing more than the limbs of trees lashed together with string. It was a wonder any of it withstood gravity, let alone wind and rain.

A badly creased woman of indeterminate age dressed all in black—her hands and arms and face nevertheless caked with soot—sat in a rough-hewn chair amid a spill of charcoal. She held up a briquette for me to inspect as I passed. Against the wall behind her a dozen black-smudged bags as large as bales of hay lay on their sides. It could just as well have been bodies as trees in those bags, and she would have given them no further thought.

A few meters away, engulfed in a poisonous cloud, a wiry, shirtless man with his pant legs rolled up to his knees shoveled a mound of coal into a blackened wheelbarrow. And then came the hat and basket weavers, a man with a stack of straw mats. Trinkets and icons and dolls carved from wood. None of it even remotely equal to the orange butterfly my mother had adored.

My shoes, which I had just polished that morning, were coated with dust.

A group of men were loitering loudly in the shade at the end of the first row of stalls, determined to share the details of their idleness with everyone around them. When they turned to look at me, it seemed to be my gray suit that most captured their attention. Several of them had responded to the heat by rolling their T-shirts up under their arms, as if they were some sort of flotation device.

"I'm looking for a gardener," I said, though among this crowd it felt as futile as asking for a brain surgeon. "If you know of anyone, tell him to come to Habitation Louvois."

On the ground beside the men kneeled a young woman in a torn dress frying scraps of pork and sweet potato in a dented tin skillet. Nearby a shirtless child with streaks of orange in his otherwise black hair watched with deadened eyes as the fat sizzled and popped. It appeared to be the closest he had been to food in days.

"And I need a woman to do the cooking and cleaning," I said. "She will have the finest kitchen on the island."

The men stared back at me, and I could see their minds silently weighing their thirst for money against their distaste for work. I needed for only one of them to let his better nature win out.

The next morning when I awoke a crowd of at least fifty men and women stood outside the gate. Under the tree where the photographers had once lain in wait for Mlle Miller I set up a chair, and one by one they came over and I asked them about their experience, and most of them offered lies and evasions. In the end I chose the only two I felt I could trust.

Raoul was older than most of the other men. Like my father, he had been a farmer, and he too had lost his land and moved to the city in search of other work. For the last decade he had worked as a gardener for several families, including one in Lyonville the Marcuses had known. His wife had died shortly after he moved to Cité Verd.

Mona had lived in Cité Verd all her life, since long before there even was a Cité Verd. In one of the shacks I had seen on my first visits she had raised her two sons. They were grown now and on their own. Her husband had gone abroad years before, looking for work. Recently the money he had been sending had stopped arriving.

When I introduced them, Mona and Raoul merely nodded, neither saying a word. I gave them a quick tour of the estate, about which they had no questions. They remained silent as I led them to their rooms in the old servants' quarters and accepted without comment what I offered them in pay.

They quickly settled in. During the hotel's final months, as the staff rapidly contracted, we had fallen far behind in our work. Raoul in particular had an enormous amount to catch up on. For Mona the cleaning was simple and straightforward, but the cooking proved to be a problem. On her first day I spent hours showing her how to use the icebox, the oven, and the stove, but that evening I found her in the yard, bent over a mound of charcoal, trying to fashion a platform on which to rest a cooking pot.

"What are you doing?" I asked.

She did not bother looking up. "Cooking."

"But why are you doing it here?"

If she was aware of my annoyance, she seemed not to care. "Why not?"

I had to squat down beside her to get her to look at me. "What's wrong with the kitchen?"

She shrugged. "I don't like it."

"It has everything you could possibly need."

She continued shaping her mound.

All my life I had heard peasant women insist that food cooked over coals tasted better than food cooked over gas. But that was just an excuse. They would rather cut down every last tree and turn their land into desert before going to the trouble of learning something new.

I spent a moment debating what I should do, before concluding that I was in no mood to return to Cité Verd and start all over again.

"Very well," I said, making no effort to suppress a sigh. "Come with me."

Between the servants' quarters and the laundry was a long, windowless building with dirt floors. Never having been wired for electricity, the space was lit by oil lamps and a few cloudy skylights. It was always dark and cheerless, resembling a barn more than a kitchen. We had been using it as a second storeroom, but it still contained the original coal stove and brick oven it had been built with, more than a century before. And there was no shortage of fuel here. Nothing would need to be cut down.

Mona stood behind me in the shadows as I opened the door.

"Is this more to your liking?"

I took her silence to mean it was.

And so, after a fashion, we settled into a routine. Dressed in his denims and blue plaid shirt, Raoul stayed busy maintaining the grounds. There never seemed to be enough time for the new projects I wanted him to begin, but at least he kept the trees and gardens from overtaking us. It was one of the many ways in which the scaling back of ambitions became my principal occupation.

Mona tended the kitchen garden and cleaned, never wavering from her schedule. Every morning at six she set out breakfast. At noon came lunch. Dinner was at five in the evening. The food could not compare to Jean's, but it was always filling and always on time. In place of elegance and refinement, we settled for the virtues of consistency.

Hector, the boy who had fetched Madame's coffee and rolls, took care of running errands. He liked to stop by at unexpected hours, banging on the gate with a stone until someone came to let him in. Unlike Mona and Raoul, he did not stay at the estate. Hector's family—or what was left of it—lived in Cité Verd, and that was where he continued to live.

Like me, Hector had lost his mother when he was young. His father had disappeared not long after. He had been raised by an aunt barely ten years older than he was. There were five of them crammed together in her one-room shack. The other three were her own children, each by a different man. Mona told me that all day long and even much of the night they could be found out on the street while their mother entertained inside. It was no wonder the boy spent as much time here as he could.

Despite my unfavorable first impressions, I slowly came around to concluding that Hector was surprisingly trustworthy for a boy his age. And unlike just about everyone else I had met from Cité Verd, he even proved to be rather clever. One afternoon a few weeks after he started working here, he brought me a radio from one of the villas that he had taken upon himself to repair. He had figured it out all by himself, despite having scarcely ever used one before. Such things seemed to come naturally to him.

Hector had been to school no more than a handful of days in his entire life, and he could neither read nor write. But there was no denying his intelligence. However bored he might pretend to be when I issued instructions, he never failed to follow them. That was far more than could be said for Raoul and Mona.

But perhaps the most valuable thing about Hector was the way his high spirits helped to counter the dark clouds that seemed to follow Mona and Raoul everywhere they went. It would never have occurred to me if not for Hector, but the estate benefited from the presence of a child. His energy served as an important reminder of the vitality of the place. More than either Mona or Raoul, he seemed to understand why the work we were doing mattered, why Habitation Louvois itself mattered. And it pleased me to think how much Madame would like him.

For pennies he was willing to get whatever we needed from the market, sparing me those unpleasant trips. When it came to more specialized items, I occasionally sent him on the bus to the capital. With electricity becoming increasingly erratic and the phones once again effectively dead, Hector was my link to the world outside. More than that, he was my one hope that, despite our recent setbacks, all might not be lost.

That summer the rains never came, and the grounds turned brown and brittle. It must have been the same everywhere on the island. The market women's baskets grew meager. I had to have Hector carry buckets of water up from the springs to vulnerable parts of the lawn that we could not reach with hoses. But there was only so much we could do a bucket at a time, and this desperate effort began to feel like a metaphor for our entire undertaking. Here I was with two old fools and one well-meaning boy, trying to sustain one of the most opulent estates in the hemisphere.

At the height of the drought, our biggest problem inside the manor house, ironically, was that the water flowed all too freely. By the time I happened to notice the stain in the ceiling of the library, it was already the size of a serving tray. Water had leached into four of the plaster ceiling panels, and an adjacent piece of crown molding had pulled away from the wall, dislodged as the water coursed past. Down it spilled, over the cornice of the bookcase and into the gap above the glass doors. There the top shelf of leather-bound volumes appeared to have acted as a sort of sponge. It was horrible to see—the pages of Madame's rare first editions swollen like the gills of a suffocating fish. Mona fetched some bowls and we lined them up, lip to lip, but by then the drip seemed to have stopped.

We did what we could to save the damaged books. I suggested we use one of the clothes irons to press out the moisture. Perhaps I should have worried about the blank expression on Mona's face. Not until it was too late did I realize she had never used an iron before. In little time she had succeeded in destroying every page.

It was hard not to feel as though this would be our fate—a piece at a time the few treasures we had left would be lost. Through attrition we would find ourselves with less and less, until at last we arrived back where we started, a vast emptiness curtained with spiderwebs.

Raoul and Hector knew no more about plumbing than me, neither one having ever lived with it before. Raoul went to check the tubs and fixtures on the second floor, but everything appeared to be in order. With the phones still out, as they had been for months, I had no choice but to send Hector into town for help.

The leak in the library was not our only problem, just the most recent. A few days before, the fountain at the center of the drive had suddenly been reduced to a dribble. We had already discovered, during the last rainstorm before the drought began, that the ceramic roofing tiles on two of the villas were damaged and needed replacing. Water everywhere was rebelling against us.

"It's a sign," Mona said one evening as she served us dinner.

"A sign of what?" I asked.

"Trouble." Given two equally plausible outcomes, Mona's predictions always tended toward the less favorable extreme.

Mouth full of okra, Hector declared, "It's a sign that everything's falling apart."

"Watch your manners," Mona scolded.

Maintaining his usual silence, Raoul never looked up from his plate.

This was the help with which I was to fight off oblivion. Was it any wonder that depression carried me straight upstairs to bed?

Even from a distance, it was clear the fighting in Cité Verd continued to worsen. Not just were more and more guns constantly joining the chorus, so too were more voices. On windless nights I could sometimes hear their shouts as they chased each other through the streets, calling for their comrades. And their screams as they were caught.

On neither side did there appear to be any limit to their brutality. For every beheaded peasant found in a ditch each morning there was a charred soldier lashed to a pole. When I sat on the balcony, I could sometimes see jeeps patrolling the road to Saint-Gabriel. I began to long for the day when they would cross paths with the boys in the windowless truck going the other way, and then all of this could end.

Chapter Nineteen

That night, no matter how I lay my head, no matter what position I tried, nothing brought me any comfort. The heat was no worse than usual, but it lay atop me like a fever, and the bedsheets provided no relief, holding on to my sweat as if out of spite.

When sleep finally came, it did so reluctantly, and the slightest sound was enough to send me back again to the beginning. First it was the cicadas. Then some sort of large-winged insect striking the shutters over and over and over again.

By the time I was awakened by the muffled rustle coming from downstairs, I was so exhausted I was no longer capable of caring. I opened my eyes and listened. A moment passed and the sound returned, barely audible over the ceiling fan. A clank. A shuffle. Most likely it was Mona. She was habitually a poor sleeper and prone to nocturnal housework.

It would be no great loss, I decided, to get out of bed and find out what she was up to.

Toeing the floor in search of my slippers, I began to have doubts. Suddenly I thought I sensed an awful lot of commotion, more than could be explained by a single old woman, even a stubbornly industrious one.

I got up silently, cautiously opening the door. Barefoot, I crept down the corridor, taking the stairs slowly, careful to remain in the shadows, away from the moonlight. At the landing halfway down, I stopped. Crouching there, I saw movement in the lobby below. My eyes needed time to adjust to the dark. It was difficult to distinguish, but I thought I counted as many as five men, darting in and out of view. On the floor beside the reception desk two more men squatted side by side, stuffing something into a sack.

I did not move or make a sound. What was I to do, one man against seven? I had no way of knowing if they were armed.

They did not talk—there was no whispering. They seemed to know what they were doing. It was as though they had known in advance what they would find here and where they would find it. If I could get outside, I thought, I could wake Raoul. Together we had a chance of scaring them off.

I managed to slip down the rest of the way unseen. At the bottom of the stairs, the sofa and a chaise longue gave me something behind which to hide. But I was running out of time. In the library, a set of French doors opened onto the side terrace. That was where I would make my escape. I need only wait for the man in there to come out. Then I saw him, rushing past. In his arms he carried three crystal ashtrays. As I got up to run, I caught a glimpse of his face.

"Georges," I said, "what are you doing?" He looked at me almost sadly, the same expression I had seen on his face the day, eight months before, that he had served me lunch for the last time.

I neither heard nor saw the man who came upon me from behind.

When I awoke it was morning, and the men and the sacks were gone. They had taken the silver and the crystal and all of the appliances they could carry. They had taken some of the vases and paintings and left others. I wondered if they had known something about their relative values, or if they had simply taken the ones they liked.

Mona wrapped my head, reprimanding me for having been so stupid.

"You're lucky they didn't kill you," she said.

"What was I to do? Just let them get away?"

"Is it worth getting killed for an ashtray?"

"It's the principle."

She rolled her eyes.

I sent Raoul to inspect the guesthouse and the villas, and he reported back that they appeared untouched. The men had known most of the valuables were here.

Hector found a locksmith who could change the lock on the gate. I had been a fool not to think of that sooner. For me, the saddest consequence was that the key M. Guinee had given me was now just a memento, no longer able to open anything. I put it on the shelf with his icons. I had arranged my father's icons there, too, hoping the two of them might find some kind of comfort in the mingling of their saints.

After the lock was taken care of, Mona brought Hector up to see me.

"I have another errand for you," I said. "I need you to find my friend Paul and ask him to come. I have to see him today."

I gave Hector money for the bus and told him where Paul lived.

"I know Paul," Hector said as soon as I named my old neighborhood.

"How do you know Paul?"

He smiled. "Everyone knows Paul."

"Why?"

Hector shrugged. "He's the man."

My head was throbbing and I could not begin to imagine what he meant. Nor did I particularly care. "Just go and get him."

Two hours later I heard honking at the gate, and Mona went down to let them in. Standing unsteadily on the balcony, I watched a red sedan with a white convertible roof roll down the drive, its headlights hooded in the bright sun, a small beaming head sticking out of one of the back windows. Paul had gotten his new car after all. And not just any car. He had gone straight to the top.

Mona made lunch and served us on the terrace overlooking the pool. Paul and I sat at one table, while his driver and another companion lurked several tables away. The driver was the same man I had met years ago. Like his car, however, he had undergone a transformation of refinement. His shoulder holster, formerly his most prominent accessory, was now just a conspicuous lump underneath his beige linen jacket. His suit was a bit boxier and coarser than Paul's, but nevertheless it was clear their operation—whatever it currently was—placed at least some value on the sheen of professional appearances.

The man wedged beside the driver, who had been sitting in the passenger seat of the car, was similarly attired. What set him apart was his size and the heavy scar embedded in his right cheek. With his sunglasses on he reminded me rather uncannily of President Mailodet's bodyguards.

Down below us, Hector splashed in the pool.

"It's been too long," Paul said as Mona poured him a cup of coffee.

"We've both been busy."

"Not so busy that we have to let"—Paul scratched his head uncertainly—"four years? pass without seeing each other."

"Almost five."

"It was here." He poked the table with his index finger. It was one of the few not bearing a heavy gold ring.

"The restaurant," I said, grimacing at the recollection. "You came for dinner."

Unshaken by my lack of nostalgia, he leaned forward, as if to share a secret. "I was drunk off my ass."

It was all I could do not to look away. "I remember."

He let loose a rollicking laugh, abandoning his earlier modesty.

"We've gotten old," he said, setting his elbows on the table.

In truth, it seemed to me that Paul had gone to great lengths to preserve his youth. Not just his stylish clothes, but also his well-manicured hair and mustache.

He leaned back, folding his hands behind his head with evident satisfaction. He seemed to have a hard time keeping still.

"Did you ever think we'd live this long?"

No doubt he meant it as a joke, but he could not help noting my hesitation. "Honestly," I said, "I never thought you would survive to twenty-five."

Paul unfurled another of his enormous laughs, slapping the table with his open palm. "Me either!"

Even I could not help smiling.

"But you," he said, more serious now. "You were always different. You're going to outlive us all."

"What makes you say that?"

He ran his index finger thoughtfully across his lips, as if admiring their shape. "You just have a knack for it."

Before I could ask what he meant, he turned, and I could see his attention shifting.

He glanced at the gardens visible around the pool. "It looks like things have slowed down a bit for you."

"Only temporarily," I said, watching Hector climb out of the pool. The hot concrete at his feet sizzled as he ran around to the deep end. "But I can see things are going well for you."

"Watch this," Hector yelled from down below. Paul and I both turned our heads.

Stepping back to give himself a running start, Hector sprinted to the edge of the pool and leaped, somersaulting into the water. Enfolded in a foam of bubbles, his dark form curled to the bottom.

"Not bad," Paul cried out as Hector resurfaced, wiping the water from his eyes.

Then Paul reached into his pocket and pulled out a handful of coins, and I regretted not having sent Hector away after he had completed his errand.

Coin balanced on the nail of his thumb, Paul gave it a quick flick. Over the banister it sailed, spinning and spinning, nearly floating, before falling with a plunk into the water twenty meters below.

Taking a deep breath, Hector dove in after it.

"You're dependent on too many things you can't control," Paul said. "A business can't work just under ideal circumstances. You have to give people things they need all the time, rain and shine. I've succeeded because I sell people the things they can't live without."

"How's your mother?" I said.

"You should come by and see her. You haven't seen the new house, have you?"

I was surprised he felt a need to ask. "No."

"It's not quite as nice as this," Paul said, "but I'm catching up."

"More," Hector yelled.

Paul sifted through the small pile of change on the table until he found the coin he was looking for. With Hector watching below, Paul brought his arm back and then he whipped it forward, never actually letting go.

Hector was too clever for such an obvious ruse. "Come on," he yelled.

Laughing, Paul picked up several more coins, dropping them one at a time into his palm. As if he were shooting dice, he gave them a shake. Then, all at once, he let them go.

Hector stood frozen as a swarm of coins twisted and tumbled in the air, shooting off sparks of sunlight. They broke the surface of the water in sudsy streaks, and Hector dove in after them, reaching out with both hands, trying to catch all of them at once.

Paul pointed to the bloody bandage in my hair. "Does that have anything to do with why you called me here?"

I nodded. My head still hurt to move.

"What did they get?"

"Everything," I said.

"Someone you know?"

"A man who used to work here. A waiter named Georges."

Paul's face turned grim. "You can't trust anybody anymore."

After lunch, Paul and I left the others behind and went for a walk through the preserve. At first he seemed unsettled by what he saw, rounding each bend as if he expected to be ambushed by the trees.

"They say the whole island was once like this," he said after I showed him one of the springs. "Can you imagine?"

Could he really have forgotten that I was the one who told him that?

"I try to," I said. "Every time I come down here, I try to imagine what it would have been like to live here then."

"Pretty miserable," Paul said, "if you ask me."

"Why do you say that?"

"Because I don't like sleeping outside in the rain." Paul stopped to light a cigarette. "And I don't think I'd look good in a loincloth."

"But think how peaceful it would be."

"Wouldn't that get boring after a while?"

"Not if it was the only thing you ever knew."

"You're forgetting one thing," Paul said, taking a deep drag. "While you're frolicking in your stream or whittling bird whistles, some other tribe"—and here he turned and pointed back toward the hills behind the manor house— "is sharpening their sticks and arrows, and they're going to come down here and rape your women and have you for dinner."

"There were no cannibals."

"That's not the point," he said.

"How is that any different from the way it is now?"

Paul dropped his spent cigarette in the dirt.

"I didn't say it was."

When he turned away, I pushed a pile of dirt and leaves over the shriveled butt.

"If I'm going to get killed," Paul said, "I'd rather be in a soft bed than on the muddy ground."

"I disagree," I said as we headed back, following the path to the manor house. "I think there was a time when it was possible to live in peace. There had to have been safe places. Maybe up in the mountains."

"You're probably right," he said. "There probably still are. But I don't think you'd want to live there."

"Why not?"

By then we had reached the upper lawn. Standing at the edge of the drive, Paul threw open his arms to embrace the manor house.

"Because you'd have to give up all of this."

He was smiling, and I decided to take it as a joke. A man with an automobile such as his could not possibly accuse me of being interested only in material things.

Ahead of us I saw his men descending the stairs, Hector trailing behind.

"There's just one thing I don't get," Paul said as he stopped to light a new cigarette. "Don't you get lonely out here?"

"Not really," I said. "I have Hector."

Paul shook his head and chuckled, and a column of smoke strafed from his teeth. "There's lots of nice girls in Cité Verd," he said, thumbing over his shoulder toward the trees. "And I know just the one for you. A regular schoolgirl. The sweetest thing you've ever seen. But the moment she wraps her legs around you—"

"Don't be crude," I said.

His eyes narrowed as he took another long draw. I could hear the paper burn. "Don't you ever need to let off steam?"

"Not like that."

He shrugged. "If I was you, I would have exploded a long time ago."

There were footsteps on the gravel behind me.

The driver opened the back door of the car, and Paul got in, followed by Hector.

"I'll take him home," Paul said as he rolled down the window. "And tomorrow someone will be stopping by with something that should fix your problem. Your security problem, that is. If you change your mind about the other thing, let me know."

"Thank you."

"It's nothing, Alexandre," Paul said as the car pulled away. "That's what friends are for."

There was no question but that he meant every word.

That night the wind blew in steadily from the bay, and just like the night before—though for a different reason—the faintest creaking of the trees was all it took for my eyes to spring open. I worried about whether I could really protect myself, and whether it would have been wiser to call the police than to let Georges and the other men get away with what they had done. But then again, the police had a way of simply compounding one's problems. I could never afford what it would have cost to convince them to care about what had happened. And for all I knew, Georges had already bought their favor.

It was dawn when the men Paul had sent arrived, and I had been awake for hours.

No more than twenty years old, both were confident and strong. They stood at the gate totally unself-conscious, thoroughly unimpressed with anything they could see beyond the wall.

The taller of the two caught my eye first. He was dressed in a wrinkled linen suit that had once been white. The cut and the collar reminded me of the one M. Swallows had once worn, but this one had to be half the size. The poor tourist who had lost it had at least been allowed to keep his shirt, or so I guessed by the fact that the young man wore nothing but a gold chain with a crucifix under the jacket. But there was something else too. An immense tattoo covered him from neck to navel. Not wanting to stare, I failed to make out what it was.

The other young man wore jeans and a T-shirt. So broad-shouldered was he that the sleeves of his shirt barely reached his armpits.

Between the two young men, more than a foot shorter, stood Hector, wearing his usual smile.

"This is my brother," Hector said, pointing to the young man in the linen suit. "You can call him Dragon Guy."

I could see the resemblance now, the long drawn-out mouth, the ears that appeared almost pinned back. But everything on Dragon Guy's face was firm and stern.

"Hello," I said.

Dragon Guy stared straight through me.

"And this is Black Max," Hector said, gesturing to the young man on his right. Black Max had a short, blunt nose and sunken cheeks and upward-slanted eyebrows. His skin was extremely dark, his name barely an exaggeration of his actual color. He nodded slightly when I shook his hand.

"And I believe you already know this man," Dragon Guy said. His voice was surprisingly soft, almost sweet. He stepped aside, and only then did I see the body leaning up against the tree behind him. The man was partly slumped over, his chin dangling at his chest. I could not see his face, but his clothes were filthy and torn.

"Go on," Black Max said, moving toward the man. "Say hello." He reached down and put his hand under the man's chin. Receiving no response, he jerked the man's head back suddenly, making it strike the tree with a horrible thud.

The beaten, bloody face barely winced. One of the man's eyes was swollen shut and the other seemed almost to have rolled back into his head. I knew he was alive only because I could hear his shallow breathing. It would have been impossible for anyone to recognize him.

"Show monsieur what you brought him," Black Max said. He moved his hand to the side of the man's head and pushed him into the dirt. Hector went around behind the tree and came back dragging several enormous sacks too big for him to carry.

"I understand this belongs to you," Dragon Guy said. Hector set the sacks down at my feet. "And this is for you as well." Dragon Guy reached down into his pants, pulling out something wrapped in an oily rag. He made it seem light, but my arm dropped under the weight.

"Do you know how to use it?" he asked.

For a moment I found myself afraid to admit that I even knew what it was. "No."

"Hector will show you."

Hector nodded gravely, as if hoping I might forget he was a child.

Squatting down, Black Max raised the arm of the beaten man, who now lay sprawled in the dirt. The arm waved grotesquely, flopping at the wrist.

I was surprised by how faintly the sight upset me. He looked even worse than the man I had watched Paul beat unconscious all those years ago. My tolerance for blood had never been great, but I had come to understand why such things were sometimes necessary. I had no desire to be ruthless, but neither could I afford to be meek.

"Say good-bye," Black Max said. "Say good-bye, Georges. Good-bye, monsieur." Still gripping the same arm, Black Max yanked Georges up. In one swift movement he threw the body over his shoulder, as if it were a sack of rice.

"Good-bye, monsieur," Dragon Guy said as he turned to leave. "And please let us know if you have any more difficulties. Any friend of Paul's is a friend of ours."

At the tree he joined his companion, and together they sauntered down the road back toward Cité Verd, Georges's body hanging lifelessly down Black Max's back.

"Come on." Hector picked up the sacks. "I'll show you how it works."

I was in no mood for company. "Later." I gripped the gun by the barrel and walked back to the manor house alone.

That afternoon, following lunch, I began the process of returning the items Dragon Guy had recovered to their rightful places. I knew exactly where each piece went. But I had been sorting through the sacks only a short time when I started to realize not everything had been accounted for. Several of the most precious pieces of crystal were missing. I looked everywhere, thinking I had perhaps misplaced one of the sacks. I went through every room, every closet, every cabinet. There was no trace.

I had Mona bring Hector to my office.

"Are you ready for your shooting lesson?" he said, flinging the door open. His preference was always for a grand entrance.

I said, "I want you to ask your brother if there was another sack he forgot to bring."

Hector seemed taken aback. "There wasn't."

"How do you know?"

"I know," he said. "My brother can buy anything he wants. He doesn't need to steal."

"I'm not accusing him of stealing," I said, gesturing for him to remain calm. I was acutely aware in that moment of a desire somewhere inside me not to hurt the boy's feelings. Where did it come from, this peculiar instinct I had to protect him? "I'm simply saying there might be another sack somewhere."

"There isn't."

I was careful to maintain the same measured tone. "I want you to ask him anyway."

Hector rose from his chair with a sigh. "Okay, but there isn't any other sack."

As I watched him leave the room, I searched my mind for something more I should have said to convince him that he had done nothing wrong.

I was sitting in the library reading, later that afternoon, when Mona came in to dust. She stood across the room with her back turned to me. "You're playing with fire, you know."

A moment passed, and she said nothing more. She did not look at me. It was as if she were unwilling even to admit she had spoken. Why, I wondered, must we play these games? I considered turning the page and going on as if I had not heard her. But as Mona herself knew best, no one could beat her in a battle of wills.

"Are you talking to me?" I said.

She reached up to swat her duster across an upper shelf. "These are dangerous people."

"I noticed," I said. "If the gun didn't give it away, the beating they gave Georges certainly did."

For the first time she turned around to look at me, and she made no effort to hide her disdain. "You don't know who they are, do you?"

"I know one of them is Hector's brother," I said, but I could tell by the look on her face that that was not the correct answer.

"They call him Dragon Guy," she said.

"I'm aware of that."

"They call him Dragon Guy," she said, "because he is fierce and because they think no one can kill him."

She relayed this with an earnestness I had never before seen from her.

I nearly laughed. "Can he breathe fire, too?"

"What did you think?" she said. "That it was just a few foolish peasants with guns? That all of this would just go away?"

Never had she spoken to me in such a tone.

She raised her duster, and the air between us, lit by slants of sun breaking through the window, looked like an exploding universe. "It's an army," she said. "There are hundreds of them, and it grows bigger every day. And all of them answer to Dragon Guy."

"That's impossible," I said.

"Why?"

"He's Hector's brother. He's barely more than a boy himself."

"How old should he be?"

Was there not some minimum threshold below which such a thing was simply implausible? "But what does he know about fighting?"

"If someone attacks you, you fight back. What else is there to know?"

"He can't possibly win," I said, fanning my book to part the cloud of dust.

"All I know," she said, "is that when Dragon Guy gives the word, all of Cité Verd breathes fire. Do you understand?"

"I understand," I said, "but I cannot believe it."

She turned to leave. "Have it your way."

When he returned that evening, Hector came to my office as instructed. But I could see in a glance that he was not happy to be there, that he was dreading the conversation to come. Knowing he felt that way made me even more anxious than I was already.

"There is no other sack," he said sullenly. "Just like I told you."

"I understand," I said, trying to put him at ease. "It must have gotten lost. I'm grateful that your brother was able to recover what he did."

Hector looked at me dubiously. Like a small child, he folded his legs beneath him on the seat.

"Your brother must be very busy," I said. "I appreciate that he took the time to help me."

Hector nodded warily.

"If not for the fact that you work here, perhaps he would not have been so willing to help."

"He's a good brother."

"I can see that," I said, feeling as if we had finally found a place where both of us were comfortable. I was glad that we could pause, for it gave me a few seconds to ponder my way forward. As much as I might have liked to, I could not afford to dismiss this as just another instance of Mona looking for trouble where none existed. Although I trusted Hector more than I trusted just about anyone else, I could not afford to take chances.

"He seems like a very good brother," I said. "And I understand he is quite powerful, too. That's why I'm a little surprised that you came here to work with us, instead of with him."

Hector's feet began to press into the cushion. "I like it here," he said.

"Why?"

"It's peaceful. And quiet. Nobody bothers you."

As he spoke, I studied his scraped, scarred hands, his clear, steady eyes. Why should he not be here for precisely the same reasons I was?

"Does your brother mind?" I asked.

"Why would he mind?"

"People can resent it when you go off on your own. Even people who love you. Some people cannot understand that not everyone wants to lead the same kind of life." With a smile I tried to show him that he had nothing to hide, nothing to be ashamed of. "We have more in common than you think," I said.

"Oh."

"Go get yourself some supper," I said, reaching across to pat his small hand. I nearly rose to embrace him, but I knew that would be going too far. "I'll see you in the morning."

The holes left by the missing crystal were impossible to hide. Madame could not help but notice. I had told her nothing about what had happened. It would have broken her heart to learn that people she had cared for and trusted had turned against her. But though I could think of no way around it, neither could I bring myself to write her the truth. Instead I filled my letters with news about everything else, in particular about how dry the weather continued to be. "We have closed all but the manor house pool and the pool at your villa," I wrote.

The others will be easy enough to refill when the guests return. I see no reason to tax the springs any further than they already are. Of course, there is nothing to worry about. We have all the water we could need, but still it is better not to waste. After all, it is only a

*matter of time before the estate will be overrun with visitors again,
and I intend to be ready. Toward that end we have been making
steady progress. Of course, there is still a great deal to be done, but I
feel everyone now understands their responsibilities. I have told you
already about Raoul and Mona, but of late I have gotten the most
help from a boy named Hector. He is only fifteen, but full of energy
and enthusiasm. And most of all, he truly loves the estate, almost as
much as you and I. I hope you can forgive my presumptuousness, but
I think you will like him very much. He possesses precisely the kind
of spirit I know you admire. All he needs is the proper education and
training. I cannot wait until you have an opportunity to meet.*

After all the flattering things I had to say about Hector, I could not
bring myself to mention Dragon Guy. I knew Madame was aware of the
fighting; she had alluded to it in more than one of her letters. But I did
not believe she understood how bad it had become. In recent nights, it
had truly begun to sound—as Mona had insisted—as if armies on both
sides were squaring off for war. But for the first time since the fighting began, I was able to go to bed feeling secure that as long as Hector
remained with us, Dragon Guy would keep us safe.

Chapter Twenty

The next morning, Hector did not come to the estate. In his place, I had to lend a hand to Raoul, who was trying to determine what was wrong with the fountain. Perhaps I should have been annoyed by the inconvenience, but I was more preoccupied with what Hector's absence meant. Never before had he failed to show up. I worried something had happened.

When it was time for lunch, we took a break. I hoped to find Hector waiting for us at the table, but Mona was there alone.

All day we worked without him, and neither did he appear for supper. It was not like him to miss a meal. Never had he disappeared without telling me.

"Have either of you heard anything from him?" I asked as I joined Mona and Raoul in the kitchen.

They both answered with silence.

"Where could he be?"

"If you find his brother," Mona said as she gave the pot a few final stirs, "I'm sure you'll find him."

"Hector is not his brother." For Mona, everything was simple: Hector's brother was dangerous, and therefore Hector was, too. But there was more to the boy than she would ever understand. I had come to see that no one understood him as I did.

Mona dropped the pot on the table as if it were an unwieldy boulder. "If you know him so well, why are you asking us?"

"I apologize," I said. "I made the mistake of thinking you might be concerned."

What had happened, I wondered, as I watched her fill our bowls as if it were beneath her, that she suddenly felt she could treat me with such disrespect?

"I'll take supper in my office," I said as I turned to go.

Mona pointed to my dish, as if to suggest I could carry it myself.

"Bring me coffee as well."

I do not know what time it was that night when the guns began their assault. There seemed to be no buildup, no first exchange. It was as if a single trip wire had triggered everyone at once. My nerves were triggered, too. Despite the distance between us and the battle in Cité Verd, I could feel each shot run through me like a charge. Sitting up in bed, I wondered how much the physical sensation owed to the darkness, which had a way of enveloping everything in a menacing kind of intimacy. Daylight could never produce this much terror.

President Duphay and his generals knew what they were doing, saving these incursions for the night. The choice had nothing to do with gaining tactical advantage. The only point was the effect it had on those of us who were merely observers, to be all the more thoroughly consumed with dread. Especially me, especially now, knowing Hector was caught in the middle of it, where I could not protect him.

As always, the guns faded as the darkness faded. By dawn it was over. But in my nerves the battle lingered. And my worry for the boy weighed even heavier on my heart. I wondered if my father had ever felt this way about me, if he ever lay awake at night fraught with worry. It was difficult to imagine. If anything, his hours were probably full of disappointment, tossing and turning as he despaired over the path I continued to follow. It was painful to consider how vindicated he would surely feel if he were to see me now.

I was still in bed, a short time later, when I heard banging on the gate. I did not waste time getting dressed. In my robe and slippers I hurried out of the manor house and up the drive. As I neared the top, I saw the flash of Hector's smile, and my knees nearly gave out beneath me. He stood with his feet on the bottom crossbar of the gate. With each hand clinging to one of the vertical bars, he swung happily back and forth, as if nothing could possibly be the matter.

"Where have you been?"

The smile dissolved from his face. Even I was a little surprised by the anger in my voice. But how could it not feel like a betrayal to see him behaving like this after having caused me such distress?

He hopped down from the crossbar. "I was busy."

"Busy? Is that all you have to say? Don't you understand how sick I was with worry?"

Hector's throat constricted, but he did not speak.

"What exactly were you doing?"

Lowering his head, he toed aimlessly at the gravel. "Things."

"You need to tell me when you're not going to come," I said. "I thought something had happened to you."

"I'm fine."

As I went to open the gate, he stepped aside, and I happened to see the sparkle of something beneath his shirt.

"What is that?"

Hector took a step back and shrugged unconvincingly. "What?"

"Under your shirt."

"Oh, that," he said, grinning as if it were a special surprise.

He raised his shirt to show me the nickel-plated handle of a pistol poking out of his shorts, reflecting the morning sunlight like a mirror. The gun looked a lot like the one his brother had given me, but newer and cleaner.

"I thought you didn't want to be like your brother," I said.

"I don't."

Having just unlatched the gate, I quickly closed it again. "I won't allow weapons here."

His eyes were sunk in dark circles. He, too, looked as if he had not slept. "What's the difference? You have one."

"I have one for defense."

"Mine's for defense too."

"Mine is locked in a drawer," I said.

Hector's hand traveled down to the band of his shorts. "I don't have a drawer."

"If you want," I said, offering my hand, "I'll gladly lock it in mine."

He shook his head.

"The choice is yours," I said. "You can come back when you change your mind."

I felt miserable as I turned my back on him, but I knew I had no choice.

I was halfway to the manor house when I heard him call out.

"Monsieur."

Somehow he had climbed up to the top of the gate. He hung there now with the crooks of his knees over the crossbar. Although his back faced the drive, he had wrenched his neck to look at me, and with a smile that seemed to be sliding away under the force of gravity, he pointed to his pistol lying in the gravel.

"Take it," he said.

I rushed forward. "Give it to me," I said, extending my hand. "And I will give you something in return."

With astonishing speed Hector swung down from the gate.

"The room next to mine," I said. "It has all the drawers you could ever need. And a bed."

The smile spread all the way to his ears. If ever I had been in doubt, at that moment I knew for certain where his allegiances stood.

PART TWO

Chapter Twenty-One

Sitting on my balcony watching the dusk fall, I happened to look down, and there they stood on the lawn below, trespassing without any apparent fear they might get caught, without any trace of impropriety. Dragon Guy stood in the middle, dressed as before, shirtless in his dirty white linen suit. He had his back to me, and I recognized the breadth of his shoulders and the peculiar shape of his head, oblong as a gourd and shaved equally smooth. The woman to Dragon Guy's right stood a full head above him; the man to his left, half a head shorter. Black Max. The estate was laid out before them, and to me they looked like surveyors come to measure the dimensions of their future.

And then Dragon Guy turned, as if suddenly remembering the house behind him. He glanced up, his hand raised to brush aside the sun. He saw me in my chair; I know because he nodded in acknowledgment. Then just as quickly he turned his back to me again.

Down the stone steps they went, Dragon Guy in the lead. Through the trees I could just barely see the red cloth wrapped around the woman's head—and just above it, the roof of Villa Bardot with its canopy of banana leaves. A long, still silence crept along, and then in the quiet I heard what sounded like a set of jalousies opening. And then that overwhelming silence again. For the length of a breath, I forgot they were intruders. For just a moment—a strange, feverish moment—Dragon Guy and his companions were our guests. Another table, I thought to myself, would need to be set for dinner. And I waited for one of the porters—whose names I could no longer remember—to appear with Dragon Guy's bags. But of course, there were no more porters, no more bags, no more guests.

Why did I not go after them? Why did I not go down to Villa Bardot and insist they leave? Perhaps I felt I owed him something. Perhaps I thought it would do no good. Whatever the reason, I did not go. Mona had just brought my coffee, and the warmth of the cup spread calm through my fingertips. I decided it would be best to wait.

That night I wrote to Madame, but I saw no reason to mention Dragon Guy. She would only grow alarmed, and without cause. He will have vanished, I told myself, even before I can post the letter.

"Dear Madame," I wrote,

I am very pleased to report that at last we have fixed all of the plumbing problems. A week ago we found the obstruction in the fountain to which I referred in my letter of several months past. The unfortunate delay was a result of the plumber, whom we finally had to replace. Despite the setbacks, all is now well. The fountain was of course a minor concern in comparison to many other projects that have been waiting longer for attention, but knowing how fond you are of it, I wanted to see to it that the necessary repairs were made immediately, before your return. I have been assured that the roofing tiles for Villa Leigh and Villa Bernhardt will arrive before the rainy season begins in earnest. As always, I hope your affairs at home are coming to a quick resolution. We await your return and the resumption of business here.

At breakfast the next morning I took care to reveal nothing to the others about what I had seen the night before. Hector came downstairs late. He had been living with us for four months now, and he had quickly developed a taste for the comforts of a genuine bed. The only problem was getting him out of it at a reasonable hour.

As was her way, Mona had been vocal in her displeasure at the arrangement, confronting me the morning after Hector's first night in the manor house. She was waiting for me the moment my foot touched down in the lobby, her mouth twisted with a sourness she had clearly spent hours savoring.

"Why is he sleeping on silk sheets, and I'm on a wool tick out back?"

I was still rubbing the sleep from my eyes. "He's only a boy. He needs someone to look after him."

"Fine," Mona said, whipping a towel from her shoulder with a snap. "You can look after his sheets too."

Raoul of course had said nothing. I could have made him sleep on the dirt, and he never would have thought to complain.

In the four months that had passed since, Mona had softened none of her objections. True to her word, she refused to clean Hector's sheets. Instead, the boy was left to wash them himself, a task I made sure he undertook weekly. I knew he saw such matters of hygiene as the most tedious of chores, but few things were more important.

But the project to which we together devoted the bulk of our time was his schooling. He would never make a better life for himself, I explained, until he learned to read and write. To accommodate his studies, I lessened his workload. In the morning he attended to whatever needed to be done, allowing us to spend the heat of the afternoon in the library, practicing his letters and sounding out words. As I had known he would, he had already made tremendous progress.

Even though I was certain Hector had not left the manor house the night before, during his brother's sudden appearance, I regarded him carefully when he arrived in the kitchen for breakfast. That I found no sign of distance or preoccupation merely confirmed what should have been obvious: Dragon Guy was not the sort of man to tell anyone anything he did not need to know, especially not his younger brother. And Hector had made it clear through his words and his presence here that he did not want any part in his brother's dealings.

"Well," I said when the last of the coffee had been drunk, "we all have work to do."

I sent Hector into town to check on the roofing tiles. It had been weeks since I had heard anything.

While Mona attended to things in the kitchen, and Raoul to the grounds, I slipped quietly outside and down the steps to the villas below.

The shutters to Villa Bardot were closed, and on the patio I could see no sign of intruders. In fact, what visible evidence there was pointed to the opposite, a long period without visitors of any kind. The pool in the courtyard was dry. A cracked terra-cotta pot lay on its side on the terrace, the spilled soil long since washed away. The talonlike remains of the plant inside were no longer recognizable.

I put my ear to the door, but I could hear nothing inside. As I strained to pick up the slightest whisper of Dragon Guy, my mind instead conjured up the once ubiquitous whir of ceiling fans, the hum of the pumps in the swimming pools. There is no greater silence than the absence of familiar sounds. If I visited each and every one of the villas, I knew I would find more of the same.

Dragon Guy had left, as I had known he would. But still, that he had gotten onto the grounds at all was troubling. It could only mean that he had somewhere managed to breach the wall. My debt to the young man did not amount to an open invitation to return whenever he wished.

We needed two hours to determine that in the vicinity of the manor house nothing had been compromised. I told Raoul we were undertaking a routine inspection, something I had been planning for months. I left out any mention of Dragon Guy. Raoul did as I asked. Being, however, unaware of the urgency, he did so without enthusiasm. I frequently had to control my own anxiety to avoid arousing his suspicion.

But with the grounds so heavily wooded, large portions of the wall proved inaccessible, frustrating much of our efforts. After several hours, we discovered that a coconut palm had fallen upon the wall near the southernmost villas—a likely casualty of the storm a month before. Even there, though, the stones had held. Wanting to take no chances, I sent Raoul for the ax, and I carried on alone.

A short distance into the forest preserve, I reached the fork where the main trail branched off into several smaller ones. As I stood there considering which direction I might choose, I could not help thinking of Madame and of our morning meetings there on the bench. I could imagine her still, in her recklessly long yellow dresses, which somehow remained yellow despite the untidiness of the paths. And her giant stick, the wood as dark as pitch, and heavier than anything I would have thought her capable of carrying. I knew I must do anything I could to ensure that nothing more happened here to put the estate at risk.

The realization came to me quickly that none of the trails in the preserve would bring me close enough to the perimeter for me to be able to get to the wall. And I could see already that the inspection would take several days to complete, and repairs several more. In the meantime, there would be little to keep Dragon Guy from coming back.

When I returned to the manor house, I could hear Hector in the kitchen talking to Mona. He was telling her a story about one of his friends, but he could not stop laughing long enough for me to make any sense of it. He was a puzzle to me, this boy who stubbornly persisted in being so carefree. Every day the only world he had ever known fell a little bit more to pieces, and he responded with a smile. It occurred to me that he was more than a little like Paul. They both had an abiding faith that things would always work out for the best. I could only hope that Hector put his faith to better use.

"He wasn't home," Hector said when I asked about the tiles.

"Where is he?"

He looked at me with a crooked smile, as if expecting me to see the absurdity of the question. "How should I know?"

"Go see if Raoul needs help," I said, and I told him about the fallen tree. "When you finish, come see me. Our lesson today will hav to be brief. I have another important job for you."

Hector hopped to his feet and drained the glass with an untidy glug.

"Mona," I said once he was gone, "I'll need you to clean up Villa Bardot."

She looked up from her chopping in annoyed surprise. "Are you expecting guests?"

"Just please see to it," I said. I told her I would take lunch in my office.

Despite the exhausting work of cutting up and carting away the fallen tree, Hector appeared restless. He sat impatiently at the edge of the chair opposite my desk, looking as though he might at any moment spring out.

"Do you remember where we left off yesterday?"

Hector wrenched the book from somewhere in the back of his pants. It was folded nearly in half, the pages torn and stained with sweat.

"What happened to the cover?" I asked, reaching out for the book.

"It fell off."

"Where? Perhaps we can fix it."

Hector shrugged. "It got lost."

"Maybe you should leave the book here between lessons," I said. "Before it gets completely destroyed."

Hector snatched the book from my grip. "It's mine."

"But why do you need to have it with you when you're out on the grounds, getting filthy?"

"We take breaks," he said. "I practice."

I smiled to show him I was pleased, but he continued to eye me warily, as if convinced I would once again try to take it away.

The book was by no means precious. I had found it in a box full of things guests had left behind over the years, a small, cheaply made paperback. Judging from the few pages I had read with Hector, it was a silly tale about an encounter between a downed pilot lost in the desert and a boy from outer space. I assumed it must have belonged to a child. Ridiculous, but it was the only thing I had on hand that Hector stood any chance of deciphering.

"Show me what you've been practicing."

Momentarily lowering his guard, Hector fanned through the pages, racing forward and then tracking back, until he found the one he was looking for. It was not far from the beginning.

"Go ahead," I said.

Hector ran his tongue across his lips. "Please," he sounded out slowly. "Draw . . . me . . . a . . . sheep."

"Very good," I said. "Go on."

Hector read another line or two, and then I asked if there were any words he had come across that he did not understand.

"What's an . . . app-a-ri-tion?"

"It's something like a vision," I said. "Something that appears as if out of nowhere."

"Oh."

I slid a piece of paper before him. "Let's try some letters."

Despite my best efforts, Hector still liked to clench a pencil as though it were a machete. "Like this," I showed him, positioning it between his fingers.

Tongue stabbing out of the corner of his mouth, he sketched out "H-E-C-T-O—." He had some trouble with the R, leaving the legs too far apart.

Placing my hand on top of his, I showed him how to pull the loop and legs together, making it tight. Then he tried again on his own.

"Good," I said. "Very good. But I'm afraid that's all we have time for today."

He looked at me glumly.

"We'll do more soon, I promise. But today I have a special job for you. Something very important. I need you to examine the wall around the estate," I said. "And when I say examine, I don't mean that you should find a spot in the shade to lie with one of your girlfriends."

Hector laughed happily, forgetting his disappointment. He was thrilled with the idea of being taken for a Casanova.

"There is only one way for you to do this," I said, "and that is to walk the perimeter. I have reason to believe the wall has come down somewhere." His expression had turned perfectly blank. It was true— Dragon Guy had not told him.

"I want you to find out where," I said. "It will be much quicker for you to do this from the outside. In some places you'll need to cut your own path, so bring a machete. But you should bring one anyway. You never know what you might run into outside."

"I know very well what I'll run into."

"I'm pleased to hear it," I said. "Then I expect you to accomplish this without any trouble. And if you find anything, let me know immediately."

I walked him over to the door and placed my hand on his head. "The daylight is half gone. You have only a few hours until curfew."

As I sat that evening on the balcony, going over the accounts, I could not help gazing out upon the grounds and observing that our once immaculate resort appeared now like a primitive settlement overtaken by jungle. Of course, this in itself was not new, but perhaps I already had a sense of foreboding about Dragon Guy, and it was causing me to reflect on the tenuousness of our existence here. Nor was it the first time the estate had faced such decay. Yet while I knew from experience that the damage could be undone, with each day our chances for a reversal were slipping further out of reach. I could not let them slip away completely. I could not bear the thought of letting Mme Freeman down, not after all the belief she had shown in me.

Down below I saw Mona crossing the drive with rags and a bucket, heading toward the steps to Villa Bardot. I had been so distracted by the dismal figures in the ledger that I had not realized how late it had grown. Dusk had arrived, and Dragon Guy and his companions had not returned. But when Mona reappeared at the top of the stairs no more than five minutes after descending them, I began to fear the mess Dragon Guy had left behind was so severe she would need a mop and bucket as well.

"Monsieur," Mona said, startling the ledger from my hands. I turned to find her standing in the corridor with the door open before her.

"I left your supper on the stove." She stepped back to go.

I called after her, and she stopped with what seemed to be irritation. I thought to ask where she was off to in such a hurry, but then I recalled her request for the night off to visit her ailing sister.

"Villa Bardot," I said, "were you able to put it in order?"

"There was no need." Her tone suggested I was foolish to ask such a thing. "It was just as I left it. A little dustier. Will that be all?"

If I appeared perplexed at the news, Mona showed neither interest nor concern.

"You had better get going," I said. "The curfew."

"I haven't forgotten."

I turned back to the ledger, thinking she had left, but when I looked over my shoulder a moment later, she was still standing in the doorway.

"Are you writing to your madame?" she said.

I told her I was.

"I wouldn't think what happens here would make for very interesting reading."

"Madame likes to be kept informed," I said curtly.

"And what does she say in return?"

"She is still occupied with business. But she is looking forward to coming back."

"If that's the case," Mona said, "I wonder all the more what you've been telling her. If she really knew what was happening here, she would know the safest place to be is oceans away."

"Thank you," I said with a tone that I hoped conveyed my lack of interest in her opinions. "Please shut the door behind you."

When she was gone, I once again took up my pen. If Mona could not see for herself why a person would remain forever attached to Habitation Louvois, there was nothing I could say to show her. I knew, Mme Freeman knew, and now Hector knew. As far as I was concerned, that was sufficient. Once the hotel was up and running again, Mona could take her indifference back with her to Cité Verd. There would be nothing more we would need of her.

"This morning," I wrote, "I discovered a palm tree fallen upon the wall in the vicinity of Villa Moreau, but there is no cause for concern. The wall held fast. It is an indication, I think, of the permanence of this place. The walls have lasted two hundred years, and they will last two hundred more—or at least as long as I am here to watch over them."

At night, of late, the estate had become particularly fertile ground for the superstitious mind. The quiet corridors, the empty offices, the restaurant with the chairs turned upside down on the tables, the club room draped in white sheets, the outbuildings in the courtyard vacant. The bullets only amplified the desolation.

With Mona gone, the kitchen was fully dark except for the faint glow of the fading coals deep within the belly of the charcoal stove. A single pot sat atop the grating. Inside I found a portion of rice and beans. A plate in the oven held two cassava cakes. This was what now passed for dinner.

Hours later, when the gunfire broke out, I awoke and turned my ear toward the shots. But it was nothing I had not heard a thousand times before, and a moment later I rolled over again to go back to sleep. I was drifting off amidst the clamor, prepared to give it no further thought, when suddenly I shot up in a panic, realizing I had not heard Hector return. It was now long past curfew.

Without bothering to reach for my robe, I rushed out into the hall.

There was no answer to my knock, and when I opened the door I found nothing but a mound of twisted sheets on Hector's bed.

He must have decided to stay with his aunt in Cité Verd. I told myself he would be safe there; I had no reason to worry.

And yet I worried all the same. Stepping out onto his balcony, I heard a squeal of tires and a few more shots beyond the trees. Dawn was an eternity away.

I did not expect to see Hector the next afternoon. Done properly, the inspection of the wall would take two full days, and since he had not come back during the night, it made sense that he would stay out and finish. But then darkness brought with it another curfew, and still he had not returned. All through the night I fell in and out of sleep, listening for his footsteps in the hall.

In the morning there was still no sign of Hector. Before breakfast I went to the kitchen to see if Mona had heard anything from him. She had not, and neither had either of the market women who had stopped by on their way into Cité Verd. Mona was going through their baskets, reading the face of each vegetable like a blind woman. How sad and meager, I thought, regarding what they had brought us. I could remember a time when women by the dozen had formed a line in the yard, waiting among the pigs and chickens for their turn to offer the provisions they had carried from Saint-Gabriel. With their fresh vegetables and the grains already locked in the pantries and storerooms, we could have fed all of Cité Verd. Now we merely needed enough for the ravenous Hector.

He will be fine, I told myself. He was smart and he was resourceful. No one could take care of himself better than Hector. He would be back at any moment, desperate to resume his lessons.

That night, Hector still did not return. I stayed up as late as I could, finally moving into his room when the tedium of mine began to wear on me. It was there, atop his mess of sheets, that I eventually succumbed to sleep.

Soon after I awoke to what I at first mistook for the pulses of a heavy, unexpected rain. I got up and raised the louvers to the jalousie, but there was no rain. Automatic gunfire was erupting everywhere at once.

I could not see Cité Verd for the trees. The capital was dark too, sporadic muzzle flashes the only light. I was watching the firing in the capital, but hearing the shots nearby in Cité Verd, and the discord between the two made it seem all the more unreal. However commonplace the fighting had become, it had not entirely lost its power to hypnotize.

I remained in the doorway until dawn, neither venturing onto the balcony nor retreating back to the comfort of bed.

For the next several nights, there was more of the same. And every morning I came upon Mona and the market women talking about the latest incidents. Cité Verd, they said, was turning to rubble. When, I wanted to know, had it ever been anything different?

Yet another radio station had been burned down. Bodies were piling up along the roadside faster than they could be carted away. And there was still no sign of Hector. He must be lying low, I decided, waiting for the worst to pass. And then he would spring on me at the moment I least expected it. And how he would laugh, delighted to have caught me by surprise.

Almost a week into Hector's disappearance, more barricades went up. The smoke of burning tires, a dizzying petroleum stench, wafted across the valley. Finally a sickening smell to complement the sickening sights and sounds.

"Dear Madame," I wrote, sitting at my desk that night with a cloth to my mouth and nose, only a candle to see by,

> *I am sorry for the lengthy gap between this letter and the one I sent you a week ago. As you have perhaps read in your newspapers, we are currently experiencing some tension. As a consequence, many of the repairs I mentioned have not yet been completed. There is no reason, however, for you to be concerned. We are safe here, as we have always been. We wait anxiously for peace and for the resumption of business as we knew it.*

The boys standing along the road glanced at me with indifference as I leaned up against the gate to get a view. I had waited until the sun had risen to come outside. The trees and underbrush along the road—and even the road itself—were slightly wet with dew and looked almost as though they had been washed and left out to dry. The boys, however, appeared not to have washed in weeks.

Perhaps ten meters up the road lay two felled trees and a wall of junk—rickety wooden tables and chairs piled upon one another, legs sticking out in every direction, like the nest of a monstrous bird. Beyond the barricade, a pyramid of molten tires continued to smolder. An odd place for a blockade, I thought. Surely they could not be expecting an invasion from the mountains.

I recognized none of the boys. They were young, many no more than Hector's age. They seemed bored, squatting on stumps discarded at the side of the road, which was everywhere littered with damp, glistening garbage.

"What are you doing here?" I asked.

A boy with a gap between his front teeth raised his head. Some sort of rifle hung from a strap over his shoulder. "What does it look like we're doing?"

"But why must you do it here?"

The gap-toothed boy turned back to his friends, sharing with them a crazy-eyed look intended as an imitation of me. I was amazed by the way he moved, as if the rifle were just another appendage, something he had been carrying all his life. He seemed unaware that it was even there; I could think of little else.

"I don't want you here."

I heard a small rock ping against the metal gate. Across the road a boy who could have been no more than twelve sifted through the dirt and stones in his hand for something else to throw. A pistol poked out of the back of his shorts, dark and grubby, as if it were an abused toy. "What makes you think we care?"

"This is my house," I said. "I live here."

The gap-toothed boy planted his feet firmly beneath himself. "This is our road. We live *here*."

"Besides"—the twelve-year-old paused to wing another pebble off the gate—"that's not your house. That's a white woman's house. You're just her servant."

To hear them laughing, clutching their stomachs as they rocked forward and back, one would have thought it was the funniest thing they had ever heard. The young one beamed with satisfaction.

I realized now that all of them were armed, in one way or another. More rifles leaned against the barricade, as casual as broomsticks. On top of a boulder balanced someone's machine gun, like a demonic lizard soaking up the sun.

"Will you still be laughing tonight," I asked, "when I'm asleep in my bed and you're curled up in the gravel?"

"He got you," the gap-toothed boy cackled with glee, roughing up the younger one's head.

The other boys were silent. I was surprised that not a single one of them made a move toward his weapon. No one's pistol cocked. It was as if the novelty of the guns had already worn off, and they had no interest even in frightening me. Perhaps they figured I was not worth the trouble.

"Do any of you know Hector?" I said. "He works here, at the estate."

The gap-toothed boy strutted forward, as if suddenly wishing to make it clear he was in charge. "He'll be back tonight."

"Was he here last night?"

The boy shrugged. Perhaps those were his orders—that he was to say nothing about the defenses, even to the point of revealing who would man them.

"If you see him," I said, "tell him I've been looking for him. I need to know he's safe."

⌗

Despite the roadblock, the roofing tiles I had been waiting months for finally arrived. Further proof of how impossible it was to predict what pieces of normalcy would continue amid the chaos. The deliverymen unloaded half of the tiles in the courtyard outside Villa Leigh. The rest they dumped on the garden path running beside Villa Bernhardt.

We could no longer afford to wait for Hector. That afternoon, Raoul and I carried a ladder from the back shed down a dozen flights of stairs overgrown with creeper, the shoots of which grew tangled with the rungs at every turn. For so dirty a job, I had found a set of old clothes folded together on a shelf in the former servants' quarters. I assumed they had belonged to the same person, but I realized I was mistaken as soon as I tried them on. The shirt must have belonged to one of the houseboys, for it was especially tight around the arms, making it difficult for me to hold the ladder high upon my shoulder. The overalls were a different matter; I had rolled them so many times the cuffs hung like weights around my ankles.

The roof of Villa Leigh was only mildly graded, allowing Raoul to move about with ease. He removed the broken tiles, and then together we mixed the mortar. I found a way to raise the bucket to him using the arm of an overhanging calabash tree as a pulley. It worked so well that I used the same method to get him the tiles.

We stopped just once, when Mona brought us lunch. Years had passed since I had last labored like this, but I found I did not mind the soreness in my muscles. By the time we had finished the roof it was evening, and we decided we would have to save the roof of Villa Bernhardt for tomorrow.

As we made our way back up the stairs toward the drive, I thought I heard voices. The commotion grew louder as we neared the guesthouse. A breeze must have picked up just then, because the moment I stepped onto the drive the stench of burning tires forced its thick, coarse fingers down my throat.

The twilight fires—the burning barricades. As constant and dependable as anything in nature. It was as if God himself had decreed this new flame as a stand-in for the setting sun, an essential element of our survival.

"Is that him?" I said, cocking my ear toward the gate. From that distance it was impossible to tell if one of the voices belonged to Hector. When Raoul failed to answer, I turned to find him, and he was gone.

"I think I heard Hector," I told Mona when I arrived at the kitchen.

She glanced up from the chicken she was gutting just long enough to shake her head. "That boy's going to find himself dead."

"I'm going to talk to him," I said.

"You do that, you'll find yourself dead." Then came the stare that withered any possibility of debate. "The only thing to do is to stay out of it."

"How can we stay out of it? They're right outside the gate."

Mona did not bother even to acknowledge the question. She had already said everything she had to say.

While she finished cooking, I went out to the terrace and stood against the balustrade overlooking the pool. The night was relatively cool for a change, and after the exhausting day I found it relaxing to look past the shimmering water to the orchid garden, just visible in the fading light. Even from afar—even in its current state of neglect—the garden reminded me of the beauty that had once existed everywhere on the estate. And in her absence, it was the gardens, more than anything else, that reminded me of Madame.

In designing and laying out the hotel grounds, the engineer and the architects had taken great care to preserve the natural surroundings. But Madame, true to her nature, had insisted upon a few exceptions, and she was not to be dissuaded. She carved out space in the indigenous landscape for her gardens—the cactus garden, the water garden, the orchid garden, and of course her rose garden, which both the engineer and the head gardener had said would be impossible to grow in this climate. She proved them wrong. She was always proving them wrong. The gardens were exactly what the estate needed, places where she could cultivate beauty according to her own taste and dictate what she would—and would not—permit to grow. And when the guests had ventured from their villas—which they did only rarely—they strolled not to the daunting forest preserve down below but to Madame's immaculately manicured gardens.

The last of the sunlight quickly faded, and soon I could make out nothing but the garden's general contours. The peace I had felt just a few minutes before was waning, and the noise at the barricade outside the gate was growing louder. It was too dangerous to go out there now. I would have to wait until morning.

Raoul did not appear for dinner. I ate alone on the terrace. More to the point, I sat at a table with a plate of food in front of me. Never had I felt less hungry.

After dinner I retired to my rooms, and although I had intended to write Madame to let her know of our progress with the roof of Villa Leigh, my thoughts kept returning to what was happening outside.

For several hours, the gunfire was continual. So too was the squealing of tires and the racing of engines, and I guessed that one of the barricades had been breached. As best I could tell without going outside, the one outside the gate stood firm. I heard little more from the boys out there than occasional shouts.

In recent months I had learned to concentrate in such a way that I could now tell the direction from which the firing of each machine gun came, even as it echoed through the valley. After the first few mysterious explosions, I had come to distinguish the charge of grenades.

I could follow the shifting of gears through the streets of Cité Verd, past the burned-out church, the phone company, the public well, even though it had been two years since I had traveled those streets myself.

And late that night, as shots crackled through Cité Verd and more distantly through the towns closer to the capital, my ear was drawn to the conspicuous sound of a car speeding up the road toward the estate, straining in low gear. I was not the only one who heard it coming.

Down at the barricade there arose a frenzy of shouting. A moment later came a hail of thuds and the shattering of glass. The car skidded to a stop and there was more shouting, and it was astonishing how loud the shouting grew, as if all of Cité Verd had descended upon the barricade. But one voice soon rose above the others, apart from the others, a scream of unspeakable agony. I opened the shutters and stepped onto the balcony, and over the top of the wall, a few meters from the gate, I saw a burst of light and smoke accompanied by a rumble of cheers.

That one horrible scream lingered and lingered, even after it had gone away.

I fell into bed then and slept for a couple of hours. When I awoke, the sun was up.

Mona had left a plate of breakfast covered outside my door, but I had no time to eat.

As I neared the top of the drive I saw shards of sunlight reflecting off something on the other side of the gate. A car, I supposed. I heard a surprising number of voices, and I was hopeful one of them might be Hector's.

As it turned out, it was not *a* car I had seen from the bottom of the driveway, but a whole fleet of them. And I counted nearly a dozen white people—almost all of them men—milling about. A few meters up the road, just before the barricade, the shell of an army jeep smoldered, everything but the metal having already burned away. The dusty gray road below the four melted tires had turned black. But the object that had captured the interest of the photographers gathered there was a dark mass propped up against the barricade. It looked like a sack of grain covered in soot. But why, I wondered, would they be interested in such a thing? It was only then that I noticed the head at rest in the middle of the road. It, too, was charred beyond recognition. I could not bear to look for the arms and legs.

The photographers all wore the same vest, upon which there were as many pockets as teeth on a zipper. Their cameras clicked and clicked and clicked.

Off to the side stood the boys I had seen manning the barricade the day before. They were watching over the scene, as if supervising. Their weapons sat in a harmless pile in the grass. Every last one of them dangled a lit cigarette between his lips. I was no stranger to the scent of foreign tobacco.

As if we had gathered here for a cocktail party, the gap-toothed boy sauntered over.

"You missed him." The boy blew a disintegrating thread of smoke through his teeth. "Hector was here all night, just like I told you."

"You're mistaken," I said. "You must be thinking of another Hector."

The photographers continued to bend over the body.

I had to look away. "Mine could not have had anything to do with this."

The boy took a long drag on his cigarette, staring at me blankly, as if inhaling required every last scrap of his concentration. Then he chuckled, coughing up clouds of smoke. "Maybe you don't know him like you think you do," he said as he walked away to join his friends. "Makes no difference to me."

Chapter Twenty-Two

As I should have guessed, among the followers Dragon Guy brought with him when he returned was Hector.

For me the night of their arrival was long and sleepless. I passed the hours on the balcony, listening to the voices and the movement down below. I saw curious shadows rising up the stairs beside the guesthouse, looking around, and then descending again. I could not tell how many there were, but the procession seemed endless. One after another they came. There was a peculiar orderliness about it, as if they had bought tickets and queued up for their turn. Everyone seemed to understand they could approach no closer than the drive; it was the velvet rope, and the manor house the priceless piece of art.

To my own surprise, I felt oddly at peace. It was as if I had known all along that this was coming. I did not welcome them—even as I watched them cycle up and down the stairs, I already understood I would have to do everything I could to make them leave. But the struggle itself and their appearance here produced in me a calming sense of the inevitable.

The next morning, Hector appeared at my office door, and by the way his eyes refused to meet mine I could tell he had not volunteered to come see me.

"Why, Hector?" I said. "Why would you do this?" But even as the words left my mouth, I understood this was not the same boy I had so recently invited here.

The differences were apparent everywhere on his body, from the new tears in his jersey to the rounding of his shoulders, which seemed burdened with fatigue and responsibility. He must have noticed I was tired too.

"We'll be using the villas," he said. He was trying to sound forceful, but he came off hoarse and uncertain. It had been less than two years since I had pulled him in off the street, and I nearly felt bad for him, this boy suddenly compelled to be a man.

"Which villas?" I said, already preparing for the worst.

"All of them."

"Not Madame's . . ."

For the first time, his eyes met mine. They contained in them something I had never seen there before. He might have called it strength and determination. To me it looked like desperation.

"All of them."

"What about your lessons? Everything was going so well." I took a step toward him, and he took a step back. "There's still so much for you to learn."

"What's the point?" He knotted his arms across his chest. "What good would it do me?"

"What do you mean?"

"What good has it ever done you?"

"It's given me a better life."

His eyes were full of pity. "You're just a servant."

"But you," I said, "you could be so much more."

He had already turned his back to me.

"He will destroy it, Hector," I said. "Your brother will destroy everything. You're not like him."

Hector opened the door, but instead of passing through, he paused on the threshold, still holding on to the knob, as if he needed its cold support. "It'll be destroyed either way."

And then the door was slowly swinging closed. "What about Raoul?" I said.

"He's with us."

It took me several tries, pushing and pulling on the heavy steel handle, before I realized the door to the kitchen was locked. Until then I had been unaware the door even possessed a lock.

"Mona!" I yelled.

"Who is it?" she said, softly but urgently from what sounded like a position just on the other side of the wall.

"Me."

"How do I know it's you?"

"Because you can hear my voice."

I heard rustling on the other side. "I need proof," she said.

After the events of the morning I had little patience for this. "Let me in," I demanded, pounding my fist against the door.

"Name the villas," she said.

"What?"

"The villas all have names," she said. "What are they?"

"There are forty of them," I said, hammering now with both fists. "You want me to name them all?"

"Forty-four," she corrected.

"Villa Bardot," I began with a sigh. "Villa Bernhardt, Villa Bacall, Villa Garbo . . ."

I started with the villas closest to the manor house and moved on from there. I had named perhaps twenty of them when I finally heard a heavy scraping and then the door swung open. Before I had a chance to step forward, Mona had reached out and grabbed my arm. She pulled me in, and as I passed the threshold I saw in her other hand a hefty steel bar, which she immediately heaved back into place.

Inside, the kitchen was even darker than usual, the only light filtering down from the small dusty windows in the ceiling. Buckets quivering with water crowded an entire counter. On the tables and in a corner of the floor Mona had stacked and stuffed everything we normally stored in the pantry: sacks of beans and corn and rice and sweet potatoes.

"What is the meaning of this?"

"I told you this would happen," she said as she returned to whatever she had been doing. "But you knew better. You didn't listen."

"What did you want me to do?"

She shrugged, exaggerating her sense of defeat. "It's too late now."

"I didn't ask them to come."

"You didn't tell them not to."

"How was I supposed—"

"If you want them to stay," she interrupted, pointing to me—as if there might be some confusion as to whom she was speaking—"that's your choice. But I'm not going to feed them."

"Did they come looking for food?"

"Let them try." From a nail on the lattice where all of her utensils hung, Mona selected a heavy knife. "They won't get a grain of millet from me," she said, halving an eggplant with a single blow.

Across the room I saw several small, twitchy shadows scratching along the floor, pecking at something. She had brought even the chickens inside.

"Not a pinch of flour," Mona said. "Nothing."

I spent the rest of the day in my rooms, pacing out to the balcony and back.

That night, like every night for the past several months, gunfire spat and pattered and the tires at the roadblocks burned. In the dark I saw muzzle flashes and ghostly shrouds of smoke. The men on the streets, including those outside our gate, clung to their barricades. Nothing seemed any different from before, except that I had lost Hector, and I could see no easy way to get him back.

Did Dragon Guy's appearance at Habitation Louvois mean he was in retreat? That seemed unlikely. The more I thought about it, the more certain I became that he was here to regroup, to prepare for some even larger battle to come. In Cité Verd, no matter how many barricades he built, there was no way to keep his enemies out. The place was too big, too exposed. Here he had walls and trees to give him cover and protection. President Duphay's army had its barracks. Now Dragon Guy's did too.

And I feared I had every reason to believe they were here to stay.

For several days, I remained in my rooms. Lethargy fell upon me like a fever, and I slept as I had not slept since I was a child. Some of those days I forgot to go to Mona, and since she would not come to me, on those days I ate almost nothing at all.

Despite Dragon Guy's proximity, I had no idea what was happening down below. The villas were invisible to me, hidden beneath the canopy of trees. Whatever they were doing was so well concealed that for short stretches I was able to forget they were even here. And that seemed to be the way they wanted it. It was as if we had come to a mutual understanding: west of the tree line behind the guesthouse was theirs; east was mine. I could see the preserve from my balcony, but I could no longer go there.

Though they remained entirely out of sight, I did occasionally hear them. Voices sometimes, but mostly prosaic sounds: chopping, hammering. They were sounds of construction, sounds of people making themselves a permanent home.

And as time passed, the noise grew louder. I could only assume that meant more of them kept arriving. But how many? One hundred? Two? It was impossible to know.

There were days that passed without my ever leaving the balcony.

I searched in desperation for any sign of Hector, still hoping I might be able to change his mind, if only I could talk to him again. Perhaps his brother feared just that, and that was why Hector was forced to stay away.

For hours at a time I watched the shimmering waves in the bay or the tossing of treetops, and the whole world—everywhere but here—appeared to be at peace.

I did not know what happened to the days and weeks other than that they slipped away and another took their place. Yet eventually even this new life grew routine. Gradually I began to leave my rooms, roaming about the manor house for signs of intruders.

One morning I found myself in the library, leafing through books I had never thought to pick up before. I discovered a collection of travel volumes—stories of voyages to the Far East, expeditions to the frozen North. And there was more than one volume of journeys to the exotic tropics. In vain I turned every page, looking for mention of Habitation Louvois. After everything we had accomplished here, was it possible the only records were the ones I myself had kept? Was I the only hope of preserving its memory?

That afternoon, with an urgency I had not felt since before Hector's disappearance, I picked up pen and paper.

"Do you remember," I wrote to Madame,

the visit from M. Gaetano, the cellist? He was a remarkable man, with hair like a flame tree. He was traveling with the smallest dog I had ever seen. I will never forget that day by the manor house pool when he gave an impromptu performance, and the guests came from across the estate, even the waiters and houseboys and maids. Everyone stopped to listen. It was the sort of magic we came to expect. Habitation Louvois was a place where things like that just happened, as if in a dream. We must never forget, so that when the time comes, we can create it again, even better than it was.

When I finished I laid my head upon the desk, utterly drained. I still believed every word, but the belief was taking its toll.

With no one attending to it, the manor house soon fell into neglect, accruing filth to such a degree that it could no longer be ignored. I did what work I could, sweeping, dusting, keeping things in order, all duties Mona had relinquished. I no longer saw her except at mealtimes. I took to brewing my own morning coffee in the restaurant kitchen, eliminating one tiresome daily round of having to prove to her that I was who I said I was. She had reluctantly given me a small sack of beans, warning me that I had better guard them, as I would get no more.

After Hector's first visit, he never returned. Of Raoul I saw not a sign. Still, a part of me would not accept that they had abandoned me. I knew how much the estate meant to Hector and how it must pain him to see his brother trample through it as if it were just another slum. And I knew how much Hector had come to depend on his lessons. I could not believe that he would give it all up, having come so far. But Hector was young, and the bonds of brotherhood were strong. My only hope was that he would come to his senses before his brother inflicted damage upon us that could not be undone.

Then there was Raoul. Never had I known anyone more stubborn. According to Mona, Dragon Guy could convince the devil himself to do good. Given what his followers considered good, that was perhaps not such a stretch, but if there was any truth to Dragon Guy's persuasive powers, Raoul was the proof.

Despite our situation, the two market women continued showing up each morning with produce. Mona taught them a secret knock. It was the only way, she said, for her to know it was them and not one of the intruders. There was also a slight variation on the knock, which the market women were to use in case they were taken hostage. Mona was leaving nothing to chance.

I was not given the option of a secret knock. Mona said she was afraid of her system becoming too complicated. I suggested a password, but she argued it would be too easy to overhear, given that Dragon Guy was likely to have spies watching and listening nearby. Instead, she tested me with trivia. If it was not the naming of the villas, it was something else having to do with the history of the estate. I decided not to point out to her that Raoul and Hector knew as much of the history as she did, and that they too could likely answer anything she might ask; I feared the security measures she would put in place if she knew.

"Have Hector and Raoul come for food?" I asked her one afternoon as I sat at the kitchen table eating lunch.

"Let them come," she said. "I wouldn't give them even a grain of rice."

And as she said it I felt a twinge of worry for the boy. Who was taking care of him? Who was seeing to it that he got what he needed? Who among them would understand how special he was?

As for Dragon Guy and his men, they were getting food somehow, that much was clear. By now they had been here nearly three weeks.

Sometimes I awoke suddenly in the night, thinking of something important I needed Hector and Raoul to attend to. Once I sprang up in a panic realizing I had neglected to ask Hector if his inspection of the wall had been a success. Another time it occurred to me that Raoul and I had never gotten a chance to finish installing the roofing tiles. It never took long for reality to set in, and when it did, I often sat up for hours, unable to fall back to sleep, imagining with dread Dragon Guy's followers resting their dirty heads and dirty feet upon Madame's clean beds.

It was a peculiar feeling to be so surrounded and also so isolated. More than once I was embarrassed to find myself engaging in imaginary debates with Hector or his brother or Raoul or one of the other men whose names I did not know and had never met, haranguing them about the various outrages they were perpetrating against Madame's estate.

But the most disconcerting moment of all came one morning, perhaps a month after their arrival, when I arrived downstairs shortly after dawn to discover Dragon Guy sitting on a chaise longue in the foyer. Hearing my footsteps, he looked up and smiled. It had been so long since I had seen anyone that at first I was convinced I must be dreaming.

But then to my consternation Dragon Guy came to life, stirring as I approached. It was as if he had been waiting there for me.

"Good morning, monsieur," he said in that incongruously soft voice of his. He pulled himself up into a sitting position. "This is quite a place you have here."

He leaned forward, and the flaps of his jacket opened. There again was his tattoo, an angry, skulking smear of color slathered across his chest. Whereas before I had caught just a glimpse, now I was granted a view of its full, terrible glory. It was green and red and blue and black, spiraling from his heart and sliding who-knew-how-far down past the waistline of his pants. A dragon, of course.

Seeing me staring, he took hold of his lapels and pulled the jacket all the way open, past his shoulders, and it slid down his back, leaving only his forearms covered. "You can come closer, if you want."

Even from where I stood the details were astonishing: individual scales that appeared to burst from his skin, and white, daggered teeth that were wet with saliva. The dragon's head was turned toward the left, belching a torrent of flame down Dragon Guy's arm.

Only now, as I looked more closely, did I see a few imperfections, spots where the ink seemed displaced or discolored. Without meaning to, I did take another step toward him, and I realized the flaws were not in the tattoo, but in the skin underneath. There were scars everywhere. Not just beneath the dragon, but on Dragon Guy's unpainted right side as well, from his collarbone to his belly and all up and down his arms. I could not conceive of where he had gotten them all. A man could not survive so many wounds. And he was in only his early twenties.

"When I was younger," he said, pressing gingerly on one of the jagged tracks, "I was reckless."

Younger? I thought. Starting when he was still on his mother's breast? "And now?"

"I'm grateful every day to be alive. Aren't you?"

Despite my failure to supply an answer, he nodded somberly, as if we were the sort of men who could agree on a great many things.

"When I was young I wasted a lot of time." He wrinkled his nose in my direction, giving his nostrils a flare. "What do you think when you look back on how you've spent your life?"

"Are you a therapist, too?"

Dragon Guy folded his arms across his chest and held himself for a moment in an awkward embrace. From where I stood, it looked as if he were strangling the dragon.

I realized I should stick with simpler words if I wished for him to follow. "What do you want?"

He came toward me slowly, dragging his fingers sleepily across the top of his head. He had that gift, so common among thugs and murderers and despots—that calm facade of humanity that obscured his true ruthlessness. He could be terrifying and charming all at the same time. "Want?"

"What do you expect to accomplish with this army of yours?"

He seemed to find the question funny, laughing with his eyes. "It's not an army."

"No?"

He looked at me with an infuriating earnestness. "It's just people."

"People with guns."

He shrugged, still smiling. "Sometimes people need guns."

We had clearly reached the limits of his philosophy.

"What about your brother?" I asked. "Why couldn't you let him be?"

"Hector made his decision."

"Bullshit," I spat.

Dragon Guy shrugged. "You wanted him to be like you. You wanted to turn him into a gentleman. This is no place for a gentleman."

"Maybe not out there." I gestured toward Cité Verd. "But it is in here."

Dragon Guy glanced around the lobby, a bemused look on his face. "Did you really think your world was different from mine?"

"I know it was," I said. "It still is."

Dragon Guy sauntered over to the open door of the library. "There's only one thing we want," he said, gazing lazily inside. "We want democracy. We want to be able to live in peace."

"What about my peace?"

"You're one of us now," he said. "Aren't you?"

I had to look up to meet his eyes. "You know very well that I'm not."

"No," he admitted. "I guess not. You still belong to that white woman."

"I don't belong to anyone."

He exhaled deeply, and his cold breath swept across my brow. "In that case, monsieur, I feel very sorry for you."

At the door Black Max was waiting. Upon reaching him, Dragon Guy placed his hand on his partner's shoulder and leaned in to whisper something. They descended the stairs together, and I could sense that they had already decided my fate.

That night, guns tore through the valley with the strength of a hurricane, and I awoke with a chill, thinking not of Hector nor of Raoul, nor even of Dragon Guy, but of Madame's orchid garden. It had been months, I realized, since anyone had tended to it.

For the rest of the night, as the sky above the trees flickered and trembled, the idea would not leave me. Against Dragon Guy's drive to destroy the estate, the garden was as good a place as any to take a stand.

The next morning, I was sitting on the terrace drinking coffee and looking through one of Madame's old gardening books. The pages were sweeping past me in a blur, and I had begun to feel increasingly sorry for the flowers, with me as their only hope. My appreciation for green and wild things was unmatched by any kind of skill or instinct for caring for them. Even with the vegetables and herbs I had tended during the period before the hotel opened, it had been a struggle for survival. As

with everything else, whatever my father had learned during his childhood in the fields, I had failed to inherit.

I finished my coffee, and I was about to give up when I happened to
raise my eyes and glance off toward the pool, and that was when I saw
Raoul, dressed as always in his denims and his blue plaid shirt. He stood
with his back to me, partially bent over, as if studying his reflection in
the water. When I yelled his name, he seemed not to hear. I yelled again
and he straightened up, reaching around to ease the pain in his back.
Then he began to walk away from me down the path, his unbuttoned
shirt trailing behind him. Gazing up at the sky as he went, his steps
slow and tentative, he appeared lost. I called out to him again as I hurried down the steps. But by the time I reached the pool, I had lost sight
of him. I called out again. There was no response, not even the crunch
of footsteps trailing away down the path.

"I don't need you," I yelled. If need be, I would save the estate entirely on my own.

For the next several days I dedicated myself to the orchids, spending all of the morning and much of the afternoon in the garden, weeding and cleaning away dead leaves and flowers. It was difficult at first,
but I found the work largely peaceful. Aside from the distant gurgling
of the water pump for the pool, I was surrounded by silence. Often, as
I worked, I found myself putting down my tools and turning my head
to listen whenever I heard a sound, no matter how faint. At least once a
day I thought I heard someone approaching, but I could never be sure
if it was that or something else, or if it was entirely in my imagination.
I began to wonder if it was Hector, wanting to be near me but afraid of
getting caught. After all these weeks apart, maybe he was realizing the
mistake he had made. Maybe he was looking for a way to come back.

I was pleased to be able to write to Madame about the progress
I was making.

Of course, I am too poor a gardener to give the orchids the full care they deserve, but already I can see the results of my efforts. The flowers are happier now, and each morning I can feel their relief at seeing me return. They may not fully appreciate my skill, but they cannot help but acknowledge my commitment. I will be sorry when Raoul completes his current tasks and is able to take over their care once again.

On the day I finished my work in the orchid garden, I was in the shed putting away the tools, and once again I thought I could hear the sound of footsteps approaching. For several minutes, until well after the sound went away, I stayed inside, looking out the window. No one was there.

The path to Villa Moreau was badly overgrown, and it was difficult to move without brushing against vines and low-hanging branches. I had to go slowly, ducking and squeezing around the foliage, making as little noise as possible. I was sure this was the direction from which the sound had come.

As I neared a bend in the path, I saw a flash of color and something suddenly came rushing toward my head. There was a cutting buzz through the air, a blur, and I threw out my hands in defense, tearing my thumb on a thorn.

I opened my eyes. A hummingbird rose from a hibiscus blossom with a gentle thrum, hovering there a moment before zipping back across the path. A tiny bird, nothing more.

Villa Moreau lay fifty meters away, hidden by trees. From forty meters I could see a corner of the roof, and I began to approach even more cautiously. At thirty meters the view was no better. At twenty I spotted a shutter covering one of the windows. At ten I could just peek into the empty courtyard.

What surprised me most was the quiet. I could no longer hear the sound that had drawn me here; I could hear nothing at all. Perhaps it was the quiet that lulled me into ignoring the danger of what I was doing. I kept going, turning off the path and down the steps, and then I stood in the courtyard, several paces from the empty pool, and I could see the jalousies of Villa Moreau and its three neighbors, and I could tell none of them had been opened.

It was thus by accident that I discovered Hector had lied when he said Dragon Guy had taken over all of the villas. In fact, in the coming days I learned he had occupied only those to the west and north. But why? The only difference was their proximity to the manor house. It was as if he were afraid of getting too close to me.

I felt something that had been constricting my chest for weeks suddenly loosen ever so slightly.

Around and around the four villas I crept, circling them one at a time, pacing up and down the paths. I had no idea what I was looking for, and yet I was certain there was something here to be found.

A few minutes later I was staring off into the trees surrounding Villa Moreau, beyond which lurked our once-impenetrable wall. It occurred to me that this was the very place where Raoul and I, while looking for the spot where the wall had been breached, had come upon the fallen tree. Fearing damage to the wall, I had ordered Raoul and Hector to remove the tree. In order to do so, they had been forced to clear a path.

It was to the path that my mind immediately raced.

Before I realized what I was doing, I had thrown myself at the brush. In an instant I was through.

There was the path, just as they had left it, only mildly overgrown.

The path, I now discovered—as if I had known all along—led not just to where the tree had fallen, but to a clearing along the wall, a spot where the ground was barren of trees and underbrush. The clearing was in fact more like a corridor; although narrow, it continued for some distance, before coming to an end in a cul-de-sac of densely packed trees just behind Villa Bacall. Villa Bacall was in one of the groups of villas just south of Villa Moreau, and it was one of the villas in which Dragon Guy's men were living.

Without meaning to, I had discovered a secret passageway behind enemy lines.

Chapter Twenty-Three

In the beginning I went out each morning at dawn. Camouflaged among the trees, I watched the courtyard outside Villa Bacall. Each morning I waited hours, sometimes until the early afternoon, before anyone appeared.

Having spent the night fighting, they were apparently not inclined to be early risers.

After a few days, I changed my approach. I began arriving in the afternoon, giving them time to rest. Crouched still and silent, I felt like a predator lying in wait of his prey. Although, in every other way, I continued to feel it was the other way around, that I was the one being hunted.

Eventually, a few at a time, they would shuffle outside with yawns and scratches and commence building fires in the courtyard. They had constructed a ring of stone not far from the pool. In it they tossed their trash and kindling and anything they found in the villas that did not suit their fancy: picture frames, shelves, hangers, drawers, even the doors of cupboards. When it came to fuel, they seemed to have a special fondness for books.

In one of the villas lived several middle-aged women. I had not been expecting women, and their presence was anything but a pleasant surprise. The last thing I had wanted to find were further signs that they were already pursuing domestic arrangements.

The women seemed to be in charge of an enormous tin pot they kept on one side of the fire. They had flat iron pans for cassava bread, and there was a wooden pestle and mortar with which they ground corn.

They had cut down some of the trees and shrubs around the villas to make room for small vegetable gardens. Now I knew at least one of the ways in which they were getting food.

Over the course of several days I counted approximately two dozen people in all, five or six for Villa Bacall and each of its three neighbors. From my spot among the trees I could hear more voices, more activity in the villas to the west and north. In my head I did the math: if what I saw here were the same elsewhere, there must be more than two hundred of them.

I came later and later in the day, after everyone had already come outside. I watched the women working in the gardens and I saw men returning from somewhere with baskets loaded with breadfruit and avocados, buckets with water. Their conversations were as dull as anything one might overhear passing through the market.

Everywhere I looked, men and boys with rigid faces sat cross-legged on the ground, sharpening machetes and cleaning their guns.

One day I arrived toward dusk, later than I ever had before, and it seemed everyone was gone. Had they already left to take up their positions at the barricade? The women too? For ten, twenty, thirty minutes I waited, just in case, but still no one appeared.

I approached Villa Bisset first, crouching behind the half-wall when I reached the terrace. The jalousies were closed and the louvers lowered, but gradually, a bit at a time, I worked at the louver with my fingernail, until there was just enough of a gap that I could see inside: a broad expanse of tiles, the canopy bed, the sunken tub, the settee. Everything was more or less as I had seen it last, a few months before. The only difference was the clutter: several bottles of rum, a straw hat, a machete, a pot and bowl. I had hoped to find something of Hector's—his book or one of his other few belongings, but there was no trace of him.

I was relieved to see the men had so far done the place no harm. And yet, it was impossible to look upon their belongings and not realize that they had already come to think of this as home.

How could they look upon this place and feel they belonged? Polished wood. Polished stone. The only coarse element was the men themselves. How could they not see that? How could they settle so easily in a place where they were not wanted?

All through the night, even as I slept, I could think of nothing other than the men in Madame's villas. They invaded my dreams as rudely as they had invaded my life, floating in and out of the rooms of the manor house while I, hopelessly anchored to the floor, could do nothing but thrash my arms, clawing at the air. As I tossed and turned in bed, the corner of the sheet wrapped around my neck like a noose.

For several days I did not venture from my rooms in the manor house. I could hardly bear to look out the window, afraid of the new horrors that might at any moment present themselves there. I spent most of these hours in bed, neither exactly asleep nor awake. If anything, it felt more like a fever state, brought on by a desperate desire to disappear from the material world.

During this time I must not have eaten, for Mona remained locked up in the kitchen. Outside there was a constant stench of smoke, a dense burn originating from something other than the tires and the cooking fires. Try as I might, I could not understand what it was. Even Cité Verd could not supply enough trash to fuel so steady a conflagration.

In one of my weaker moments, I decided it must be the smell of hell surfacing upon the earth.

In addition to the smoke, there were drums, a heady, endless thumping I could not block out, no matter how many shutters I closed, no matter where in the manor house I tried to hide. Even with a pillow over my head the beat burrowed its way into my chest and into my skull.

Not until dusk each evening did the drumming finally cease, and then only because it was time for them to put down their instruments and pick up their weapons.

In my moment of greatest despair, I wrote Madame another letter. This time I told her everything: about the corpse and the burning jeep; I told her about Dragon Guy and his followers and about Hector and Raoul's defection and about Mona locking herself up in the kitchen. I mentioned that the four closest villas remained unoccupied, and that I had found a place among the trees behind Villa Bacall where I could spy on the intruders, and it was as I caught myself nearing a description of the men's belongings in Villa Bisset that I stopped, understanding there were some things she could not know.

I burned the letter in the stove.

But even during the worst of it I was aware that I could not continue to absent myself forever from what was happening. Nearly six weeks had already passed. It was obvious they would never leave on their own.

A bit each day, quietly with one of Raoul's machetes, I cut a path from the space in the trees behind Villa Bacall to the path leading to the forest preserve, a distance of perhaps twenty meters. Dressed in the clothes I had found in the old servants' quarters, I worked for a week, starting at dawn and stopping just before I knew the intruders were likely to appear, stumbling sleepily out of the villas. Had I not needed to remain silent and unseen, the work would have taken no more than a day.

It was to the path to the preserve that every path among the villas led. Reaching it gave me access to wherever I might wish to go, but I did not yet wish to go far. Instead I moved a little bit north and hid among the trees and underbrush near Villa Bernhardt, where I could watch men trudging back and forth from the preserve, bearing baskets of fruit they had just picked. It was there that I learned Villa Bernhardt had gotten its new roof after all, and I took comfort in thinking that Raoul was still taking care of at least some things. During a period of near constant discouragement, it was the one thing that allowed me to believe all might not be lost.

O ne afternoon, after a long morning of cutting and clearing my new path, I settled down to take a break in my hiding spot among the trees.

In the courtyard of Villa Bacall, an old man with a flannel patch over one eye was chipping away with a hammer and chisel at a small cottonwood log. He worked contentedly, singing to himself a song I had never heard before.

> *The cannons fire,*
> *We are not afraid of them.*
> *Oh, Ogou, war!*

I wondered if he had chosen the song on purpose, or whether it had simply come to him without his having considered the reason. The way he worked, never pausing to regard his progress, reminded me of so much else about this occupation. If there was one thing at which Dragon Guy and his followers excelled, it was being able to act without ever asking why. I could not help wondering if it was that very instinct that had kept them alive this long.

I could not say what it was that kept me there. Perhaps I was just exhausted. Maybe I was willing to be captivated by anything. Squatting in the brush for what I later realized must have been at least an hour, I ignored the pain spreading down my back and the stiffness swelling in my legs. The song went around and around.

Gunshots are fired,
We are not scared of them.

Only when the log was at last fully hollowed did the old man finally stop singing. Then he got up, his knees cracking like twigs, and sauntered into Villa Bernhardt. He came back a moment later with what looked like a goatskin, inelegantly hacked into a lopsided polygon. Curling his tongue in concentration, he stretched the skin across one end of the log, securing it with rope. He tested the drum with a few tentative hits.

The old man was in the process of adjusting the tautness when a second man sat down beside him, arranging several glass vases in a semicircle on the ground. Neither said a word to the other, though it seemed clear they were working in concert. Between his fingers the second man held mallets made of stick and fabric.

The old man settled down behind his drum. With the heels of his hands he beat out a rhythm. The man with the mallets joined in.

The others arrived from every direction, already dancing when they entered my view. How was it that they seemed to know just what to do? There was no hesitation, no discussion. Within just a few minutes, the patio around the pool, which had been almost entirely empty, was suddenly trampled in bodies. Never had I seen so many of them in one place. There must have been at least a hundred.

I marveled at how carefree they seemed, as if this were the most natural place in the world for them to be throwing a party. Their feet moved instinctively. They tossed their heads and bodies, swaying to the music. The ground shuddered beneath me. Soon they ran out of space on the patio and the dancing spread toward the trees, coming closer and closer. I waited, hoping to catch a glimpse of Hector, but he was not there.

Rising to my hands and knees, I inched backward out of the cavity. Not until I was sure no one could see me did I get to my feet.

The drumming and shouting chased me back to Villa Moreau, pushing me from behind. No doubt it would have followed me all the way up to the manor house. But just then a breeze blew through, carrying with it the smoke I had been inhaling for weeks—but stronger now than it had ever been before. It was earthy and heavy, and soon it filled the air.

With my head still swollen with the thumps of the drums, I turned around and headed back down the path I had cut to the forest preserve, following the corrosive smoke. It grew thicker and thicker, until I had to cover my mouth with my sleeve. I did not have to worry about anyone seeing me now.

As it turned out, I did not have far to go.

Just beyond the fork, in a clearing along the north trail, ran an enormous mound of earth perhaps ten meters long. And there was the smoke, escaping like steam from a poorly covered pot. As I drew closer, I felt the heat pressing against me like an outstretched hand, urging me to stop. After several more steps I could bear to go no farther.

Hell after all.

The next morning over breakfast I told Mona what I had seen.

"They're burning the trees," I said. "They're turning the preserve into charcoal."

"You're a fool," she said. They were words that even a month before she would never have spoken to me. But it was undeniable that our circumstances had changed.

"If we knew what they were planning," I said, "there might be something we could do."

"If we knew," Mona said, "we would be no better off than them."

"I thought you wanted me to get rid of them?"

Mona shook her head. "It's too late for that now."

"There has to be a way," I said.

Mona pushed a forkful of rice through the last clumps of yolk on her plate. "Mark my words, the army will come. And when they do, I intend to say that I have been in my kitchen. I know nothing," she said, "and that will be what saves me."

Chapter Twenty-Four

Each night, as darkness fell, Dragon Guy and his men continued slipping back out of the estate to resume their clashes in the streets with President Duphay's troops. Each night, from my balcony, I could hear them at the roadblock outside the gate, telling each other jokes and singing obscene songs while they waited to be attacked. My daily schedule began to mirror theirs: up all night and then asleep at dawn.

What did I do during those hours? I had grown adept at following the muddled movements of men and guns. Most of all, I listened for signs that Dragon Guy was finally weakening. It had to be only a matter of time before he ran out of men. If not men, certainly bullets.

I ate little, sometimes waking and going straight to the blind behind Villa Bisset without stopping first at the kitchen. I sat for hours, observing the activity in the courtyard, occasionally moving to a different blind for a view of different villas. It grew so routine that I seldom paused to consider my purpose. What was the point of the notes I was taking? Only, it seemed, that information gave me comfort; it fed the illusion that if I knew enough, I would somehow be able to get them to leave.

One night, while Dragon Guy and his men were out fighting, I decided to leave the safety of my rooms. By the light of the moon I got dressed and made my way out of the manor house. This time I did not use the path I had cut behind Villa Moreau. Tonight, for the first time since Dragon Guy had come to stay, I followed the cobblestones to Madame's private villa.

Unlike all the rest, the courtyard outside Madame's villa betrayed none of the usual signs of habitation. There was no fire ring and no pots and pans. The trees had been spared and there were no vegetable patches. In fact, the trees here had been recently trimmed and someone had thinned out the undergrowth. The stones appeared recently swept. Somehow they had even managed to fill the pool. It was as if the place were being preserved for some special purpose.

Nevertheless, I entered Madame's villa feeling a sense of dread. Yet, from the moment I stepped inside, it was as though Madame had never left. Her perfume bottles stood at attention on her dressing table, along with her old mother-of-pearl brush. Her display of photos in gold and silver frames remained arrayed in a perfect fan on the credenza, as though no one had thought to look at them, lacking even the mildest curiosity about whose home this was. The bed was made. Who among them would know how? I was sure Dragon Guy, until the day he arrived here, had never in his life slept on anything other than a pallet.

Hector. Who else could have taken such good care of things?

In the wardrobe I at last found traces of Dragon Guy—a soiled shirt hanging as though it were a handmade suit. At least he owned a shirt. Beside it dangled an orange dress. There were two pillows on the bed, and each one smelled of someone different. But neither belonged to Hector. It was not here that he slept.

Looking around, I found it inconceivable that a man such as Dragon Guy could so easily take Mme Freeman's place, that such a change could amount to so little. A different wardrobe, a different scent. Everything else the same.

And where, right now, was Mme Freeman? Did she have any idea of what was happening here? No doubt she had been reading about us in her papers; she knew the general outline. Perhaps she was even hoping Dragon Guy would prevail. After everything President Duphay had done to destroy her hotel, she could not be blamed for wanting to see him flee in disgrace. But she could not understand the cost at which that would come. Dragon Guy was anything but a savior, especially for Habitation Louvois.

Even if Madame did not know all of the details, she at least knew the estate and the capital, the terrain upon which the battles were being fought. That was more than I knew of her world. Among the magazines left behind over the years by our guests were one or two dedicated to homes and gardens around the States. Inside were pictures of houses that looked nothing like the Marcuses', nor any other home I had ever seen. What surprised me the most was how bland the majority of them were, white the most common color. Occasionally brick. Somehow, despite all the flowers in neat, vibrant beds, the places seemed lifeless, as if no one actually lived there. And yet I could not help noticing that none of them were ever surrounded with walls.

I found it impossible to imagine Madame strolling such flat, treeless expanses of grass. And what did the stores she shopped in look like? The streets she drove down? Was her company in one of those featureless glass towers? The photos on the credenza showed faces against backdrops of mountains and oceans and beaches, views of Madame and her friends and family on vacation. But on vacation from what?

I closed the wardrobe and returned everything to where I had found it. One thing was certain: she could never know what was happening here. I would have to live with my failings, but I could not live with her discovering that I had allowed a man such as Dragon Guy to poison her most private sanctuary.

On my way back to the manor house I struggled in the dark to avoid tripping on the overgrown underbrush along the paths. I was nearly at

Villa Bardot and the last set of steps before the drive when I noticed someone coming toward me. Whoever it was had not yet noticed me, for I had only just turned the bend—but there was nowhere to hide. And then it was too late.

"Is that you, François?" she said as she reached the bottom step.

"Yes," I said.

She came toward me swiftly, tall and lean. "How do you expect to heal when you're out here limping around?" she said with gentle reproach. "You should be in bed."

And then she stood directly before me, a young woman with a red kerchief wrapped around her head. I realized she was the one I had seen with Dragon Guy that first day he had arrived. And I knew in an instant the orange dress in Madame's wardrobe belonged to her.

"I couldn't sleep," I said.

She folded her arms across her chest. She was a head and a half above me, and I could make out her face no better than she could mine.

"Your leg will never heal if you don't rest."

"Of course," I said.

She reached out and took my arm, and I assumed a limp as she eased me down the path. I let her lead, and she directed me to Villa Garbo, bringing me right to the door.

"I'll help you into bed," she said.

"No," I said. "I can manage from here."

"Very well." She took my hand in hers, and I was surprised by the roughness of her skin. "Get some sleep," she said, "and if I hear you've been out wandering around again, you're going to have to answer to me." And then she bent down and kissed me on the forehead. I recognized her wild scent.

※

I drew a map of the estate, a crude rendering—rectangles and squares to represent the manor and guesthouse, the villas and outbuildings and various other structures. I was reminded of the hotel blueprints from all those years ago, and I was surprised how much I had retained from them. Lines of varying thickness marked the drive and the paths. I made note of the villas Dragon Guy had occupied.

What I realized was that the estate was made up of three parallel sections, all virtually identical in size. The boundary of the first was formed by the drive, and within it was the manor house and the pavilion, the discotheque and casino, the outbuildings and the easternmost villas, those Dragon Guy had left unoccupied. The next section, to the west of the drive, contained the guesthouse and the rest of the villas, and it extended down to the path leading to the preserve, which itself formed the last of the sections.

I knew the hole in the wall was not in the first section. Had it been, at one time or another I would have seen Dragon Guy coming and going. I also knew the hole was not along the south wall of the second section, because it was there that I had cut my path. I knew, in fact, that the hole was not anywhere along the southern wall, because if it had been, Dragon Guy would have used the path leading to the preserve to get to it, and I would have seen him from my blind behind Villa Bacall.

That left only the northern wall, which meant the hole must be deep in the preserve, where the wall butted up against Cité Verd.

The slums gave Dragon Guy the cover he needed.

The next morning, while Dragon Guy and his soldiers slept, I snuck into the preserve. It took me only an hour to find the spot where feet had beaten down a trail off the main path.

The hole was just where I expected it to be. Yet how quickly my satisfaction turned to disappointment. What had I expected? Something dramatic, I suppose. Looking at it now, I could not help but laugh at how insignificant a thing it was. Nothing more than a gap where the wall had crumbled, the stones falling inward, scattered by the back and forth of Dragon Guy's men. Two meters wide, no more. That was all it took to transform an impregnable wall into a turnstile.

But it was all there, all the pieces I would need to put it back together again.

That night, after Dragon Guy and his followers had left to continue their fight, I returned to the wall. Down the rugged paths I struggled to navigate an old wheelbarrow in which I had collected a trowel, a bucket filled with glass bottles, and a half-full sack of cement I had found in the shed. With water from the spring I quickly mixed the cement, and then I set to work fitting the stones back into place. The bottles I broke, planting the shards along the top of the reconstructed wall.

Then came the fire. If anyone on the other side saw the flames, they did not come to investigate. The wall baked until dawn, and then, just before I knew Dragon Guy would return—or rather, try to return—I tamped down the embers and I went home to bed.

Chapter Twenty-Five

Watching from the balcony as they made their way down the drive, it struck me how well each man's weapon seemed to fit his bearing. The strongest—or those who otherwise managed to hold themselves the most erect—possessed an assortment of assault rifles and machine guns, some with pistols in reserve, tucked into their waistbands. Most of the others, thin and ragged, carried whatever they had been able to obtain: shotguns, revolvers, rifles.

But then there were the stragglers, dragging their feet as if they were something old and useless, carrying nothing but machetes.

It was a subdued procession, not at all the triumphant return of conquering warriors. In all there must have been close to two hundred of them. And that did not appear to include any women.

At the lead marched Dragon Guy in his white linen suit, Hector at his side. I knew Raoul was somewhere among them. Who else could have unlocked the gate to let them in? And why had I not thought of that? Had I learned nothing from everything that came before?

Now that I had taken away their hole in the wall, they would come in through the front gate, like welcome guests.

In the coming days it became clear how much else would change as well. And how quickly. It was as if they had been waiting for such an invitation all along.

The next afternoon, just about two months after they first arrived here, several of Dragon Guy's men appeared at the manor house, entering the library as I was sitting there reading.

"We can fit two dozen or so here," one of them said, surveying the room. I had never seen the man before: short, with a long continuous brow shadowing his eyes like a promontory.

I rose from my chair, and the short man's brow rippled toward me.

"Did Dragon Guy send you to talk to me?" I asked.

"Who are you?"

"I'm the manager."

The man's brow folded in on itself. "The manager of what?"

"The estate."

He looked at me uncertainly. "I could use a cup of water," he said.

"That's not what I do."

"Never mind." Turning around, he led the others back out to the corridor and on to the ballroom.

Their move-in was fast but orderly. They had prepared in advance who would go where, and the men transported their few belongings without difficulty. They passed me in the halls with their small bundles, most of them failing even to notice me.

In the club room and the library and the ballroom and in the rest of the other rooms on the first floor they laid out their bedrolls. The outbuildings became dormitories once again. Others settled into the suites upstairs, Madame and M. Gadds's old offices. Mine they left alone. But on the second floor their numbers were smaller, only one or two men to each room. Through the walls I heard the shifting of furniture and footsteps coming and going in the hall.

That first night, at odd hours, I awoke to officious knocking on my neighbors' doors and obsequious voices addressing "colonels" and "majors" and "captains."

A mad scrambling up the stairs in the dark of the morning carried a "message from the general." The message itself was muffled with the closing of a door.

Apparently, my neighbors were men of rank, Dragon Guy's lieutenants. In addition to the private rooms, they were apparently privileged with staying behind when the fighting commenced.

As had become my habit, I too spent that first night awake, listening to the sounds of the battle beyond the gate. But while my neighbors were preoccupied with whether or not they were winning, I spent the night trying to find ways to ensure they would lose. Even now, with the manor house fully invaded, my goal struck me as no less improbable than theirs.

But what, in fact, was I to do, one man against hundreds? There was no force I could bring to bear, no sort of coercion of which I could conceive. So I asked myself, what would Senator Marcus do? Or Mme Freeman, if she were here? I knew already what my father would say, that Dragon Guy and his followers had just as much right to be here as I did. But I had sworn to serve the estate, not to provide shelter and haven for anyone who might seek it. And in any case, I disagreed. They had no more right to invade my home than I did theirs, and I would not sit idly by and let it happen.

In the dawn, heavy with exhaustion but no closer to a solution, I shuffled out to the balcony to watch Dragon Guy's soldiers return, as limp and hushed as the morning before. They drifted together in small clusters, speaking quietly of—I could not guess what it was they spoke of. Judging by their mild expressions, it could have been something as banal as the weather. It occurred to me how much they resembled common laborers coming back from the field. They could have been carrying picks and hoes instead of arms, and nothing else would have been any different.

Within a couple of minutes, the soldiers had passed, their day finally over. And I was left alone with mine. At this dark stage my day seemed to offer neither beginning nor end.

I was about to go back inside—perhaps to sleep, perhaps to piece together some sort of plan—when suddenly I heard a cry. I looked up again to find more movement at the top of the drive.

The second wave of men progressed so slowly it was possible to study every bloody shirt, every bandaged head. That first morning I counted eight men, some limping, some dragged or carried. I wondered how many more had been left behind, their bodies without hope of recovery.

By the time the wounded reached the end of the drive, the others before them had disappeared, as if—in order to be able to continue— the living had to forget the dying and the dead.

But I was not so lucky. Even after they were gone, the wounded remained with me. They followed me to my wardrobe. They trailed me to the basin. They watched me in the mirror.

That day, I did not leave my rooms. Never before had they seemed so confining. If before I had felt surrounded, now I was trapped, and nowhere I looked—even as I opened the shutters and gazed upon the capital and the surrounding hills of Lyonville—did I see a way out. I thought about writing to Madame, but what was there to say? Whereas in the past I had gotten through difficult periods just by thinking about her possible return, in our current situation the notion had become so absurd that it moved me to anger. I could not bear the thought of her seeing what had happened.

I sat a long time at my desk, drawing aimless circles on the page.

It was the smell that finally roused me, sometime before nightfall, a smell so common and yet—given our circumstances—so unusual: onion and garlic frying in oil.

It was the smell of dinner.

There was no one in the hall when I peeked my head out the door, and no one on the stairway as I peered over the banister and no one in the lobby when I got to the bottom. I heard nothing coming from the library or the club room. A vast emptiness lurked behind the closed ballroom door. But as I made my way down the corridor to the south wing, I began to hear a murmur coming from within the restaurant.

From the doorway I saw that every table was full, and for a moment I imagined a dark sea of tuxedoes and gowns and Madame standing beside a table in conversation while Georges swept by with a tray of silver serving dishes. I almost expected to find a maître d' waiting to greet me.

But no one looked up when I came in. The men were hunched over their bowls, like pigs at a trough. They had not bothered with table-cloths or napkins. Everywhere I looked, cups rested in rings of water on the naked wood. They had brought in extra chairs, six men squeezing together around a table built for four. Near the verandah a man in a buttoned shirt from which the sleeves had been ripped reclined in a wing chair, a tarnished spoon balanced on one of the arms.

In the back corner, the kitchen doors shot open and a tall rolling cart emerged. At its helm limped an old woman whose green T-shirt struggled to withstand the pull of her tremendous breasts. With every one of the woman's steps, the cart jerked forward in sudden, graceless bursts, like a car in a fit of stalling. With each jerk, the enormous pot balanced on top slid closer and closer to the edge.

At a table near the entrance, the old woman came to a stop and the man seated closest to her held up his bowl. Rising to her toes, the woman managed to dunk her arm into the pot and pull out an immense ladle, inside of which something wet and lumpy quivered. She filled his bowl with a single dripping scoop, snailing a trail of greasy blots that led back to the pot.

For each of his dinner companions she did the same.

A young man at the next table called out as she went by. "You forgot me. Come on," he whimpered as she moved on without stopping. "Just a spoonful. Give me a bean. I'll settle for a single bean."

"If you want to eat like two men," the old woman rasped, not bothering to look at him, "you should work like two men."

Circles of laughter rose up from the neighboring tables like startled crows, and the young man got to his feet with a self-effacing sigh. He was a broad-shouldered boy of perhaps eighteen, strong and full of energy.

As he approached the doorway the young man fixed me with a sneer. "What are you looking at?"

"I thought you were someone else," I said. Though they shared no similarities other than an approximate age, I had allowed myself for just a moment to believe he was Hector. Observing the malice afflicting his face, I realized what a mistake I had made.

Without warning, the boy's shoulder slammed into mine. Only the wall at my back kept me from falling.

When I looked up again, the old woman with the cart was standing in front of me. I thought at first that she had come to help.

"Well," she said, already losing patience, "what are you waiting for?"

She gestured with the still-dripping ladle toward the chair the young man had just vacated.

There were five other men at the table, and several of them looked up with curiosity as I sat down, almost as if they recognized me and were surprised to find me here. They could tell by my suit that I was not like them, and as far as I was concerned, that was all they needed to know.

"Where's your bowl?" the woman asked, hovering gloomily above me. Globs of what I now realized was rice slid helplessly down the sides of the ladle and back into the pot, like prisoners dragged along by their chains.

I looked around at the dishes spread out in front of the other men. Dented tin and a few hollow gourds.

"My bowl?" I said, deciding I had no choice but to play along. "I must not have brought it."

Turning away brusquely, she lowered the ladle back into the pot. It seemed I would not be eating after all. I was uncertain whether to be disappointed or relieved.

"You can use mine."

Before I even knew who had spoken, a thin metal vessel was pressed into my hands, still warm on the outside from being held. The inside had been scraped clean.

"Go ahead."

I looked up to thank him, meeting a dead, milky eye.

"You can use this too." He wiped a spoon on his elbow and handed it over.

The woman looked down upon this transaction with dull disapproval. "Next time you'd better remember to bring your own."

"I will." I would have agreed to anything just to bring the encounter to a close.

Grudgingly she dipped the ladle back into the pot. In the bowl, the red of the beans and the white of the rice converged in a murky, gray mass.

"How are you, monsieur?" said the man to my left. The scar on his chin twitched as he chewed, as if it were doing the talking for him.

I committed to only the briefest of glances. "Well, thank you."

A man sitting across the table greeted me with an enormous grin. He had a broad, flat face and square, yellow teeth resembling kernels of corn. "This must be a strange sight for you."

"Pardon?"

"Not your usual clientele," said Corn Teeth with a chuckle.

I did not care for his overly familiar tone, and I could not imagine what grounds he might have for thinking he could condescend to me. "Have we met before?"

The other men at the table glanced at each other with lowered gazes, as if surprised and embarrassed by the question. Corn Teeth leaned back in his chair. "I don't believe we've ever spoken, but—"

"I didn't think so," I said curtly.

"I didn't mean to interrupt your meal," he said with exaggerated deference, sharing an outraged look with one of his neighbors. With a grating shriek, he pushed out his chair. Everyone else but the dead-eyed man who had lent me his bowl did the same.

As they cursed toward the exit, flinging glances at me over their shoulders. I considered thanking them for so kindly leaving me in peace.

"Good, isn't it?" Dead Eye snuggled his head on the table, staring longingly at his bowl.

"Here," I said, shoving it toward him. "You have it."

He immediately perked up. "Really?"

"I've lost my appetite."

"If you insist," he said, wiping the spoon on his elbow.

Every night, the fighting seemed to pick up where it had left off the night before. Each morning began with the same procession of the living and the wounded. Somehow, no matter what happened, no matter how many men he lost, Dragon Guy's army never seemed to get any smaller. If anything, it grew.

Along the paths between the outbuildings, pigs and chickens roamed. There was always something underfoot. Until now, I had not realized how many children had accompanied their parents here. The grounds began to feel less like an army encampment than like a small city. One day I discovered a group of children chasing each other through the yard beside the casino. There were twenty or so boys and girls, in ages ranging from about six to twelve, all of them perfectly oblivious to what was going on around them. That was their privilege, as children, but I could not conceive of how Dragon Guy could be so reckless as to assemble a playground in the middle of a battlefield.

I felt drawn to the children, although I could not say why. Perhaps it was simply that I sensed they were the only ones here, other than me, who had no particular place in Dragon Guy's plans. Their caretaker was a young woman with a round, soft face and a delicately pointed chin perched below her mouth like a tiny ebony knob on a jewelry box— features not so much pretty as they were doll-like. Unlike most of the other women here, she looked remarkably unravaged. But the thing that most distinctly set her apart from the others was that she was without question the only person here, besides me, for whom a book was something other than fuel for a fire.

The first day I came upon them, the young woman was sitting on the casino steps, a small hardbound volume balanced upon her tightly clenched knees. Whenever she turned a page, she paused to glance up at the children. It seemed to me to be with genuine fondness that she raised her eyes—and her plump arm to deflect the light—to make sure that all was still well. I was curious to know what the book was, but from where I was standing—among the trees along the path—there was no way I could read the spine.

A long time passed before I heard her speak. "Come, children, come," she said, kind but firm as she stood up and brushed at the back of her dress. It was blue with a faded pattern of irises across the waistline. "It's time to resume your lessons."

She stood aside on the steps until the last one had gone inside. Then she closed her book, as if she were folding a delicate handkerchief, and went in after them.

Standing out of sight in the entryway, I listened to her lead them, letter by letter, through the alphabet. It was the only thing they accomplished that afternoon, but in the end each of them could recite it without making a single mistake. This was the most heartening thing I had seen in a long time. And yet how could it not also be bitter, reminding me of those lost afternoons in my office with Hector, watching him study the pages of his book and shape his mouth into words?

I decided this was to be my comfort, that there was at least one responsible person among Dragon Guy's ranks, one person committed to something good in the midst of all of this destruction. And, perhaps, one person who might be willing to help me make them leave.

⁂

Following Dragon Guy's occupation of the manor house, nothing changed for Mona. She remained locked in her kitchen. The dust on the paving stones outside the door showed where numerous sets of feet had stood, trying and failing to gain entrance.

"It's me," I said one afternoon as I knocked softly, not wanting anyone passing by to overhear. "Open up."

"Mona." I knocked more loudly. "It's just me."

I could hear not even the slightest movement inside.

"Go ahead," I said, "ask me whatever you wish." When still there came no response, I began listing the names of the villas. Usually she cut me off midway through, but this time I had to struggle to get all forty-four.

"That's all of them, Mona." I knocked again. "This is enough. Let me in." I pounded on the door with my fist. "What's it going to take to convince you?"

"Nothing," she whispered hoarsely through the crack. "There's nothing you can say to make me open that door."

That night at dinner I found an empty chair at a table with four other men. Once again I caught the not-so-subtle elbowing and whispering. It was as if a man in a suit were the most exotic creature they had ever seen.

"Good evening," one of them said as I sat down.

I nodded without looking to see who had spoken, hoping to make it clear I had not come here for conversation.

"She works at the laundry," one of the younger men was saying. He was thin and frail, with sunken eyes streaked with yellow. There was nothing healthy about him.

The young man beside him scratched his bicep, running his fingernails over a deformed tattoo—a bird, I thought, but the color appeared to have run, making it look like a bloated chicken. His smile was gummy and warm. "What's her name?"

"They call her Lulu."

The smiling young man smiled even more brightly. "Lulu the laundress."

"I think I know her," said a man sitting across the table. His black, scraggly beard hung crookedly from his chin, like some sort of moss from a tree. "She's small and light skinned."

"No," said the skinny young man. "She's dark and almost as tall as me."

The smiling young man clapped his skinny friend on the back, laughing joyously. "Ah, she sounds like a beauty—a beauty!"

The skinny young man looked around the table self-consciously, as if afraid he were being mocked. "She is."

"Yes," said Moss Beard. "Too beautiful for *you*. What a girl like that needs is a mature man—one that knows how to take care of her."

The skinny boy puffed up his chest to little apparent effect. "I've been with plenty of girls."

"Of course you have," said the fourth man at the table. He gave the young man a grotesque, squishy wink. As that half of his face folded in on itself, I noticed he was missing most of his left ear.

The smiling young man put his hand on his friend's shoulder and squeezed it enthusiastically. "Have you talked to her?"

"Yes."

"What did you say?"

The three men watched expectantly as the skinny young man pushed the spoon idly around his bowl, as if he were setting the hands of a clock.

"Well?" the smiling young man said, nodding encouragement.

The skinny young man sighed. "She was carrying a basket of clothes—"

"And?" Moss Beard and One Ear shouted simultaneously.

"—and she dropped a shirt, and I brought it to her." The young man paused to look at his friend, who nodded for him to continue.

"What did you say?"

"I said, 'You dropped this.' "

Moss Beard leaned forward, combing his fingers through his gray whiskers. "And what did she say?"

"She said—" The skinny young man paused to look at us. "She said, 'Thanks.' But it was *how* she said it," he added.

The two older men were already laughing. " 'Thanks,' " One Ear lisped, lewdly licking his lips.

At last the old lady with the cart limped to the table, mercifully halting the crudeness before it could degenerate any further.

"Where's your bowl?"

I turned around, and she saw my face.

"You again!"

"I must have lost it," I said, daring to hope for another act of mercy.

"What do you mean, you 'must have lost it'?" The ladle fell back into the pot with a suck and a gurgle. "You don't even know? Is eating that small a matter to you? If you lost your pants, would you go wandering around naked until someone pointed it out to you? Or is it your plan to show up here every meal expecting someone else to take care of you? You've got too much to do to keep track of your own bowl, but you expect everyone else to be looking out for you?"

"There are extras in the kitchen," I said. "There are hundreds of bowls and plates—"

"That's how it is with you?" She folded her arms across her chest. "No reason for you to worry—there's always an extra lying around."

I began to get up. "I could show you where they are."

"Oh, no you don't." She dragged the ladle out of the pot, threatening to thump me on the chest. I tilted back down into the chair.

"Myriam!" she shouted. "Myriam!"

Almost instantly the doors to the kitchen in the far corner of the room sprang open and an immense figure appeared there, glancing around the dining room with pronounced displeasure. Over her significant torso Myriam wore one of Jean's old aprons, streaked with stains of every conceivable color. Never had Jean appeared in the dining room wearing one, and not even in the kitchen would he have worn anything so filthy. Myriam looked as though she had come fresh from a slaughter.

The cart woman waved her ladle, finally catching Myriam's eye.

"Our prince here has lost his bowl, and he wants us to give him a new one."

Without a word—or even a discernible expression—Myriam pushed her way back into the kitchen, and before the doors had stilled she had returned. In her enormous hand, pinched between her meaty thumb and index finger, she held a bone-white china bowl twined with an inlay of gold leaf. It was a lovely pattern, selected by Madame herself, but it had not been designed to be tossed around like a tin cup, and I was not convinced it was going to survive the trip across the room.

Myriam wove around the tables and errant chairs. She did not slow as she reached the table, and I gasped as I saw the bowl leave her hand. When I opened my eyes, it was there in front of me on the table, rocking in a circle like a spun penny. After another half turn it finally came to a rest.

"Here you go, sweetheart."

I let my breath go.

The cart lady dealt me my slop and limped away.

"At the rate you're going," Moss Beard said, turning from me to the skinny young man, "the only way you'll get into her drawers is if you trip on them in the street."

Chapter Twenty-Six

Each afternoon, the older children gathered at the tennis courts, two dozen teenage boys in undersize T-shirts wearing the solemn faces of old men. On any given day there were three or four instructors, young men themselves, who all grew beards to make themselves look older. They fashioned lumpy enemy soldiers out of tablecloths and old clothes stuffed with grass. It was difficult to see how the clothes cast aside for this purpose were any worse than what most of these men wore themselves. The boys learned to beat the dummies with sticks and fists. But whenever the instructors' attention was elsewhere the boys turned to pushing and hitting each other, an exercise they appeared to enjoy a great deal more. Somehow the instructors never seemed to notice.

Then came the weapons. At some point each day, one of the instructors brought out to the tennis courts a crate of old guns, which the boys practiced taking apart and reassembling and running around pointing at one another. In lieu of bullets, they made explosive gurgling sounds with their throats as they dodged behind the straw dummies, taking improbable shots. Almost as much as they loved shooting did they enjoy dying, staggering about like drunks, watching imaginary pools of blood trickle through fingers splayed across their chests. Sometimes, after the formal lessons were over, I saw boys practicing their death pirouettes and crumbling to the ground, while others stood off to the side offering tips and critiques.

I never saw the boys fire actual ammunition. I assumed there was none to spare. For target practice they threw rocks. But so easy did they find it to hit the dummies while standing still—even from great distances—that they preferred to throw while weaving and scrambling in unpredictable squibbles; firing sidearm while in midair; diving and tumbling and hurling from their knees. Even so, they rarely missed.

To counter these discouraging sights I found myself more and more often taking walks leading past the casino, where at certain hours I knew the younger children would be outside playing, their teacher reading quietly on the steps. I envied her ability to find peace under circumstances such as these. And I wondered where she had acquired the books. Madame's library, perhaps. If so, was it possible she could read English? I knew without a doubt that she and I were the only two people among the hundreds here who had finished school—perhaps we were the only ones to have attended at all. What could someone with her education and disposition have in common with these people? None of these men could mean anything to her. She must find them repellent. Like me, she had probably spent her whole life trying to get away from them. And yet here we were, surrounded.

But an opportunity to talk to the schoolteacher and ask about her books never arose. Over the course of several weeks I learned little more about her than her name: Mlle Trouvé, which the children some-times sang out in affection: *Mademoiselle Trouvé, Mademoiselle Trouvé, she sits and reads while the children play.*

On Sundays I saw Mlle Trouvé at the pavilion, where a man in a makeshift collar—fashioned, it seemed, from a dinner napkin—led morning services. The pavilion was too small for even a fraction of Dragon Guy's followers, so most of them made do with a seat on the grass. Not all of them came. Still, on no other occasion could I see so many of them in one place—usually well over two hundred. There seemed to be more every week.

I had a favorite spot at the base of a shady tree on the periphery, which the grizzled priest—whose shapeless collar gave him more than a hint of menace—had no trouble reaching with his voice.

The benches inside the pavilion were reserved for Dragon Guy and his inner circle, including his younger brother and Black Max. Although I had come to feel a certain fascination for the services, what had first brought me to them was a realization that it might be my only chance to see Hector.

Despite everything that had happened in the almost two and a half months since Dragon Guy had appeared here, I still could not bring myself to blame Hector. Perhaps he *had* played some part in deceiving me. Perhaps he had been aiding his brother all along. Perhaps he had even been the one to show Dragon Guy the hole in the wall. Perhaps he had done even more than this.

Whatever he had done, he had done out of desperation, and not because deception was the direction toward which his heart inclined. I could believe he had duped me, but I knew better than to imagine his devotion to the estate had ever been anything less than sincere. And that was why I continued to believe that if I could just get rid of Dragon Guy, we would be able to recover the things we had lost.

Each Sunday, from my spot under the tree, I could see the boy sitting beside his older brother. It was remarkable how much he seemed to have aged, all the while wearing the same tattered jersey and flimsy sneakers. The hardest thing of all was seeing the sadness that seemed to overtake him the moment he sat down. It was not just the solemnity of the service. In fact, I had never seen a congregation more prone to outbursts, weeping and laughing, shouting and clapping. But each week Hector sat perfectly still and perfectly silent, sapped of all his former energy. I could not help wondering, as I watched him stare abstractly off toward the trees, if he was sitting there wishing he could take it all back and return to the way it was.

At moments like these it was hard not to think of what it must have been like for my father when I was Hector's age. Those hours he spent in church watching me drift through services, and how much of the time that he would have liked to devote to worshipping he instead had to spend on thinking of ways to keep from losing me. Now here I was in his role, and Hector was in mine. And yet although I had countless reasons to have given up on Hector, to have stopped caring, to have turned against him, I never did. Was it possible that the same was true of my father—that he had continued to love me, even through his disappointment?

Hector was not the only one who had trouble staying attuned to the priest's sermons. His brother was even worse, hopelessly fidgety and impatient. In truth, it always surprised me that Dragon Guy bothered to come at all. Aside from his jewelry, there seemed to be nothing even remotely pious about him. Everything about his restless manner suggested he was here out of some sort of obligation. Perhaps even powerful generals needed to keep up appearances.

On Dragon Guy's other side sat his girlfriend, René-Thérèse, who discreetly touched his arm whenever she saw his attention straying. In those moments she reminded me of Mme Marcus, and how at any social occasion she could be found standing at the Senator's elbow, feeding him the names of every minister's wife and the ages of every one of her children. She had done as much as anyone to make him the man he became. I wondered if the same could be said of René-Thérèse.

At every service Mlle Trouvé sat in the grass, accompanied by several older women. They could have been relations, but I thought it just as likely that they were merely part of the group of women who lived together in the former maids' quarters near the laundry. By chance I had seen Mlle Trouvé coming and going from there on several occasions. To my dismay, among the women she sat with was the limping old lady from the dining room, whose eye I had to be careful never to catch. But there was little chance of that, given the rapt attention she paid the priest.

The women's gazes never wandered; their voices never faded during the hymns. Although I was not myself devout, I found their devotion comforting. It suggested—or so I hoped—that however anarchic things seemed, perhaps some higher principle continued to circulate among the baser currencies.

Much as his appearance suggested, the warrior priest delivered fierce, fiery sermons. His was a scripture I remembered from my childhood, full of bombast about the poor, oppressed masses, and I often thought how much my father would have liked this man, who wielded holiness like a club.

Before this crowd of misfit soldiers, Dragon Guy's priest spoke of hope, of a new day, of God's grace for those of his creatures who followed the path of righteousness—the latter uttered without any trace of irony. Since their arrival it was surely the least trodden path in all of Habitation Louvois.

I was aware that the priest was not their only spiritual guide, nor likely the most popular. From men in the dining room I learned of villas where lazy-eyed seers stinking of rancid herbs read cards by candlelight, hoisting bowls of chicken blood and communing with the dead. Somewhere deep in the preserve they had even built a peristyle, providing a proper place to enact their delirious worship. On nights when the fighting with President Duphay's army was less intense and some of Dragon Guy's followers were able to stay within the walls of the estate, the drums never ceased, and it was all too easy to imagine them tripping over each other as they staggered around in various states of possession, recalling scenes from my childhood of some of our neighbors' more grotesque nocturnal gatherings. There was no way to live on the island without encountering it, but that did not make hosting it in my own home any more bearable.

Upon taking over the manor house and the guesthouse and the out-buildings, Dragon Guy had also decided it was time to move his people into the two remaining groups of vacant villas—a wide berth being yet another of the privileges I had surrendered. These new additions quickly came to take on the feel of a marketplace. There were barbers and seamstresses and basket makers and rum distillers and knife sharp-eners. Bartering was the chief form of payment, but there also seemed to be a great deal they got for free. As in the dining room, where every man was allotted his bowl of slop, there was a villa where one went each day to receive one's quota of charcoal, of which there appeared to be a limitless supply—thanks to the preserve's endless bounty.

So greatly had they expanded the cutting and burning of Madame's trees that virtually the entire forest now wore a permanent shroud of smoke—it seeped up through the turf as though the earth itself were raging in fire. During daylight hours I could barely see Cité Verd from my balcony. I could scarcely see the sky. Watching the smoke was like witnessing my mother's last breaths. The preserve was slipping away, and I could do nothing to save it.

Whatever charcoal they did not use themselves they stuffed into sacks and threw onto their shoulders to carry to the market. They treated the trees like a pestilence, something to be eradicated at any cost. Never mind that the trees were just about the only thing keep-ing them alive. All they could see was what the trees bought them in exchange, guns above all else.

I could only assume it was also the trees that bought their other supplies, including rice from the coast and coffee from the mountains. The rest of their food they grew here. Before becoming slum dwellers, most of them—like virtually everyone in Cité Verd—had been farmers in the countryside, and the women had been able to turn almost every available patch of ground into garden. I doubted they had ever seen such fertile soil. Swaths of the immense lawns along the drive were now barren of grass, seeded instead with yams and onions and eggplants. The water came free, too, flowing endlessly from the springs. They had discovered ones even I never knew about. Someone had gotten the water flowing again in almost all of the villas, the outbuildings, and the casino.

Now it was their turn to grow accustomed to luxuries.

And yet, despite all of this, it was clear the estate was nearing collapse. By now there must have been nearly three times as many people living here as there had ever been, even at the hotel's peak. Three, four hundred? It was hard to guess. I could measure their numbers only by the devastation they wrought. I wished my father could see what really happened when walls and gates came down and everyone was let in. Was this his utopian dream? Everywhere I looked I saw peeling paint and crumbling walls. Among the outbuildings there were no more paths; the constant trampling of the grass had left nothing but dirt. Everything of value in the manor house—the vases and paintings; all the silver and crystal; even the chandelier—every bit of it had disappeared. Whatever was left that they had no use for—and that could not be sold or burned—they dumped in piles out near the stables, as if its mere presence offended their senses. Their own garbage, however, bothered them not in the least. They left it wherever it happened to fall, sowing fields and pastures of trash.

I often asked myself what reason there was for continuing to stay. What good could I possibly do? Despite the priest's call for faith and hope, I had almost none. And yet, I could not bring myself to leave. Even if I had somewhere to go, I could not abandon a place I had sworn to protect.

Nor could I abandon Hector.

It was during one of my daily walks following the midday meal that I encountered Mlle Trouvé on one of the lower paths among the villas. I had just come down the stone stairs beside the guesthouse as she was heading toward them. Mlle Trouvé had a way when she walked of drawing her shoulders and elbows in toward her body, as if trying to make herself smaller and more difficult to see. I wondered where she was coming from, alone and unhurried. As I watched her shrink toward me, a picture came into my head, so vivid it was as if I had been there to see it myself: Mlle Trouvé reading quietly by herself on the bench in the preserve that Madame and I had for so long shared.

A few steps before we met, I stopped. Against her chest she held a small brown book. I knew then that what I had imagined must be true.

"It's beautiful, isn't it?" I said.

She stopped suddenly, as if surprised by the sound of my voice. I realized then that prior to this we had never actually spoken. Did she have no idea who I was?

"The preserve," I added. "It's my favorite place in the entire estate."

She glanced at the steps rising before her and then hesitantly back at me. "Is it?"

"Yes," I said. "It always has been. It was—*is*—Madame's as well."

Mlle Trouvé smiled quickly. "I see. Well"—and she placed her foot on the bottom stair—"good-bye."

"Do you have one?" I asked.

She paused to look over her shoulder.

"A favorite place in the estate?"

Shuffling her small feet on the narrow stone, she turned around to face me. Her tiny mouth twisted nervously. "I couldn't say." With a nod she started back up the steps.

"Perhaps I could show you." I recalled the tours Madame had given to her rich and glamorous guests when the hotel first opened, full of shimmer and sparkle. Why should Mlle Trouvé not be afforded the same opportunity? For someone like her would it not be all the more rewarding? Who could better appreciate the beauty of what we had made than someone who had spent her life in a place such as Cité Verd? As had been the case with my mother, raising a family in our squalid neighborhood. As had been the case with me. We were drawn to the things we did not have, things that seemed out of reach, that we knew would make our lives better than they were.

In my tour for Mlle Trouvé, there would be no room for discotheques and ballrooms; this would be a tour of the places that went unmentioned in the travel brochures—the quiet, peaceful spaces where one could escape from the world and find true tranquillity. Where one could be immersed in a pure sort of beauty utterly untouched by the clamor and desolation all around us.

"Another time," she offered from the top of the steps.

"Of course." I took them two at a time after her. "When?"

By the time I made it to the top, she was far across the lawn.

That night at dinner I found an empty chair at a table with the smiling young man and his skinny friend. Their crude companions from previous meals were thankfully nowhere in sight.

The smiley one pointed at my bowl and gave me a thumbs-up. "How have you been?"

"Fine," I said. "Okay." There was something about him I found oddly appealing. Perhaps it was simply his ability, rare among this group, to be friendly without forgetting our differences.

The skinny one was silent and sullen, and I wondered if things had not been going well with his laundress.

"My name is Marc." The smiling man pointed to his skinny friend. "This is Louis."

Louis nodded wanly.

"Don't mind him," Marc said. "He is heartsick."

"I'm sorry to hear that."

Marc smiled. "It's the sort of pain that gives a man pleasure."

"Is it the woman?" I said. "Lulu?"

Marc slapped his knee in delight. "You remember her name! Yes, Lulu is not making it easy for him. I've tried to tell him the difficulties he experiences now will make it all the much sweeter when it does happen."

"Does she not like him?"

"Oh, you know women. They are moved by winds we never feel. She loves him—she just doesn't know it yet."

"He looks unwell," I said. Louis had folded his arms into a pillow, upon which his head now lay. He seemed to be moaning. "Maybe we shouldn't talk about her anymore."

"Oh, no no no," Marc said. "The worst punishment of all would be if he could no longer hear her name."

Across the dining room I saw the old woman with the cart making her way toward us. I was uncertain whether she had seen me come in, but somehow she always seemed to know who had been served and who had not. It occurred to me that Mona would like her. The two could have been sisters, dour and humorless.

When she arrived at the table, the woman showed no sign of remembering me, filling my bowl with the same mechanical gesture she used with everyone else.

"Thank you very much," I said.

She glanced at me suspiciously, as if I might have just picked her pocket.

Marc elbowed me gently, wearing a devilish grin. "I keep telling Dragon Guy we should take her out of the kitchen and put her on the front line. President Duphay would surrender just at the sight of her."

"Do you know Dragon Guy?"

Marc shrugged guiltily, as if I had caught him in a lie. "I was only joking. In any case, I shouldn't say such things about Claire. She's a widow, you know. Her husband was killed in the fighting."

"That's terrible."

"That's the way it is. We're all missing something. We seem to attract misfortune."

"You too?" I said, surprised by how easily he had drawn me in.

"I have a wife and daughter. My little Evelyn is six years old. They live in the States now, but I'll be joining them soon, God willing."

"Have they been gone long?"

"Two years. Almost three. I prefer not to count." He was still smiling, but for the first time I noticed the lines on his face. "It already feels long enough without knowing the number."

"It must be difficult, living apart."

"It is difficult. It would be one thing if we were living apart on the island. But instead she's living in a completely different place. What's it like there? I have no idea. I can't picture it. I see their faces, but what are they doing? Where do they live? All I can imagine is our house in Cité Verd, but I know it's nothing like that."

I thought of the magazines in my office and for a brief moment I almost told him about them. "I have the same problem," I said.

"Is your wife there too?"

I did not intend to lie. My tongue was pressed against my teeth, ready to say the word. But the word never came, and instead I felt my head nodding, and once it started it felt somehow as if it were true.

"How long has it been?"

I did not need to stop to count. I knew exactly how long it had been since Madame had been here last. "Five years and seven months."

"I shouldn't have asked. I don't want to think about five years. Five years is impossible. It's simply out of the question."

That quickly, his smile was gone. I wanted to take it all back now, say it was a mistake, a misunderstanding. But it was too late for that.

"I don't know how you manage," he said, shaking his head.

"I think about how wonderful it will be when she comes back."

"*Back*?" He sounded surprised. "The way things are, who would ever want to come back?"

I had to remind myself that he knew nothing about Madame— nothing about me. I doubted he could even fathom what our lives had been like before, despite the fact that he now lived here himself.

"It will get better," I said. "Everything will be like it was."

He gave his head a shake. "I hope it gets better than that. Other- wise what's the point of all this?"

I lowered my eyes and gave the bowl a stir. "The hardest part is the wait between letters."

Suddenly I felt his hand on my arm, squeezing tightly. "You too?" he said, nearly crushing me. "Have you not been getting letters?"

"It's been a long time."

"How long?"

I tried pulling my arm away. "A year. Maybe more."

His fingers started to loosen. "Is that all?"

Finally I was able to free myself. "I'm not sure." I could still see the impressions of his fingers on my skin. "How long has it been for you?"

Elbows on the table, Marc brought his hands together and set his chin on top. He gave me a weak smile. "I'm still waiting for the first."

"It's a wonder anything gets through," I said with as much sincerity as I could muster. "What's not lost, the censors destroy."

"Just one," Marc said, "so I would know they made it."

There was nothing I could think to say.

"You hear stories about the crossing," he said. "Terrible stories. Boats that sink. People drown. Sometimes you hear about people getting dropped off on deserted islands and starving to death. I don't believe it," he said, "anything that awful. How could you believe it? Still, though, it makes you worry."

"I'm certain everything is fine."

For a long moment he regarded me carefully, searching my eyes for assurance that I meant what I said.

I felt myself crumbling under his gaze. "I should go."

Concern spread across Marc's face, and he gestured toward my bowl. "You haven't finished yet." He gave me one of his gummy smiles, as if to show me he felt no sadness about the turn the conversation had taken.

I tried to smile too.

"There's a young lady I recently met," I said, looking from Marc to Louis, who raised his eyes at the mention of the girl. "I wonder if you know her. Perhaps she is a friend of your Lulu. Her name is Mlle Trouvé."

"Ah, yes," Marc said, grinning happily. "Garcelle. Yes, she is a sweet girl. But I don't know that she'd be right for you."

"Oh no," I said. "I wasn't thinking of that."

"She is very proper. Some say she is haughty. Claire is her aunt."

"Claire?"

He nodded over my shoulder, and when I turned I saw the lady with the cart.

Marc winked at me. "Perhaps it would be best not to mention this to Claire."

"I was just curious," I said. "She seemed like a very nice young lady."

Marc gave me a sad little smile. "I know how it is. You don't have to explain. There comes a time when a man has to go on living. Am I right, Louis?" he said, turning to his friend. "We must find comfort wherever we can."

⁂

The next morning I awoke later than usual to the jarring snap of something large and sturdy breaking down below. Then came the shriek of splintering wood.

Only partially dressed, I staggered onto the balcony. Across the drive, scattered on the grass, lay the entire contents of the guesthouse: the long oak table surrounded by overstuffed chairs, an ottoman atop the sideboard, the grand piano and its stool separated from one another by an armoire and a pile of leather-bound books.

At the edge of the drive a man stood with his foot planted in the middle of an overturned buffet table. With four lazy blows of a hammer he knocked off each of the legs.

By the time I reached the drive, another man was climbing into the open piano with a pair of wire cutters.

"What do you think you're doing?" I yelled.

The man pulled his head out of the piano, regarding me with curiosity. "Who are you?"

Nearly out of breath, I reached past him and grabbed hold of the prop supporting the piano lid. "You have to stop."

He watched with bemusement as I closed the lid.

"This doesn't belong to you," I said. "It belongs to Madame Freeman. I demand that you put everything back."

The man with the wire cutters shrugged. "Never heard of her." But warmly, as if we were old friends, he came over and put his hand on my shoulder. "You know how it is. We've got a lot to do."

"You don't understand."

He had his arm thrown over me now, and I smelled the rum on his breath. "We're brothers, you and me."

"No," I said, "we're nothing of the kind."

His smile took a menacing turn, and he freed his arm from around my shoulders.

Reaching down, he gripped the edge of the piano lid and threw it back. Despite the weight of the wood, the lid seemed to sail, stopping only when the hinge could go no further. With a snap and a groan, the metal separated from the wood. The upright lid wobbled for a moment, uncertain which way it should go. Finally it began its long retreat, landing with a crash that caused the strings inside to thrum.

I must have been a peculiar sight, running down the path half dressed. Had I paused to think about what I was doing, I might have stopped and turned back. Did I really expect Dragon Guy to do something to stop the destruction? But it had been years since I had run like this, and momentum kept me going.

As I neared Madame's villa, I heard voices. There was a loud splash of water, then laughter. They must have heard me as well, for they were waiting when I rushed around the corner to enter the courtyard.

Two men with machine guns hanging from straps around their necks stood side by side. One of them threw out his arms to stop me.

The last thing I saw was the other man raising the butt of his gun to my head.

I awoke in my room as dusk was working its way through the louvers.

"How are you, monsieur?" Hector said, sitting in a chair with his back to the window.

Gingerly I touched my head, feeling the dry clumps of blood. It was almost the same spot as the last time. "More or less as you would imagine."

"That's a pretty nasty lump you have."

"Are you here to tell me I had an accident?"

"An accident, monsieur? No, no. A misunderstanding. My brother asked me to come and apologize."

CHRISTOPHER HEBERT

I tried to sit up, but my head was throbbing.

"Does he expect me to accept his apology?"

"We have to be careful, monsieur. These are dangerous times. You should be careful, too."

"I'm aware that a great deal has changed around here," I said. "But it has not changed so much that I find myself in need of advice from a sixteen-year-old boy."

"I'm just trying to help."

"If you want to help," I said, "you could stop your brother from destroying everything in sight."

"No one wants to destroy anything," Hector said. "But there are some things more important than your precious estate."

It was painful to look into his eyes and see the cold indifference there. "You don't have to pretend," I said. "You don't have to do what your brother says. I know you love it here."

Hector got up from the chair, and with the light at his back I could no longer see his face.

"What other choice do I have?" His voice was gruff, and yet he could not stop himself from sighing. "We're at war. We're fighting for our freedom." As he came forward I saw that he felt sorry for me—for my pitiful inability to understand.

"War?" I said. "What is this war you keep talking about? Wars have strategies and purposes and aims. Wars have battles and campaigns. This is not a war. This is just shooting. This is nothing but mindless, brutal violence. This is a power struggle, nothing more. Your brother wants to topple President Duphay. Fine. But what does he propose to put in his place? How is all of this going to make anything better? Nothing is going to change. There's just going to be more death. Don't fool yourself," I said. "You're too smart for this. You're just going to get all these people killed."

My head suddenly felt like a bucket of stones. I had to close my eyes. I could no longer sit up straight.

"You might be right, monsieur."

I felt my head lift and a pillow slide underneath.

"But it's still something," Hector continued. "And it's more than you or any politician has ever done. What did you ever do to make things better?"

"I built this place," I whispered through the crushing pain.

"What good did that ever do any of us?"

"If I had not built it," I said, "you and your brother and everyone else would already be dead."

"Goodnight, monsieur," Hector said. "My brother is expecting me."

Hector had been gone just a few minutes when there was a knock on the door.

Claire limped over to my bedside table, setting down a supper tray.

"Thank you," I said.

Closing the door behind her, she said, "I put a little extra in the bowl."

Chapter Twenty-Seven

What was most surprising was how quickly life came to seem routine. Each day the children went to school at the casino. The older boys and the newest recruits drilled on the tennis courts. I kept up my walks along the grounds and took my meals in the dining room with the other men, never forgetting my bowl. Though I often saw Marc and Louis, I found other places to sit.

One evening after sunset I saw the skinny young man sitting with a young woman on a bench in the pavilion. Partially hidden behind a lattice woven with vine, he leaned in and kissed her. Was she Lulu the laundress? I wished I could hear their voices, whispering in each other's ears. I wondered what sorts of promises they were making. What could love feel like at a time like this? Perhaps they were imagining their future together. But what could that future possibly look like? Had they picked out the villa in which they would raise their family and tend their garden? Did they think this would last forever? They were so young—how could they understand these brief lives they were living were not their own?

There was only one person who I thought understood. Alone she sat each afternoon on the steps of the casino, tending to the children, as removed as it was possible to be from Dragon Guy's kingdom. It could not have been more clear that she did not belong with these people. And it occurred to me that no one, perhaps not even Mlle Trouvé herself, was aware that something else was possible, that there existed a world where she could be happy. Or at least it had existed, and could exist again. And only I could show it to her. Not Dragon Guy, not Black Max. No one but me.

Alone I often saw Mlle Trouvé walking the villa paths, always with a book in her hands. The only time she was not alone was during mass. I wondered how Dragon Guy had ever gotten her to come here. No words, no matter how grandiose, could have persuaded her to join such a futile cause. There could be no allure for her in such brutish men. I could imagine her, the beloved teacher, standing in a clean, pressed skirt at the front of a classroom, holding up a picture for her students, a forest of raised, eager hands. Had they kidnapped her—Dragon Guy and Black Max kicking in the schoolhouse door? No; she would have had plenty of opportunity to escape. The only reason could have been that she came for the children, knowing only she could protect them.

As she prayed each Sunday in the grass outside the pavilion, I thought I felt Mlle Trouvé asking for forgiveness—not for herself but for everyone else, for all of those too blind to realize what the future held. I could see, all around me, signs of that future approaching. In the corridor outside my rooms, the rugs were wearing low. All night long there was shouting in the room next door. Sometimes I was able to catch a few words, but rarely enough of them to derive any meaning.

Despite living in such close proximity, I had little idea who my neighbors were, aside from their ranks. I had seen some of their faces when we happened to pass one another on the way to or from the stairs, but I seldom saw them anywhere else. They did not dine with the other men. They did not socialize. Some of them went to the Sunday mass at the pavilion, but not all. Some of them I was quite sure I had never seen, although I occasionally heard their voices.

There was one in particular, sharper than the rest, who even through the wall conveyed more than a hint of menace. Whenever he spoke, everyone else instantly fell silent, no matter how animated the discussion had been just moments before. I eventually learned he was a colonel, and I did not need to be present in their private meetings to understand he was the one the others most feared. Perhaps even more than Dragon Guy.

I recall one night, not long after they had moved into the manor house, when the fighting was especially intense. A messenger came running to the colonel's office. Outside my door he paused, and I could hear him breathing heavily as he tried to collect himself. However well he succeeded, the moment the colonel's door opened, the boy lost his composure. "I told him, Colonel," he blurted, still standing in the hall, where I could not help but overhear. "I gave him your orders, but he won't listen. He refused—" and there was a strangled sound as the boy was yanked inside.

The door closed like a thunderclap. The colonel's voice was calm but stern. There were others in the room with him. I heard them arguing, but each time anyone dared open his mouth, the colonel's voice returned them to silence. They seemed to know better than to contradict him.

With so little possibility of debate, the discussion did not last long. The door reopened, and the boy stepped out again into the hall. And then, for the first time, I heard the colonel's voice clearly, without a wall between us.

"Tell him," he said softly, carefully, as if searching for just the right words. "If he disobeys me again, I will have his head."

The boy tried to say something to indicate he understood, but the words got stuck and came out as little more than a gurgle. In his eagerness to get away, he stumbled. I heard his feet trip on the rug. No matter how clumsy he was, I wished just then that I could follow him, wherever he was going. I did not need to know whom they were discussing to share the boy's terror.

I often wondered if these men ever thought about me, troubled about the secrets I might overhear. At first I was careful to sit in the part of the room farthest from their voices; should they take it upon themselves to kick open the door, I wanted them to see my innocence. I kept my water glass full, lest they think I had been pressing it to the wall.

But soon it became all too clear that they considered my presence to be of no consequence. In me they saw not the slightest danger.

Late one afternoon, a few days after my encounter with Dragon Guy's guards, I was sitting on the balcony when I saw Hector down below, crossing the drive to the guesthouse. For the last several days I had not been able to stop thinking about our conversation. Since all of this had started, it had become easy to forget how young he was— that he was still just a boy. As hard as it was for everyone else to resist Dragon Guy, I could not imagine how difficult it would be for his own brother. But I knew Hector's better nature, and I knew I had to keep trying.

If Hector heard me calling out to him, he showed no sign. After a few more steps he disappeared inside the guesthouse. I waited for him, bent over the railing, but when a few minutes had passed and he still had not come back outside, I got up and went downstairs.

From the front steps, the guesthouse was quiet. The entire estate had been quiet all day. I knocked at the front door, but no one answered. What would I have said if they had?

The smell hit me the moment I turned the knob. Faint yet fetid, it seemed to seep from the wood. The open door released the rest, a queasying stench of decay that poked its wretched fingers up my nostrils. From down the hall came a rumble of coughing. A murmur of voices snaked from corner to corner. As I approached the drawing room, the coughing continued, growing louder and hoarser. I detected other sounds too—jumbled and indistinct, like the hum of a crowd heard from a distance. The corridor was lined with refuse: piles of filthy rags and empty baskets. Beside a broom made of palm fronds lay a mound of broken glass.

I saw the first man just as I was reaching the doorway to the drawing room. He was lying on a low table, his head wrapped in a rust-colored bandage. His eyes were closed. I came forward softly, trying not to wake him. Next to him lay another man. At first I could see him only from the neck up, dirty and unshaven but not visibly injured. As I turned the corner he rolled his head toward me, parting his bloodshot eyes.

The drawing room was the largest in the guesthouse, occupying a full quarter of the first floor. The northern wall was mostly glass, a series of broad, tall, arching windows, one after the next. The shades had been lowered, projecting a foggy yellow pallor across the otherwise darkened room, making it look like an old photograph. There were three rows of men, one each along the east and west walls, and one in between, cutting the room in half. All of the men were laid out on makeshift beds of varying lengths and heights, many constructed of a familiar glossy, black-lacquered wood. It was all here: Madame's piano and priceless antiques stripped into cots and gurneys.

Between most of the men there was room enough for a single person to stand. But there were also seven or eight men side by side on the dining room table, separated by only a few inches of bare mahogany. Nowhere on any of the beds was there a single sheet. Those had been turned into wrappings, which I saw now encircling arms and legs and feet and hands—or whatever it was that remained of them.

There must have been sixty or seventy beds, but that seemed too few. I had never seen so much blood, staining not just the men themselves but the beds and the floor and even the walls. A few heads turning to look at me led to a few more, until half the room was gazing at me with both curiosity and indifference, as if eager for distraction but sorry it came in no other form than me.

The last to notice me were the two women in dirty dresses and head scarves at the far end of the room, facing the windows as they examined one of their patients.

"What do you want?" one of them asked, glancing distractedly at me over her shoulder as she ground something in a mortar.

"Nothing."

She had already turned back around, as if I had not spoken.

Throughout the rest of the guesthouse I found more of the same. Every room on the first floor was filled with beds and sick, wounded bodies: more men in the dining room and a ward of women in the library. In the kitchen several women with blackened fingers were grinding herbs and making poultices while a pot boiled over on the stove.

"Are you lost?" one of them asked.

"I'm looking for Hector."

She dropped a rag in the boiling pot. "Haven't seen him."

"Try out back," said another.

The corridor off the kitchen led to the back patio, an otherwise short route made treacherous by the trash spilling underfoot. I had not been in the yard behind the guesthouse in some time—since long before Dragon Guy's arrival. Yet despite everything I had seen of late, I was still surprised to stand beside the empty pool and find not a single flower. The grass was mostly gone as well. Alone, barefoot in the dirt with a shovel at his side, an old man with a raw pink patch of skin covering the right side of his face peered down into the hole he was digging, as if trying to measure its depth. All around him, rectangular patches of dark soil showed where many more such holes had recently been filled. At the edge of the patio, a six-foot bundle lay wrapped in yet another stained sheet.

"The service is over."

"I see."

The old man stabbed his shovel into the earth. "There's still time to pay your respects."

Seeing me standing there uncertainly, he came forward and took me by the arm. When we were just a few inches from the body, he lowered his head and closed his eyes.

I tried to tell myself that people did it all the time, praying for strangers. In a place like this, one did not always have the luxury of a face to identify the dead. And what did it matter, really? The dead all wanted the same thing.

I, too, closed my eyes and lowered my head. The smell made it impossible to forget what was at my feet.

In the self-imposed darkness an image began to draw itself in my mind. I did not want it there, and I fought it back, but it would not go away. So I opened my eyes, and for a moment everything was better. But when I closed my eyes again, the image returned. I could see nothing but Senator Marcus. His fine features, his carefully clipped mustache. But he was not dead. He was asleep in his bed, utterly at peace.

Very well, I said to myself, holding my breath, and I prayed. I prayed for the Senator's soul, and for the soul in the bag, and for Hector and Mlle Trouvé and Mona and Madame, and even for Dragon Guy and all the doomed souls he had brought here with him, and I hoped—despite the abundant signs to the contrary—that it might do someone some good.

Sitting on the balcony that evening, I was relieved to find the image of Senator Marcus gone. But I was left now with all those men wrapped in rags soaked in their own blood. I tried to put them out of my head, too. But I had nothing to replace them with. When I tried to think about how things had once been, I could see them only as they were now. There were no more gardens. After three months of their presence, there was not a single thing on the estate anymore that shone. Not even the lifetime supply of floor polish Paul had sold me could erase the traces of what had happened here. That blood would always remain.

And as dusk came on and—like every night—I watched Dragon Guy's men march up the drive to resume their endless battle, I felt a numbness come over me. How many would return in tatters and how many not at all? So futile did the entire exercise seem that I failed to see the point. I doubted if they knew themselves what awaited them outside the gate, no matter how many times they had gone out there. One could see the same blankness on a goat tethered to a stake, oblivious that the knife ground against the whetstone was intended for him. Nor was I sure anything would have changed if the men had known. It was a brutal fate, and this was a brutal place, but they were brutal themselves. Even the sad little men I had come to know at supper were brutal in their own sad little ways. Their lives were no more than this. What was the point in mourning them? Why bother trying to save them when they were too stupid to save themselves? These were the same people who had plagued me all my life. I had thought I had escaped them; maybe I had been a fool even to try.

If the fighting was more vicious that night than usual, I barely noticed. It was all the same to me whether there were ten guns firing or ten thousand. I laid my head down on my feather pillow, and I went to sleep. And I slept as I had not slept in years. Nothing—not a single sound—penetrated, and even my dreams left no impression.

And when I awoke in the morning, just as the sun was rising, I felt oddly refreshed. The blood had been washed away after all. Standing out on the balcony, I looked down upon the canopy of trees below, blotting out the villas and their inhabitants. For once there was no smoke, and it occurred to me that from my old window in Senator Marcus's attic the distant green oasis on the mountainside would appear no different today than it had then, no less inviting.

I had been out on the balcony only a few minutes when I heard the commotion at the gate. The goats were coming back from the slaughter. And as I turned to watch them bump and bleat back down the drive to their beds—much more slowly than they had gone out—I thought to myself, Let them do what they will. Let them kill themselves, if that is what they want. But may they do it quickly.

That morning, an unmistakable pall clung to Dragon Guy's men, apparent even from so great a distance. Not until they were almost below me did I see why. At the lead, where I had never seen her before, strode René-Thérèse. The woman who ordinarily carried herself like a queen shuffled now like a penitent. Beside her walked two men I did not recognize, struggling to bear a stretcher between them, upon which lay the still form of a man dressed in a white linen suit. How strange, I thought, that nowhere did I see a single spot of blood. One panel of the jacket had fallen away from Dragon Guy's chest, revealing the intense green dragon. René-Thérèse gripped the fabric in her fingers, as if trying to keep the creature from flying away.

Instead of dispersing as they usually did upon reaching the end of the drive, the men clung limply together, watching the stretcher bearers stumble up the steps to the guesthouse with Dragon Guy. Two of the nurses stood waiting in the doorway. The grim looks with which they beheld their coming charge told everyone watching everything they needed to know about their leader's fate.

Soon there was shouting in the lobby, and the noise grew steadily louder as the men stomped upstairs. There were voices everywhere, and I found myself clinging to the arms of my chair until they passed, slamming seemingly every door on the second floor, except for the one belonging to the colonel. The manor house trembled and I did too, before allowing myself one deep, hopeful breath.

Perhaps the dragon was not invincible after all.

Almost no one showed up for breakfast. Among those who did, there seemed to be a sense that only silence would be permitted. In no case would I have dared to speak. Now more than ever I knew I must hold my tongue and wait.

For the rest of the day, everyone hung about in a suspended state, waiting for the dreaded news they thought might come at any moment. Me as much as anyone else. But I did not take part in the endless speculation.

Black Max had been shot alongside his friend, and he was already dead. No one saw it happen. There were some who insisted it must have been one of Dragon Guy's own men who did it, someone trusted, someone close. If that was true, was the traitor still among us? For the first time since they arrived here, I saw them eyeing each other with a suspicion they normally reserved for me. I could not have been more happy to share.

Never could I have imagined their idyll could crumble so quickly.

For once, I was glad when the evening darkness began its lazy creep over the mountains and the nightly assembling of arms commenced upon the lawn. They would not take the night off to sit at the side of their leader, waiting for him to die. Indeed, they seemed more eager than ever to fight. I could not wait until they were gone, taking their fury with them. From within my office—even with the shutters closed—I heard snatches of speeches trying to inflame them further.

"Dragon Guy is worth a hundred men," one of them boomed, as if he were shouting through a horn. "Tonight we will kill a thousand."

"Destroy them all," screamed someone else, sounding as if blood were already running from his lips.

And then came the chant, bursting from every hysterical throat: "Duphay shall pay."

Before they began their frantic march up the drive, I peeked out just once, and what I saw was more than two hundred men raising their weapons to the heavens, and their cry for revenge was like a cannon. In the center of it all, Hector stood, silent and still, like a boy lost in a crowd.

Chapter Twenty-Eight

The news that Dragon Guy was dead reached me in my sleep. It was not yet dawn when I heard the sobs and sprang up out of bed, hurrying to the balcony. There were two women clinging to one another on the lawn below, their necks entwined like birds. Each was the only thing keeping the other erect. Their cries were loud enough to wake the entire estate.

The mood around the manor house was grim, even worse than the day before. In seemingly every corner, small groups of men and women huddled, talking in low voices. No one seemed to have any idea what to do, and so they did nothing. Here and there men paced in silence, staring absently at the walls. They collected under every shady tree, like fallen fruit.

As word spread, so too did the rumor that perhaps Dragon Guy had been dead all along, and that only now were they telling us. That the men suspected such a thing gave me hope I had until now not dared to dream.

The blood pounded in my ears. Without Dragon Guy, would there be nothing to keep all of this from unraveling and his army from fleeing?

Throughout the day, the words "What now?" were on nearly everyone's lips, but it was their eyes—both heavy and quick—that gave away their fear. And then there was me, doing everything I could to keep my rising hope to myself. I struggled to remain still, abandoning a letter to Madame after getting no further than the salutation. When at last my rooms grew too constrictive, I went outside, making certain to keep my eyes low to the ground.

At the door to Mona's kitchen I knocked quietly.

"Mona," I whispered, but she would not answer.

It was difficult to keep from yelling the news to her, loudly enough that everyone would hear.

School had been canceled at the casino. The restaurant was empty; even Claire was gone.

The one familiar face I finally came across as I was walking along the paths was Marc's. I was unaccustomed to seeing him without his skinny friend, and I wondered if Louis was off somewhere seeking comfort in the arms of Lulu.

It was clear that Marc, too, was in distress. "What will happen?" he said. "What will we do?"

"I wish I knew," I said. But he continued to look at me expectantly, as if certain I possessed the information he so desperately needed. I added, "All I know are the rumors."

His eyes opened wide in anticipation.

"I've heard this will probably be the end." I did not wish to lie to Marc. I liked him too much for that. But in fact this had already begun to feel like the truth. As I said it, I felt my mind spinning on, putting together the pieces to come, assembling a list of what needed to be done. The repairs, the planting, the painting, the cleaning. It was not too late. Hector would come back, and together we could fix the estate so that Madame would never have to know what had happened. By the time she returned, it would be just as it was. Perhaps not *just*, but close enough that she might once again feel she was home.

"Is it true?"

"It is," I said, and I meant it. "I'm sure of it. And do you know what that means?"

He did not try to disguise that he did not.

"It's time for you to go find your wife and daughter."

Something changed in his face. A brightening. An opening. I could see the idea did not displease him, and I was relieved. First Marc, and then the others would follow.

"What if I can't find them?"

"You will."

He thought about that for a moment. "What about you?"

"What about me?"

"Your wife," he said. "There's no more point in waiting. She'll never come back now."

Having created this deceit, I had no choice but to agree. Inside, though, I was beaming; with Dragon Guy gone, there would be nothing to keep Mme Freeman from coming back.

Just then, over Marc's shoulder, I spotted a boy running toward us up the path. He could have been one of Mlle Trouvé's students, but not one I recognized. As he drew closer, Marc heard his footsteps and turned, and I saw that the boy was waiting to say something.

"What do you want?" Marc said with uncharacteristic irritation.

"Aren't you coming?"

"Coming where?"

"There's going to be an announcement."

"Wait," I said, reaching out for Marc as he started off after the boy.

"Later."

"Promise me," I said.

He brushed me off, waving for me to come along. "We'll talk about it later."

By the time we arrived at Dragon Guy's villa, the boy had long since disappeared into the crowd. Everyone was there: half-dressed men who appeared to have come straight from bed; women holding paring knives and laundry baskets. Even the children had come, drawn in by the promise of some rare kind of excitement. They were packed in around the pool, filling every last space. In front of me I could see almost nothing but heads. Perhaps three to four hundred. I saw them, and my head fell into my hands. Dear God, I thought, How could I possibly get rid of so many?

"What do you think is happening up there?" Marc asked.

Every once in a while there was the briefest of openings, and I thought I could see the edge of some kind of structure. I could not tell what.

I gestured to Marc to stay where he was. "I'll go and see if I can get a better look."

Squeezing through a gap, I made my way toward the edge of the courtyard. There, beneath the sunlit canopy of a mombin tree, was a low stone bench. That little bit of height made all the difference. Beyond the heads, beyond the pool, directly in front of Dragon Guy's villa, a small wooden platform rose above the patio. It was impossible to hear over the crowd, but on one corner of the platform an old man was kneeling, weakly tapping nails into the boards below him. He was all there was to see.

For several minutes the old man continued to hammer. Several times he dropped a nail, and it was painful to watch him searching, his failing eyes of little use. When at last he was finally done, he wobbled to one knee. Using the hammer as a cane, he pushed himself unsteadily up the rest of the way. He had aged so much so quickly that at first I did not recognize him. It was as if the last three months had for him stretched into years. Even now, as he turned around and faced the crowd, only his blue plaid shirt gave him away.

"Raoul," I yelled. "Raoul." But with all the noise there was no way to get his attention.

At the back of the platform he was met by one of Dragon Guy's guards, who lifted him up by his armpits and then lowered him to the ground, as if he were a child. In an instant, he was gone from sight, and there was no way for me to go after him.

Just as quickly, the noise evaporated too. It was eerie how suddenly it happened—as if someone had flipped a switch.

Hector ascended the stairs to the stage slowly, like an old man himself, unsure of his footing. As he made his way to the center, he looked at us with a strange uncertainty, as if he did not know how he came to find himself there. One might have mistaken him for someone strolling unawares into a surprise party. Seeing him here now, I realized how much he had grown in recent months. At sixteen, Hector had nearly reached the height of his brother, and he was almost equally broad and strong. But he was still a boy, and no matter how big he had grown, he could not help looking small up there all alone.

No one in the crowd dared to speak. What did they make of him? I wondered. Was he anything to them other than Dragon Guy's little brother? Would they try to resist when he told them it was time to leave, to go back to Cité Verd?

Hector lifted his arms awkwardly, stiffly from his sides, forcing them to fold across his chest. He was trying to look like a defiant warrior. Where had he learned such a pose? It was nothing I had ever seen on his brother. Where did a boy who had grown up in a place like Cité Verd, utterly cut off from history and the rest of the world, find a model upon which to build such an image?

"Today," Hector began, "we have lost something great." I was surprised by the sound of his voice, coarse and deep and confident. But there was no denying that it suited the somber expression on his face. "But if you came here to mourn," he said after a suitable pause, "you have come to the wrong place. Dragon Guy was a brave soldier, the most courageous among us. And I know all of you loved him like he was your brother. He was your brother as much as he was mine. But we are at war, and there is no place in war for sentiment."

Around me, I saw many of the men and women sharing glances, but no one was willing to risk so much as a whisper. "This was not our first loss," Hector continued, and as an afterthought he raised his fist into the air. It was an odd moment for such a gesture, but he appeared to have little idea what else to do with his hands. "It will not be our last," he added. "Many of our comrades have been killed. But I ask you to remember this: for every blow we've suffered, we've dealt two in return. That's how it is when the weak fight back."

As his eyes swept the crowd, I felt a strange unease come over me. Where had he found these words?

"*They* are strong," the boy added with another pump of his fist, "only when the fight is easy. Our courage increases their cowardice. That is why even though the man who calls himself our president can offer pay and uniforms and weapons, it is *our* army, not *his*, that continues to grow. Look around you. Look into the face of your neighbor." Everyone around me did as he commanded. They were transfixed. "That is the face of a soldier. That is a face François Duphay fears. Even those who once said it was impossible to fight back have joined us now. And we hold out our arms to welcome them. It is never too late," he thundered, "to join the side of the right and good."

As the aphorisms continued to fall from his lips, my bafflement grew. I could more easily believe he was somehow reading these words—despite his still almost complete illiteracy—than that he was making them up. What had happened to the boy I knew?

"There has never been a time when we've needed them more than we do now. M. Duphay understands that desperation is a poor battle companion. He knows that if he does not crush us now, we will crush him. From this day forward, all our efforts and all our energy must be focused on the fight ahead. We have God on our side, we have right on our side." He clenched his arms and brought together his fists. "We have everything we need."

Even as his voice rose and swelled, it was lost in the storm of cheers. Hector stood at the very edge of the stage, his face displaying none of the fire of his words. It was as if he were not aware that it was he everyone was applauding. But I knew that was not so. This platform, made of scrap boards and bent nails, could just as convincingly have been made of marble and topped with a golden throne. Despite his conviction and bearing, I could imagine him practicing his proud, expansive beneficence before Madame's gold-framed mirror. His eyes gave away the rest: the quick, subtle scanning of faces, searching for proof that the crowd had embraced him. And as his eyes traveled in my direction, glancing from man to man, I thought to climb down from the bench and lower my head, slipping unseen behind someone else. But when the moment came, I froze. His eyes locked on mine, and mine locked on his, and both of us wanted to look away, but neither of us could. So long were we stuck together like that that others in the crowd began to turn their heads to see what it was that had stolen Hector's attention. Were they simply curious? Was it jealousy?

The letting go happened in an instant. Suddenly aware of the attention he was attracting, Hector tore his eyes away and raised his hand. The applause, which had only just begun to wane, roared again. Hector lowered his arm and took a step backward, and there to meet him was René-Thérèse, wearing as usual her red head scarf. In her outspread hands she held a bright yellow garment, which she proceeded to drape over Hector's shoulders, affixing the corners of the cape across his throat with a familiar brooch. And as Hector turned to walk away, he glanced once more in my direction, bestowing me with something between a wink and a smile. Then he disappeared back into the villa, the cloth of one of Madame's favorite dresses billowing slightly behind him.

Just like that, the day that had begun in sorrow for everyone but me had completed its reversal. Yet whereas I had worked to guard my optimism, the men and women surrounding me in the courtyard saw no such need. That which they had lost—even things that could not be replaced—Hector had somehow given back.

How was it possible? How was any of this possible? Could that really have been Hector, the boy who ran my errands, the boy I was teaching to read? How could such a transformation happen? And how could they so readily embrace him, offering up their allegiance? Did they imagine the mere fact of their shared blood meant that Hector and Dragon Guy were one and the same? Could they not see he was just a child? Or were they desperate enough to have accepted anyone who happened to step onto that stage?

I did not go looking for Marc. There was no longer any point. Hector had seen to it that there was nothing I could say now to convince anyone to leave. Was that it, an opportunity that lasted no more than an hour? Had that really been my only chance? And how was it possible that, given the same chance, a boy could turn himself into a king? Could it really be that I had misjudged him all along?

A hand fell on my shoulder. René-Thérèse, her face proud and regal again, looked down at me from her great height. She took hold of my wrist. "Hector would like to see you."

This, our second walk together through the villa paths, passed in silence. I had no words to offer her for Dragon Guy. What was there to say to someone mourning a loss you yourself did not regret? And besides, why should she not offer her condolences for what had been visited upon me? The way she looked at me, courteous but cold, made it impossible for me to know whether she had come to realize it was me she had escorted that night so long ago. And even if she had, would it have given her cause for anger? There had to be a code for forgiving someone so soundly defeated as me.

Back at the courtyard, the crowds had already dispersed. Alone in front of the door, a fat, shirtless man wobbled out of his wicker chair. When he stood, he was even taller than René-Thérèse. There was no mystery about his function. Without needing to be asked, I turned toward the wall and raised my arms.

"Is this really necessary?" I asked.

"After what happened to Dragon Guy," René-Thérèse said blandly, "we can take no chances."

Having found nothing of interest in my possession, the thug stepped aside.

René-Thérèse pressed her fingers into the small of my back. "Go ahead."

Like a cat in repose, Hector lay sprawled on Madame's chaise longue, the ceiling fan spinning effortlessly above him. I felt as if I were watching some crude parody of ancient Rome—an absurd emperor lost in self-reverence. Yet it was just as he said: there was no trace of sentiment. No sign of Dragon Guy. Even his brother's unworn shirt was gone from the wardrobe. There was nothing about Hector that did not belong here, and yet it appeared he had changed neither himself nor the room. All of Madame's belongings remained. It was as if the people in her photographs had become Hector's friends, Hector's family. There had never been a Dragon Guy. Still in its spot on the wall across from the sofa, Mme Louvois's painting somehow appeared more brightly lit than ever before. Had the evening sun that had been fixed above the bay for nearly two hundred years circled round to midday? What would Mme Louvois have thought of all of this? I imagined she might have been pleased—in a wicked sort of way—to see that her husband, having lost his island, was now losing his home as well. But what about the general's servants—his wife's models? Would they have welcomed Hector as their king?

"How did you get it to work?" I asked.

As if half asleep, Hector slowly turned his head and glanced up at the ceiling. Such problems as a lack of electricity could not be made to concern him. "You can't expect us to tell you all our secrets."

For the first time I noticed we were not alone in the room. In addition to René-Thérèse there was an older man sitting at the table. He had eyes like melting ice cubes, cold and remarkably clear, with a faint halo of light, piercing blue. Around his neck he wore a string of white seashells. I had never seen him before, but I had the distinct impression that he knew me.

There was one other person, too. At Madame's desk a young woman was hunched over a tablet of paper. The scratch of her pencil was almost as steady as the fan.

"Good afternoon, Mlle Trouvé," I said.

Her pencil came to a sudden stop. "Shall we continue, sir?" she said, turning to Hector. "We were almost done."

Hector rolled back onto his side, head propped up on his folded arm. "Where did we leave off?"

Mlle Trouvé lifted the page. "'I'm giving you one last chance to retreat.'" Her voice was tired and flat.

Hector closed his eyes. I thought I saw his lips move, silently repeating the words.

René-Thérèse sat down on the sofa, leaning back and folding her long, thin legs beneath her, like a deckhand stowing unneeded sails. From a basket on the end table she selected a mango. As I watched her work at the peel, I realized she looked less like a widow than like a bored, idle girl.

"Just leave it there," Hector said, nodding decisively. "There's nothing more to say."

With Hector's eyes still cast upon the ceiling and René-Thérèse's on the fruit, Mlle Trouvé looked to the man in the shell necklace, who in turn nodded his assent. Only then did Mlle Trouvé put down her pencil, making it clear whose opinion it was that mattered.

With a long, creaking stretch, Hector rose from the chaise longue. René-Thérèse had worked the skin from the fruit and Hector sauntered over to her, snapping open the blade of a knife he had hidden who knew where. The mango lay cupped in her open palms, and Hector lifted it with a stab, raising the slippery fruit to his lips.

And then he turned to me with a smile. "It's good to see you again, monsieur."

At the desk, Mlle Trouvé was collecting her things. I scanned her face for traces of the shame she must have felt at being used like this. Even I was surprised they could be so crass, exploiting the most moral and intelligent person they could find. Then again, given their success with Hector, why should they stop there?

The young woman's expression was perfectly blank, as if her greatest wish were to pretend none of this were happening. I could not blame her.

"Is this some sort of joke?" I said, shifting my gaze back to Hector. "Your brother is dead, and this is how you behave?"

Hector blinked for a moment in silence, as if struggling to get his eyes to focus. "This is no time for sentiment—"

"I heard that already," I said, gesturing toward the stage. "But you seem to have plenty of time for acting like a buffoon."

Mlle Trouvé started toward the door, and for a moment I considered following her.

Instead I took the rest of them in, one at a time. "Pardon my saying so, but you are fools. All of you."

René-Thérèse and the man in the shell necklace received the news with curious indifference. All they seemed to care about was Hector's reaction. As if the boy and I were opponents on opposite ends of a tennis court, they turned to look at him. The ball was his now. They wanted to see what he would do with it.

There was no wicked return. No dramatic backhand. It was as if the ball had struck him square in the chest. Watching Hector's face fall, I realized it was more true than ever that I was the only one who truly cared for him. Army or not, I was all he had left.

"Do you not understand what will happen?" I said. "President Duphay knows you're here. They will come. You have children here. And women."

A sneer slid across his face. "You're just afraid of what they'll do to your precious estate."

In fact, it was only then that I realized I had not been thinking of the estate at all; I had been thinking of Hector.

I came forward and grasped his arm. "Please," I said. "Don't do this."

Hector lowered his eyes upon my hands as if they belonged to a leper. "What do we have to lose?"

"Everything," I said. "We will lose everything."

⌖

Below my balcony Hector's army assembled at dusk, and I do not know how so many men managed to make so little noise. It was as if they were gathered for prayer, rather than battle. And indeed, standing at the front of his nearly three hundred troops, Hector bowed his head. His men did the same.

And then Hector lifted his eyes, and he touched his hand to his heart. "Tonight," he shouted, and his voice seemed to catch. "Tonight," he tried again, "we will turn the moonlight red."

Tonight they did not march up the drive. Instead they rushed past Hector like a waterfall over a precipice, screaming for blood.

Chapter Twenty-Nine

In the morning, on the grass around the guesthouse, too numerous to count, lay the bodies of the injured and the dying and the dead, with nurses scurrying from one to the next in a futile effort to tell them apart. The men who were still among the living clung to their comrades' sides, offering encouragement and bonhomie. It was strange how even the faces of the grievously wounded cast a determined peacefulness, as if desperate to prove how pleased they were with how things had turned out. Despite the carnage, the mood was almost gleeful. It was just as Hector had said: for these men, bloodshed had become an end in itself. They were content to keep on fighting until everyone and everything was dead.

A young woman with dreadlocks and a baby on her hip told me where to go, pointing down the path. Second on the right.

The sun had only just risen and the courtyard was empty, but I could hear voices coming from inside one of the villas. A man came out and emptied a tin cup into the dust, scratched his crotch, and then went back inside.

The villa I was looking for was the farthest from the path. The room was badly lit and became more so as my body blocked out the scant bit of rusty light that had been sneaking in the partially open door. Raoul lay on his back in bed, his unbuttoned shirt twisted and bunched around his waist and arms.

I knocked, and his eyes fluttered open. He struggled to rise up on his elbows.

"Who's there?" he said hoarsely.

"It's me."

He pivoted slowly, laboriously swinging his legs over the side of the bed. "What time is it?"

"Early."

"Is there water?"

On the desk stood a crystal vase smudged with dust and fingerprints. I poured the last of the water into a cup.

Hunched forward over his knees, Raoul gripped the side of the bed with both hands. He let go with one to take the cup. He drank slowly, but still some of the water dribbled from his mouth.

I placed the cup back on the desk, and when I turned around again I saw him struggling to get up.

"Take my hand."

His body felt as slight as a blanket. As I helped him up and guided him, arm in arm, toward the door, I marveled at the ease with which we were able to slip into this intimacy, as we never had before. With everything else that had changed, perhaps it was only natural that this would too.

Once outside, he paused to catch his breath, leaning against the patio wall with his eyes closed.

"This sort of thing is meant for younger men."

For a moment I did not know what to say. I was quite certain those were the first words he had ever volunteered in my presence.

"That's true for both us," I said.

His expression was dubious. "You? You're still a young man."

"I wish I felt that way."

"Look at me." He scratched his white-whiskered chin with his sleeve. "This is what an old man looks like. Do you feel like this?"

If I told him sometimes I did, I knew he would not believe me, and I was not about to put so unprecedented a conversation as this at risk.

He pointed toward the corner of the patio, where two bedraggled chairs squatted side by side in the shade.

"They've been working you too hard," I offered as I helped him over, curious to see if he would continue.

Settling into the chair, Raoul chased away a yawn.

"Do you know," he said sleepily, "I'd never been in one of these before. The whole time I was working here, I never went inside. A glance through the doorway once or twice. That was all."

"You could have," I said. "I wouldn't have stopped you." Perhaps a lot would have been different, I wanted to add, if you had ever bothered to speak.

"Do you ever think about what it would have been like to be one of those people? Lying about all day like a lizard. Nothing to worry about but that your skin didn't burn."

"I know what it was like," I said. "I was there."

He rolled his head toward me, squinting in my face. "I mean what it was like to *be* one of them, not just to *see* them."

"It was paradise."

"Was it?" He seemed not at all convinced. What did he know of paradise?

"You'll never understand what a paradise it was."

He leaned back and closed his eyes, as if he were trying to conjure it up in a dream. I was almost sorry to have to interrupt.

"Raoul," I said, "I need your help."

He opened one eye cautiously.

"Talk to Hector," I said. "He refuses to listen to me."

"What am I supposed to talk to him about?"

"He's making a terrible mistake," I said. "He's going to get hurt. He's going to get all these people killed."

Raoul shared a bemused smile. "What did you expect him to do?"

"I expected him to come to his senses."

Raoul sighed.

"He's just a boy," I said. "He has so much potential."

"For what?" Raoul scratched his head. "Did you think he would be just like you?"

Why not? Given the alternatives, would that be so wrong?

"This fantasy you and everyone else here is living," I said, "it's not real. There isn't going to be a happy ending."

Raoul looked at me as if that were the most ridiculous thing he had ever heard. "It's no less real than what you were living before."

"Not to me," I said.

He shrugged, acknowledging the impasse. "I bet if you ask any of them, they'll tell you they like it better this way."

"How would they know what it was like before?"

He regarded me with a strange, almost amused curiosity. "Do you really not know?"

"Know what?"

"They said you didn't, but I couldn't believe it." He could see all over my face that I had no idea what he was talking about. "Look around you," he said. "How could you not recognize them?"

"Recognize who?"

Raoul placed his hand on my knee. With the other he pointed to a man across the courtyard. I could not tell if it was the same one I had passed on my way in.

"He worked in the kitchen," Raoul said.

"Where?"

"Where do you think? The hotel."

I tried to make out his face, but there was no way to be sure. "He's too far away."

"I could call him over," Raoul said, raising his hand to wave.

"No."

"Over there," he said, pointing to another villa, "live two of your houseboys."

"I don't believe it."

"A couple of days ago at lunch I saw you sitting with one of your old drivers. Half the women around here were maids."

"That's impossible," I said. "I knew the drivers. I knew every single one of them. I may not have known all the others, but I couldn't be expected to know them all."

Raoul shrugged.

"How would you know, anyway? You weren't here then. You never knew any of them."

"Everyone knows."

"I can't be expected to remember them all."

"They remember you."

"What is that supposed to mean?" I said, noting the unmistakable relish with which he related this.

"Like you said," he replied with a shrug, "I wasn't there."

I got up and walked over to the patio wall. From there I had a better view of the man who had supposedly worked in the kitchen. Even as I began to process what Raoul was telling me, I could not begin to shape it into any sense. If it was true, what did it mean? Whatever it was, something had clearly shifted beneath me, just as Raoul had known it would.

"They're lying," I said, knowing they had tried to make me out to be some kind of monster. "Whatever they said about me was a lie. My only crime was expecting them to work."

Raoul spread his arms to stretch. "It's getting late," he said, glancing at the brightening sky above the treetops. "Claire should be here soon. She said she'd bring me some food."

I had no memory of getting up. I was certain I never said good-bye.

The rest of the morning and the day, each in turn, lifted away, and evening lowered itself in their place. I found myself in my rooms, sitting stiffly at the edge of the bed, holding on like a man at sea, struggling to withstand the roiling waves. Even my office felt menacing, as if something unseen lurked in every corner.

Fully dressed and covered with a blanket, I still could not get warm. All around me mosquitoes buzzed with electricity, oblivious of the cold. If I was truly so despised, why had all of this remained hidden for so long? That question pressed against my skull like the weight of the ocean upon a sinking stone. Had Hector hated me too? What about Mme Freeman? For her, too, was I anything more than just a fool who did her bidding?

In my dreams that night I saw my father, and I awoke understanding I had been utterly abandoned, just as I had abandoned him.

As I sat alone eating breakfast the next morning, Marc came over to join me. Ever since my conversation with Raoul, I could not stop scrutinizing every face I saw, trying to divine in their expressions the grudges they held against me. But how could I know, now that I had lived with them for so long, whether I recognized them from the past or from the present? All I could see of Marc was Marc, the simple young man who never stopped smiling.

Leaning discreetly toward my ear, he said, "I've been thinking. You're right—it's time I went to find my family."

I could barely summon the enthusiasm to nod.

"I'm going to start by finding the man with the boat," he said, opening his hands before me, as if the plan lay written there. "He was the one I paid to take them. Someone will know his name and where he lives. He's probably still doing it. There's always a need for that kind of business. And I'll bet he remembers my wife. The picture I had is gone, but her mother will have another. Someone as beautiful as my wife is someone you don't forget. Especially not when she has a beautiful little girl, too. And I remember he had a son or a nephew—maybe he was a younger cousin—that worked with him. If I can't find the man himself, I'll find the nephew. He was the one I gave the money to, and I'm sure he could tell me where to start. Maybe I could even get him to take me there, to where he dropped them off. I know she wouldn't have gone far. She would have wanted to stay near the water. And she knew I would come for her. She'll be expecting me."

"Of course," I said, though I knew it no longer mattered. The exodus I had hoped for was no longer possible, not as long as Hector was willing to accept the cost of martyrdom.

"Do you think so?"

"Of course," I said. "Of course." But my mind was elsewhere. "Marc," I added after a moment, "there's something I have to ask you."

He raised his eyes distractedly.

"Did we know each other before?"

"Before what?"

"Before all of this."

He seemed not to have any idea what I was talking about. "I don't think so, why?"

"I thought not."

He nodded in agreement, as if he were just as pleased as me to have this matter resolved.

His eyes suddenly lit up again. "Why don't you come, too?"

"Where?"

"To find your wife. You should come with me."

I shook my head. "Not yet."

"Then when?" His eyes were nearly pleading. "You can't still believe she'll come back?"

In truth, I was no longer sure how to answer. "I don't know."

"Come with me," Marc said. "They might even be in the same place. They might even know each other."

I was still thinking about what he had said before, about Madame not coming back. It was not the first time he had said such a thing, but for the first time the idea continued to linger, and I could not seem to push it away.

"No," I said distractedly. "I think that's unlikely."

"How can you know?"

"She's in the north," I said. "My—*mine*." I could not say the word.

He looked puzzled. "Have you heard from her? Did you receive a letter?"

"Yes," I said, realizing my blunder. And then I said it again, as if to convince myself it was true.

"I'm so happy for you," he said. Only then, as I watched the sadness overtake him, did I understand what I had done.

"It means the mail is starting to get through again," I said, trying to undo the damage. "You'll probably hear from your wife soon. And then there will be no need for the man with the boat."

He smiled weakly but he was no longer listening. It was as if he had heard me say, *Your wife is dead.*

Marc pushed back his chair and stood. Just like that, without intending to, I had added another enemy.

There were more than the usual number of guards at Hector's villa. Four of them sat at the edge of the stage, and by their movements I could see they were playing dominoes, but they had situated themselves in such a way that no one checking up on them from inside could see. When the moonlight caught me passing into the courtyard, they rose quickly, reaching for their guns.

"I'm here to see Hector." After what had happened to Dragon Guy, I knew this was where he would be, not out on the streets.

"Is he expecting you?" one of them asked.

"No."

I gave myself over to their rough hands.

Two lamps in distant corners of the sitting room glowed dully. In the dim light, little clouds of smoke circled each other like boxers waiting to strike. Madame's dining table had been moved to the center of the room, and around it I counted seven men in addition to Hector. With one exception, I was certain these were men I had not seen in all the time they had been here. Perhaps that was why I knew, beyond a doubt, that the four who looked familiar did so because I had known them before. Seeing them here now, with their cigars and their grimaces, I felt again as I had all those years ago when coming upon Senator Marcus and his colleagues in his study—as though I had walked in on something I was not supposed to see.

Sitting next to Hector was the man in the seashell necklace.

"This is a surprise, monsieur," he said, a sharpness in his voice that I immediately recognized. "We weren't expecting you."

So this was the colonel, the man with the office next door to mine. He was also, I was suddenly quite sure, a former waiter, one of Georges's colleagues. And then I realized who the others were. In appearance, there was little to separate Hector's lieutenants from the rest of the men I saw each day on the grounds. There were the same scars, the same scraggly beards. One of the younger ones had a broken tooth that pierced his cigar. Him I could not forget. He was the gardener we had arrested after he snuck onto the grounds with his pockets full of drugs. Beside him in sullen stupor sat one of the guards who had proven so useless the night of our grand opening. He had been equally useless on many other occasions too, until I was finally forced to fire him. And there was the pool boy who had nearly ruined Mlle Miller's visit.

I did not recognize the other three, but I could only assume they also counted themselves as victims of my unreasonable demand for basic competence and honesty.

"You must be kidding me," I said, turning to Hector. "This is your high command?"

The colonel displayed a tight, withering smile. And then he nodded toward the broken-toothed houseboy, who rose and went to the writing desk to fetch me a chair.

"I came to speak to Hector."

"Of course," the colonel said, gesturing for me to sit. With a false, ungracious smile, he stood and signaled to the others to do the same. "We'll give you a few minutes." Gesturing impatiently, he shooed the others toward the door.

Hector watched them go with slow, sad eyes, as if I were something to be feared. After all that had happened, I could not help feeling hurt. I had tried to give him everything—a new life, a future. Everything I had struggled for myself had been his for the taking. From the moment I met him, I had never been anything less than a friend.

"What do you want?" he whispered as soon as we were alone.

I slid my chair a few inches closer. "You have to end this," I said. "It's not too late."

I had never seen him look more miserable. He kept shaking his head, over and over again, as if there were someone else talking who I could not hear, someone he desperately wanted to silence. "What choice do I have?"

"You can't win," I said. "You can't let the army come. Think of all these people. Think of yourself. It's not too late to save them."

"Since when do you care about them?"

"I care about you," I said. "And I've gotten tired of watching people die."

He took a deep breath and closed his eyes. "It doesn't matter," he finally said. "We can't just give up."

I felt a hand on my elbow, tugging me tentatively from behind. I did not need to look to know who it was.

"Let go," I shouted, and he did. Just as useless a guard for Hector as he had been for the hotel.

The colonel was waiting for us on the patio, fingering the shells on the string around his neck. "Gerard will see to it that you make it back safely."

With a jerk I once again pulled my arm from his grasp. "I'll take my chances on my own."

Chapter Thirty

I ran into Louis the next morning at breakfast, just as he was leaving. He asked if I had seen Marc.

"No one knows where he is." He seemed distraught.

"He mentioned something about going to look for his wife," I told him, not sure how much was appropriate to say.

One of the men in Louis's group called out impatiently from down the hall, and Louis waved for him to wait. "Do you think he'll be back in time?"

"Back?" I said.

"For my wedding."

Smiles had been so rare of late that it felt strange to suddenly find one on my face. "Are you getting married?"

My smile was immediately dwarfed by his. "Tomorrow."

"To Lulu?" I said. "The laundress?" I would not have thought such news would please me so, but it had been a long time since we had experienced anything worth celebrating.

I offered him my hand in congratulations. After a tentative pause, he accepted, first brushing his palm against his pant leg.

"How could he miss it?" I said.

Louis's face lit up with relief. "You should come, too."

"Of course," I said. "Of course."

He was about to walk away for good when I raised my hand and gestured for him to stop. I hurried to close the distance.

"There's something I want to ask you," I said.

He eyed me warily.

"I've been wondering if we knew each other before. Before all of this, I mean."

He seemed to be doing the same sort of calculation as I had just a moment before. "Yes, monsieur."

"You were a houseboy?"

He shook his head. "A porter."

Of course. How could I not have recognized him? He looked exactly the same—as if he had not even aged. The skinny boy who could never keep his shirt tucked. Always quiet. The clerks often failed to see him standing there, ringing their bells while he shifted uncomfortably and invisibly beside them, one shirttail hanging out like an oar in the water.

"Of course," I said with a smile. He had been so frail then. Despite his sloppiness I had never yelled at him, never raised my voice. Of that I was sure. There was nothing he could possibly hold against me.

I knew just where to look and found the box easily, high up on the shelf in the back of the closet. Sitting at my desk, I pulled off the top. My fingers did not have far to dig. Around the edges, the brochure had turned the color of a tea-stained saucer. Some of the creases had frayed, but it was nonetheless intact. "The Wedding of Your Dreams."

What would that look like, I wondered, the wedding of Louis's dreams? I doubted he had ever dreamed of any kind of wedding at all. What did he know of rose petals and horses and champagne?

Setting the brochure aside, I picked up the otherwise blank sheet of paper I had long ago addressed to Madame. I began to write.

> *I am sorry that it has been so long since my last note. Several times I have sat down to write to you, but I have found it difficult to know what to say. By now you have no doubt heard that our troubles continue. Yet having just written these words, I realize how ridiculous they must sound. When have our troubles ever ceased? Still, however accustomed we have become to these difficulties, it is true that the situation we now find ourselves in is the most dire we have seen. I must confess, I have held back some of the harshest realities in the hopes of sparing you. Things have reached such a state, however, that I can no longer do so in good faith. The truth, Madame, is that you would no longer recognize Habitation Louvois. I fear you would be heartbroken even to glance upon it. I have done my best, but it was not enough.*

I put down my pen. I could not go on.

❊

That afternoon, I went for a walk, and for the first time since our encounter in Hector's villa, I allowed my course to take me past the casino. I had been waiting to explain to Mlle Trouvé how well I understood what she was going through, how difficult I knew it to be to find oneself so compromised. She needed to know that there was someone here who cared.

It was recess time, and Mlle Trouvé was sitting in her accustomed spot on the dusty steps while the children played in the grass. Seeing her again now, I could not help wondering if it had been recognition that had first drawn me to her, all those months ago. Was it possible she was one of the many maids Raoul said had come back? No. If I had forgotten the others, it was because they were so forgettable. Even dressed in their hotel uniforms, they had never been anything but what they had since become. This had always been their fate. Mlle Trouvé was different. Within her she contained something far larger and far better than the circumstances in which she found herself.

Out of the corner of my eye I saw one of the children playing in the grass—a little girl in a light pink dress—turn too quickly toward one of her classmates and catch her foot on the uneven ground. She landed on her side, and initially it appeared everything would be fine—she would dust herself off and her friends would laugh and together they would resume whatever it was they had been playing. But after the girl had taken a moment to examine the dirt on her hands and the scratch on her knee and the circle of classmates gathering around her, she suddenly broke out in a bitter sob. I realized by the way she held her hand to her head that she had struck a stone.

In an instant, almost simultaneously, her classmates' worried expressions turned toward their teacher, anxious to see what she would do. But somehow Mlle Trouvé appeared not to have noticed, either the fall or the little girl's bawling. It was not until another of the children—a little potbellied boy with slightly bowed legs—ran over and patted her on the knee that Mlle Trouvé seemed to awaken. Dazedly lowering her eyes to discover the child waiting at her feet, a look akin to horror crept onto her face.

Mlle Trouvé reached the girl quickly, and it did not take long to soothe her. Holding the girl in her arms, she gently touched her head.

"You'll be fine," I heard her say. "It's just a scratch. . . . Just a scratch."

And soon the girl was smiling and holding on to Mlle Trouvé's hand as they walked together over to the steps and sat down. In a moment, I was there as well, smiling down at the little girl, who suddenly stopped her breathless reconstruction of the fall.

"Mademoiselle," I said, turning to the young schoolteacher.

She seemed surprised by my appearance. Wanting to assure her that there was no cause for alarm, I said, "I was sorry we didn't have a chance to talk the other day. I looked for you after you left Hector's."

She nodded.

"I know how difficult this must be for you," I said. "I understand. I've long thought that you and I have a great deal in common."

She looked up at me uncertainly, a question forming on her lips that she seemed unable to complete.

"For the good of the children you have made incredible sacrifices. I have made sacrifices too."

"I see," she said. An uncomfortable look came upon her face, and I noticed her gaze straying. Only then did I realize the children had stopped playing. Behind me on the grass they had assembled, listening in on our conversation.

"Children," Mlle Trouvé said, getting quickly to her feet, "it's time to resume your lessons."

"I'm sorry if I intruded," I said, watching as she led the children up the stairs to the casino.

"Good-bye, monsieur." She left me there with a quick, distracted wave.

After she left, I remained out on the casino lawn a short while longer, replaying in my mind our clumsy conversation. Almost none of the things I had wanted to say had managed to leave my mouth. *You and I have a great deal in common.* She must have thought me mad. What I had wanted to say—what I thought she alone could understand—was that all the things we had endured were about to be over. The end was upon us. And it was time for us to decide what we would do. Hector and his followers had made their choice. If they wished to die here, taking their stand, there was nothing more I could do to stop them. But for Mlle Trouvé and the children and me it was not yet too late. Or so I hoped; I had wasted our best opportunity, and there was no way of knowing how much time we had left.

I started off down the path, walking in no particular direction. It did not matter where I went; I just needed to keep moving, to retain what little momentum I still possessed.

In that state I arrived at the pavilion. There I discovered that some of the women—Claire among them—had begun putting up decorations for the wedding, stringing up scraps of colored paper and the blossoms of the few flowers Hector's followers had not already killed. They were the sort of impoverished adornments one saw in Cité Verd on such occasions, when the last scrawny chicken was sold off for a package of streamers and a few crooked candles. The sight reminded me of the scraggly shrubs Paul's mother had planted outside their door, hoping to produce some small simulation of gaiety. I was happy for Louis and his bride. How could I not be?

And yet, as I gazed upon the pavilion, what stood out the most was not the decorations but the peeling paint and the warped, weathered boards, the cracked slats of lattice and the vines choking every pillar. No matter how many times we cut them, the vines always grew back. And the fresh paint faded and the wood continued to rot. And I realized now—as I had refused to for months—that no matter what happened, Habitation Louvois would not be rescued. Never again would it be as it had been before. Who would be foolish enough to try, after all of this? There would be no more hotel, no more parties, no more photographers lying in wait beyond the gate. And I realized as well that Marc had been right all along: Madame would never again return. There was nothing for her to return to.

I had been blind not to see it. I was probably the last to understand. Madame herself must have decided long ago. Possibly years ago. Possibly she knew even as she was leaving that last time, foreseeing what the future held. Or at least she had suspected it. She had cut her losses and slipped away, without even saying good-bye.

Had she already forgotten us? All those letters I sent—how many had remained unopened? Perhaps at first she had read them dutifully, intending to respond, but over time they became nothing more than a painful reminder of what we would never have again. Were we anything more to her now than a figure in a ledger, long since written off?

But the question that made me stop and rest in the shadow of the pavilion was this: What if we had not come here? What if M. Guinee had never brought me to this place, never shared it with Mme Freeman? Would Dragon Guy and Hector still have found it? Would they have known it existed? If Madame and I had never built the hotel, would the forest have remained as it was, untouched, unseen, a permanently preserved memory of our past? Maybe it would have gone on forever, like the story my mother had passed on to me. If so, that meant it was not Dragon Guy, but Madame Freeman and I, who were responsible for the destruction of Habitation Louvois. The things we had done to save the place had ensured its ruin. Did that mean we were somehow responsible for all these lives, too? If so, that was another burden Madame had excused herself from bearing; she had left it entirely to me. But what more could I do than I had already done?

After dinner, I did not go up to my office, as was my habit. Instead, I went out to the terrace overlooking the pool and breathed in the still evening air. I was out there a long time, and I could not remember when I had last felt such calm. I felt as if I had been freed of some enormous weight. I no longer had to worry about disappointing Mme Freeman. I no longer had to worry about anything. All that was left was for me to do as she had done and take leave of the place. I still hoped Hector and Mlle Trouvé might come with me. Who knew what lives they might have ahead of them, if only they could start over somewhere else? But regardless of what they decided, I knew I must go.

In the courtyard near the laundry, they had built a fire, an enormous one with flames feeding off limbs and trunks it must have taken several men to carry. To the side, with their backs against the door of Mona's kitchen, three men were pounding on drums, and I stood for a while on the path, watching the dancers lose themselves to the deadening beats. At least some of Hector's army, it seemed, had been given the night off. Was the battle going so well for them that they could now take turns fighting?

In the middle of it all, like totems unsure of their purpose, stood the lovers, Louis and Lulu. The young man did not see me; he could see nothing but the glowing flesh of his bride-to-be. Indeed, she looked lovely, like a woman ready to embark on some bold new adventure. Perhaps it was for the best they had no idea what lay ahead of them. I was not going to be the one to spoil the moment.

It was time to head back to the manor house. I had one last piece of business to attend to, one last letter to Madame to finish, one final request. I did not need much. Just some kind of work. And a visa. I had enough money left for airfare. For Hector and Mlle Trouvé too, if they would come. How could Mme Freeman refuse, after everything we had been through together?

But as I turned to go, I happened to see a familiar face peering out from between the flickering peaks of fire. Mlle Trouvé's expression was odd, both intimate and cold. It was as if she had been expecting to find me here, as if she had heard my thoughts, as if we had come by mutual agreement, so that we might have a moment to speak in private about some vital business. Despite the party going on around her, she seemed completely alone, standing with her arms folded across the front of her faded dress. For whom but the two of us could such a celebration have afforded privacy?

She watched me as I made my way through the crowd. In a moment I was at her side.

"I'm sorry if I interrupted you today," I said. I was relieved by the lack of anger on her face. "I didn't mean to frighten you. It's just that I cannot help but feel that Dragon Guy and Hector have forced our fates together."

The schoolteacher continued to stare into the flames.

This was the closest I had ever stood to her, the clearest I had ever seen her face. For the first time I noticed the soft, faint, delicate hair outlining her cheeks and jaw.

"We have very little time left," I said. "We're all in great danger."

She gave me what I interpreted as a cautious nod, and I was about to go on, to say the other things I needed to say, when something happened for which I was wholly unprepared.

She smiled.

And not just any smile—it was beatific. It unfolded like a gift. Mlle Trouvé had surprisingly small, neat teeth, like a child. And the smile so warmed me that for a moment I managed to forget that it made no sense, that there was nothing in what I had said that should produce such happiness.

I could have watched her like this forever, letting the fire consume itself and the coals cool to ash and everyone in our midst evaporate along with the smoke. The world could produce only one such smile, and it was hers.

And my heart fell a little bit when her lips came together once again.

"I'm ready," she said. "We have come so far. We are not afraid to die."

It was dark and the trees wore bibs of smoke and the manor house was huge in the shadows. "It's okay," I said. "I know you're not one of them. I'm not either. I'm like you. I'm on your side."

Finally she turned to look at me squarely, and only then did I feel she truly saw who I was. I could see her considering what I had said, and I hoped she could find a way to trust me, that we could return again to that smile.

And then her mouth fell open again, and I saw the gloss of her tiny teeth.

That was the moment something hit me from behind.

My head whipped back and I stumbled forward, falling just a meter from the fire. When I got up again, my hands and knees were covered in ash.

"Forgive me, monsieur," came a man's voice, laughing somewhere in the crowd.

I turned, trying to find him, and then I was struck again, and again I fell toward the flames.

A different voice this time, from a different direction. "Clumsy me."

A foot came down on my back as I tried to get up.

The laughter spread, and I felt bodies closing in on me from all sides. Then I heard another voice—Mlle Trouvé's—yelling at everyone to get away. She grabbed my arm and pulled me up.

We met with little resistance as we pushed our way through the crowd.

"Going so soon, monsieur?" someone called after me. "Just when the fun was getting started."

We did not stop until we reached the manor house pool. There Mlle Trouvé released my arm. "Go," she said, giving me a push. "You have to go."

"We must stick together," I said. "That's our only hope. Please trust me."

"Why can't you understand?" Anger was scrawled across her face. The flames leaped behind her, punctuating her words. "I do not wish to be saved."

Chapter Thirty-One

All along the road to the capital burned-out chassis mingled with garbage, and no one seemed to notice them. It was as if a car were just another useless nothing someone might indiscriminately let slip from his pocket.

Our progress was slow. The bus was constantly stopping to maneuver around another barricade of twisted furniture and melted tires.

I got off at the central market. The taxi drivers stirred without urgency as I approached their waiting cars. The man at the front of the line had a neck like a broomstick and an equally skinny mustache. Opening the back door to his car, I announced I was going to Lyonville. Before I could get in, a man dressed in khaki pants and dark sunglasses came forward, placing his hand on my shoulder.

"I'll take you," he said.

I nodded toward the broomstick-necked man. "I'm perfectly content with him."

"You'll come with me."

It would have been wrong to say he was rough, but he was unequivocal as he led me—never letting go of my shoulder—to his car, farther down the line.

The new driver had a mustache too, but his sprouted heavy and wild. Even without being able to see his eyes, I knew it was me he was watching in the rearview mirror. The merengue on the radio was almost too low to hear.

At the very bottom of the road into Lyonville we encountered the first of the checkpoints. The two guards, both wearing army uniforms, sat in old wooden chairs in front of a gate adorned with fawning posters of President Duphay. Cradling their guns with a gentleness I doubted even their girlfriends knew, the soldiers came around the sides, and one of them flung open my door.

"Out," he yawned. He smelled faintly of tamarind as he led me over to the garden wall at the side of the road, jamming the hollow opening of his gun barrel into the back of my head. I wished I could close my eyes, but I was afraid the things I might not see would be even more unsettling than the things I could.

The driver lit a cigarette as the other soldier climbed into the backseat of the car. "Did you see the end of the match?"

"I don't want to hear about it," I heard a muffled voice say.

Chuckling, the soldier at my back clunked the heavy steel against my skull. I gritted my teeth and waited for the sting to pass. "He lost a bundle."

"A goal like that," the driver said, "I'd give both my legs to be able to make a ball do that."

Crawling backward out of the car, the other soldier rose too quickly and the roof clipped the hat from his head. "You wouldn't be saying that if you lost money on it." He picked the hat up from the dirt with a frown, smacking it several times against his thigh.

The driver dropped his cigarette, grinding it out with his shoe. "How about paying the toll so we can get on with it?"

I reached into my pocket and brought out my money. I was in too much of a hurry to argue. "How much?"

The man with the gun to my head slid the bills from between my fingers, taking every last one. "That should be enough."

There was no point in objecting. The driver was already whistling himself into his seat.

Back on our way, we soon passed the road leading to my old neighborhood. I wondered what it looked like now, whether it too had been besieged. I was tempted to ask the driver to go back, if not to my father's shop then at least to the cemetery. I should not leave until I had a chance to say good-bye to my parents. I felt I owed them an explanation, perhaps even an apology. They needed to know this was simply a world that had no place for me. I had never belonged here, and now that Habitation Louvois was lost, I never would. I was sorry to have to leave them like this, knowing I would probably never come back, but it was the only thing left for me to do.

Even for that short detour, though, there was no time. I could no longer see the capital below. The air had grown cooler. We had already passed the road to Senator Marcus's old house.

"Are you sure this is the right way?" I asked after we had passed the third checkpoint and continued climbing.

"Of course." The driver's voice betrayed offense at the suggestion that he might be lost. "You're going to Paul's house."

He must have seen the surprise on my face.

"Everybody knows Paul," he offered in explanation.

The car lunged forward. I was thrown back against the seat. The driver pitched back too, his arms stiff as branches.

Up we sped along the narrow street. Around a bend he swerved to dodge a pothole, and I hit the door with the full force of my body. Face pressed to the glass, I saw three girls in blue-checked school blouses standing at the curb, and my eyes were drawn to the white ankle socks so bright above their black leather shoes, and then to their faces. As I flew past, one of the girls—the tallest of the three—met my eyes, and I hung on to them as if they were the last living thing I would ever see.

The windows in the front were open and the wind stuffed itself into my mouth like a gag. The engine raced, and I could see a needle on the dashboard quivering in the red.

"What are you doing?" I finally managed to yell.

But the car was already slowing down.

We stopped in front of a low, whitewashed wall overhung with bougainvillea. Through the bars of the gate I saw a sprawling white house that looked like something from a magazine: airy and modern, with a terra-cotta roof and windows arranged asymmetrically in seemingly every available space. Between the trees flashed ribbons of blue sky. Somewhere beyond the endless patchwork of windows was a cliff overlooking the capital.

"Tell Paul that Céline says hello," the driver shouted before squealing out of sight.

There was no bell, but I had been waiting only a moment when a man wearing a holster over his white polo shirt passed through the front door and the portico.

"Who are you?" he asked.

"I have an appointment with Paul."

He spun around wordlessly and began walking back up the drive. I saw him unclip a radio from his belt. There was a burst of static and then a voice at the other end. The conversation ended without a clear sign of what was going to happen. The man waited back under the portico, leaning against a pillar, thoughtfully turning the pages of a newspaper, as if his principal duty were to monitor the daily events of the world.

Finally the voice came over the radio again. An alarm sounded and the gate clicked open. The man put down his paper and nodded for me to follow.

In the marble foyer a muscular young man wearing a thin, violent smile and pink tank top stood waiting. "This way."

An arched ceiling reached high above the lengthy hallway, edged with a delicate floral motif. We passed a vast polished ballroom and a brightly upholstered sitting room. A woman's touch was everywhere apparent.

At the end of the hall my escort slid open a set of glass doors, and he stepped aside to let me through.

It appeared at first glance that I was alone in the room. Directly in front of me another set of glass doors, flanked on each side by small lemon trees in fluted ceramic pots, looked out upon the garden and the pool. Beneath my feet a rich burgundy rug stretched out to the far ends of the room. At one end huddled a wing chair and a small teak table supporting a white porcelain lamp. The tassels at the other end of the rug pointed toward a massive mahogany desk.

Paul stood up to greet me. "Alexandre, I'm glad you made it."

In the three years since I had seen him last, Paul had undergone yet another transformation. Whereas for me the arrival of our fifth decade had expanded the cavities around my eyes and rubbed the hair away in patches around the crown of my head, Paul had not only retained but improved the compact body of his youth, which seemed perfectly molded to his soft, neatly tailored suit. A tie was fastened tightly around his neck. Never before had I seen him wear one.

The room was cool despite the light bursting through the gauzy drapes.

"What happened?" Paul said as I came closer, wincing at the cuts and bruises on my face. "Another run-in with a waiter?"

"Yes," I said. "With several."

The man sitting in front of the desk glanced disinterestedly over his shoulder at me, remaining seated.

"Come." Paul waved me toward him. "Come. There's someone I'd like you to meet. This is Charlie." He gestured affectionately to the seated man. "He's my right-hand man. I'm nothing without him."

"Pleased to meet you," I said.

Charlie nodded.

Paul put his hand on the man's shoulder. "Could you excuse us for a minute, Charlie?"

My escort was waiting for Charlie at the door, and when he stepped out into the hall, the doors closed behind him.

"I'm glad you came," Paul said, as if genuinely surprised that I had.

As if I really had a choice. "I've been worried about you." He smiled. "We get so caught up in our work, we forget the little things that would bring us pleasure."

Given the circumstances of my visit, I could only assume we had very different ideas about what constituted pleasure.

"Your house is beautiful."

"That's kind of you to say." Paul took a seat and motioned for me to do the same. "Of course, it's nothing compared to yours. I owe most of the credit to my wife."

"I wondered if you'd gotten married."

Paul scratched his head and gave me a quizzical smile. "In fact," he said, "I sent you an invitation."

"I—," I began, but the air escaped my lungs as if from a punctured balloon. I could not allow myself to wither before I had even begun.

"I must not have received it," I said. "You know how it is with the mail."

Paul brushed away the disappointment. "It doesn't matter. I'd like you to meet her," he said. "She's a beautiful girl."

"Is she the one from the restaurant?"

"The restaurant?"

"I thought it might be the one I met—I don't know how many years ago."

Paul laughed. "Oh, no no no. A lot has changed since then."

Indeed, in that time he had evidently gone from petty criminal to king of Lyonville. Not quite as rapid an ascent as Hector's, but impressive nonetheless. All around me it seemed great men were suddenly attaining great heights. Meanwhile, I slid closer and closer to oblivion.

"How is your mother?"

"My mother?" Lifting a silver letter opener from his desk, Paul bounced the tip against his open palm, frowning at its dullness. "She passed away. Almost two years ago."

"I'm sorry," I said. "I hadn't heard. I can't remember the last time I was in the neighborhood. I lost touch with everyone."

"I know how hard it is to get away. Even living this close. I try to

CHRISTOPHER HEBERT

go back when I can. We're building a school there. Or will be, soon.
Charlie is from the neighborhood. Some of the other guys, too. They
keep me connected."

"Everyone back there must be very proud of you."

Paul put the letter opener down. "You know how it is. Pride is easy,"
he said with a shrug. "It costs almost nothing, especially compared to
what it can get you in return."

"Oh?" I had not expected so complicated an answer to so idle an
observation.

Paul stood up and sauntered over to the French doors overlooking
the garden. It looked as if he were preparing to deliver a lecture on
some great philosophical truth. I felt myself growing weary even before
he had begun.

"Consider your father," Paul said. "He was honest and he had prin-
ciples. He never did anything just for what it might get him. It took me
a long time to understand how rare that is."

Having been unprepared for the turn the conversation had taken, I
suddenly found myself uncertain of what to say. No one could deny my
father was a righteous man, but he was also miserable, and it is unfair to
admire the one and ignore the other. It is the real world we must live in,
not the world of our ideals.

Paul smiled warmly, still looking as though he were genuinely glad
to see me. He took his seat again. "Do you know why I asked you here,
Alexandre?"

Behind me I could hear the men outside in the hall. Charlie was
waiting to be let back in. "I'm desperate," I admitted. "I would have
come even if you hadn't invited me."

"It's a terrible mess," Paul said, falling away from me as his chair
tipped back. "Madness on all sides. It can't help but end badly."

Suddenly my hand was shaking on the arm of the chair. I tried
tightening my grip, but it still would not stop. "I need a visa," I said.
"And one for Hector, just in case. I've written to Mme Freeman, but
there isn't time." The calm I had so carefully been guarding was quickly
slipping away.

Paul demonstrated his sympathy by lowering his eyes. "I'm sorry it's come to this."

I tried to say that I was too, but nothing came out.

Paul said, "You've been like a father to him."

A father? I had taken Hector in and tried to give him a better life, and then I had let him slip away. And now, eight months later, I was in danger of losing him for good. "If so," I said, "I was as poor a father as I was a son."

Paul folded his hands together on top of the desk. "It's not easy being a father."

I thought to myself, must we do this? My sigh surely revealed my impatience, but Paul seemed not to notice.

"Do you have children?" I asked, as I knew I was supposed to. In fact, the possibility had not occurred to me until now.

Paul smiled with modest pride. "Two. A boy and a girl."

I started to congratulate him, but then I stopped myself, fearing he would feel obliged to lecture me further on the topic of fatherhood.

"I have no doubt that you're an excellent father," I said, hoping we could leave it at that.

Paul spent a moment staring at his open palms. "It's kind of you to say, but it wasn't me I was thinking of." And then I realized his gaze had shifted. He was looking at me with an unusual intensity. "I was thinking of our fathers, yours and mine. I've been thinking about them a lot lately."

There was no time for this, but what could I do?

Paul tapped his thumbs thoughtfully together, another of the genteel gestures that seemed to have come along with his success. "What do you remember about my father?"

"Your father?" I said, trying to hide my annoyance. "Very little. Almost nothing." And then as an afterthought I added, "Except for his laugh."

Paul smiled. "His great big rolling-around-in-a-chair laughs." A strangely wistful look came into his face. I was not used to this sort of nostalgia from him. Nor was I convinced that this was a fitting occasion for it.

"He was like a kid himself."

I would not have put it in those terms, but I could see it being true.

Paul said, "I was eight or nine when he left. My mother didn't talk about it. She made it clear she didn't want to answer a lot of questions about him, so I didn't ask."

The same had been true of my father and me.

A silent moment passed between us, and I asked, "Why are we talking about this now?"

Paul leaned forward over his desk again. "They were best friends," he said. "Our fathers. Did you know that?"

I answered with another shrug. I had never thought about it in those terms, but I failed to see why it mattered. In truth it was difficult to imagine anyone being my father's best friend. "I remember them spending a lot of time together."

"They grew up together," Paul said. "Like you and me. And in a lot of ways they were as different as you and me. My father was the one that was always laughing and having fun. He was always enthusiastic about things. He had all these dreams and plans. All of them completely unrealistic. But even though they were so different, my father really looked up to yours. He admired him. Your father had his shop, and that was a big deal."

I could think of nothing to say in return. There were aspects of my father that I admired too, but it was difficult to separate them from the things that had always driven me away.

Paul asked, "Do you know what my father did for a living?"

I shook my head. Did he not see how little time I had left?

"He worked in the dockyards. Sort of like where I started out, actually, only less—"

"—illegal?" I suggested, hoping to move things along.

Paul's grin seemed to concede that was what he had in mind. "From what my mother told me, he didn't have the stomach for more adventurous things. He may have been a dreamer, but he didn't like to take risks."

It was clearly there that the paths of father and son diverged. "At least in that way he was like my father," I noted.

Paul nodded distractedly. There was evidently a different point he was trying to make, and he did not wish to be sidetracked.

"My father liked the docks. The work was grueling and the pay was pitiful but he loved the camaraderie. He loved people. He loved joking around and telling stories."

"I remember," I said reluctantly. "There was never a quiet moment when he was around." And my father, I saw no need to add, contributed only silence.

"It's true," Paul said with a nod. "And maybe if he hadn't been the kind of guy he was, he might never have disappeared."

I shook my head to show that he had lost me. I had hoped we were nearing the end of this detour, but the intensity of his concentration suggested we were only just getting started. Finally I understood the restlessness Hector felt when he was in this position in my office, waiting for me to stop talking and wasting his time.

"Everyone remembers it a little differently," Paul said. Everything about his leisurely tone suggested that he thought he had all the time in the world. "But the general outline is the same. It began when a couple of university boys started showing up at the docks. They came at odd hours, whenever my father's boss was away, smoking their imported cigarettes, wearing their tailored suits. Everyone else smelled trouble, but not my father. He was the same with them as he was with everyone else, only too glad to make friends. These were rich boys from the hills. Professional students. Never had a job of their own. The sort of kids who solved all the world's problems without ever leaving the library. They had pamphlets and philosophies. They especially had ideas about people like my father. The exploited class of workers, the ones who provided all the labor and got nothing in return."

"Communists?" It came out in a gasp. Any sentence containing Paul's father and Communists could not help but sound absurd. "Are you trying to tell me your father was a Communist?" Of all the ridiculous things Paul had said to me over the years, this topped them all.

"It was the usual thing," Paul said. "Rich people were the enemy of the worker. Until then I doubt it had ever occurred to my father that anyone was his enemy. He was poor, but there was no bitterness in him. All his get-rich-quick schemes, they were just dreams."

Although I had things I was tempted to say on the subject of my own father and bitterness, I held back, realizing this would all go more quickly if I remained silent.

"Of course, these university boys were rich themselves, but I'm sure my father never thought about that. For all their talk, they didn't know the first thing about poor people's lives. Of course, that didn't stop them from telling my father what he should be doing to fight back."

"Why your father?" I said. He seemed the least likely choice.

"They went to the docks because they wanted to organize a strike. I'm sure they'd gone to other places too, but everyone else just slammed the door in their faces. But my father would never slam a door in anyone's face. He swallowed every bit of it."

"I find it hard to imagine," I interrupted. "I never saw your father angry—"

"I don't think it was anger," Paul said. "I don't think he ever really saw it like that. I think he just liked talking. He was an endless optimist, enthusiastic about everything. I think he thought it would be fun. He never thought about where it would lead. He must have been their dream come true," Paul said with a shake of his head. "He was totally guileless. Even as a child I remember I could always see right through him."

"That was one of the things I always liked about him," I said. "He was probably the only adult I trusted."

With a thoughtful smile Paul leaned back in his chair, swiveling a bit from side to side as his eyes scanned the ceiling. The silence went on so long that I raised my eyes too, but I saw nothing there.

"Of course," Paul finally said, "there was another reason I suspect he was so willing to go along." As he paused to consider how best to say whatever was to follow, I could see the pensive movement of his tongue across the sharp bottoms of his teeth.

"The first time those university boys showed up at the docks, they weren't alone." Paul slowly urged the casters of his chair forward a few rotations. When he reached the desk, he carefully folded his hands together on the blotter. "Your father was with them," he said, his eyes suddenly boring into mine. "He introduced them."

"*My* father?" I said with a start.

"Who knows, even if your father hadn't been there, my father might have gone along. But the fact that he was made it that much easier. He would have done anything your father said."

"You must be mistaken," I said, suddenly feeling my skin prickle with cold. "My father was never involved in anything like that."

Paul's face had turned stony. "He was. They both were."

I could not believe what I was hearing. And Paul's confidence only made it seem all the more inexplicable. "Your mother told you all of this?"

"She told me some, but most of it came from other people who knew them."

I folded my arms across my chest. "This is impossible."

Instead of being angered by my skepticism, Paul seemed bemused. "Why is it so impossible?"

"*My* father?" I said, driving my thumb into my chest. "*My* father? He would never have had anything to do with people like that."

Paul truly seemed to be enjoying my frustration. The amusement settled deeper into his face. "How can you be so sure?"

It was as though he thought being a Communist were of no greater significance than being left-handed. "Have you met my father?"

Paul shrugged, still unmoved by my protestations.

"How long is this supposed to have gone on?" I said, making no effort to hide my incredulity.

"A few months after they met my father," Paul said, settling comfortably back into his chair, "the house of one of the university boys was raided. The kid's name was Clement."

The name meant nothing to me.

"In his house the police found a pile of correspondence Clement had been having with other Communists, mostly in the States. There was one letter in particular they made a big deal about, something

Clement said about requesting 'material' that his comrades were supposed to send. The police claimed the 'material' was explosives, and that they'd uncovered some sort of plot to overthrow the government."

"That's absurd. My father would never—"

Paul gestured for me to wait. "—I said that was what the police claimed. Really it was nothing more than some pamphlets the kid had ordered. But it gave them the excuse they needed. They cracked down on everyone," Paul said. "There weren't many of them anyway. A dozen university boys in different parts of the capital. The police closed the newspaper they'd been putting together. Not even a newspaper, really. It was mostly poetry and other bullshit masquerading as politics. They arrested all the leaders. They made up charges when they had to. Eventually they arrested my father, too. He wasn't a leader, of course, but they knew about him. The secret police had been following Clement for a long time, and at his trial agents testified that he was constantly receiving literature sent from known Communists abroad. They said he regularly went to pick it up at the docks. They probably suspected my father had been Clement's inside man at the docks all along."

"This is ridiculous," I said, throwing up my hands. "It's impossible. I never heard anything about any of this." I could hear the voices again in the hall, and I was tempted to get up and let Charlie back in. Let him be Paul's audience, if that was what he was looking for.

"We were kids," Paul said. "Besides, it wasn't the sort of thing that got publicized. The papers printed what they were allowed to print, and things like this were better left alone."

And yet I was supposed to believe that somehow all of these details had been preserved for the day Paul would come looking for them. Is that what this is, I wondered, a story Paul had invented to give his father's disappearance a more romantic luster?

Paul's fingers opened and closed, opened and closed. He seemed to be exercising the tension out of his fists. "They say he was tortured. The police did everything they could to get him to talk, but he never mentioned your father."

"Why would he?" I said almost breathlessly.

"I told you already. He was one of them." It was the first time Paul had shown any impatience.

I pushed back my chair and started to get up. "This whole thing is impossible."

Paul shrugged. "You can believe what you want."

But I was angry now, and I had a great deal more to say. "What does any of this have to do with why I'm here? You invite me here under the pretext of wanting to help, and instead you hand me something I cannot possibly believe. I know my father," I said, stabbing my finger into the air between us. "I know he would never have been involved in anything like this. He is literally the last person in the world who would ever be involved in this."

"Did it ever occur to you," Paul said, a newly sharpened edge to his voice, "that there are things about your father that you don't know? Did it ever occur to you that what you saw was only part of it? Did it never occur to you to wonder what happened before you came along? Did you never wonder what happened to make him so bitter?"

"I know what made him so bitter," I said. "He lost his land. My mother died of malaria."

"Why is it so hard to accept that your father might have believed in something? For someone who supposedly refused to discuss politics, he had a lot of strong opinions. Especially when it came to rich people. Do you really think there was nothing in the world he wanted to change? Is it really that crazy, wanting to stand up for yourself?"

"Yes," I said. "It is when you're doomed to fail."

"Fine." Paul waved his hands, signaling defeat. "Okay." He shrugged resignedly. "All I can do is tell you. What you do with the information is your business."

"What I cannot fathom," I said, "is why you're so willing to accept it. Does it not bother you at all to think of your father being involved in something like this? What you've become is exactly what they would have despised."

He leaned over the desk until I could smell his sweet breath. He gave me a long moment in which to savor it. "That's true," he finally said, "but success like mine doesn't come without strings. I said a long time ago when we were kids that I would never be anyone's servant, and I've held to that. But I'm not so vain or stupid that I've forgotten that all of us are here not by the grace of God but because someone with more money and power than us has decided to let us. That's as true of me as it is of you. I owe my business and my fortune to monsters like Mailodet and Duphay. I've benefited from them as much as anyone and more than most. That's because, unlike your senator, I've never given them any reason to question my loyalty."

At the mention of Senator Marcus, a shudder coursed through me, and I felt my chest tighten. I could not bring myself to speak.

"But that doesn't mean I have to like them," Paul said. "And in fact I would like nothing more than to see M. Duphay dragged out into the street and shot. I would volunteer myself to pull the trigger. So to answer your question, I mostly believe my father was a fool, and the people he got mixed up with were scum, but it pleases me to think there might also have been some part of him that was willing to put a bullet in a tyrant's brain."

I slumped back into my seat. "You still haven't told me where you got this information. What makes you so sure of it?"

Paul folded his arms across his chest, and for the first time he looked at me not as if I were an old friend but as if I were a disagreeable chore he hoped would soon be over.

"Look around you," Paul said. "We're not children anymore. You wanted to know what this has to do with your situation? It has every-thing to do with your situation. I called you here because you need my help. So that's what I'm offering you."

"How is this supposed to help?"

"That's up to you." Paul leaned back in his chair, recollecting his thoughts. It was clear he would not let me go until he had said precisely everything, and precisely to his satisfaction.

"My father got three years," he said, signaling that his story was not yet over. "Most of the others did too, including Clement."

"And that's why your mother said he disappeared," I said, supplying the ending for him.

Paul gave no indication of having heard me. He seemed intent on finishing without me. "Clement died in prison. Most people say he was murdered on orders from the president. The newspapers didn't report it, of course. They just said he died of 'unknown causes.' " Paul leaned forward again, letting his elbows land solidly on the desk. "My father wasn't killed. He got sick. It was probably pneumonia. Of course, it was a forced-labor prison and a cesspool. So basically they killed him, too. Only no one had to go to the trouble of actually stabbing him."

Paul was silent then, and I was too. And I realized, looking into his eyes, that he felt he had already said as much and more than was required of him. I could see there, too, a catalog of the innumerable ways I had failed him over the years, starting with when we were children, but most of all when we were older and I could have done better. My crimes were greater than just having missed his wedding. Years ago in the hotel restaurant I had been ashamed and done everything I could to distance myself from him. How many times had I asked for his help? And when had I ever given him anything in return?

"Why did no one ever say anything? Why did my father and your mother not tell us the truth?"

Paul's expression was not unlike the ones I had seen reproduced on my father and M. Guinee's saints. This was all he had wanted. The only thing he had ever asked of me was that I trust him.

"What else were they going to do?" he said. "However much he'd bought into it before, your father had no choice. After the arrests there was a decree. Everyone was paranoid about communism. They made it illegal. You could get sent to prison just for talking about it, even in your own home."

Suddenly it seemed Paul's air conditioning had fallen to some arctic setting. The cold swirled along my spine, and just then I felt my thoughts drifting elsewhere, exiting the room and the frigid house, speeding down the twisty hill as quickly as I had gone up, crashing amid a pile of dominoes on the table outside my father's shop on the day he died. *He was a one-man revolution*, René had said. But who was he talking about? Paul's father or mine?

Or maybe it had been someone else entirely. Where did it end? If what Paul had told me was true, if this really was my father, someone I thought I knew, someone I thought I had understood, where did that leave me?

And that was the moment I began to laugh. I tried to stop, but that only made it worse. I could not help myself. I shook my head and then I laughed some more. I laughed not because there was a single thing about this that was funny but because at that moment I was remembering all the time I had spent alone at the estate, thinking about that figure from our ancient history, General Louvois. And of course there was nothing funny about General Louvois either, nor about his legions of dead, nor the death he had inflicted upon us. But really it was General Louvois's young wife and even more specifically his infant son that caused me to laugh, although they were not the least bit funny either. I was laughing because laughing was what I had always imagined them doing, the ghosts and descendants of everyone who had arrived upon our shores as conquerors and left in defeat, who spent the rest of their lives and centuries watching us crumble and destroy ourselves while they sat in warm splendor in their garden gazebos. And I was laughing to think of the shame with which I had often imagined the farces and comedies their writers must have composed, their actors on stage in blackface, their audiences rolling in the aisles. I laughed now to think of the countless times I had asked myself, how could all of this not serve as proof to them of how right they had been in their efforts to subdue us? *See*, I had imagined them chuckling, *do you see what barbarians they are*?

And the least funny part of all, I realized now, was that they were not laughing. They never had been. Not once. Mme Louvois and her son, sitting in their garden gazebo, had not thought of us at all. For them, we ceased to exist the moment their ships passed over the horizon. They had their own struggles, their own changing world to be concerned with.

No, the reason I was laughing, the reason it was all so excruciatingly unfunny, was that I understood now that all along the only one who had been laughing was me.

My determination to escape the desolate place I was from had itself followed the path General Louvois had laid out for us. I had thought I was turning my head and refusing to bear witness, but all along I had been laughing, while everyone else around me, even my father, had continued fighting. Because it was not true that by defeating General Louvois we had vanquished our enemy. We had vanquished merely one of its manifestations. The interminable upheaval that had remained with us ever since was not a confirmation of our savage natures, it was in fact a badge of our resolve never to succumb, even in those instances when we were our own oppressors.

"But the main reason I called you here today, Alexandre," Paul said, drawing me back from some distant place, "is that I thought you should know President Duphay is sending his army to you. It will be hours, not days. And I'm telling you this because I consider you a friend, but more than that I'm telling you out of loyalty for our fathers. And now you know why. Because after my father died, it was your father who supported us. My whole childhood, and he never asked for anything in return. Without him we would have starved. And this is what I owe him. That is why you're here."

"Is there no way to stop it?"

Paul shrugged, unburdened now of his responsibility. "They're coming with everything they have. One way or another, they're going to bring this to an end."

Paul leaned back, and the soft leather of the seat bottom shushed beneath his shifting weight. "I already bought you as much time as I could."

I sank back into my chair, feeling that heaviness too.

From that position, the slightest bit removed, I noticed for the first time how clean Paul's desk was. It was immaculate. So shiny was the surface that it was as if nothing had ever touched it, as if it were impervious to any of the violence of the material world.

It was not as if I had not seen this coming. But only now did I understand that Hector had seen it too—he had seen it right from the start. And not only had he known, he had accepted it. Everyone had accepted it, everyone but me. I alone had resisted, thinking there might be some other way out.

For Hector, it had all been inevitable. That his brother would be forced to begin the war. That he, a mere child, would have to see it through. I understood that now. He was willing to die for the very people I had spent my life trying to escape. And what was true of Hector had been true of Senator Marcus, just as it had been true of the slaves who defeated General Louvois, just as it had been true of our fathers. In the end, all that was left were the battles one chose and the consequences one accepted. Apparently Mlle Trouvé understood that too, and she was prepared to take her stand, children in tow.

"So what's it going to be?" Paul said, reaching for the phone. "Do you still want that visa?"

How strange, I thought, taking it all in one last time, that Paul's office would turn out to be so much like M. Rossignol's. Tidiness was one of the last things I would ever have expected Paul and Senator Marcus's old friend to have in common. But perhaps that was how it was with men who had survived for so long embroiled in chaos. Their prize was a certain clarity. But what one did with the clarity remained the thing that mattered most. And as I gazed upon the finish of Paul's desk, seemingly free of even fingerprints, I was reminded of M. Rossignol's last words to me, and I hoped somehow that he would learn how wrong he had been.

Perhaps this so-called war was inevitable, and perhaps certain sacrifices were necessary, but I felt equally sure that there were some things that could be saved.

"Do you have a piece of paper?" I asked Paul.

As he slid open one of his desk drawers, I reached over and from a shiny brass stand at the top of the blotter I removed a pen.

Chapter Thirty-Two

In the light flooding through the louvers, I could see a bit of shine on the knees and cuffs of my suit. I had managed to get rid of the dirt and soot. The first time I wore the suit, Senator Marcus's maid had shown me how a dab of vinegar could return softness to wool, and ever since I had made sure to keep a small bottle in my wardrobe. I laid the pieces out on the bed, straightening the arms and legs and smoothing out the flaps over the pockets. Despite its age, there were no tears or holes. It had been handmade by the Senator's favorite tailor, and the stitching still held. The lint did not come off as easily as it once had, but when I pulled on the pants and the jacket and looked at myself in the mirror, it seemed to me the old suit had lost none of its dignity. About the cuts on my face there was little I could do.

The benches were already mostly full when I arrived at the pavilion. Here were the men with whom I had often seen Louis dining;

there the women who spent their days gossiping with Lulu at the laundry. Through the innumerable traces of displaced seams, the women's dresses told complicated histories of former incarnations. To add luster to the sun-bleached fabric, many of them wore flowers pinned to their chests and pressed into their hair.

Despite its peeling paint, the pavilion itself looked lovely.

I was still looking around when I spotted Marc coming up the path with the priest at his side, struggling to fix his misshapen collar.

"Well?" I said as they reached me. "How did it go? Did you find her?"

"Later," Marc said coolly. He kept going. Still at his side, the priest glanced back at me, sensing strife and eager to piece together what Marc and I were talking about. I felt equally at a loss.

Lulu was impossible to miss, standing uncomfortably by herself near the back of the pavilion. Somehow she had gotten hold of an actual wedding dress, whiter than ivory. Where were the stains, the rips? Even the fit was perfect. For so skinny a girl a dress like this could not have been easily altered. The thin tulle sleeves supported a lattice of delicately needleworked white petals and flowers. The way Lulu's arms were wrapped around her stomach, she appeared to be enveloped in vines. A self-conscious smile appeared on her painted lips and disappeared as Louis, ignorant of even the most simple wedding customs, led Marc and the priest over to her. Did no one here understand that bride and groom should not see each other before arriving at the altar? Not even the priest?

Every time I tried to get closer to Marc he moved farther away, as if we were at opposite ends of the same pole. The sorrow on his face had no place at a wedding. I could only guess his search had not gone well, and I was sorry. Still, part of him must have known all along that his wife was dead. If I had used him, I had also tried to save him. And I was willing to save him still.

Marc was not the only one keeping his distance. The men with whom I had shared so many meals walked past me as if I were invisible. Were they afraid I would recognize their voices, taunting me by the fire? I saw them, and I smiled. I called out to them by name: Hervens, Haute Pierre, Jersey Lynne, Owen-Sam, Alain, Jean-Joseph, Red Bean, Hugo. None of them dared to raise his eyes. I stood out as much as Lulu in her white dress. Perhaps more.

No one thought I would have the courage to come.

The priest entered the pavilion first, calling for everyone to take a seat. Marc found a spot in the back, buried in the shade. Below him in the grass I tried to catch his eye, but he kept turning away.

Had this been one of M. Gadds's weddings, the music would already have started. For our guests he had standing arrangements with a string quartet from the capital, two young men and two young women who had studied at the university and owned their own tuxedoes and formal dresses.

Not until he had taken his place at the makeshift altar did the priest appear to realize what was missing. With an awkward flourish he gestured toward the bandstand, where only now did I notice a teenage boy in an unbuttoned shirt squatting on a stump behind a tall drum. Quietly, almost accidentally, the boy's fingers began to brush against the skin. In the middle of the drum he traced soft circles. The sound was like someone sweeping.

There was movement at the back of the pavilion, Louis and Lulu debating their next move: whether they should go up one at a time or together and—if one at a time—who should go first. Who knows how long they would have remained there, arguing under their breath, had Claire not finally stepped in, rushing toward them from her seat in the front. The old woman took the couple's hands and brought them together, guiding the two of them forward. Did she really know no better than this? Louis should already have been at the altar. And was there no one to give away the bride?

I watched Claire return to her seat, and that was when I found Mlle Trouvé. Like the other women, the schoolteacher had brought out for the occasion her finest dress. It was the blue of a cloudless sky, with sleeves that only just capped her softly rounded shoulders. The neck of the dress was uncommonly high, rising partway up her throat. On another woman it would have looked coarse and inelegant, but for Mlle Trouvé the collar was a pedestal upon which to place her gentle face. I knew my mother would have approved. It was something she might have made herself.

As Louis and Lulu took their tentative first steps down the aisle, the heads of the assembled turned to watch. And just then the peculiar brushing of the boy with the drum started to change, taking on a more familiar form. *Bum ba da um da da da da da da dum.* I closed my eyes, imagining the notes bowed from twin violins.

To the slow, careful thumping of Pachelbel's Canon, Louis and Lulu reached the altar, and when they turned around to face their friends, both of their faces were flushed.

Suddenly I was aware of a crowd forming around me on the grass, pressing in from every side. Barefoot in jeans and T-shirts and shabby dresses, they encircled the pavilion, sliding their elbows along the rail, vying for a better view. If these were the uninvited, they seemed indifferent to the slight. Two little girls weaving among the adults crashed into my legs and ran off in laughter.

With a cue from the priest the drumming came to a stop.

Then God said: "Let us make man in our image, after our likeness. Let them have dominion over the fish of the sea, the birds of the air, and the cattle, and over all the wild animals and all the creatures that crawl on the ground." God created man in his image; in the divine image he created him; male and female he created them. God blessed them, saying: "Be fertile and multiply; fill the earth and subdue it. Have dominion over the fish of the sea, the birds of the air, and all the living things that move on the earth." God looked at everything he had made, and he found it very good.

The word of the Lord.

Already, the crowd on the grass was growing restless. Then came the psalm, and I could barely hear over their chatter. Even the bride and groom's attention seemed to wander. By the time the gospel came, I was probably the only one listening.

> *Jesus said to his disciples: "Not everyone who says to me, 'Lord, Lord,' will enter the kingdom of heaven, but only the one who does the will of my Father in heaven. Everyone who listens to these words of mine and acts on them will be like a wise man who built his house on rock. The rain fell, the floods came, and the winds blew and buffeted the house. But it did not collapse; it had been set solidly on rock. And everyone who listens to these words of mine but does not act on them will be like a fool who built his house on sand. The rain fell, the floods came, and the winds blew and buffeted the house. And it collapsed and was ruined."*

Finally it was time for the vows, and Louis took both of Lulu's hands in his. The pavilion fell silent.

"I loved you the first moment I saw you," Louis said.

"It's true!" a man shouted from the crowd.

"If I could have, I would have married you before we even met." Louis seemed about to say something more, but before he could get it out there arose a cheer from inside the pavilion that soon spread far beyond me in the grass.

And then it was Lulu's turn, but she could not manage to say anything at all before breaking out in tears. Unbidden by the priest, she moved toward the man who was to be her husband, and he toward her, and they met in the middle with a kiss. The bare-chested man beside me clapped me on the back with an exclamation of satisfaction.

I could not tell what it was the bride and groom slid onto each other's fingers, but it gave off no sparkle as they bounced down the stairs into the sunlight and were swallowed by the crowd.

Without my noticing, they had prepared a feast. Around the manor house pool there were tables full of food and a plank of roasted pig. The supply of rum had been replenished and the bottles were making their way from hand to hand. Everywhere he went, someone was trying to pour a drink down Louis's throat, and he never stopped smiling. One after another the older men took him aside with an arm around his shoulder and solemnly pressed their sour-smelling advice to his ear. I kept looking for Marc, but he seemed to have slipped away. No one could tell me where he had gone.

"If you see him," I said to one of his friends, "tell him to come see me. It's important."

"*Important*," he repeated with a smirk. "Right."

I knew I was on my own.

Of everything I had seen since Dragon Guy brought them all here, this was perhaps the most peculiar. There they were, mingling by the pool with empty cups still in their hands, as if they expected a waiter to come and top them off; laughing and talking with a practiced ease, as if they had never known days that were anything other than this; casually reaching out for another bit of meat, as though an infinite supply of hors d'oeuvres lay waiting on silver platters in the kitchen.

As I walked among the crowd, it struck me how much my parents would have enjoyed this moment, how at home they would have felt here. Only now, with so much behind me, was I able to understand that however much my mother might have appreciated the beauty of what we had built, not until now—with so much of that beauty destroyed— would she have felt she belonged. The hotel in all its splendor would have had no place for her.

After everything I had accomplished, it was the thing I never intended—the thing I fought against—that would have pleased my parents the most. The realization did not disappoint me as much as I would have thought. After all, watching the celebration of Louis and Lulu made me happy, too, and I wondered if this was the sort of marriage Mme Freeman had imagined for me. It did not matter now. It was clear that was not the life I was meant for.

Just then Hector—with the colonel beside him—stepped up to the side of the pool and raised his gourd of rum, as if it were a holy goblet.

"To Louis and Lulu," he said. "For reminding us what we're fighting for."

Around the pool there arose a cheer, and I was glad they could have this moment when everything was just as they had dreamed.

Toasts were offered in every direction. Louis and Lulu were too full of smiles to speak.

While everyone's attention was turned toward the bride and groom, Hector snuck a glance at me, and our eyes met, just as they had the day he made his very first speech, on the stage outside Madame's villa. I did not know what I expected to see. Perhaps he did not know either. None of this was how either of us would have planned it. And yet we both understood this was how it must be. And as I watched his still-boyish head nod ever so discreetly, telling me in a way I could not fail to see that whatever happened was for the best, I did not think it foolish to believe he was also thinking back to that morning so long ago when he had stood in the foyer, staring up at the chandelier, contemplating a whole new world of possibilities that he had never before imagined. Although for his part he might have gladly accepted having to do it all over again, I knew that if I had been given a second chance, I would never have let him go back to Cité Verd. I would have kept him here beside me, where he could have remained the boy he was meant to be.

So far away were Hector and I in that moment from the wedding party and everything else surrounding us that we were the last to notice when—out on the road, beyond the gate—the gunfire suddenly erupted. It was as if our heads had surfaced from under water at the exact same second, birthing us in the same foreign world of sound. Booms and cracks and pops. But even those among us who had heard the very first shots seemed not to know quite what to make of it. The face of the man beside me appeared to register the sounds only as something vaguely recalled from a memory. It was as if he had never imagined such things could occur in broad daylight.

"Hector!" I yelled, but the colonel was already sweeping him back to his villa.

The wedding guests were fleeing, a mass of them making for the paths that would lead them toward their own villas. A smaller group dashed up the steps to the manor house. Soon only the bride and groom remained, sitting side by side on a bench, still holding hands.

In Louis's eyes I saw panic and fear.

I said, "Come with me."

Moving quickly, we passed the orchid garden and I led them down the trail to Villa Moreau. And when we reached the courtyard and I pointed toward the trees, they looked at one another in confusion, but they did not resist.

By now, Raoul and Hector's path had largely regrown, and there was little sign of where it had once been. Lulu struggled to get through the thick undergrowth in her dress, and Louis had to stop several times to untangle branches from her hem. And when at last we reached the hollow cavity near the wall, they looked around perplexedly.

"Where are we?"

"You'll be safe here," I said. "No one will find you."

As I turned to go, Louis was helping Lulu to sit down in the tall grass.

When I stepped out of the trees and into the courtyard of Villa Moreau, Hector's men were emerging from their quarters. I was struck by how little change was required for them to turn back into soldiers. Yet when they had taken up their rifles and machetes, there seemed to be little agreement about what they should do next. Some of the men were yelling that they must go to the barricade. Others insisted they take up positions inside the estate. One way or another, they knew they could not stay where they were.

Upon reaching the path, they were joined by other soldiers from other villas, and together they made their way back to the drive, still not knowing what to do when they got there. And then they arrived, and it was clear the decision had already been made for them.

It was some of the men beside me, at the front of the pack, who first saw the men running toward us from the gate, four in front and one limping along in the rear, struggling to keep to his feet. The men with me were quick to reach for their guns and take aim, and I have no doubt they would have fired, had not the men in their sights thrown up their arms just in time, waving frantically that they were friends, not enemies. That was the moment we understood the barricade had fallen.

And then there was silence. As suddenly as they had started, the guns out on the road ceased, and there seemed to be no one coming in pursuit of the men retreating from the barricade. And where, I wondered now—as the men from the barricade finally reached us, shouting about platoons of troops and artillery assembling on the road—were Hector's precious lieutenants now that the real battle had arrived?

Although I had never been in close proximity to one before—nor seen one, except in pictures—somehow I knew the throaty thrum of the tank as soon as I heard it. I knew little about such things, yet still I was surprised by how quickly it moved, rushing forward and crushing the gate in a single motion. As the tank crested, first rising up and then tipping downward, its turret swinging in a wild arc, the others around me took off running.

But if it was cannon fire they were fleeing, they could just as well have stayed put; following its dramatic entrance the tank appeared to have nothing in mind but rest, coming to a slow, lazy stop.

The way the soldiers spilled down the drive, like water from an overturned cup, they must have come by the thousands. I did not stay to count. The trees beside me to the west and behind me to the south erupted as Hector's men opened fire. The army's response was equally sudden, and I do not know how I managed to get away. In an instant the air was alive with bullets, and the dirt and the grass and the gravel and the trees and every material thing was eating them up.

I made for the manor house, aware of the shots kicking up at my heels. Inside, the scene was no less frantic. Men were racing simultaneously up and down the stairs, and from every direction—and seemingly every mouth—came ceaseless shouting. A thousand competing plans were hatching at the same moment, with no one left to carry them out.

At the top of the stairs, the men broke off down the corridor. The door to my rooms was closed, as was the door to the colonel's office.

But the rest were open, and the men were scurrying through, rifles at the ready.

Once inside, I locked the door behind me. I did not need to go to the shutters to know the army had advanced farther down the drive. In addition to their guns, I could hear their voices now, and from the balconies of the other offices Hector's men were firing down upon them.

I stayed low as I crept across the floor. My progress was slow. So loud and close were the guns that it was difficult to keep from recoiling every time one of them went off. Eventually I reached my desk. But even once I had managed to slide the key from my pocket, my hands were shaking too much for me to be able to fit it into the lock. I needed both hands, one to steady the other.

The pistol was still wrapped in the same oilcloth in which Dragon Guy had delivered it. Not once having touched it since then, I had never had time to develop a proper feel for the thing, and even now—with bullets thunking into every part of the manor house—it felt wrong in my hand.

As I started to close the drawer, I spotted something else tucked in the back, half buried by a bundle of paper. It was Hector's gun, the nickel plating just as shiny and polished as it had been the day he handed it over for me to keep, a little more than a year ago. Seeing it there, I felt a sickening knot tighten in my belly. How I wished now that I had thought to give it back.

It was clear I could not stay in the office, even if I had no idea where else to go. The tank had begun firing now, and even though the manor house was not the target, I could feel the floor shake with every shell. Should the tank choose to swivel this way, I knew I might never be able to come back; there would be nothing left to come back to.

I saw my father's icons on the shelf, M. Guinee's key, my books and the boxes of records from the hotel. All I had left of Senator Marcus was his suit, which I was already wearing. On top of the desk I spotted a small pile of Madame's letters, tied with a piece of yellow ribbon.

There was room in my pocket for just one item. And so I chose Hector's gun, hoping it was not already too late.

This time the stairs were clear. At the bottom I discovered a dozen of Hector's men squatting in clusters on either side of the broad front entrance, taking turns firing. Three men bunkered behind the front desk popped up as if spring-loaded into a child's toy, spraying the circular drive with bullets. And then, just as quickly, they ducked back down. The front of the desk looked as though it had been chiseled away.

There were bullet holes everywhere—high up on the wall, in the hallway mirror, in the ballroom door. It seemed that no angle, no amount of cover, could provide any safety. A blue china vase missing its upper half sat in prim indifference on a pedestal beside the library. The saw teeth cutting across its middle looked so serene and perfect they could have been sculpted by the artist himself. But not everything had been touched so superficially. On the floor between the settee and an armchair lay a man with a small purple smudge in his neck. It looked like a stain, like a drop of wine spilled on a tablecloth.

Huddled there at the bottom of the stairs—just as I was the night of Georges's robbery—I could not decide what to do. I watched from behind as one of the men beside the entrance slowly raised his finger. A moment after the first came another. The others waited nervously for him to finish his count. The instant his third finger rose, the man pivoted toward the doorway and the others did the same, swinging the barrels of their rifles ahead of their bodies, shooting without taking time to aim. I got up to run just as one and then another of them fell.

Safe now around the corner, I glanced back. Those still standing had pulled back their guns and returned to their positions against the wall, pausing to catch their breath. The two men I had seen fall lay still on the floor. The only part of them that moved was their blood, blooming atop the marble.

Once again the leader began his count for all the others to see, firing his fingers out like pistons—one, two—his concentration unbreakable.

For the first time, I saw his face. It was Marc. He had found a place to put his anger, and I knew there was nothing I could do or say now to stop him.

There was an explosion of bullets, and I fled, knowing better than to look back. I ran down the corridor as fast as I could. This part of the manor house seemed completely empty, so I was not prepared when I stepped on to the verandah and suddenly found myself surrounded. There were five of them, but their pulsing, sweaty faces made them seem like one. Reflexively, I raised my hands.

Both pistols were still in my pocket, weighing me down like stones. I do not know why they did not shoot. I tried to stop, but I lost my balance and stumbled to the ground. Several of the barrels followed me down, still pointed at my head.

"It's *him*," one of the men said. "It's just *him*."

When I looked up, they had already dispersed, returning to their posts behind the low wall. The army had not yet made it this far. Down below, the charred pig glistened on its platter. On the surface of the pool floated the party's abandoned vessels, scratched tin cups and hollow gourds, too insubstantial to sink.

Even before I reached the back of the manor house, I could hear the shouting. Soldiers were pouring onto the grounds surrounding the outbuildings, and there were women and children everywhere. There was too little space for so much chaos, and the soldiers were swinging randomly with the butts of their guns, using them as clubs. I watched with sinking horror as one of the laundresses—a friend of Lulu's, still wearing her purple floral dress—took a blow to the head and tumbled lifelessly to the cement.

Some of the women had weapons, too, but they were outnumbered. Every minute there were more soldiers. I heard shots coming from up above and then one of the soldiers down below fell with a cry against the wall of Mona's kitchen. I saw with relief that the door was still barred shut.

Mlle Trouvé stood barefoot on the top step leading up to the casino, calling out to the children below her on the grass. Given how little time had passed since the invasion began, she must have run straight here, abandoning her shoes along the way. Seeing her so disheveled, I was struck by how much like a child she was herself.

"Hurry," she shouted to the children as they bumped and stumbled their way toward the door. But it was taking too long, and the youngest among them could not keep up. Down the stairs Mlle Trouvé went, collecting one under each arm.

"Let me help you," I said.

She did not answer. There was no time. We could hear the voices of the soldiers getting closer.

Up and down the steps we went until we had gathered together every last child. When they were safely inside, we scurried in after them, closing and locking the door behind us. At that very moment I heard the crunch of heavy boots kicking through the dust and pebbles outside.

"They're here," I said.

Mlle Trouvé was nearly gasping, trying to catch her breath. "Let them come."

In her shaking hands a rifle trembled. Had it been in here all along?

As I watched, feeling the hope drain out of me, she pulled back the bolt handle to make sure the chambers were loaded.

It was just the two of us, with our backs to the door. The children were huddled at the other end of the room, crouched behind the bar. Although the electricity had been shut off, there was enough light coming through the windows that I could just make out our surroundings. Mlle Trouvé and her students had made themselves at home here. The roulette table was piled high with books. There were balls and toys in the craps pit. In the center of the room they had cleared a space to sit on the floor, pushing the blackjack tables up against the wall.

Mlle Trouvé closed her eyes and let her head fall back against the door. All her breath escaped in a long, exhausted sigh.

Out on the grass I could hear the chink and rattle of guns and gear as the men took up positions. An indecipherable squall of noise burst from a radio not far from the window.

I put my hand on her shoulder. Up and down it surged.

"All we need are some desks," I said. "We'll have ourselves a proper school."

Beyond the walls of the casino, men squawked at one another through the static, relaying orders about what was to be done. I could only hope that someone among them, either the men outside or the men at the other end—was holding the map I had drawn in Paul's office, an exact replica of the one I had made shortly after Dragon Guy appeared here, and that he saw that the building he had surrounded was the one they had promised to preserve. I had given them everything else. This was what they had given me.

I said, "I'll buy the books myself."

Mlle Trouvé was silent. Suddenly I realized how quiet everything had grown. There were still occasional pops in the distance, but outside the window I could hear two birds chittering to one another in the trees. It was over. It was done. And this was my compromise, one that I hoped my mother and father might both accept: the charred remains of an idyllic past, along with the promise of something better to come.

As for Mme Freeman, there was nothing to say except that what was lost had never really been ours to begin with.

"The children will have a home here," I said. "They will be safe. And so will you."

Beside me, Mlle Trouvé was crying.

Chapter Thirty-Three

In the morning the army was still removing bodies. I was afraid to look too closely, for fear of whom I might see. The soldiers ignored me. They seemed not to see me at all. It was my life's role to be always invisible.

They did not bother to wash away the blood. They did not sweep up the bullet casings. They had no interest in the scraps and junk Hector's men left behind. They were careless even about the weapons. In their hurry, they barely seemed to notice the estate at all. Or at least what was left of it. They had taken to its ruination with glee, breaking every window they saw, kicking in every door, blowing holes wherever they could, smearing the walls with blood. Now that the battle was over, they were ready to forget.

An officious-looking man with a blunt chin and shiny shoes was overseeing the cleanup with an air of impatience. When I asked what would happen when they were done, he gave me a curt glance and said, "I don't intend to wait around to see."

"But what about me?" I said.

"What about you?" And he turned to catch a passing soldier, into whose ear he commenced yelling orders.

When I went to find them, Louis and Lulu were gone from the cavity behind Villa Moreau. There was no sign that anyone had trampled through the trees and underbrush to get to them. All I could do was hope they had found their own way out.

As I made my way along the path, I passed several of Hector's men handcuffed in a row between two armed soldiers. Among them hunched the colonel, his eyes no longer so cold and clear. His eyebrow was stiff and streaked in crimson. Around his neck was a long, curving gash. The string of seashells was gone.

"What do you think of your gardens now?" he slurred through a swollen mouth.

The soldier walking alongside him raised his rifle and struck the colonel between his shoulder blades. He staggered on the stones, and I reached out to keep him from falling. But he would not accept my hand.

I did not begrudge him his anger, but neither did I see any need to offer a defense. I had done what I could. We had men enough who had dedicated their lives to destruction. We had far fewer who had ever committed themselves to saving anything.

Some shots rang out from the direction of the preserve, and the soldiers hurried the prisoners up the path.

The door to Madame's villa was closed. The courtyard was strangely peaceful. It seemed to be the only place other than the casino that they had left untouched. The guards and thugs were gone now. Only the stage remained, looking like something constructed for some itinerant piece of children's theater.

Inside, all the shutters over the windows were closed, and the darkness felt wet and heavy. With no fresh air to lead the way, the sticky tobacco smell still lingered above the table. Everything about the place felt trapped. In the center of the room, above the chaise where he had briefly lain like a pampered king, Hector hung bound and gagged. They had wrapped the rope around the mount of the ceiling fan.

The plaster above was filthy with muddy prints. I could think of any number of people they might have belonged to. Soldiers under orders from President Duphay. Or the colonel and the rest of the flunky high command, who had no further use for him. His was a sacrifice everyone demanded—even Hector himself.

I had not wept at the death of my father. I had not wept at the death of M. Guinee. I had not even wept over the tragedy that had befallen Senator Marcus, for whom I had such great respect. All of the tears I had stowed away I left at Hector's feet.

I cut him down myself. It was not easy. It had taken several men to get him up there, but I could not bear to let anyone else touch him. On Madame's bed I laid him out. I took off his soiled clothes and washed him. He seemed so much smaller now, so much more like the boy I had known. And yet I was surprised at how well he filled out my suit. With the necktie tightened and the collar closed, he was perfect again.

The drawers of the dresser were empty. Despite his ascension, Hector had never acquired anything more than the red-and-white jersey he had been wearing ever since the day I first met him. Even before I opened the wardrobe, I remembered it was empty. I had seen for myself, on the day of his coronation, that Hector had purged his brother's unused shirt, the only item either of them had ever hung there. There was, he said, no place for sentiment. And yet I opened the door anyway, somehow knowing exactly what I would find. Standing on a chair, I reached directly for the very top shelf. Stuffed into the back corner, where no one who was not looking for it would ever see, was not only the shirt, but also the filthy linen suit. All of it folded as poorly as any boy would.

In the back of the jacket were two singed and bloody holes.

And on the very same shelf, tucked into the same back corner, was the dirty, creased children's book from which Hector had been learning to read. In it was a scrap of torn paper with which it seemed he had marked his place. He had very nearly reached the end. I opened it up, and there was a passage underlined in lead: "You become responsible, forever, for what you have tamed." There was no way of knowing, just by looking at the line, who might have drawn it. Hector? The child who had left the book behind? But if the scrap of paper were there to mark the passage and not Hector's place in the book, did that mean Hector had finished it? The pages toward the end were as dirty as the rest, but it was impossible to know for sure.

I fanned through the rest of the pages, but I saw no other markings. Until, that is, I went to close the book, and then I happened to notice, on the inside of the back cover, a wild mess of scribbling. I immediately recognized his handwriting. There were some of the words we had practiced making together: book, pencil, brother, tree, desk, chair. But also some words I would never have taught him.

And last of all, on the bottom, were two names. His and mine.

I decided, then, that he had finished the book. How could he not, given his determination? And the thought brought me comfort. Even if the story was as silly as it appeared to be, I liked to think he carried it with him throughout this ordeal, and that it reminded him of what we briefly had.

I placed the book upon his chest, and on top I folded his hands.

Around the bed I scattered the rest, whatever remained of Mme Freeman's belongings: her photographs and books and even her bottles of perfume. And against the headboard, behind Hector's head, I leaned Mme Louvois's painting. It seemed fitting that the general's wife should be the final witness. Present at the start of all of this, and now also at the end.

The flames were still small when I walked out the door, but by the time I reached the drive there was smoke in the sky overhead.

Mona had finally left the kitchen. I found her in Raoul's villa, sitting beside him on the bed.

"Well?" I said.

The two of them looked up in silence, their faces worn blank with weariness. I could not imagine what I must look like. Dragon Guy's shirt hung from me like a tablecloth, wet with sweat and soil. There would be a great deal more of that to come. All those piano pieces and antiques in the guesthouse, previously crafted into beds and gurneys, need now face their final transformation. Wood and nails. That was all we required. We would have more desks than even Mlle Trouvé and her students could fill.

I said, "There is a lot of work to be done."

ACKNOWLEDGMENTS

I owe a great many thanks to my indefatigable agent, Bill Clegg, to my brilliantly insightful editor, Terry Karten, and to some wonderful readers who helped make this book what it is: Augustus Rose, Genevieve Canceko Chan, Peter Ho Davies, Michael Knight, and most of all, Margaret Lazarus Dean, without whom there would be only paper and ink.

My family and friends provided love and support throughout the long writing process. For their encouragement, counsel, and assistance I especially want to thank Sharon Pomerantz, Patrick O'Keeffe, Raymond McDaniel, Lynne Raughley, Valerie Laken, Julie Barer, Shaun Dolan, and Sarah Odell.

I owe gratitude as well to the teachers and mentors who provided guidance and inspiration along the way: Eric Horsting, Jacqueline Spangler, Eileen Pollack, Nicholas Delbanco, Peter Ho Davies, and Charles Baxter. And, going all the way back to the beginning, Deborah Weiss.